Pawsitively
Secretive

A Witch of Edgehill Mystery

Book Three

MELISSA ERIN JACKSON

Ringtail
PRESS

Ebook ISBN: 978-1-7324134-8-1
Paperback ISBN: 978-1-7324134-9-8

Front cover design by Maggie Hall.

Stock art via Designed by Freepik, iStockPhoto, Shutterstock.

Interior design and ebook formatting by Michelle Raymond.

Paperback design and formatting by Clark Kenyon.

First published in 2020 by Ringtail Press.

www.melissajacksonbooks.com

To Boorito

Previously in the Witch of Edgehill series ...

Two months ago, Amber Blackwood's best friend, Melanie Cole, was fatally poisoned. Their small cat-loving town of Edgehill, Oregon, was thrown into upheaval amidst the first homicide in decades. Edgehill lost not only a beloved resident, but the director of the town's annual Here and Meow Festival. After Melanie's death, Kimberly Jones, an acquaintance of Amber's from high school, assumed the role. The scandal also left two other committee seats open: finance chair and volunteer coordinator. Ann Marie became the head of the volunteer department, and Mayor Deidrick's seventeen-year-old daughter, Chloe, became her assistant. The finance chair remained open.

While trying to solve Melanie's murder, the chief of police, Owen Brown, learned Amber's biggest secret: she's a witch. No one else aside from Edgar—Amber's cousin and fellow witch— knows. Though nervous about Amber's abilities, the chief has seen how her spells can get him answers that normal police work can't always provide. The sudden thaw in their interactions, however, has sent the small-town rumor mill into overdrive. The chief is married, his wife pregnant with their second child, yet people whisper more may be going on between Amber and the chief than meets the eye.

Last month, a member of the cursed Penhallow clan, Kieran

Penhallow, traveled to Edgehill to find and steal the grimoire of Amber's late mother, Annabelle, a prodigy of time and memory spells. She had created a spell that allowed a witch to go back in time. Ever since, Penhallows have been searching for the grimoire, determined to use its hidden secrets to prevent their clan from having ever been cursed in the first place. Annabelle knew that the rewriting of history could cause irrevocable harm, and she worked the rest of her life to keep the book hidden via elaborate cloaking spells. She and Amber's father died at the hands of a Penhallow who had been after the grimoire.

Edgar had been tasked with keeping the book hidden until Amber turned eighteen. Due to a series of spells and attacks from the Penhallows, his consciousness was melded with that of a Penhallow, slowly driving him into madness. The location of the grimoire, up until last month, had been locked away so deep in Edgar's mind that even he hadn't known where to find it. When Amber found the book hidden on Edgar's property, the decades-old cloaking spells on the coveted grimoire dropped, and the cursed Penhallow had come after it, with Amber in his sights.

Amber, her younger sister Willow, their paternal Aunt Gretchen, and Edgar managed to stop Kieran from stealing the book, but it came at a price. The magical attack on Edgar's property nearly cost Amber her life when Kieran used his magic to choke her, and both Amber and Edgar's cars had been torched. Worst of all, Jack Terrence—owner of Purrcolate, and Amber's recent love interest—had witnessed everything. After the dust settled, and Kieran had been cured of his curse, Jack decided he found this witchy world of Amber's too difficult to handle.

He asked Aunt Gretchen to remove all memory of that night's magic, and Amber's connection to it, from his mind.

With her complicated and often dangerous past, Amber fears that guarding her secrets—and those of her parents—will keep her forever isolated.

CHAPTER 1

Amber Blackwood's magic was restless.

Though the clouds were a dark and dreary slate gray, the voice of Kimberly Jones was chipper as Kim drove them toward the center of town. Given Kim's tendency to hit the brakes for any minor disturbance in the road—such as a streetlight turning yellow a mile ahead, or a leaf falling on the sidewalk— Amber often volunteered to drive. But, thanks to the events of a few weeks ago, Amber had found herself without a vehicle.

"The Hair Ball is proving to be even more stressful to coordinate than the Here and Meow," Kim said in her signature breathy way. "Just the other day, Ann Marie said she saw Janie Howard, you know, the newest cashier over at Holly's Harvest? Well, Janie was supposed to help with some of the decorations for the Hair Ball because she majored in artistic something or other, and she's back in Edgehill now because her mother has a bad case of gout. Or was it arthritis? Anyway …"

Amber tuned back out, letting Kim's voice become a dull hum in the background. She watched the passing landscape out the window, trying to ignore how antsy her magic felt beneath her skin. This always happened on the eve of a bad storm. Though they were well into March and had a relatively calm winter, as far as Oregonian weather went, this felt like a storm for January, not nearly spring.

The impending storm was a big part of why she'd asked Kim for a ride, rather than making the trek on the bicycle she'd pulled out of storage a couple weeks ago. She hadn't ridden her bike this much since she was a teenager. As she cruised down deserted residential sidewalks in the evenings and wove in and out of traffic on her lunch breaks, she'd fallen for her feline-obsessed town all over again. It was still the town of her childhood, but it had evolved bit by bit over the years, just as she had. Grocery shopping, unfortunately, had proven to be a nightmare, but at least she was getting her cardio in. She'd lost four pounds and her calves looked great.

Calves that thanked her today for opting to carpool with Kim to the mayor's house. Her calves and her itchy, twitchy magic. Amber wished she could release some of the building pressure with a simple spell or two, but if Kim had an overactive brake foot now, Amber could only imagine what would happen if she changed the color of Kim's steering wheel or dashboard for a few moments. They would surely get into an accident.

For the briefest of moments, Amber wished Kim knew her secret—wished she *could* change the color of the dashboard and that Kim's only reaction would be "Ooh, try orange next!" She wished Kim could understand her the way Willow and Aunt Gretchen did.

Her thoughts strayed to Jack. Jack, who had learned all her secrets on the same night Amber had lost her car to the magic of the cursed Kieran Penhallow. And, once the threat of Kieran's magic had been dealt with, Jack had asked Amber to make him forget. It had been too much for him. *She'd* been too much for him.

He'd known her secrets—known her—and rejected it all.

So, no, Amber would never have someone like Kim know her secrets. Amber's parents had kept even more secrets than Amber had and had taken dozens more to their graves—because it was better to die with Blackwood secrets than to share them. Amber knew this was true. Deep down, she knew her parents had been right to choose safety over all else.

But it made for such a lonely existence.

"And *then*," Kim said, "Nathan told me that the centerpieces we had planned on are on backorder, and they likely won't be back in stock for another two months which simply won't do. The Hair Ball is only two weeks away! I don't know what we're going to do. I really need an assistant, but I don't have time to find one. My mom was saying she thinks little Abby Dryal might be a good fit, but we went to high school with her brother—do you remember him?"

Amber turned to look at Kim, but gasped as Kim suddenly slammed on the brakes, the seatbelt tightening on her chest. Amber's back hit her seat as the car came to a complete halt in the middle of the road. Luckily, no one was behind them.

Kimberly laughed nervously, fluttering a hand in the air as if trying to wave away Amber's brush with a heart attack, then continued driving. "Sorry, sorry! I thought that squirrel was going to run into the street, but he went up a tree instead. Ha. Anyway, what was I saying? Oh, yeah, do you remember Brian Dryal? He was really into found art when we were in high school. Like he made his own shoes out of old car tires or something weird? Well, Brian ..."

Amber sighed, her heart still thudding hard thanks to their near miss with the supposed squirrel, and prayed to whoever was listening that they'd make it to the mayor's house before the storm hit. Amber couldn't imagine Kim was a calm driver during lightning and thunder either.

She supposed that part of the reason why Kim was even more chatty and anxious today than usual was because the Here and Meow Committee was meeting with Mayor Deidrick himself. Kim had attended the pre-Here and Meow meeting with mayors in the past, of course, including *this* mayor last year, since she'd been on the committee in some capacity for a couple of years now. This would be the first meeting with Kim leading the whole thing. The committee's last head chair, Melanie Cole, had died two months prior at the hands of the former financial leader, Whitney Sadler. Kim had assumed the role after Melanie's death and had tried to do Melanie proud ever since.

Since his election as mayor nearly two years ago, Mayor Deidrick had done his best to be as hands-on with as many events as possible in Edgehill. This was partly due to the fact that the last mayor had committed the worst faux pas in the history of the world during his first—and last—term: he opted to only attend the first day of the three-day Here and Meow Festival, and then sent his assistant in his stead for the following two days.

A rumor started to circulate that the old man "didn't even like cats," and that was it: Mayor Proust was out, and the much younger, charismatic, cat-loving Frank Deidrick was in. It had been a landslide.

A political newcomer and lifelong resident of Edgehill, Victor Newland, had tried for the position as well. It had been a contentious campaign season; Victor Newland had been out for blood. For months, both Victor's and Frank's faces had been plastered all over town. Then, one day, Victor abruptly dropped out of the race and Frank ran nearly unopposed.

"It's just so sad, you know?" Kim said now.

Amber had no clue what Kim had been talking about. "Sorry. I zoned out there for a minute. What's sad?"

Kim made a sympathetic cooing sound and removed her hand from the steering wheel just long enough to pat Amber's knee. "Oh, it's okay, hon. I'm amazed you're keeping it together as well as you are, if I'm being honest. You've been through so much lately."

Kim wasn't wrong—and she didn't even know the half of it.

"I'll be more focused at the meeting," Amber said. "Promise."

"Oh, I'm not worried." When said in Kim's usual dramatic tone, it sounded like she was the exact opposite. "Everyone already knows what's going on with you; you have everyone's support. I swear. Truly. Just go at your own pace, okay?"

Amber nodded and looked out the window at the passing landscape again. People were out walking their dogs, ducking into Edgehill's many cat-themed restaurants and shops, or stopping to talk to friends. A perfectly normal day.

None of them knew that sitting beside Kimberly Jones was Edgehill's resident secret witch. They didn't know Amber had two cloaked grimoires hidden in her studio apartment, one that was so highly coveted, witches had killed over it. They didn't know Amber's aunt and sister, who'd recently left town, were also witches. Or that the Blackwood parents had been killed by a cursed witch. Or that there were other Penhallows out there somewhere, possibly on their way to Edgehill, who wanted to claim the book Kieran had come so close to taking.

A book with a powerful time-travel spell in it that could rewrite history for witches and non-witches alike.

Absently, Amber put a hand to her throat, remembering how Kieran had tried to choke the life out of her with his magic. She had nightmares about it nearly every night.

Despite her wildly caterwauling thoughts, she stifled a yawn. She really needed to sleep.

"Oh my God, Amber. Have you heard?"

"Heard what?"

"John Huntley might perform the last night of the festival!"

Amber blinked again. She was a total dunce when it came to pop culture, but even Amber knew who John Huntley was. "The country singer slash actor?"

"Mmhmm," Kim purred.

"How'd *that* happen? Isn't he on the cusp of superstardom?"

John Huntley had just finished up a season as a bad-boy vampire on some ridiculous TV show Amber had unabashedly binge-watched recently. He'd been such a fan favorite that the writers were apparently scrambling to add him back into next season despite unmistakably being reduced to ash in the season finale.

"Get this!" Kim said, grinning. "He's a huge fan of cats.

He's got three of his own that go on tour with him and he donates large chunks of money to animal rescue organizations every year."

And he was a dreamboat. It was unfair that so much genetic luck had been crammed into one person.

"Edgehill will be swarmed with women if John Huntley shows up for the festival," Amber said. "Even worse than when Olaf Betzen was here."

"I'll be at the front of the line!"

Amber laughed. Remembering pieces of that last season— namely when John was shirtless, bloody, and scowling—she grinned as well. "I'll be right behind you."

"I thought you were dating Connor Declan," Kim said. "Are you telling me that tall glass of water is back on the market?"

Amber frowned slightly. "If he was ever *off* the market, it had nothing to do with me."

"Really?" Kim sounded genuinely baffled. "I heard he's been talking about you to people all over town like some lovesick teenager." She paused thoughtfully. "Rumor had it that you and Jack were an item too, though. Is *that* one true?"

Something twinged in Amber's chest. "Nope."

"I need better sources," Kim said, huffing. "Are the two of them close? Connor and Jack, I mean. I didn't think so, but Ann Marie said she's seen the two of them chatting it up lately. I guess Connor comes in to Purrcolate a lot and he and Jack get into these long conversations. Dina over at the Catty Melt mentioned that she saw the two of them meeting for lunch there a couple times last week, too."

Amber's brow furrowed. Other than the time Jack had

given Connor a ride back to the Sippin' Siamese the night of Connor's birthday celebration, Amber hadn't known the two to be on friendly terms. Now they were getting lunch together on a regular basis?

Maybe they had bonded over the fact that Amber Black-wood was a terrible date.

"Weird," was all Amber said.

They cruised down tree-lined Scritch Boulevard, branches almost forming a canopy over this stretch of road. Leaves were just starting to grow back now that the promise of spring was near. Tiny buds dotted branches.

The little patches of sky that peeked through the branches were still dark, so dark the clouds were nearly purple. Perhaps once they arrived at the mayor's house, Amber could duck into the bathroom and change the color of the walls a few times to release this buildup of magic. This storm was sure to be a doozy.

There was a sudden break in the foliage as Kim's car followed the road's curve. The mayor's house, which sat nearly in the dead center of Edgehill, appeared on the corner. It was three times larger than any other residence in town. It was a modest house as far as mayoral homes went, but it was the most impressive building in Edgehill aside from the sprawling Victorian-like Manx Hotel a few blocks away.

The house was two stories, had a large wraparound front porch, and was painted a sunny yellow.

Once Kimberly parked at the curb, she hunched down to peer at the house through Amber's window. The second floor's balcony was lined with a white wooden railing, and a tabby cat laid on the middle of it, tail twitching as he watched the world go by.

"I've never actually been in there," Kim said. "Have you? Last year was at the Community Center."

"Nope," Amber said. "I used to babysit Chloe when I was in high school, but they were in a tiny apartment back then."

Kim sat up straight. "I've always liked the Deidricks. Good for them, you know? He went from being a single dad in an apartment to being *mayor*. He's full of perseverance and gumption and all that. Can't believe he's *still* single, though. I really thought he and Francine Robins were going to become a thing, but even someone who works as closely with him as Francine can't seem to crack that nut."

Amber snorted.

Kim flushed. "Oh! I didn't mean for that to sound so dirty!"

Francine Robins had only been living in Edgehill for a few months before she'd landed a job with Frank. She'd started off as his campaign manager and then, once elected, had become his right-hand woman. They were seen together in town so often, people had started to speculate that the perpetually single Frank Deidrick had finally snagged himself a girlfriend. Frank hadn't grown up in Edgehill like Kim and Amber had, but he'd been a resident here for sixteen years. And in those sixteen years, Amber was fairly certain Frank had never been in a truly serious relationship.

He'd shown up with little one-year-old Chloe one day and had never left. Chloe's mother, Shannon, had died in some tragic way—the most common theories were either a car crash or an accidental drowning—and Frank's heart seemed to have shut itself off from loving anyone again. Other than being a devoted father to his daughter, of course.

While he'd clearly folded himself into Edgehill easily, his personal life had been a subject of conversation in town for years. Even Amber, who had helped him out while she was in high school, babysitting the always well-behaved Chloe, had never learned much about the Deidricks' past. Chloe seemed happily clueless about it, and Frank had always skirted the subject with the agility of a politician. Amber had wondered if his dirty laundry might get aired during his election campaign, but nasty Victor Newland hadn't uncovered anything before he mysteriously dropped out. Nothing of note had ever surfaced about Frank, and Amber liked to believe that was because there had been nothing for anyone to find.

"Ready?" Kim chirped from the driver's seat.

Amber nodded, emerging from her ever-bouncing thoughts, and the two climbed out of the car. They walked up the short brick path to the door, either side lined with neatly tended grass. Glancing up, Amber met the semi-interested gaze of the tabby watching them from his perch on the second story's railing.

"I'm so nervous," Kim muttered, smoothing down her already-smooth brown hair that hung around her shoulders in wide waves.

"You'll be great," Amber assured her. "Mel would be proud."

Kimberly stopped walking abruptly, hand to her chest, eyes welled with tears. "Do you really think so?"

Amber faced her, taking Kim's free hand in hers. "Absolutely. You've made the best of a horrible situation. She loved this festival and she would be grateful that you've been working your butt off to make sure it runs as smoothly as possible. I mean ... John *Huntley* might grace one of the Here and Meow stages? Mel would be ecstatic."

Kim nodded, doing her best to get her emotions under control before she actually started crying. She took a fortifying breath and gave Amber's hand a squeeze. "She'd be proud of you too, you know. Melanie was a fighter and so are you. Life might be kooky right now, but you've got people around you who love you and are here for you, okay? We'll get through this together."

Amber fought her own sudden flood of emotion, surprised at how suddenly it worked its way up her throat and burned her eyes. "Together," she agreed, giving Kim's hand one more squeeze.

They walked the rest of the way to the mayor's front door and Kim gave the black door a quick series of confident knocks. It was pulled open seconds later by the mayor himself, a bright smile on his face.

"Welcome, ladies!" he said, ushering them inside with a grand gesture. "Come on in."

As Amber stepped in after Kimberly, following the sound of happily chatting voices and laughter somewhere deeper in the house, Amber wondered how truly together she and Kim—she and *anyone*—could ever really be.

CHAPTER 2

The mayor gave them instructions on how to find the rest of the committee, then excused himself and ducked down a hallway. They didn't need directions; it had been easy to find, thanks to an uproarious guffaw from Nathan. When Whitney Sadler and Susie Paulson had been on the committee, Nathan had been practically mute. He was a nice stay-at-home dad who was always exceedingly willing to help out the committee in any way needed, but he'd done so quietly. Now, it seemed, the reason why he'd been so quiet had been more about the company and less about his personality. He had a goofy, braying laugh that always made Ann Marie snort, which in turn got Chloe giggling.

Amber supposed they all had sensed something about Whitney and Susie was off, even if they hadn't been fully conscious of it. Any person willing to plan the slow poisoning of another—regardless of the reason—was a psychopath.

If they had only sensed this about the pair sooner, Melanie might still have been here. She'd be giggling alongside Chloe at Nathan's ridiculous laugh.

One of the few positive things that had come out of all this was that Ann Marie had become the head of volunteer services when Susie Paulson was removed, and then Chloe had joined as Ann Marie's assistant. Amber hadn't seen Chloe once she no longer needed a babysitter; she was happy she was able to spend more time with the girl now.

"Oh, hey, ladies!" Ann Marie said, waving from her spot beside a table laden with snacks.

Kimberly squealed and met Ann Marie halfway across the room, hugging her tightly. They were both brunettes, the same height, and had similarly bubbly personalities. Amber was fairly certain the pair had seen each other a couple days ago, yet they greeted as if it had been months.

When they disengaged, Ann Marie smiled warmly at Amber. "Hey. How you holding up? Do the police have any leads on who vandalized Edgar's place?"

Nathan, Kimberly, and Chloe all turned to her, expressions curious.

Chief Owen Brown knew the vandals in question were fictional, since he had been aware of Amber's secret for a while now, but no one else did. She still wasn't sure how she felt about all of this, but he hadn't run into the *Edgehill Gazette* office yet, telling any reporter there who would listen that they had a witch in their midst.

The truth was, it had been *one* vandal, and by vandal, she meant a cursed Penhallow witch.

"Nope," Amber said, offering a bewildered sigh. "The chief thinks it might have been some kind of gang initiation. I mean, hardly anyone goes out to that part of town, and most kids are scared of the place, so he doubts it was actually locals."

Ann Marie had a hand to her chest. "A gang. Goodness. We don't have *gangs* in Edgehill."

"I bet it was kids from the town that shall not be named," Chloe offered.

"Of course it was!" Ann Marie said.

Nathan lowered his voice a fraction and voiced something truly upsetting. "I had to go into Marbleglen last week to check their flower stock since the ones we need for the centerpieces for the gala might not be available in time."

Ann Marie shuddered, then placed a hand on his arm. "I'm sorry. There was no other choice."

Nathan nodded solemnly. "The name of the shop I went into was called Garden Variety."

"That's not even clever!" Ann Marie said. "Ugh, that Marbleglen."

The group at large sneered at the name of Edgehill's rival town.

After a short bout of silence, Kim clapped her hands once and dispelled the tension. "Well!" she chirped. "Let's take a few minutes to grab some snacks and use the facilities if necessary and then we can get started, hmm?" She looked around the room. "Chloe, hon, is your dad around?"

Before Chloe could reply, the crisp, clear voice of the mayor sounded as he walked into the dining area. "Sorry, everyone. Had to take a quick call." He slipped his cell into the front pocket of his button-up shirt and smiled at the small group assembled.

Mayor Deidrick wasn't handsome in the classical sense: he was of average height, had brown eyes, neatly cut brown hair streaked lightly with gray, and sported a few extra pounds in the middle. Amber thought her own father might have looked something like the mayor had he reached the same age. But what the mayor didn't have in dashing good looks, he made up for with that X factor of politicians. Whether it was the way he carried himself, his thousand-watt smile, or his charming personality, Amber couldn't be sure. She supposed it was all those things. In the wrong person, Frank Deidrick's collection of attributes might come off as smarmy or overbearing—like a salesperson confidently convincing you to purchase something you both know you don't need. But in the mayor, it resulted in an affable man who smiled easily and listened with great attention.

"What did I miss?" he asked.

Kim beamed at him. "Nothing yet, sir! We're going to get started in just a few minutes."

He playfully wagged a finger at Kim. "Now, what did I tell you about calling me sir, Miss Jones?"

Kim giggled. "Sorry … Frank."

Grinning, he said, "That's better." His daughter stood nearby, and the mayor slung an arm over her shoulder. Chloe was a few inches shorter than him and tipped her head back to offer him a grin of her own. "You all right, kiddo?" he asked softly.

Chloe's smile faltered a little and she nodded, looking away. "Yeah. I'll be okay."

He squeezed her shoulder gently. "Promise?"

"Yeah," she said.

He squeezed again and gave her a little shake. "Promise, promise?"

Chloe tried not to smile, but her efforts were in vain. "Yes, Dad. Geez."

Frank kissed her temple and then unhanded her quickly, seemingly anticipating how much Chloe would be embarrassed by the affectionate gesture in a room full of people. The girl, who had lighter hair and eyes than her father, turned beet red.

"*Dad*," she hissed.

Unfazed, he rounded the oblong wooden dining table that could easily seat ten and took a seat in the middle. Chloe semi-glared at her father and sat across from him.

Amber's magic was calmer here inside than it had been in the car, but she still felt jittery, so she opted to skip the snacks and took a seat beside Chloe. She did her best to ignore the mayor across from her, who was making silly faces at Chloe—who also attempted to ignore him, but she eventually caved and cracked up.

"I'm fine, Dad," she said, laughing.

He nodded, satisfied.

After a few minutes of perusing the snack table behind them, Ann Marie, Kim, and Nathan joined them at the table, their plates piled with fruits and pastries. Kim sat on Chloe's other side, while Nathan and Ann Marie sat on either side of the mayor.

"So, Kimberly," the mayor said, hands folded on the table, "how do you like being the head of the committee this year?"

"Oh!" Kim said, hastily putting down a blueberry scone that Amber had a sneaking suspicion was one of Jack Terrence's. "It's been great, even though I wish I'd come into the position under better circumstances."

"Speaking of, and not to step on toes or anything," the mayor said, "but what do you think of creating a memorial for Melanie at Balinese Park? We could unveil it during the Here and Meow. The park is in need of a revamped rose garden—do you think she would have liked to have one named after her?"

Kim leaned forward at the same time Amber did, to better see around Chloe between them, and they grinned at each other, nodding in unison. Kim turned her attention back to the mayor. "She would have been delighted. What a lovely idea."

The mayor nodded. "I'll get started on that right away."

Kim's chair creaked slightly as she bent over to grab her bag. She pulled out a file folder and plucked a few papers out of it, then deposited the bag back onto the floor. "So far, we're right on schedule for the Here and Meow preparations, with the exception of the centerpieces needed for the Hair Ball. We're working on getting those, but otherwise, everything should be ready in two weeks for the gala. I also just finalized the list for all the businesses selected for the Best of Edgehill competition."

Kim took the topmost sheet and passed the rest to her left toward Chloe. After Amber took hers, she slid the remainder of the stack across the table to Nathan. Once everyone had one, Kim said, "Eighty percent of the tickets for the gala have already sold."

The gala had been the mayor's brainchild—and one he'd used as part of his campaign to win his election. The idea had been popular with prospective voters and with the Here and Meow Committee alike. The first gala had been held that following March and was a roaring success. It was already proving to be even more popular in its second year.

Everyone who purchased a ticket to the elegant evening got a fun night of dancing and food, but they also were purchasing the chance to vote for which businesses in town would be given the "Best of" designation during the three-day Here and Meow Festival.

There were twelve categories this year, up from last year's eight: coffee, treats, pizza, comfort food, healthy eats, clothing, home decor, weekend hangout spot, entertainment, nightlife, hotel, and leisure. Over the course of the last few months, the committee—with votes submitted by Edgehill residents thanks to ads placed in the *Edgehill Gazette*—had narrowed the list down to two or three per category. At the gala, each business was encouraged to attend and present their best offerings. Those in attendance voted on their favorites, and each of those businesses received a "Best of Edgehill" label and several perks.

One such perk was having a Scavenger Hunt Bingo square. During the festival, a scavenger hunt was held, and each participant was given a Bingo-like card with twelve squares on it. Every visit to one of the "Best of" shops earned the attendee a stamp. A card with all twelve stamps was then turned in at a designated location, and the attendee received a commemorative pin. The design of the pin would change every year; the artists who got to design the swag and the Here and Meow logo were also chosen during the gala. The pin from last year had already become a collector's item.

Aside from the added foot traffic that came from attendees attempting to complete their cards, each "Best of" shop was to create a featured item that would be offered for free to any attendee who spent at least ten dollars in the shop in question. The Here and Meow provided a huge uptick in business for Edgehill in general, but the "Best of" designation was so lucrative, a few of the chosen businesses last year had made almost as much in three days as they had all year.

Attending the gala was not only a fun experience for the wealthier residents of Edgehill, but it was also an opportunity to give businesses a boost they otherwise wouldn't have had. Last year, the candy shop Lollicat, owned by Olivia Dawson, had been named "Best of" in the treats category and had done so well during the festival, the business was now opening franchises in three other cities in the country—and Olivia's online store was so popular, it wasn't rare for her shop to sell out completely around major holidays.

Amber noted that Jack Terrence's shop, Purrcolate, was on the list not once, but twice—the only business to be up for the prize in two categories. He was in competition with both the hateful Paulette Newsom of Clawsome Coffee for the coffee category, as well as Betty Harris of Purrfectly Scrumptious for the treats category. As much as she'd hoped to avoid Jack—say, for all of time—she knew she would have to see him in a couple weeks at the gala at the very least, but likely much sooner. Her traitorous heart hoped he won the coffee category, not only because Paulette was terrible, but because she truly wished to see his business do well.

She was torn about the treats category, because as much as she adored his scones and had a feeling that getting the "Best of" label would be the kick in the keister he needed to convince him to take his pastry business to the next level, Amber absolutely adored Betty and Purrfectly Scrumptious. People already traveled far and wide to Betty's shop for her sinfully delicious cupcakes, regardless of the time of year, but

Amber would love to see the woman get all the recognition she deserved.

Contestants for "Best of Edgehill" Competition

Coffee: Purrcolate, Clawsome Coffee, and Coffee Cat

Treats: Purrcolate vs. Purrfectly Scrumptious

Pizza: Patch's Pizza vs. Cateroni's Corner

Comfort food: Catty Melt vs. Mews and Brews

Healthy eats: The Milk Bowl vs. Holly's Harvest

Clothing: Angora Threads vs. Shabby Tabby

Home decor: Pawterry House vs. Hiss and Hers

Weekend hangout: Point and Pounce vs. Purrfect Pitch

Entertainment: Tell Me a Tail vs. Feline Groovy

Nightlife: The Applaws vs. Just Kitten Comedy Club

Hotel: The Manx vs. Tropical Purradise

Leisure: Feline Fine Day Spa vs. Claws and Paws

Emceed by: Henry and Danielle of 98.9 K-Mew

While Amber looked over the impressive array of participants this year, she couldn't help but notice that Chloe beside her was more focused on the phone in her lap than she was on the sheet of paper on the table. Amber couldn't tell what the girl was looking at, but if she had to guess, she would have said she was messaging someone. It looked more like a series of texts than anything, but even that didn't seem quite right.

Chloe looked up suddenly and caught Amber's gaze. The girl flushed, muttered an apology, and powered off her phone, which she tucked under her thigh.

Flicking a look toward the mayor, Amber saw that he was

eyeing his daughter, his brows pulled together. Amber couldn't tell if the look was one of annoyance or concern, but she supposed most parents of teenagers looked at their children that way most of the time. His gaze slid to Amber and he offered a slight shrug of one shoulder, as if to say, "What can you do?" and returned his attention to Kim who was still chattering away.

Amber knew that Chloe, in her senior year of high school, was gunning to be valedictorian, participated in a handful of school clubs, and was in the running to be Miss Here and Meow. And, of course, she was Ann Marie's assistant for volunteer services for the festival. She was also turning eighteen in a month and there was a rumor that she'd already started getting college acceptance letters. The girl had a lot on her plate and she was on the precipice of her first major life change— Amber figured both father and daughter were a ball of nerves for different reasons.

After another twenty minutes or so, while the mayor was in the middle of asking Kim something, someone cleared her throat from the hallway behind Amber. "Excuse me, Mr. Deidrick?"

Frank slammed a hand on the table. "What did I tell you about interrupting my meetings, Ingrid?"

Everyone at the table, Chloe included, flinched. Amber's shoulders were bunched up by her shoulders.

"I'm … I'm very sorry, sir," the woman said.

The group was frozen like statues, but Amber turned her head slightly and spotted a middle-aged redhead standing in the doorway, her face a brilliant red. Her head was bowed, like a small child who had just been scolded.

21

The seconds ticked by in silence.

"*Out* with it, Ingrid," the mayor said. "As you can see, we're busy. It's terribly rude to keep all these people hostage."

"You have a phone call, sir," she said quickly. "It's … Francine. Again."

"And I told you I do not want to speak with her—especially not now."

"I know, sir, but she says she won't stop calling until she talks to you," Ingrid squeaked out. "And she said if that doesn't work, she'll just show up."

When Amber glanced back at the mayor, she saw his nostrils flare. His fists were balled on the table.

Frank pushed his chair back. "I'm sorry, but I have to take this. Please continue without me; Chloe can catch me up on anything I miss." With a nod and another apology, he stalked out of the room. Ingrid had already fled.

"*Awk*-ward," Chloe sing-songed, breaking the tense silence.

Kim chuckled nervously. "Why don't we take a little break and see if he can join us again in ten minutes or so, hmm?"

Nathan and Ann Marie were up in an instant and were beelining for the snack table again. Kim busied herself with pulling more things out of her bag.

With everyone distracted, Amber turned to Chloe. "You okay?"

Chloe's gaze had been glued to her phone again, but she quickly turned off the screen and offered Amber a small smile. "Yep, all good. Dad just gets grouchy sometimes. Okay, a lot."

Interesting. Motioning to Chloe's phone with her chin, Amber asked, "And that?"

Chloe shrugged good-naturedly. "Just making plans with a friend."

She scanned the girl's sweet, heart-shaped face for a moment. "Well, in that case, where can I find the restroom?"

Chewing her lip and staring at Amber as if she'd just asked her to answer a complicated math equation, Chloe finally said, "Down the hall, make a left toward the staircase, then go up and it'll be the second door on your left."

Amber would have thought there would be a restroom downstairs but didn't question it and excused herself from the table. Once closed inside the bathroom—decorated in a beach theme that was all soft blues and creamy whites—Amber peeked out the window. The rain had started in earnest since her arrival here. The bathroom faced the backyard, and the trees there were still stark and bare, buds only just starting to sprout up on branches that were swaying in the wind. Their spindly limbs looked almost sinister with a backdrop of such dark, heavy clouds. A bright burst of lightning lit up the sky on the horizon.

"One-Mississippi, two-Mississippi, three—" *CRASH.*

Amber flinched as thunder rumbled so loud, she could have sworn she felt it in the soles of her boots. The lightning electrified her magic and sent it zipping through her blood stream. She looked around the room to find some small object she could use her magic on to dispel some of it so she could at least settle her stomach and claim some of those pastries downstairs before Nathan and Ann Marie ate them all.

She had just picked up a small, smooth seashell out of a decorative dish on the counter when a soft knock sounded.

Brow furrowed, Amber put the shell back and opened the door. Chloe stood on the other side, a look on her face that reminded Amber so much of the five-year-old Chloe who had just secretly eaten her weight in cookies while Amber was focused on making dinner, that Amber almost laughed.

But a look such as this on a seventeen-year-old's face was much more worrying.

"Chloe? What's wrong?"

"Can I come in?" she asked, as if Amber lived in their upstairs bathroom and Chloe had stopped by to visit.

Amber stepped aside, then closed the door behind Chloe. "Should I run the tap to drown out our conversation? Don't they do that in movies?"

Chloe laughed slightly at that, then plopped onto the closed toilet lid. She let out a long weary sigh.

Amber leaned her hip against the counter, crossed her arms, and jutted her chin at the teenager. "All right, girl, spill. What's going on?"

Thunder rumbled outside and they both flinched. Rain pelted the bathroom window.

"So …" Chloe sighed again, hands on her knees. Then she wrinkled her nose. "It's about a boy."

Amber grinned. "Okay, so I absolutely want you to dish every detail, but I would like to state for the record that my love life is currently abysmal, so I would take all my advice with a grain of salt."

"It can't be *that* abysmal," Chloe said. "I heard you were dating *two* guys—at the same time."

Good grief. This was a definite downside to living in a small town. Amber wasn't even going to bother to ask how Chloe had heard such a thing. It hardly mattered at this point. "I was only half dating one of them and it fully didn't work out. I'm too weird to date."

"Oh, I don't know," Chloe said, giving Amber a once-over. "Guys like weird."

Amber snorted. "Does *your* guy like weird?"

"Ugh. We only have like eight minutes before the break is over so I can't go into everything, but we can talk about it all later. I mean, if you want to? I know we haven't seen each other as much lately, but you've always been one of my favorite people to talk to."

Amber was so touched, her eyes welled up a little. "I just sort of want to hug you right now."

"No hugging! We only have seven minutes now."

Amber shook out her hands, mimed zipping her lips and throwing away the key, and then gestured for Chloe to continue.

"You're such a dork," Chloe said, laughing. "Okay, so there's this app called Scuttle that's basically a place to chat and share stuff anonymously. Mostly younger people use it but there are adults and stuff on there too. Anyway, I've been talking to a guy on there for a while now. Like … three months? He's super sweet and a really good listener. We tell each other everything, you know? I like him a lot. *A lot*, a lot. And he really likes me too, but he's been kinda pushing me lately to meet him."

Five hundred red flags were flapping in the wind in Amber's head. Maybe even a red banner whipping about in a torrential gale that would put the storm outside to shame.

"Okay, wait, before you say anything," Chloe said, hands out in a placating gesture, "I know this sounds like it could be dangerous. But he's sent me pictures—well, *a* picture—and we've talked on the phone a couple times. He lives in Belhaven. There are chat rooms on Scuttle for different interests—like movies or TV or whatever. I was in one of the chat rooms and posted a picture of myself and there was an Edgehill sign in the background. He freaked out because, like, what are the odds that two people from really small towns so close together happen to find each other?"

Amber pursed her lips.

Chloe started talking fast—whether trying to get in as much information during their break as possible or wanting to dominate the conversation so Amber couldn't voice her concerns, Amber wasn't sure. "He's a little older—nineteen—and he's still in Belhaven because he's working on an online course to get his AA and then he's going to transfer to a college outside Portland. He's almost done and plans to move in the next six months, so we're kind of running out of time to meet in person while he's still close by. I don't feel nervous about the guy at all. I've gotten to know him so well. The problem is that my dad doesn't want me to date until I'm like ninety. He'll be so mad if I tell him; he's so unreasonable about certain things. But I'm going to be eighteen in a month—technically an adult—and then he can't really tell me who I can date. I'm going to college; he won't even *know* if I'm dating."

"You said this guy has been *pushing* you to meet him?" Amber said when Chloe paused long enough to suck in air.

"Pushing is strong," Chloe said. "We just really get each

other, you know? And he's so hot—what if I wait too long to meet him and some other girl snatches him up?"

"If he's meant to be with you, he won't be distracted by someone else," Amber said.

Chloe huffed. "I knew you'd say that." After a pause, she said, "You want to see his picture?"

Amber wasn't sure how seeing this guy would help, but her curiosity got the better of her and she nodded.

Chloe pulled her phone out of her back pocket, tapped the screen a few times, swiped a few more, and then held the phone up for Amber to see. The young guy smiling back at her *was* attractive, and had a wide, easy smile. The background behind him implied he was standing outside—maybe at a park or in his yard at home—but the majority of the greenish backdrop was blurry. The boy had his hands clasping the back of his neck and he was grinning up at the camera. Maybe his mother took it. Two bracelets made of brown wooden beads ringed one wrist. As cute as the boy was, there was something … staged about the picture. Didn't kids these days only take selfies?

As Amber studied Chloe, who had retracted her arm and was staring wistfully down at the smiling boy, the red flag in her mind snapped in the wind again. "What's the urgency?"

Chloe glanced up. "I told you. He's moving—"

Amber shook her head. "Try again."

The girl sighed. "He's going to be in Edgehill tonight." She started swiping at the screen again. "He's really sweet, too. Look, he got me flowers."

Chloe held out the phone to Amber again and showed her a photograph of six red roses in a thin glass vase. A tan-colored card was tied around the vase with black ribbon. When Chloe pulled her hand back, gaze focused on her phone, she said, "The card says, 'To my Kitty Cat—" she glanced up at Amber for a second—"he calls me that since I come from the quote-unquote cat town." She rolled her eyes good-naturedly. "To my Kitty Cat, you make every day brighter. Love, Snugglebear."

Chloe flushed.

"Snugglebear?" Amber asked. "Anything to do with Belhaven High's mascot being a bear?"

Laughing, Chloe nodded. "I know it's all kind of silly, but it's sweet, too, don't you think? He wants to give me the flowers tonight."

Another boom of thunder rumbled outside, mirroring Amber's thoughts. "You can't go out in *this*." She waved vaguely at the storm outside.

"We planned to meet at the arcade," Chloe said, as if she hadn't heard anything Amber had just said. "That's what you're supposed to do, right? Meet in a public place?"

Amber sighed.

"Bethany is going, too! That's who I was talking to earlier during the meeting," Chloe added, clearly sensing that if Amber had been on Chloe's side when this conversation started, she surely no longer was. "I'll be safe. I promise. I'll text when I get there and when I leave. Bethany and I will stick together. No going to a second location with a guy or anything. I'm not dumb, Amber. I promise I know what I'm doing."

"Then why are you telling *me* this and not your dad?" Amber asked.

"Because he doesn't want me to date," Chloe said. "I just told you that."

"But he *is* a reasonable guy even if you don't always see it that way," Amber said. "I couldn't in good conscience know you're going out with some guy you've never met in person before and not let your dad know."

Chloe stared at her with her mouth slightly agape, her brow furrowed. She looked like Amber had just kicked her in the gut.

"I know you're mad at me right now, but either you tell your dad about this, or I do," Amber said. "It's not that I don't trust you or your judgment—you're one of the smartest people I know—but that doesn't mean I trust anyone else. I would never forgive myself if we didn't tell your dad where you were planning to go and something happened to you."

Jaw clenched, Chloe folded her arms across her chest and stared up at the window being pelted by rain.

Amber moved to squat in front of Chloe, who still sat on the closed toilet lid. "Hey. Look at me."

It took the girl a moment, but she finally did, her eyes rimmed with silver.

"Do you like this guy?" Amber said. "Deep in your gut, do you like him?"

Chloe nodded.

"Is he important to you?"

She nodded again.

"Tell your dad that. He's worried about you—you're all he's got. That's what makes him so protective. But we're protective of the things and people we love," Amber said. "He would be more hurt that you didn't think you could tell him any of this. Plus, if you have to sneak around to do something, there's likely a problem with it. So tell your dad. Let him know how much this means to you."

Chloe sniffed hard. "He'll probably want to go *with* me on the date. I'll be stuck with Bethany bored out of my mind while Johnny and my dad talk about football or something dumb."

Amber laughed softly. "Would that be so bad, though? To not have to hide that part of your life from your dad? He's your biggest fan, you know."

Chloe rolled her eyes at that, but she managed a watery laugh. "Okay, maybe it wouldn't be the worst thing if the two of them got along."

"Thatta girl," Amber said, standing up, then held out a hand and helped the girl up. "Just be honest with him. He'll listen."

Chloe still looked dubious.

"And, in case he doesn't, call me, okay?" she asked. "We can talk about this as much as you want if he shuts you down. You still have my number?"

She hit a few things on her phone, then swiped up on her screen. "Yeah, I've got it. And I've had the same number since I was twelve."

"Good. Call or text any time. Day or night," Amber said.

The girl nodded.

Once Chloe had splashed water on her face and gotten herself under control, Amber led them out of the bathroom, but came up short almost immediately. Mayor Deidrick stood in the hallway, looking even more startled than Amber felt. Her mental red flag, though, gave another frantic flap. The mayor looked nearly as guilty as his daughter had earlier. Had he been listening at the door?

The rumble of thunder that sounded moments later told her that even if he *had* been listening, the raging storm outside had likely drowned out a lot of their conversation.

"Hey, Dad," Chloe said shakily, moving to stand beside Amber. "Could I talk to you about something?"

His posture relaxed at the question. "Of course, pumpkin."

Amber's chest twinged at the nickname; her own father had called her that when Amber was around Chloe's age now. The memory spell she'd inadvertently cast a couple of weeks ago had allowed her to relive one of the moments when her father had called her that. Somehow it felt as if it had happened just yesterday and, at the same time, a lifetime ago.

"I'll see you downstairs in a bit," Amber said, and gave Chloe's arm an encouraging squeeze.

Once on the stairs, Amber glanced up just before the landing above would be obscured from view, and she saw the mayor drape an arm around Chloe's shoulder as they walked slowly down the hallway. *Please let him listen to her.*

The meeting went on for another half hour, but neither the mayor nor Chloe came back down. As they packed up, Ingrid bustled into the room to help clear the plates and uneaten snacks. The mayor didn't even emerge to bid the committee members goodbye. Amber had to hope that meant he and Chloe were having a deep heart-to-heart and had lost track of the time.

Kim and Amber ran to Kim's car, their coats draped over their heads in an attempt to shield themselves from the rain. Amber's magic was even twitchier outside. Thunder rumbled.

As Amber stared out of the rain-streaked passenger-seat window and toward the house, she hoped forcing Chloe to air her secrets to her father had been good advice.

CHAPTER 3

"Do you have plans tonight?"

Amber tore her gaze from the dark upstairs of the mayoral house and focused on Kim. "Uhh ... no?"

"I know you can be kind of a homebody and life has been kooky for you lately, so no pressure, okay?" Kim said, turning in her seat a little to face her. "But me and the rest of the committee are going to happy hour at the Sippin' Siamese. Want to come? If not, I can drop you off at home first. It's totally okay."

Amber was growing increasingly aware of how aware everyone *else* was that she was a recluse. Some part of her had hoped people would think she was busy with Very Interesting Things and that was why she wasn't often seen about town in the evenings or on weekends. Instead, they'd all been sensing the truth: she stayed home with her cats.

Rain still pelted the windshield, but the booms of thunder had become less frequent. The clock on Kim's dash said it was just after 4:30.

"Oh gosh, that's a long pause," Kim said, laughing nervously. "You really don't have to go. It would be great if—"

"Sure," Amber said, nodding once.

Kim abruptly stopped talking, eyes wide. "Really?"

"Really."

"Oh, yay!" Kim said. "Are you okay with heading over there right now?"

Amber looked down at herself. She wore dark jeans, a dark top, black boots, and a dark gray peacoat. Her choice in wardrobe colors was as bleak as the weather. She could only assume that her damp hair was windswept—and not in a sexy model way. But who cared, right? She was off the dating market as long as only non-witches resided in Edgehill; she had no one to impress. "Yep, I'm ready."

Kim let out an excited squeak. "Oh, I'm so glad. Happy hour at the Siamese is so fun. And since it's Thursday, there's even a line dancing lesson at 5:30 if you want to try that! Ann Marie has got some serious moves."

"Sounds fun," Amber said, hoping her flat tone didn't dampen Kim's chipper mood.

But Kim was already chatting happily about the last time the whole committee met at the Siamese. Amber got the impression the group had started to hang out more since the dramatic departure of Whitney Sadler and Susie Paulson. Had Amber been invited—and didn't remember—but had always turned them down? Or had no one asked, assuming she'd have said no anyway? Both possibilities were depressing in their own right.

The last time Amber had been to the Sippin' Siamese had been the night she and her younger sister, Willow, had joined Connor Declan and his friends for Connor's birthday celebration. Though Amber had originally been going to the Siamese to see Connor, she'd run into Jack Terrence, Purrcolate's pastry chef. They'd had a nice chat that had solidified her crush on him, but the evening had been cut short when word spread through town that an older woman had been found dead at the Manx Hotel—the same hotel where Amber and Willow's Aunt Gretchen had been staying.

Amber still got chills when she thought about how scared she'd been, sure the dead woman would turn out to be her aunt. That had started a series of events that eventually culminated in the terrifying night on Edgar's property where the cursed Penhallow had nearly killed Amber. She'd lost her car *and* her budding relationship with Jack Terrence that night.

If Jack was there again tonight, Amber vowed to walk home in the storm. Getting struck by lightning would be far better than seeing the lack of memory in Jack's eyes.

The drive to the Siamese took nearly twenty-five minutes, thanks to the ever-present rain. The bar was located on Korat Road. On one side of the street were a handful of shops and restaurants—only about half of them still in business—while the other side was lined with empty, fenced-off lots choked with overgrown grasses or copses of dense trees. At least Kim wasn't prone to slamming on the brakes in slick conditions; she just drove like a grandma—which was more than okay with Amber.

Once they'd parked in the gravel lot a few doors down from the bar, positioned a little behind what had used to be a diner, Amber and Kim made a mad dash across the wet sidewalk, running past the boarded-up shop fronts. It was a testament to the Siamese's great beer, food, and dancing that it was still open—and packed nearly every night—despite how many other businesses around it had folded.

Both the podium and the outdoor patio area were deserted. Kim pulled open the door and warm air, laughter, and loud music poured out. They stomped their feet on the already-soaked black mat just inside the door and shook out their coats. Dozens of sopping umbrellas rested against the entrance walls and were heaped on the floor, the bar's warm yellow light reflecting dully off their slick surfaces.

Kim led the way through the crowd that was thankfully less robust than it had been the last time Amber was here, but she guessed the place would be packed as the hour grew later. They walked past the smaller front bar, all the stools occupied, with a row of people standing behind them, some with arms in the air, trying to catch the eye of one of the two busy male bartenders.

Pushing her way through the side door that led into the second room, which had an additional bar, a mechanical bull, pool tables, and a dance floor, Kim confidently strode ahead, quickly finding their party at a table with a perfect view of the mostly deserted dance floor. Ann Marie and Nathan were deep in conversation, Nathan's arm around the waist of a petite blonde with a pixie cut. The pair's backs faced the dance floor, while Ann Marie stood in front of them, her hands waving about as she talked.

Nathan noticed Amber and Kim first and he grinned, waving them over. "Blackwood! You made it!"

Amber stopped before the group and shrugged, smiling. "This must be your wife?" she said, holding a hand out to the blonde.

Her smile was wide and, as she shook Amber's hand, said,

"I'm Jolene. Nice to finally meet you. I work graveyard shifts in Belhaven a lot, so when I am in town, I'm passed out."

"NICU nurse," Nathan said, grinning down at her with nothing less than total admiration.

Jolene nodded. "I miraculously got the night off, so Nate dragged me out of the house. We have the babysitter for another three hours, and my challenge for the evening is to get so tipsy that my lovely husband has to carry me out of here over his shoulder like I'm a sack of drunken flour."

"And since she only drinks once every three months and weighs one-ten soaking wet, that time will likely come sooner rather than later," Nathan said. "First round is on me. What do you ladies want?"

After their orders were placed, Nathan wandered to the bar on the other side of the dance floor.

While the four women were making idle chitchat until their drinks arrived, Ann Marie suddenly gasped. Amber and Kim stood with their backs to most of the bar, while Ann Marie and Jolene had their backs to the DJ booth in the corner.

"Don't look now," Ann Marie said, "but is that Francine Robins?"

Amber wasn't sure how literal "don't look now" actually was, so she glanced over her shoulder. Sure enough, Francine Robins was standing near the back wall, chatting up a very attractive guy wearing butt-hugging jeans, a black button-up, a black Stetson, and a huge belt buckle. He looked like he belonged in a sexy tractor commercial. Francine was a leggy black-haired woman who was at least five-eight. She wore a white sundress and an amazing pair of black-and-red strappy shoes. Amber was almost positive the woman couldn't dance in those things, but Amber herself wouldn't have even been able to walk in them.

"I haven't seen her here ... ever," Ann Marie said. "I figured she and the mayor spent most nights snuggled up on the couch together but pretended in public that they were just colleagues."

Just as Ann Marie finished that sentence, the gorgeous cowboy slipped his hand behind Francine's head and brought his mouth to hers. Francine most definitely didn't push him away. In fact, the make-out session went on for so long, Amber and Kim quickly turned back around, and Ann Marie and Jolene diverted their gazes.

"Welp, there goes *that* theory," Ann Marie said.

"If it's true the mayor hasn't put the moves on Francine, that's his loss," Jolene said. "She's a knockout. Did you see those shoes? Get it, girl! Giddy. Up."

The four women erupted in laughter just as Nathan arrived with their drinks.

"What'd I miss?" he asked, smiling wide, gaze bouncing around the group. The question only made them laugh harder.

"Nothing, babe," Jolene said, and got up on her tiptoes to kiss his cheek.

Kim and Ann Marie shared a quick, quiet look that only Amber seemed to notice.

Nathan, content to ask no further questions, set about distributing the drinks.

Amber had said, "I'll have whatever Kim is having," seeing as Amber drank even less than the tiny Jolene. Kim's drink of choice was Vodka and Red Bull, neither of which were things

Amber would even drink separately, but she needed to get out of her slump, and if this was what normal, well-adjusted people her age drank, then she would drink it, too.

It was decidedly horrible. She chugged the foul thing down anyway.

Before she knew it, Kim was dragging her by the hand onto the dance floor for the night's first line dancing lesson—the beginner's lesson. Even with the alcohol cruising through her system, Amber was so nervous, her knees were nearly knocking together. Luckily, the instructor was extremely easy to follow, and most of the people on the floor were just as clueless as Amber was.

When the lesson ended, Kim and Nathan on either side of her—Ann Marie already knew the dance, so she was holding their table—it was time to put her retention skills to the test. Copperhead Road started and Amber and Kim shared an excited squeak. Amber only screwed up twice, colliding with Nathan when she went the wrong way. But she was laughing and he was laughing and Kim beamed at her, clearly thrilled that she'd gotten Amber to come out tonight.

A bubbling sense of appreciation for the goofy chatterbox was suddenly so overwhelming, Amber felt a lump form in her throat. She wanted to shout her thanks at Kim, but the song ended and soon the floor was swarmed by more people, as the lesson for the advanced group was due to begin. Ann Marie hurried onto the floor, and Jolene stayed her ground, while Amber, Kim, and Nathan hurried off.

They had just reached their table when Amber's phone started to vibrate in her back pocket.

Brow furrowed, she slipped it out, expecting to see Willow's smiling face—hardly anyone else called her—but it was an unfamiliar number.

"Hey, you okay?" Kim asked, gently touching Amber's elbow, seeing as Amber had just been staring down at her ringing phone for several moments as if she'd never seen it before.

Since so few people had her number, she automatically assumed most phone calls were from someone who was trying to reach her because of dire circumstances. Had something happened to Willow or Aunt Gretchen? "Sorry, one sec," she said to Nathan and Kim, then hit accept and pressed the phone to her ear.

"Amber?" came a semi-frantic sounding male voice. "Is this Amber Blackwood?"

She pressed a couple fingers to her free ear in an attempt to drown out the sound of people chatting, laughing, and the instructor calling out, "Five, six, seven, eight!" "Yes, this Amber."

"This is Frank Deidrick."

Amber blinked several times. Why was he calling *her*? "Hi, Frank," she said loudly, brows pinched. "What can I help you with?"

"Have you seen Chloe?"

Her heart rate ticked up. Without saying anything to Kim and Nathan, Amber strode for the back door that would let her out onto the patio. She might get lashed with rain, but it would at least be quieter out there. She scanned the bar as she walked, mostly hoping *not* to see Jack Terrence. Francine and her hot cowboy were gone. *Good for her.*

40

Once the door was open and the biting air hit Amber's flushed face, she realized that she'd left her jacket inside draped over the back of a chair. She shivered, but stepped outside anyway, letting the door clank shut behind her. The rain had mercifully stopped, but the temperature had dropped several degrees during the hour she'd been in the bar.

"Sorry, Frank," she said. "Did you ask if I'd seen Chloe?"

His breath whooshed out. "Yeah. She and I had a long talk this afternoon and she agreed it would be best to have this Johnny kid come by the house tonight so I can meet him. She said she would call him and invite him over here for dinner at six. Ingrid and I had been prepping the meal for the last half hour while Chloe showered and got dressed. But around five forty-five, I realized she hadn't come down yet or confirmed that he would be here by six. I went up to her room to make sure everything was okay, but her bedroom is empty. The window is open and her car is gone."

Amber squeezed her eyes shut and leaned against the damp wall behind her. "Has she ever snuck out before?"

"Never," he said. "And in this storm? What was she thinking? I've called her half a dozen times and she hasn't picked up."

Silence descended on them, and Amber listened to the dead air on Frank's end of the line. Then something clinked on his side. The first image that came to mind was ice dropping into a glass.

"Um ..." she finally said, "can I ask why you called *me*?" Some part of her already knew why.

"Because she confided in you about this boy first," he said, the bitterness in his voice as biting as the wind ruffling the hem of her too-thin shirt. "Did she tell you where they were going? Or anything about Johnny?"

Amber wracked her brain to remember her conversation with Chloe. "Oh, maybe she's sticking with her original plan. She said she and Bethany were going to meet him at the arcade. She said she was going to Bethany's first, and then they were going to the arcade together. They may already be there by now if it's after six."

He heaved out a breath. "Okay, well that's a start. Thanks."

"*I would never forgive myself if we didn't tell your dad where you were planning to go and something happened to you.*" That was what she'd said to Chloe, and yet, even after telling her dad, she'd slipped out her bedroom window anyway.

Amber could only wonder if Chloe would have described the conversation with her father as merely "a long talk." Chloe Deidrick was one of the most level-headed people Amber had ever met—even when the girl was very young. What had her father said to her that would make her lie to his face, then sneak out of the house in the middle of a thunderstorm?

"Have you called the Williamses?" Amber asked. "Maybe Bethany's parents know where they are."

"I tried calling both Bethany and her mother, but no one answered."

"I'm over at the Sippin' Siamese right now; I think the Williamses live pretty close to here. I'll head that way," Amber said, walking to the patio door. "What kind of car does she drive? I'll keep an eye out for it; they may have headed somewhere other than the arcade."

"It's a black four-door Honda," he said. "There's a bobble

doll of a purple cat on her dash—like a hula girl, but as a cat. It dances around as the car moves." With a shaky sigh, he added, "I got it for her birthday last year."

"It'll be okay, Frank," she said. "Let me know if you hear from her, okay? I'm sure she's fine."

The call abruptly ended.

Teenagers snuck out all the time, didn't they? Sure, this was rare for Chloe, but that didn't mean this wasn't just a case of late-onset typical behavior. Chloe was fine. She was a lovesick girl who had likely been forbidden by her father to date unless he met and approved of the boy first, and Chloe decided not to subject the boy to it. So she snuck out. She was likely playing Ms. Pac-Man or laughing at one of the boy's silly jokes or interrogating Bethany in the bathroom about what she thought of him.

When Amber reached the table where she'd left Nathan and Kim, Kim was still sitting there, watching the advanced lesson. Nathan was on the dance floor now, wedged between Jolene and Ann Marie, and looking completely baffled by what was happening around him.

Kim's brows shot up as Amber approached. "Everything okay?"

"Not sure," she said, and grabbed her coat, slipping it on. She buttoned up her peacoat. It was still damp, and a chill seeped into the fabric of her long-sleeved shirt. "I've gotta go. I'll call a cab, okay? I don't want to ruin your night."

"Don't be silly!" said Kim, popping out of her chair. "I'll drive you."

A song suddenly blasted out of the speakers and the

instructor counted, "Five, six, seven, eight!" The dancers all surged to the right in unison. Poor Nathan surged left, his substantial weight almost knocking the guy next to him off his feet.

Amber turned her attention back to Kim. "You don't even know where I'm going."

"Doesn't matter," she said, pulling on her coat, too. "You're not going out into that nasty weather alone. Nuh uh! Don't argue. Let's go." Turning to the dance floor, she waved her arms in the air enthusiastically, like she was guiding a plane onto the tarmac. Nathan spotted her first. With a series of elaborate hand gestures, Kim mimed that she was going to take Amber home.

Nathan frowned, then nodded and waved. Amber waved as well, then followed Kim back out of the bar.

By the time they emerged out the front doors, the rain was back to a light drizzle. It was so quiet and deserted out on Korat Road—the only sounds were the muted hum of music coming from the Siamese, and the light tap of their shoes on the wet sidewalk—that it made Amber's ears ring.

"I'm sorry I'm making you leave early," Amber said.

"Nonsense," she said. "Now, what's going on?"

Kim's eyes widened a little more with every new detail Amber told her. They climbed into Kim's car and she cranked up the heater. It smelled a little like a wet dog.

"And now he has no idea where she is," Amber said, buckling her seatbelt.

"That seems really unlike Chloe," Kim said. "I don't know her *that* well, but she's always been so well-behaved and respectful. Her dad must be worried sick."

"He is," Amber said. "But this is new ground for them

both. Chloe has never liked a boy as much as she likes this one. You remember how intense high school crushes were—"

"Oof, girl, you don't even know …" Kim muttered.

Amber let out a surprised laugh. "Frank has never had to deal with her acting out before, so he's especially worried. I'm sure she's fine, though."

Amber hoped that if she said that enough, it would be true. "Okay, so where should we go? Bethany's?"

"Yeah. They're not far from here, right?" Amber asked.

Kim nodded and pulled out of the gravel lot. "Her mom and I are in a book club together. I'll call her."

The Williamses lived in a little tucked-away neighborhood off Korat Road. It wasn't as isolated as Edgar's house, but it was one of those places that was hard to find if you weren't looking for it, and the unpaved road that branched off Korat was unlit and surrounded on both sides by a dense copse of red alder, Douglas fir, and western hemlock trees.

Kim used her hands-free settings to call Bethany's mom as she turned left onto Blue Point Lane, her little car bumping along the semi-uneven ground. The thin gray trunks of the red alders stood out amongst the thicker fir trees. The alders' branches had been stark and bare up until a few weeks ago, and now they hung with reddish catkins and small brown cones. In the dark, they looked like dangling, fat human fingers. It wasn't full dark yet, but it was getting close, and Kim's headlights shone bright on the wall of trees on either side of the road.

"Hey, Kim!" came the crisp, clear voice of a woman through the speakers, and Amber jumped. "What's up?"

"Oh, hi, Grace," Kim said, sounding startled, too, as if she hadn't expected her to pick up. "Have you seen Chloe Deidrick tonight by any chance?"

"Uh … no, I haven't," Grace said, likely confused as to why Kimberly Jones was asking about the mayor's daughter. A bit of rustling followed. "Oh dear. Looks like I've got a couple of missed calls from her father. Bethany's been sick all day with a stomach bug; she hasn't had any visitors."

"Hi, Grace, it's Amber Blackwood," Amber said, chiming in. "Do you know if the girls had any plans to go to the arcade?"

Now Grace sounded truly confused. "No, not that I know of. Is everything okay? Has something happened to Chloe?"

"We don't know," Amber said, gaze focused on the trees alongside the road. "She snuck out tonight and Frank has no idea where she is. She isn't answering her phone."

"Goodness!" Grace said. "That doesn't sound like Chloe at all."

Kim slammed on the brakes suddenly and Amber let out a grunt as the seatbelt tightened across her chest. The grunt was more due to surprise than pain. When she focused out the windshield, she expected to see an animal of some kind in the road that had triggered Kim's excitable brake foot, but instead she saw a parked car, its headlights illuminating the path before it. It was dark four-door. The car's hazard lights were on, throwing silent bursts of yellow light against wide leaves and hanging catkins.

"Is that …" Amber said.

"Hello?" Grace said. "What just happened? What's going on?"

"I'll call you back, Grace!" Kim said and hastily disconnected the call. Kim inched forward and stopped behind the dark sedan that was pulled off to the side of the road.

Now that they were closer, Amber could clearly see that it was a Honda and that a back tire was flat. It wasn't hard to get a flat out here, what with the unpaved road riddled with potholes and rocks. Without saying anything to Kim, Amber threw her door open, pushing aside overgrown foliage, and climbed out. She hurried around the side of the car and toward the parked one, noting that the driver's side door stood open.

Amber's boots squelched in the thick mud. The drizzle had ramped up to a light rain now.

Slowly, Amber approached the open car door. "Chloe?"

No answer.

Heart in her throat, Amber worried she'd find the girl slumped over in the seat. That the airbag would be deployed, a dead deer lying by the car's hood—which would be smashed in and smoking. She imagined Chloe thrown from the car, her body expelled through the windshield.

But then she remembered the flat tire. At seventeen, Amber wouldn't have known how to change a flat, but perhaps Frank had better prepared his daughter for such things. Yet, the tire was still flat, and it didn't look like she'd attempted to change it. Had Chloe tried to walk the rest of the way to Bethany's house and something had happened on the way?

If Chloe had run into car trouble, why hadn't she called her father? If the discussion with him had gone as poorly as Amber suspected, perhaps Chloe's father had been the last person she'd wanted to talk to. She hadn't called Amber either, though.

Chloe could have called a friend to come get her; the girl

surely had several people who'd drop what they were doing to rescue her. Like the mystery boy, for example.

When Amber finally peeked into the car, she found it empty. The purple cat on the dash swayed lazily from its perch. Definitely Chloe's car. The girl wasn't in the front *or* back. Her purse still appeared to be on the passenger seat. Amber pulled her own phone out of her pocket and called Chloe. The call went directly to voicemail. No blue light from a cell phone's screen lit up from inside the car.

Amber turned around at the sound of Kim's approach, the mud sucking at her boots. "She's not here."

"Oh my God, Amber," Kim said, eyes wide. "What do we do now?"

"You call the mayor and tell him we found her car," she said, then she made a phone call, too.

The chief picked up on the first ring. "Hi, Amber. I'm a little scared to ask you how you are, given the hour. And considering how hectic your life has been lately."

"Hey, chief. Can't say things are much better today," she said. "I think Chloe Deidrick is missing."

"Deidrick? As in the mayor's kid?" the chief asked, at full alert now. "Why are *you* calling me about this and not Frank himself?"

She could tell he'd been sitting when he answered her call and was on the move now. Something creaked. A door slammed shut. The click of heavy soles on a hard surface. Amber explained the events of the evening, ending with the fact that the girl had crept out of her window without telling anyone where she was going. "Frank went to the arcade and

Kim and I headed for Bethany's house. We found Chloe's abandoned car on the side of Blue Point Lane. We called Bethany's mom and she hasn't heard from or seen Chloe; Bethany has been home sick all day."

The chief cursed softly. "All right. Stay put. Garcia and I are on our way."

Kim was waiting for Amber in her car, and once they were both closed inside, Kim cranked up the heater. The rain had picked up steam again and pattered against the windshield.

"Frank is on his way," Kim said in a soft, faraway voice, gaze focused on Chloe's abandoned car. "He sounds so worried."

"The chief is on his way, too."

They waited in silence for ten minutes. Amber knew then how worried Kim was based solely on the fact that she wasn't speaking. Every couple of minutes, Amber would either send Chloe a text or call her. Texts went unanswered; calls went to voicemail.

Had Amber broken the girl's trust by encouraging her to come clean to her dad? The thought that Chloe didn't feel like she could call Amber when she was in trouble made her stomach churn.

The storm had already driven Amber's magic haywire, but now, it itched to be used to help find Chloe. Could she use that dashboard cat to conduct a locator spell? Or something from the girl's purse? Amber knew now that her Henbane half—her mother's half—had been skilled in memory and time magic. Her magic was still a wild, unskilled thing, but maybe her cousin Edgar could help her figure something out.

The mayor arrived first. He was out of his car and hurrying

49

toward Chloe's with such speed, Amber wasn't sure he'd even taken the time to turn off his car. Amber had scrambled out to warn the mayor not to touch anything in the vehicle until the chief and Garcia could examine its contents, but Frank came to an abrupt stop several feet away. He put his hands on his hips, staring at the car as if it specifically had done something to Chloe. By the time Amber reached him, his boots had sunk an inch into the thick mud. He didn't seem to notice.

The rain came down harder now, plastering his short hair to his forehead. He didn't seem to notice that either.

"Hi, Frank," she said tentatively.

Slowly, his head swiveled until his flat-eyed gaze met hers. Amber involuntarily took a small step back, her boots squelching. After several intense moments of him staring at her, he finally said, "*What* did you say to her?" The question was simple enough, but his tone held nothing short of an accusation.

Her head reared back. "*Excuse* me?"

"You filled her head with romantic nonsense," he said. "And now she's gone."

"*I'm* the one who told her to talk to you in the first place," she snapped, magic zipping around under her skin. Amber had been having a rough couple of months and the mayor's tone was making her far angrier than she should have been. "She wanted me to keep it quiet so she could sneak off and meet him in peace and I said she needed to include you in her plans for safety reasons, if nothing else. What did *you* say to her that made her sneak out? This isn't normal behavior for her. If you're looking for someone to blame, try yourself."

The way he clenched his jaw implied he was weighing the consequences of decking a woman—one of his constituents, no less. He stalked toward her, invading her space. He peered down at her. "Don't tell me about my own daughter. You haven't spent a significant amount of time with her since she was *twelve*, Amber. You don't know what's normal for her. You just happened to show up when she was vulnerable so she confided in you. Anyone who showed up tonight could have filled that role. Don't pretend you have some lasting relationship with my daughter just because you're lonely."

That one stung, but she refused to show it.

She and the mayor were practically nose-to-nose now, rain beating down on their heads.

"So even *you* admit that if given the chance to confide in a near stranger or her own father," she gritted out, "she'd choose the stranger? What does that say about *you*?"

His jaw wobbled at that. One second ticked by, then two. And then the fight seemed to drain out of him entirely, his shoulders slumping. "You're right," he said softly, backing up. "She tried to talk to me. I …"

The fight drained out of Amber now, too. In a matter of seconds, suddenly the man appeared so much older. "What happened, Frank?"

He tipped his head back, eyes closed as rain ran over his face. He sighed and stared at her with red-rimmed eyes. "I gave her an ultimatum. I said the only way I would allow her to keep talking to him would be if I met him first. I threatened to turn off her phone and put parental restrictions on her internet use."

"*Oh, Frank* …" she said.

"I know," he said, gaze turned now toward the car and its blinking hazard lights. "I pushed her too hard. I always push too hard."

"Let's not get ahead of ourselves," came a familiar voice from behind her.

Amber turned to see the chief and Garcia approaching, both of them in black rain slickers and sporting wide-brimmed hats. They were far more prepared for this weather than she and the mayor were. Amber peered around the men to see Kim still in the driver's seat, her phone pressed to her ear. She gave Amber a little wave to let her know she was still there, and for Amber to take her time.

"Why don't you start at the beginning, Mayor Deidrick," the chief said while Garcia moved on to the car alone.

Amber stood back a few feet, not sure if the chief still needed to talk to her too. She would likely catch pneumonia by the time the evening was over, but she couldn't get herself to leave. Even though she knew most of what Frank had said to her had been fueled by fear—and anger at himself—Amber still couldn't dispel the guilt that sat heavily on her shoulders. *Had* she said the wrong thing to Chloe? The *what ifs* were going to give her an ulcer.

"The reality is," she heard the chief say after the mayor finished his version of the story, "teenagers this age *do* run away sometimes."

"Not my teenager," Frank said.

The chief held up his hands. "And that very well might be the case. I'll file a missing person report tonight; we will treat this seriously."

"I don't have to wait twenty-four hours to report her as missing?" Frank asked.

The chief shook his head. "Nope. Common misconception. But, again, roughly ninety-eight percent of people who go missing are found within a week—alive and well. It's only been two hours at most since you last heard from her. The best thing you can do right now is go home in case she shows up there. I'll get all my available officers on this tonight—paperwork will be filed, and what canvassing we can do will be done—but we'll have a better idea of what we're looking at by morning. If I have any more questions, I'll give you a call. But also remember that we're going to be limited in what we can do right now because of the weather."

Frank looked peeved, but he eventually nodded. "Okay, yeah. But *first* thing tomorrow morning—"

"First thing," the chief agreed.

"And you need to find out who this Johnny kid is," Frank said. "I don't know a last name. I just know he's from Belhaven."

"We'll get on that, too," the chief assured him. "But if she was primarily talking to him on Scuttle, well, we'll have our work cut out for us."

Frank nodded again, then turned for his car. His gaze snagged on Amber, still standing there waiting, shivering and soaked through. "I'm sorry, Amber. I ... I'm sorry I said any of that. I didn't mean it. Thank you for telling her to come to me."

He walked away before she could respond.

When he was out of earshot, Amber asked, "Do you really think she just ran away?"

With a weary sigh, the chief said, "It's really too soon to

tell. I saw cases like this constantly in Portland. Most show up no worse for wear."

"And what about the two percent of people who *aren't* found in a week?" she asked, a pit forming in her stomach.

"My officers and I will do what we can tonight," he said.

It wasn't an answer.

"Get on home, Amber," he said. "And get out of those wet clothes before you catch your death." He paused, taking in her appearance which had to be somewhere in the vicinity of "drowned rat." Water dripped steadily off his hat's brim. "Could you hocus pocus the water away? Like a ... magic dryer?"

He looked truly invested in the answer and she laughed softly. "I probably could, but that might be even more work than using an *actual* dryer."

"Huh," he said. "Well, try to have a better night. I'm sure Chloe will show up by morning."

But as the sun crested the horizon the following day, chasing away the last remnants of the evening's storm, the Edgehill rumor mill swung into full gear. And everyone was saying the same thing: Chloe Deidrick was still missing.

CHAPTER 4

Tourists and Edgehill residents alike were in and out of the Quirky Whisker all morning. In addition to the news that the mayor's daughter snuck out during a storm and hadn't been heard from since, the rumor mill was spreading stories at varying levels of ridiculous about what might be going on in the Deidrick household behind closed doors.

Henrietta Bishop had come in for her usual weekly supply of sleepy tea—three days early—and then casually asked if Chloe was pregnant and had run off with the father of the baby once the mayor forbade the girl from seeing the boy again.

Dina Regrath, the manager of the Catty Melt, came in under the guise of buying one of Amber's animated cat toys for her son, and then asked if it was true that Chloe had a drug problem and that she'd been taken to rehab in the dead of night, the runaway story fabricated to save face.

There were theories about the mayor's past catching up with him—everything from escaping the mob to being a fugitive from a heinous felony. There was a rumor that Chloe's mother Shannon hadn't died sixteen years ago and had actually been in hiding. *Maybe Shannon had been in prison until last night and kidnapped Chloe*, someone said. *Maybe she's part of a cult that the mayor didn't approve of, so he stole her away when she was a baby, but Shannon and Chloe have been in touch for years, and her mother finally showed up to bring her home,* someone else suggested.

These were all bits of rumors and speculation Amber had heard over the years about the mayor and his mysterious past, but to hear them all again in one afternoon was exhausting.

She knew dozens of people had come to *her* shop because Amber had been one of the last people to see Chloe, and because Amber and Kim had been the ones to find the girl's car. Amber wondered if Kim's phone had been ringing off the hook. She worked as a teller at Edgehill Savings and Loan, so Amber assumed not as many people could come in to pepper her with questions as they had been doing with Amber.

Just before noon, Betty Harris from Purrfectly Scrumptious across the street stopped by. Amber was always happy to see the woman, but if Betty—the queen of usually *accurate* Edgehill gossip—threw another wild theory at her, Amber might scream.

With Lily and Daisy Bowen helping the last few customers in the shop before they closed for lunch, Amber was free to chat with Betty.

The woman gave Amber a scan from head to toe and then offered Amber one of her signature tongue clicks. "You look beat, sugar. You okay? Everyone and their mother has been through this shop of yours today."

Amber groaned. "I'm about ready to pass out."

"Anything I can do to help?" she asked.

With a sigh, Amber shook her head. "No, but thank you. They're all just worried about Chloe, and since they can't harass the chief or the mayor, they're asking *me* every conceivable question instead."

"You and that chief sure turned the tide on your rocky relationship," Betty said.

"He's not so bad once you get to know him," Amber said. *And once you confess to him that you're a witch and that's why weird things have a tendency to happen around you.*

Betty smiled, her white teeth a sharp contrast to the deep brown hue of her skin. "Well, I'm sure the chief appreciates you fielding the nonsense so he and his officers can focus on finding that poor girl."

Amber wasn't sure if it was the barrage of loopy theories she'd heard today, or if she had just begun to doubt her earlier conviction that Chloe was okay, but dread had been creeping in all morning. Sure, the chief had said that teens ran away all the time, but Amber couldn't shake the feeling that something—or some*one*—had happened to Chloe.

"You hear the mayor called an emergency town hall meeting for tonight?" Betty asked.

Amber blinked. Somehow, even with all the visitors she had today, no one had mentioned that. "No. What time?"

"Six sharp," she said. "You want to ride with me and Bobby?"

"That would be great," Amber said. "Thanks."

After giving Amber's arm a light squeeze, Betty headed for the door. "We'll pick you up around five-thirty; we'll be right out front." The bell above the door chimed as she pushed it open. "And I may or may not have an Oreo Dream waiting for you."

Amber salivated at the mere thought of it. "You're the best, Betty."

Her smile was wide. "Oh, I know."

As promised, at five-thirty, Betty and Bobby pulled up outside the Quirky Whisker in their old, tan Chevy truck. Betty said it was Bobby's pride and joy even though it wasn't remotely practical for a town like Edgehill. But, as she had said once, "When you've been married as long as we have, you pick your battles."

The truck ran well enough—though it was a bit bumpier than Amber was used to, as if the wheels might rattle right off the thing at any moment—and both the body and the inside were pristine. It was clear how much Bobby loved it.

Amber locked up her shop and hurried to the truck idling on Russian Blue Avenue. As she let herself in, Betty slid to the middle of the brown leather bench seat.

"Hey, sugar," Betty said.

"Hey, guys. Thanks for picking me up," Amber said, shutting the door with a rattling clang.

"Of course," Bobby said, pulling out onto the street. As the truck bounced amiably down Russian Blue, he said, "How you doing? Terrible business, this situation with the mayor's little girl."

"I'm okay," she said. "Worried like everyone else."

"Our niece ran off a few months ago," Betty said. "Girl is fifteen. Got upset with her parents over something and just up and disappeared for three whole days. My sister was beside herself."

"Where had she been?" Amber asked, watching streetlights slowly click on as dusk approached.

"An estranged cousin's," Betty said. "Oh, before I forget!" She hinged forward to pick up her monstrous purse off the ground. She plopped the thing in her lap, then rummaged around until she found what she'd been looking for: a small pink box.

Amber took it and peered through the plastic window on top. Inside sat a single cupcake. The frosting was a perfect swirl of vanilla sprinkled with Oreo crumbles. "You angel."

Betty and Bobby both laughed.

"Give it a try," Betty said. "I tweaked the recipe recently. I'm thinking of using it as part of my entry for the Best of Edgehill competition at the Hair Ball."

Amber didn't have to be told twice. She peeled off the little round sticker holding the box closed. The Purrfectly Scrumptious logo featured a cartoon rendering of Betty and Bobby's Maine coon, Savannah. Her fur was thick and gray, her whiskers full, and the hint of a little pink tongue rested against an upper lip, her eyes closed in feline delight.

The scent of sugar, chocolate, and cream filled Amber's senses as she flipped open the lid, and she briefly closed her eyes in delight, too.

Then she cut a playfully offended look at Betty. "You're not trying to butter me up so I put in a good word with the committee, are you?"

"Darn tootin' she is!" said Bobby, laughing.

Betty swatted at his arm. Then she wagged a finger at Amber. "It's only fair since you've been fraternizing with my competition!"

Amber snorted. "I am not fraternizing with anyone! Besides, your competition is not even talking to me right now, so you're safe on that front."

"Oh, sugar," said Betty, patting Amber's knee. "I'm sorry I made fun. I didn't realize ..."

"That's okay. Now hush so I can try your cupcake."

Betty laughed again.

Removing the chocolate cupcake from the box, Amber peeled down a portion of the paper wrapping and then took a giant bite of both cake and cream frosting. Once she'd bitten down, she realized the cake was a swirl of both chocolate and white cake, little pieces of Oreo mixed in. Amber groaned. "Betty. This is amazing."

"Yeah?" she asked, as if she didn't know her cupcakes were so good they were nearly criminal.

"I told her as much, but she doesn't listen to her stuffy old husband," Bobby said, but he was smiling to himself.

"Yes, really," Amber said. "Definitely bring this one to the gala."

Betty nodded, satisfied.

They chatted easily about nothing in particular until they reached the Edgehill Community Center, which had only just been cleared of its "infestation" a week ago. Amber still had no idea what the chief had said to the mayor to convince him that what had attacked the people attending the junior fashion show last month had been insects, but Frank had bought it, closed the community center down, and had it fumigated.

Only the chief, Amber, Willow, and Aunt Gretchen knew that the real culprit had been weaponized magic.

The lot was half full when Bobby pulled his truck in, cruising slowly past the steady stream of people walking in the opposite direction to the center's front door. Once he'd parked, Amber brushed off her shirt to make sure she wasn't covered in chocolate crumbs. As the trio walked to the center, Betty looped her arm through Amber's, a gentle hand patting Amber's forearm.

The front door's peaked white awning, supported by four columns, had a banner hanging from it as it always did on nights like this. "Town Hall Meeting Tonight!" it said, swaying gently in the light breeze.

The oval-shaped hedges dotting the small front lawn in intervals stood vigil amongst the patchy grass. While Amber and Jack had gone through the staff's side door of the red-brick building on the day of the junior fashion show, today she strolled in through the propped open white doors with everyone else.

The small auditorium was filled with folding chairs facing the stage across the room. An aisle was created between the two columns of chairs, and a good deal of the seats were already occupied. Edgehill had an active community; residents loved their feline-obsessed town and the meetings often had a healthy turnout, regardless of what was on the agenda. Today, though, Amber suspected the room would be at capacity.

Amber, Betty, and Bobby were wandering down the middle

aisle looking for a seat when someone called Amber's name. It was Kim Jones, who stood next to a waving Henrietta Bishop. Amber saw Henrietta's mass of curly red hair first. Amber waved back and led the Harrises toward her friends. Amber sat between Kim and Betty, Bobby taking the aisle seat. Henrietta leaned forward to see down the row and greeted Betty and Bobby.

"Oh my God, Amber," Kim said in a stage whisper. "How many people have been calling you?"

"Nearly every person in town has shown up at my shop today. I called you at lunch to check on you, but you didn't pick up," Amber said.

"Amber. Oh my God, I nearly chucked the thing in the river!" she whisper-hissed.

Betty leaned forward to address Kim. "There were so many Nosy Nancys coming and going from Amber's shop today, I almost put up a barricade so no one else could get in!"

Henrietta winced. "I was totally one of those Nosy Nancys."

"Oh, I was too," said Betty.

"You actually bought something though, Hen," said Amber. "And Betty brought me a cupcake, so all is forgiven."

Kim frowned. "I want a cupcake."

"You know where to find me, sugar," Betty said. "And you usually do every Friday."

Kim gasp-laughed. "How dare you share my cupcake addiction with the world!"

Betty just grinned at her.

Within twenty minutes, the Center, as Amber predicted, was full, with even more people standing in the back and along the outer walls once there were no more chairs available. When the mayor stepped out onto the stage, everyone gave him a warm round of applause. Amber wasn't even sure why; she supposed everyone just wanted him to know that they cared about him and Chloe both.

As the mayor approached the podium in the middle of the stage, he raised and lowered his hands, gesturing for the crowd to quiet down. Hundreds of chairs creaked as people settled in.

"First, I just wanted to thank everyone for coming out tonight—and on a Friday night, no less." The crowd clapped again. "As you all know by now, as of last night, just a little over twenty-four hours ago, my daughter Chloe snuck out of the house and hasn't been seen or heard from since. In a town as small and close-knit as ours, you know how rare it is for someone to completely slip everyone's radar. None of her friends have seen or heard from her. No one has seen her around town. I'm her only known living family, so it's not as if she's with a relative somewhere."

Betty placed her hand on Amber's knee just long enough to give it a sympathetic squeeze.

"Last night, after six in the evening, two residents found Chloe's abandoned car. Her purse, coat, and umbrella were found inside. The only item missing is her cell phone. The phone appears to be off, as we have been unable to track its location so far.

"A missing person report has been filed. The chief and his officers are hard at work trying to find where Chloe might be."

There was a commotion off to the right. Chairs creaked

under shifting bodies. Voices rose. Someone was loudly shushed. And then a man stood up on the right side of the room and stepped into the aisle a few rows back from where Amber sat, waving away the people around him trying to get him to sit back down. Amber recognized him instantly: Victor Newland.

"How are we supposed to trust that you can keep our children safe, Mayor Deidrick, if you can't even protect your own daughter?" Victor shouted into the silent auditorium.

Frank froze, his features so rigid, they might as well have been carved into stone. "Please have a seat, Mr. Newland."

Victor did no such thing. "Melanie Cole is the first homicide Edgehill has had in decades. And only a year into your term. Less than a month ago, a maid was killed while having the audacity to think she was safe at work. And, in this very room, while friends and family cheered on their talented, creative children, a ... *swarm of exotic insects ...*" He looked around the room then, expression one of exaggerated disbelief, his arms out wide. He got a smattering of chuckles in response. "A swarm of insects sent dozens of people to the hospital. Two residents had their cars set on fire by a band of hooligan teenagers from Marbleglen. Even people from other towns see that things are falling apart here in Edgehill, Mayor Deidrick. Now we're seen as an easy target. These are all problems that started when *you* took office."

Frank's hands were balled into fists, but there wasn't even a hint of a twitch in his stone-like features. His intense gaze was homed in on Victor like a laser. Perhaps he hoped if he glared at him long enough, it would incinerate the man where he stood.

"And now," Victor said, shrugging dramatically, his tone falsely concerned, "the mayor's daughter is missing. Maybe she was kidnapped, maybe she ran away. Maybe he staged this whole thing to garner sympathy points because no one trusts him to keep us safe anymore."

"I would *never* hurt Chloe," Frank finally snapped, a finger jabbed in Victor's direction. His tone was so fierce and sharp, Amber heard several intakes of breath around her. Very few had seen the quick shift from a calm Frank Deidrick, to a furious one. "How *dare* you even imply that it's a possibility. You lost a mayoral race. I lost my daughter. *Sit. Down.*"

The room was so quiet now, Amber was sure she'd be able to hear Kim and Betty blink—but of course they were so startled, their eyes were stuck open.

"I'm only saying what everyone else here is thinking," Victor said, not needing to raise his voice. Then, without another word, he turned and walked out of the auditorium. A chorus of boos—much louder than the smattering of laughter he'd gotten earlier—followed him out the door.

Creaking filled the room again as people turned back in their seats to face the now crestfallen mayor standing on the stage, his shoulders sagging just a bit, as if his display of anger had zapped what energy he had left.

"We're on *your* side, mayor!" someone called out.

An upswell of agreement followed. It bolstered Frank a bit.

"I called this meeting because I wanted to ask for your help," Frank finally said. "At eight a.m. tomorrow morning, we're going to conduct a search of the woods around Blue Point Lane. That's where her car was found. We're looking for anything that might give us an idea of where she is or what might … or what might have …" He cleared his throat. "What might have happened to her. It will be muddy out there, courtesy of the storm, so keep an eye out for anything that might have gotten buried in the mud. Things of interest might have been washed farther out than we might anticipate since the rain was so heavy last night.

"If you would like to participate—if I *haven't* lost your trust—you can meet us on Korat Road. I know this is a lot to ask—to give up your Saturday morning—but I hope to see you there. We'll be coordinating outside the Sippin' Siamese; the folks there are supplying us with refreshments, too."

"We'll find her, mayor!" someone called out.

"I hope you're right," he said, bowed slightly, then walked off stage.

Amber had been woken by one of her usual Kieran Penhallow nightmares and lay in the dark, staring at the ceiling. It was just a little after 3 a.m. This time, rather than reliving the way Kieran had lifted Amber by her throat, his magic a physical thing, Amber had watched from afar as Kieran did the same to Chloe. The girl kicked and thrashed in the air. Amber tried to run for her, but she was caught in sucking mud. Mud that turned to quicksand, pulling her under until it covered her head. She had woken with a gasp. It had startled Tom, who hissed, sprang off the bed, and then underneath it. Alley, who had been asleep with her head on Amber's shoulder, had lightly pawed the side of Amber's face as if to ask, "You okay?"

"I'm fine, Alley," she'd said, her voice a little hoarse. "Just another nightmare."

Alley had seemed satisfied with that and had gone back to sleep.

Every time Amber closed her eyes, she saw Chloe again, thrashing and scared.

So around four, Amber got up and continued work on a series of cat toys she was tasked with making for the Hair Ball. They would be used as part of the centerpieces. The theme of the gala was "springtime," in honor of the Here and Meow happening in May, so Amber's creations were all playful kittens, most featuring a ball of yarn. Some lay on their backs with the yarn clutched in their paws. Some balanced on the yarn with all four paws, or just one or two. She called those her yoga cats. Some had yarn balanced on their heads, while others sat with yarn draped over heads and noses and pooled at their feet.

She was keeping them small, no bigger than two inches, and was foregoing enchantments for now. If the Quirky Whisker had been nominated for a Best of Edgehill designation, she'd have been enchanting the daylights out of the things, but at the moment, her life and her magic were in such upheaval, all she could picture were rogue cats darting across tables, launching into the overly coifed hair of fancy ladies, and doing the backstroke in tomato bisque.

When early morning sunlight crept in through her window, warm light spilling across her window bench seat, she decided to shower, get dressed, and walk to a coffee shop for a caffeine pick-me-up. She preferred Purrcolate's coffee but seeing Jack

Terrence right now would do nothing to help her already frayed nerves, so she'd need to come up with another plan.

After she was ready, she fed the cats an early breakfast—to Tom's great pleasure—and went downstairs into her shop. She pulled her closed sign down and took it with her behind the counter. Checking once over her shoulder to make sure there wasn't anyone wandering around Russian Blue Avenue on this chilly morning, she turned back to her small chalkboard, swiped a hand over it, and watched as the message changed.

Her bespectacled cat logo now sported a detective's cap and held a magnifying glass. The handwritten message said, "*Participating in the canvass for Chloe Deidrick. Join us outside the Sippin' Siamese. Shop closed today until further notice.*" The sign's wooden edges tapped lightly against the glass as she hung it back up.

She left her purse upstairs, taking only her wallet, cell phone, and keys with her, and let herself out of her shop. She had just turned the key in the lock when she heard someone behind her.

"You're up early."

Yelping, she whirled around to find Connor Declan standing on the sidewalk. "Goodness, Connor! You have *got* to stop sneaking up on me."

He held up his free hand, the other wrapped around a steaming cup of what she guessed was coffee. It was from Purrcolate; she could see the pointy cat ears protruding from the top of the "o" from the space in between his fingers. "Sorry! I was just taking a walk to kill some time before the search this morning. I usually go for a run on Saturday mornings but I couldn't get myself to go today. Guess I'm just full of nervous energy."

Amber narrowed her eyes. Connor's house and Purrcolate were both southwest of her shop, and the spot where Chloe disappeared was decidedly closer to both of those locations than the Quirky Whisker. Why was he taking a walk on this side of town at six in the morning, and why had he appeared just as she was leaving? She mentally shook her head. She was being paranoid.

Then she remembered her magicked blackboard and wondered if he'd seen anything. She involuntarily looked over at her sign, the cat on her logo now dressed like a feline version of Sherlock Holmes.

"Plastic toys, elaborate chalk drawings ..." Connor said. "You didn't major in art in college, did you?"

Amber hadn't gone to college at all. She'd graduated high school and immediately started working. She pinched and scrounged and worked three jobs for a while—some in Edgehill, others in Belhaven. The job that changed her life was becoming assistant to the elderly Janice Salle. Back then, when Amber was an exhausted and still-grieving twenty-two-year-old, Janice had been the owner of the Quirky Whisker, but under a different name. She sold curiosities as well, but hers had been decidedly lacking in magic. Janice didn't have any living family left, and with her failing health needed all the help she could find. Amber did everything from stocking shelves and putting in orders to refilling their inventory, balancing the books, and cleaning the store at night. The upstairs had been nothing more than a glorified storage area then.

As Amber had gotten more and more competent at the job, Janice gave her more responsibility. A little over a year after Amber started at the shop, Janice passed away in her sleep.

The news was relayed to Amber by Janice's lawyer that evening—though Amber had already suspected something had happened to the woman when she didn't show up to the shop that day. What had been the true shock was the lawyer informing Amber that Janice had left her the shop in her will. The building was bought and paid for—Amber needed only to maintain the space, pay the necessary property taxes, and keep the business afloat.

Life had been Amber's teacher, not art professors at a university.

"I inherited my mother's artistic nature," she said to Connor now.

He watched her carefully. She really had no idea what to make of Connor. There had been some semblance of a spark between them when he asked her to come to his birthday celebration last month, but he also had a spark with Willow. A spark that the two had been ignoring since high school. Amber couldn't get in the way of that—she honestly wasn't even sure if she wanted to.

"I wonder what else you might have inherited from your mother," he said, taking a slow slip of his coffee without taking his eyes off her.

She swallowed. He couldn't possibly know anything about her *witch* traits, could he? "Meaning?"

He shrugged nonchalantly. "You Blackwood women seem

to have so many more layers than I first thought. Just curious what else there is to know about you."

Was he flirting? Was he here for a story?

"Not much," she said, then turned away, heading down Russian Blue. She was sleep-deprived and was in desperate need of coffee. Her gut told her this wasn't a social call. All she knew was that if he found a way to interrogate her about Chloe's disappearance, she was likely to snap.

As predicted, Connor jogged to catch up and walk along beside her. "The nearest coffee is two miles away. You planning to walk there?"

"Yep." The exercise and brisk morning air would keep her awake long enough to mainline some caffeine. After the search in the woods, Amber was sure to be so exhausted, the nightmares just might give her a night off.

He jogged ahead of her and whirled around, a hand out. Amber came up short.

"Let me drive you. Consider it a happy coincidence that I happened to be in the neighborhood when—" he started to say, but when Amber crossed her arms and raised an eyebrow, he sighed. "Okay. Fine. I've been looping your block for the past half hour hoping I'd run into you before you left for the search."

"Why?"

"My editor—"

Amber groaned and stepped around him.

"Wait," he said, and hurried to catch up. "There are several reporters in town from other areas, including a very nosy woman from Marbleglen. My editor wants the *Gazette* to have the upper hand and land the story before anyone else—*especially* before Molly Hargrove."

Amber didn't know who Molly Hargrove was, and she didn't care. "We don't even know if there *is* a story yet."

"We have to prepare for the possibility that there is," Connor said. "The more information we get out to people about what may have happened, the better chance we have of finding Chloe. She might not even be in Edgehill anymore. A thorough, well-researched story could get traction online, and that traction could make all the difference."

Dang it.

They stared at each other.

"What do you need from me?" she finally asked. "I've retold the story a zillion times already."

He fought a smile, clearly knowing he'd won. "Make this retelling one zillion and one? Being able to use a couple of direct quotes from you would really help. I'll buy the coffee."

Amber supposed if telling the story again could help Chloe, she couldn't say no. "Fine. But I also want a muffin. Maybe two."

Connor chuckled. "Deal. Jack made these—"

"Not Purrcolate," she said quickly. Likely *too* quickly, given the cocked brow Connor aimed her way. "I was thinking Coffee Cat." She mentally winced just saying it.

Connor wrinkled his nose. Coffee Cat was a bit more hoity-toity than most Edgehill residents preferred, but the place was wildly popular with tourists. They sold elaborate coffee concoctions, artisanal waters, and overpriced snacks and sandwiches. It had opened two years ago, and while most

Edgehill residents had been convinced the place would fold in six months tops, it had thrived. And now it was even in the running for Best of Edgehill at the Hair Ball. "Coffee Cat it is. But, uh, my car is back this way."

His slate-gray Jeep was parked in the lot by her building, taking up the space where she had once parked her own car.

Amber liked to think the inside of one's car said a lot about them—or at least the current state of their life. The inside of Connor's car was immaculate. She wondered if his desk at work was this orderly. She imagined him living a minimalist lifestyle, his apartment sparsely furnished.

Amber's own car had always been in a state of mild chaos.

Once they were buckled in, he smoothly maneuvered them out of the lot and down Russian Blue. Their silence felt charged, but Amber couldn't say with what. He was, at least, a much more relaxed driver than her brake-happy friend Kim.

What had Connor been like in college? Given his goofy friends—particularly the drunken Wesley Young—she had to imagine he wasn't as rigid as his car's interior would imply. Not that she was one to judge.

Coffee Cat was in one of the more business-heavy parts of Edgehill, on Chartreux Way—home to the Milk Bowl, the *Edgehill Gazette*, and Sadler Accounting, among others. Amber wondered how Derrick Sadler was faring after the events of a couple months past. He'd lost his mistress and his unborn child to his wife Whitney—and now Whitney was in jail. Did he visit her? Did he bring their daughter Sydney? He'd gone from living a double life to being a man on his own, raising a ten-year-old.

Amber couldn't remember the last time she'd been in town this early in the morning—especially on a weekend. A few people wandered around, but Amber figured many of them were tourists. Most residents likely were trying to catch as much shut-eye as possible before they had to be on Korat Road.

Because of this, parking was exceptionally easy to find, and soon they were walking up the sidewalk to the café. In silence. Still. He'd left his coffee cup in the car; Amber wondered if *he* would be unable to sleep later, due to all the caffeine he was putting away this morning.

Two doors down from the accounting office, and next door to the Milk Bowl, a black-and-white awning stretched over the sidewalk, shading the heavy wooden door. In the large plate glass window to the right of the door, a giant white logo took up most of the space. "Coffee" was written in looping cursive and arched over the top of a white coffee cup, a black cat with its paws on either side of its face peeking out from the depths of the cup. The C in the word "Cat" made up the coffee cup's handle, the rest of the word following in the same looping font.

Connor pulled the door open for her. As she stepped over the threshold and onto the rustic, creaky wooden floor, she was hit not with the scent of coffee, but of sugar and spices. It smelled more like Purrfectly Scrumptious than a coffee shop. The color palate was all warm brown, deep green, and soft beige. The dark-wood counter stood to the right of the space and took up most of the wall. Gleaming planks of wood with wide gaps between them were overlaid on the front of the counter. It reminded her of the side of a log cabin. The walls behind the counter and directly across from the front door were painted with black chalkboard paint. Someone with even more impressive chalk skills than herself had drawn the menu items of the day on the wall, interspersed with drawings of leaping, sitting, and sleeping cats. The wall opposite the door was slowly being turned into a chalk mural of a meadow filled with cats.

The wall to the left was lined with a single dark brown leather bench seat and round wooden tables were spaced out periodically before it. In the available space in the middle of the room were plush deep green chairs positioned in front of small tables.

Amber was very annoyed by how absolutely inviting and cozy it felt, despite the fact that it was her given right as a lifelong resident to despise this place on principle, simply for being the kind of over-the-top artisanal café she would expect to find in a city like Los Angeles or even Portland, not in a tiny town like Edgehill.

"Do you know what you want?" asked Connor, startling her. She had been so taken in by the charm of this snooty place that she'd forgotten all about him.

"Not a clue," she said, and led them around the maze of chairs and toward the counter where two thirtysomething men with matching ridiculous handlebar mustaches manned the counter. There were two couples in the far corner, near the chalk mural, but no one at the counter.

As Amber and Connor walked up, one of the mustachioed men spotted them and smiled wide, placing his folded arms on the smooth wooden surface.

"Good morning, you two!" he said, even more chipper than Kim when relaying a juicy piece of gossip. "Is this your first time to Coffee Cat?" Then he stood to full height, gaze focused on Amber. "You're Amber Blackwood, aren't you? You're on the Here and Meow Committee? What an honor! We're so excited to be in the running for the Best of Edgehill. Your coffees are on the house this morning!"

"Oh, no, you don't have to do that," Amber said.

"I insist," he said, waving away her protests. "I know a lot of the locals are a little reluctant about this place but give me a chance to turn you into a Coffee Catter." He turned to the side so he could address them and look at the menu board at the same time. "We have your standard choices, of course, but if you want the true Coffee Cat experience, I suggest you try one of our signature mochas or lattes."

Amber eyed the board. Under mochas, she saw, "Raspberry white peppermint, toasted marshmallow, Black Forest cherry, and strawberry white mocha." She had no idea how to feel about any of those. The lattes sounded more like dessert flavors than those of a drink. "Brown sugar cardamom, snickerdoodle, spiced pecan maple, caramelized honey, white chocolate toffee nut," to name a few, as well as ones that were truly baffling, such as "iced oat milk matcha latte," and a concoction with ginger, cinnamon, and vanilla that was blended with something called "moon milk."

The man at the counter laughed. "Your eyes glazed over there for a second. How about you tell me if you want something sweet or something with a unique spice array, and I'll choose one for you."

Amber was terrified. What in the world was a "unique spice array" and why was it in coffee? "Sweet," she said.

"Same," Connor said, though his tone was mildly ashamed, as if he'd just admitted to committing an atrocious crime.

"Coming right up!" the man said and turned toward the machines and ingredients laid out behind him.

Amber and Connor shrugged at each other helplessly and found a spot on the bench seat—Amber in the booth, and Connor across from her in a wooden chair positioned on the other side of the round table. She wiggled out of her belted trench and draped it on the seat next to her.

They both folded their arms on the table's surface, looked at each other, looked away. Amber slid her arms off the table and sat up straighter, her hands in her lap.

"So ... uhh ... why don't you tell me about last night," Connor said. Amber wondered if the guy did better with talking about his stories than he did making "normal" conversation. That, or Amber just made him deeply uncomfortable. She supposed either one was likely. "Start with arriving at the mayor's house and then what happened through to finding Chloe's car. Is it okay if I record this?" He reached into the pocket of his black peacoat—which he hadn't taken off—and pulled out his phone. He placed it on the table.

Amber stared at it a moment, then nodded. "Sure."

He tapped his phone a few times, got to the app he needed, then hit record. She went through the whole story again, only stopping briefly when the barista brought them their drinks.

Amber's came in a small glass mug, the drink inside beige with a half inch-ring of what might have been cream or foam.

The lip of the glass was ringed in a thick layer of what Amber guessed was cinnamon.

Connor's looked more like a milkshake than a coffee. It came in a tall glass, the drink inside a dark brown that was swirled with darker lines of chocolate. A light brown-colored foam filled the top inch of the glass, and a healthy dollop of whipped cream crested high above the rim. The cream was dotted with a cherry and a few chocolate chips.

Though she knew he was mostly listening to her, he was also deeply engrossed in his drink. He had muttered a soft "Oh my God" after the first sip, though she suspected it had been involuntary. Amber's drink had been gone in five minutes flat. She guessed hers had been the snickerdoodle latte and desperately wanted to order ten more.

But she would be vigilant. She would not be a traitor. She was still rooting for Purrcolate, after all, regardless of how things had gone between her and Jack.

When she got to the end of her story, she hesitated. She remembered the mayor's anger and the hurtful things he'd said to her. Was that the kind of thing to share with Connor? Would it paint the mayor in an unfair light? Especially when she knew what the mayor had said had been fueled by fear more than anything else. She didn't want Connor to take anything she said and twist it out of context. Yet something about the whole exchange hadn't set well with her.

"Can I ask that this next part not be on the record?" she asked.

His brows furrowed, but after a moment's hesitation, he

reached out and hit the stop button on his phone. With his glass empty, he folded his arms on the table again. "What is it?"

"Well … Frank was really upset when he got to the site. I mean, it's completely understandable, given that his daughter was missing in the middle of a storm. But Frank has always been such a mellow guy, you know, and he … he said some really nasty things to me. Got right in my face. I can't explain it but there was something really off-putting about how … vicious he was. I swear, if he wasn't the mayor and had a reputation to uphold, he very well might have hit me."

Connor's brows shot up. "Really?"

"He apologized as soon as he realized he'd crossed a line with me. He admitted that he'd gone too far with her and given her an ultimatum that she clearly didn't like. Chloe taking off after all that sounds like a typical teenager reaction … but in a storm? I can't help but wonder if that conversation had been a bit more tense than he let on." She sighed, shaking her head. "I know he loves Chloe. But …"

"But who knows what things are really like in that house," Connor said.

Amber nodded.

Had Frank threatened more than Chloe's access to her phone and internet? Had she run away not to be with this mystery boy, but to get away from her own father?

"Do you know anything about Chloe's mother?" Amber suddenly asked. She supposed all the theories she'd heard lately had burrowed their way into her mind. "Any idea how she died?"

Connor shook his head. "We're looking into it. The details around her death are sketchy at best."

Amber recalled the mayor being nose-to-nose with her. "*Don't pretend you have some lasting relationship with my daughter just because you're lonely.*"

His words had been meant to wound. He'd searched for Amber's weaknesses so he could make her feel as low as he did. He had been around her enough and heard enough about her to know she led a fairly lonely existence here in Edgehill. Somehow, the man who would listen to your smallest of problems with attention and compassion, could also be the type of man who could take those same details and throw them in your face.

Had the mayor turned that quick anger onto Chloe during their talk? Had his actions and biting words scared her enough that she'd lied to his face and then crept out a window? Had Frank's wife been scared of him, too?

Connor spoke up, giving voice to the thought Amber already had forming. "It makes you wonder if Frank Deidrick fled to Edgehill to escape painful memories of his young wife's death or if he was running from something much worse."

CHAPTER 5

On the way to the meeting spot on Korat Road, Amber's phone chirped. She'd been clutching it, her keys, and her wallet tight in her fists, and gave a start when the sound interrupted her thoughts. It had been silent in the car again except for a classical music station kept at low volume.

"Sorry," she said to Connor, though she wasn't sure why she'd said it, and found a text from Kim.

Morning, Amber! I didn't wake you, did I? I'm still putting on my face, but I can pick you up in twenty if you want to ride over with me.

Shooting a quick glance toward the driver's seat, she typed, *I'm actually riding there with Connor right now.*

Connor DECLAN? So my sources were right!

They were not! You need to fire them all.

We'll talk about this later.

Hoping to redirect her, Amber asked, *Has there been any news since last night?*

Not that I've heard. We're hoping NOT to find anything today, right?

Guess it depends on what that something is.

Ugh. Right. Well, I'll see you soon, okay?

Cars lined both sides of Korat Road, soft sunlight glinting

off hoods and windshields still dotted with morning dew. Connor had to drive past both the Sippin' Siamese *and* the turnoff for Blue Point Lane to find a spot. The trek back to the bar where everyone was meeting took nearly ten minutes. Connor, mercifully, had finally started to talk. Amber had brought up Willow and suddenly the guy had all kinds of things to say. Amber would have to call her sister later to share this little tidbit of news.

Edgehill police cruisers were mixed in with civilian cars. Amber was mildly surprised to see police vehicles from both Belhaven and Marbleglen. Even a couple from Portland. Had the chief called in favors to his old cop buddies from the city?

The Sippin' Siamese's patio was scattered with people bundled down in coats and hats and nursing cups of steaming coffee. More still were inside, given the murmurs coming from beyond the bar's propped-open front door. A gaggle of police in uniform, including Chief Brown, stood talking on the sidewalk in front of the windows of the Siamese's front room. The mayor stood with them, his brow furrowed and arms crossed as he nodded periodically at what the officers were telling him. Perhaps he was being debriefed on how the search would go.

Amber's gaze skirted over the collection of officers, then snagged on their feet—they all had muddy shoes and pant hems. Chief Brown didn't notice her as she and Connor walked past them, nor when they stopped a few feet away. Her traveling partner had clammed up again. She pulled her phone out of her pocket to text Kim so she would know where to meet her, and also to give Amber something to do other than scrounge for another conversation topic that lit the guy up as much as the topic of her sister did.

Connor's attention was across the street anyway, where a news van was parked. A group of people were clustered together, talking in even more hushed tones than the police nearby.

"Friends of yours?" she asked, after hitting send on her message to Kim.

"Hmm?" he asked, and turned to her, as if emerging from a daze. "Oh, uh, yeah. My editor is over there with a few co-workers."

"You can go," she said, when it became clear that he very much wanted a change in company. "Kim should be here soon."

"I just want to check in really quick," he said, but he was already moving away. "I'll be right back." Then he hurried across the street, not sparing her a second glance.

That Connor Declan was an odd duck.

She watched how he'd grown decidedly more animated as soon as he was around his colleagues. Then her gaze snagged on a man off to the right of Connor's group. There was nothing remotely familiar about him, but she supposed there could be people from nearby towns here. A friend of one of the out-of-town cops, maybe. But something about the guy seemed off. He was dressed casually enough and appeared to be alone.

Instead of checking his phone or awkwardly making eye contact with strangers—the nervous energy of someone who was in an unfamiliar place surrounded by unfamiliar people—this man seemed too calm. Amber thought of the men in movies who were dressed a little *too* nicely and then strolled into the wrong part of town and were immediately labeled as cops by the locals. *That* was what was wrong with him. He seemed too alert, too calculating. As if he owned that little strip of sidewalk he stood on.

He must have felt her gaze on him, because his sliced over to her. She could only hold it for a moment, and then she swallowed and looked away. She pulled out her phone, but she didn't see any new messages from Kim. When she looked across the street again, the well-dressed man was gone. She scanned the sidewalk but couldn't spot him.

The only consolation she had was that she didn't *think* he was a Penhallow—but given the way her last couple of months had gone, she couldn't be truly sure of anything.

She scanned her side of the street, hoping for some sign of Kim. To her right, the gaggle of officers was still deep in conversation with the mayor. And beyond them, making their way up the sidewalk, were … Jack and Larry Terrence.

Oh crap.

She took several steps back until she was pressed against the outside wall of the bar. She hoped the cluster of uniformed officers shielded her.

Please go into the Siamese. Please go into the Siamese.

The brothers stopped just past the patio and peered into the bar. Amber couldn't hear anything they said, but she saw Larry shake his head. Then they kept moving toward her terrible hiding place. She tried to assess, on a scale of one to ten, how embarrassing it would be if she dropped to her knees and crawled under the officers' legs to hide, like a bored kid hiding from his mom in a turnstile of clothing at a department store.

No more than a six, right? Anyone who knew the details of her recent past with Jack Terrence would likely assist her.

Closer. Closer. Amber took in Jack's handsome face—his dark hair and his day-old stubble. Oh, the stubble was new. And it was working.

No. She quickly shook her head. *No, he's not a good match for you, Amber. Stop ogling his pretty face.*

Larry spotted her before Jack did, and Amber froze. He smiled at her tentatively and raised a hand in greeting. Poor Larry had seen Jack and Amber go from smitten to cold-as-ice in the matter of a day and neither Jack nor Larry had any idea why—both for different reasons.

Kim! Where are you? Save me!

Her phone chirped in her hand at that moment; a message from Kim.

Parked but still need to walk to the Siamese.
Oh my God, Amber, there are so many people here! This is wonderfully terrible.

"Dang it, Kim," she muttered to herself.

Amber was going to be forced into another awkward conversation with Jack, which would be made even more awkward by the presence of his brother. Up until now, Amber had done a rather bang-up job of avoiding Larry Terrence altogether. Which was sad, as she and Jack's brother had just been forming a friendship.

But Amber had a knack for making lots of *almost* friendships. It was the real, lasting ones that she struggled with.

Panicked, her gaze swung back to the chief and his fellow officers. On impulse, she tapped into her already haywire magic and, with a tiny flick of her wrist, sent a burst of air toward the chief's currently exposed neck. He gave a shiver and looked over his shoulder—whether he had sensed her magic, or he had instinctively turned to find the source of the gust, she couldn't be sure. All that mattered was that he'd noticed her.

She gave him a pointed look that hopefully made him think she had something truly urgent to share with him. His brows bunched up, but a moment later, he placed a hand on the mayor's shoulder, said something close to his ear, and then broke away from the group to move her way. The timing was perfect: just beyond the chief's broad frame, she saw the Terrence brothers come up short. Then a pair of women a few feet away waved them over. Jack hardly paid Amber another moment's glance as he greeted the women, but Larry squinted at her suspiciously.

"Amber?" the chief asked, craning his neck so his face was in her line of vision. "Earth to Amber."

She focused on him. "Sorry. Hi."

"Hi." Standing to full height, he cocked his head. "You all right?"

"Eh."

He chuckled. "Fair enough. Well, I'm glad you're here. I have a ... favor to ask of you."

"Oh?"

He glanced at the officers to her right, then lightly jerked his head to the left. "Come with me."

She did so, his big frame shielding her from the Terrence brothers as she walked by. She could feel Larry's gaze on her; she did her best to ignore him.

Amber and the chief walked halfway up the sidewalk, the crowd much thinner here as this was not only getting too far from the Siamese, but it was exceedingly farther from Blue Point Lane.

"There's an alley coming up here in a second," the chief said in a low tone. "Turn in there."

He was creeping her out a little. She thought of the mud on his shoes and pant hems, and a lump formed in her throat. Had they already found her? Had her body been discovered in the woods during a preliminary search and the police had been debriefing the mayor on how best to tell all these people the worst possible news?

After turning left into the alley, they silently walked to the end of it. When they reached it, Amber whirled to face him. "You found her, didn't you?"

He cocked his head again. "What? No. Actually, the opposite. We canvassed the woods last night and came up empty. We've been in and out of this area since four this morning. A couple of officers from Portland brought in sniffer dogs. Nothing. Whether that's because there's nothing to find, or because the rain washed away any hint of evidence ..."

Amber's shoulders sagged and she rested her back against the brick wall behind her. "So what's with the clandestine alley meeting?"

"Normally, we would never let civilians canvass what could potentially be a crime scene. At least not this soon," he said. "The mayor called that town hall meeting without consulting the department first. Once we found out about it, we did our best to conduct our own preemptive search. We tried calling this off altogether, honestly. I dang near begged him to. Asked him to give us a week, then three days. He won't budge. I could fight him on it—the guy isn't above the law—but I'm not sure raising a stink is worth it at this point. I'm trying to make the best of an already bad situation."

None of that answered her question, but she let him keep talking.

"He threatened to get a gang of private investigators in here if we didn't step up the search. We've barely had time to breathe; most of my officers haven't slept. We're doing all we can," he said, and she noticed the bags under his eyes then. "I've met my fair share of up-and-up PIs, but I've met some real sleazebags who will do anything they think is necessary to get the information they've been paid to find. Depending on who he gets in here … well, they could make things even more difficult for us."

"And this is where the favor comes in?"

He nodded, then glanced behind him down the length of the alley, the mouth of which was still deserted. All she could see was part of a large white van on the opposite side of the street. He turned back to her, then leaned a shoulder against the wall, blocking her from view, she realized, from anyone who might walk by.

Though, at this point, she was sure everyone in Edgehill had seen the two disappear into an alley together and were already speculating that she and the chief were doing something inappropriate down here.

He quickly reached into a pocket and pulled out a plastic zipped bag with a tube of lipstick in it and handed it to her.

She took it cautiously. *Lady in Red,* said the round label on the base.

"This is Chloe's," he said. "I was thinking you could do one of your … what do you call them … locator spells on it?" He said the last few words in a hushed whisper as if they were the foulest of curse words.

"Really?" she asked, blinking rapidly.

"Really," he said. "Between the mayor's influence, the growing media interest in this, and the threat of possible PIs invading the town, we need something to appease Frank enough to get him to back off a little. If something truly terrible did happen to Chloe, things could get ugly here."

She looked down at the tube in her hand. "Can I touch the actual canister? The more direct the contact, the better."

He sighed. "Can you magic away your fingerprints afterwards?"

"I have no idea."

Groaning, he said, "I feel like I'm setting myself up for disaster here, but yes. We need a lead. Anything. Your fingerprints being on her lipstick could be explained away by that conversation you had in the bathroom with her at her house. Maybe you touched it then."

Amber nodded. "Okay, give me a second."

He blanched. "You're going to do it *here*?"

"Oh, don't get your panties in a twist," she said, smiling to herself at the appalled expression on his face.

Opening the bag, she reached in to take out the thin gold canister. Then she folded and stuffed the empty bag into her pocket. With a calming breath, and the canister held between thumb and forefinger, she closed her eyes.

"Is it ... is it working?"

"Shh!" she said. "I haven't even started yet."

Conducting a locator spell varied in difficulty depending on what—or who—she was looking for. The spell used to find her cell phone had been conducted so often, it had become second nature, hardly needing a full thought. All she had to do was picture her cell phone and her magic did the rest.

When it came to people, however, how much the person *wanted* to be found—assuming they could be found at all—had a way of interfering with even a perfectly executed locator spell. Amber supposed she could still locate Chloe if she had met her end, but it would depend on how long it had been since she'd passed away. Amber's magic could latch onto what remained of Chloe's life energy, but only if that energy was still there to find. Amber had been able to tap into Melanie's life energy at least partly because Melanie's body had been preserved in the morgue. Amber couldn't say the same for Chloe.

Her stomach roiled.

Blowing out another steadying breath, she told herself to concentrate. The chief staring at her wasn't helping, and her magic felt as jittery as the rest of her.

Memory magic is your birthright, she reminded herself. *You inherited memory magic from the Henbanes.*

When she instructed her magic to remember her conversation with Chloe, suddenly she was *there* again. Rain lashed the bathroom window. Chloe, alive and healthy, sat on the closed lid of the toilet, while Amber stood with a hip resting against the counter. Amber focused on Chloe—her heart-shaped face and light brown hair and eyes. The way she was prone to turn beet red when embarrassed.

Though her mind told her she stood in a bathroom in the Deidricks's house, she could still feel the lipstick tube held tight between two fingers. The brick wall against her back. The chief's piercing gaze boring into the side of her head.

Where is Chloe Deidrick? she asked her magic.

She was pulled, almost literally, out of her memory and the Deidricks's bathroom. Her eyes snapped open and she involuntary took a step forward. The feeling was similar to what happened after she conducted a spell for her cell phone; a tug in the direction of where the item was hidden. Except this was ten times stronger.

She wasn't sure how long she could fight it. What if she started sprinting down the sidewalk toward the location, unable to get her feet to listen to her?

"Is it happening?" the chief asked.

"Yeah," she said. "It's strong. How soon can you get this search started? My magic won't let up until I find what I'm looking for. It'll get more insistent until I do."

"I can get them moving in ten," he said. "That enough time?"

"Guess it'll have to be," she said, wincing slightly. She felt like a piece of metal being yanked toward a powerful magnet.

"On it," he said, then jogged away. Thankfully he slowed to a causal strolling pace once he reached the mouth of the alley, which hopefully made their alley meeting slightly less suspicious looking.

Though, didn't people who had secret meetings always leave a place separately to keep people from making assumptions? Which was exactly what would happen anyway. Great. She really hoped the chief's wife didn't catch wind of some kooky rumor about her husband and Amber having a secret romantic rendezvous in an alley on the morning of a search for a missing young girl. It sounded tacky on so many levels.

As much as she had grown to like—and trust—the chief, he was one of the last people she had romantic feelings for, regardless of the fact that he was married, and she adored his son Sammy.

But none of that would matter if some busybody got it in his or her head that Amber and the chief were up to no good. People were already starting to make wild speculations about the rapid shift in their relationship from animosity to best buds.

Thankfully, she'd only heard one person suggest that perhaps she and the chief had an "enemies to lovers" kind of chemistry that had finally tipped over to the "lovers" side. Amber gave a violent shudder.

Her magic tugged her forward, reminding her that she had more important things to be worried about right now. She dropped the lipstick tube into her pocket.

Just as the chief had done before her, she slowed when she reached the mouth of the alley, gave herself a little mental pep talk, and then strode out onto the sidewalk, turning right. She had almost reached the assembled group outside the Sippin' Siamese—the mayor was standing on a table in the patio of the bar and had just brought a megaphone to his mouth—when her phone gave a chirp.

She pulled it out to see several missed texts from Kim.

Where are you?

Someone said you and the chief just snuck off together?

The chief is here and looking very haggard and you're nowhere to be found!

Amber?

Amber fired off a quick reply, wincing as her magic gave her another yank. She stumbled forward a half step but held her ground. *I'm outside the Siamese now. Where are YOU?*

"Thank you all for coming this morning," the mayor said into the megaphone.

There were at least one hundred people here. Amber could only imagine how much damage this many pairs of feet could do to potential evidence—none of that had occurred to her until the chief had said as much.

Amber stood at the back of the group assembled on the sidewalk and had to rise onto her tiptoes to see over the sea of heads. Soon there was a minor disturbance in the group ahead, and Amber soon realized it was because Kim was making her way through the crowd against the flow of traffic to get to her.

When Kim broke free, she let out a puff of air. "Oh my God, Amber. I never thought I'd find you in all this madness." Her friend wore jeans, black boots, and a puffy black jacket. Her long brown hair had been stuffed up inside a fuzzy pink knit cap, which was held down by a pair of plush white earmuffs. It wasn't nearly cold enough for such attire, and she looked a bit closer to a snow bunny ready to lounge in a ski cabin than she did someone preparing to trek through mud in mid-March, but nonetheless Amber was happy to see her.

"Sorry," Amber said. "I had to talk to the chief."

Kim wrinkled her nose. "So I heard. Too bad he's a happily married man. He's kind of hot. I like the idea of you snagging someone like that."

Amber took Kim by the elbow and gently turned her around so she was facing the same way as the rest of the crowd. "I much prefer having *your* company."

Kim beamed.

"These fine officers here," the mayor said, pulling their attention toward the bar's patio. They both stood on tiptoe to get a better view. The mayor motioned to the group of officers huddled just outside the gate of the patio. Several waved a hand in acknowledgement at the residents waiting on either side of the street. "These officers will be sending people out in waves and will be giving you assignments on where best to search. There are a lot of you here, so please be patient while they sort everything out. For now, they've asked me to have everyone on *this* side of the street start making their way toward Blue Point Lane. Those across the street will get their time as well—just hold tight."

The mayor put the megaphone down on the table, then jumped off.

Amber's magic gave another lurch and she let out an involuntary grunt.

Kim cocked her head. "You okay?"

Amber rubbed her stomach. "Just nerves, I think."

"Oh my God," she said. "Me too. I had this really weird dream last night about Chloe. Well, at first I didn't know it was Chloe, because she was in the form of a pink duck, but eventually …"

Amber let her friend ramble on as the group slowly inched forward. Since there was more open space across the street—one of the fences surrounding a field had toppled over—the group on that side had become increasingly larger. There were still thirty to forty people in Amber's group, but maybe that was an easier amount for the police to tackle first.

It took a good ten minutes to reach the mouth of the dirt road that was Blue Point Lane. They crossed the street as a group, then huddled together near the weather-beaten street sign. Amber's magic was nearly thrashing now—being so close to where Chloe's car had been found—that the niggling worry in Amber's gut had started to morph into full-on dread.

Here, Chief Brown took over, telling the group that they'd be broken into groups of ten and would be paired off with an officer. This group as a whole would be starting closer to the neighborhood where Bethany Williams lived, and would be fanning out into the woods on either side of the road. The bigger group still waiting across the street from the Siamese would be fanning out starting halfway down Blue Point and would work their way back toward Korat Road.

The chief then assigned certain officers to groups of people. Once an officer had been assigned ten people, the group started down the road. This kept happening until the only people left were Kim, Amber, and the chief.

"Our group seems a little small, no?" Kim asked, in a tone tentative enough that it was clear she didn't want to offend a man such as the chief, who had the power to arrest her.

"We'll be searching the area about halfway down the road—right about where you two spotted the car. Since you two were the ones who found it, I was hoping being there again might jog your memory," the chief said. "There may be something near the site that we missed."

Kim relaxed at that.

Amber's magic lurched again and this time she couldn't ignore it. Against her will, her magic yanked her forward, powering her legs to move up the muddy, rock-strewn road.

"Guess she's really anxious to get started," she heard the chief say behind her, followed by an awkward laugh. The chief clearly had *not* missed his calling as an actor.

They both hurried to flank her. Amber's strides were long and determined. She hoped her magic would at least give her some warning before it inevitably caused her to veer into the foliage growing tall and thick on either side of the road. Kim was on her right side, and if Amber's magic suddenly caused Amber to head that way, she was sure to knock the thin brunette clear off her feet and into a mud puddle.

"What kind of thing should we be looking for, chief?" Kim asked.

The chief replied, but Amber didn't register what he'd said. Her magic's pull kept getting stronger, making Amber's mind grow fuzzy with it. She felt like a plodding robot being driven forward by mechanics and wires, not anything resembling thought.

"This is where the car was found," the chief said, a pointer finger angled ahead of them, his voice cutting through her magic's fog. Miraculously, her magic eased up a little and allowed her to stop—but it was more like pulling the emergency brake on a car that was still in motion. "You can't see the tire tracks, of course, as the storm washed those away, but Garcia and I left a marker here." He gestured to a small flag, its pennant attached to a thin wire stand, the orange material speckled with mud.

As they made a semicircle around the marker, Amber heard the rustle of people in the woods behind her and to the left. The call of "*Chloe!*" echoed around her like erratic bird song.

Red alder dominated this stretch of road, their thin, pale trunks patterned with gray blotches of lichen. The trees were dense here, the trunks so close together it looked like a wall of white that stretched on forever. Smaller green shrubs grew at their bases. Could Chloe truly have gone in there? During a storm, no less? It was intimidating on a dry day in broad daylight.

Though her magic had settled when she stopped before this flag, Amber knew there had to be more her magic could give her. The fact that it still hummed beneath her skin told her it wasn't done, just that the biggest energy signature from Chloe was in this location.

Kim had taken a few steps to the right and was hinged at the waist as she examined something on the ground.

"Anything?" came the chief's voice, nearly right in Amber's ear.

She jumped. "Maybe. Just ... take a step back?"

He did so. Relaxing her shoulders, letting her hands hang

loosely by her sides, she closed her eyes. Her magic perked up, like the way Tom did when he heard the crinkle of the treat bag. It was tense, ready, waiting.

Where is Chloe? she asked her magic again.

She was abruptly yanked forward, as if someone had a rope tied around her waist and suddenly pulled with all their strength. Her eyes sprang open and she started forward, her boot narrowly missing the orange marker flag.

"Amber?" Kim asked, but Amber couldn't stop now.

She knew Kim and the chief would follow.

Amber pushed aside the red alder branches as she ducked under them, trying not to picture fingers snagging in her hair as the reddish catkins brushed against her. The foliage beneath her feet didn't crunch, as everything out here still felt so damp, but she and her companions were definitely making noise. Like a heard of elephants. The farther in they got, the more the calls for "Chloe!" seemed to come from all sides.

Surely if the girl was out here, she would have heard someone by now. Which didn't bode well for her.

Branches clawed and snatched at Amber's face, but she kept moving forward, her magic telling her where to go. The sounds of Kim and the chief seemed to grow softer and softer the farther she went. Kim might have called out for Amber to slow down, but Amber couldn't have even if she'd wanted to. Her magic had full control.

Tug. Under a hanging branch.

Tug. Over a wide shrub.

Tug. Around a tree with a much wider trunk than a red alder.

98

And then her magic put on the brakes so abruptly, Amber almost pitched forward into the slowly moving stream ahead of her, the banks of which were covered in moss. Amber could easily see the bottom of the stream, the bed littered with rocks.

The stream ran straight for quite some distance to the left—the direction the water flowed—and, to the right, it disappeared around a bend. The drop into the stream was only about half a foot, but the moss looked slick.

Tug.

Before Amber could protest, her magic forced her down the slippery bank and into the stream. She considered it a small miracle that she hadn't lost her footing and landed butt-first in the sure-to-be-chilly water. The stream only lapped a few centimeters up the side of her boots, and the current was virtually nonexistent. She began to walk up the very slight incline against the flow.

Kim had reached the bank, given the "What on *earth* has gotten into her?" Amber heard behind her. But soon after, there were a few grunts and then the muted splashes of more boots hitting water.

"*Chloe!*"

"*Chloe, are you out here?*"

"*Chloe!*"

When Amber reached the bend in the stream, her magic put on the brakes again. The water was a little stronger here, lapping over the tops of Amber's boots. She frantically scanned the trees, the ground on either side of the stream, and the water itself, half expecting to see Chloe lying in a heap somewhere.

Instead, Amber's gaze snagged on something glinting near the shore. At first, she thought it had merely been sunlight reflecting off the water, or a smooth rock close to the surface, but something about it looked different. The moment that thought materialized, Amber's magic released its hold on her and she nearly sagged to her knees in relief.

She hurried to the spot, finding a rock roughly the size of her head, water flowing around either side of it. And, wedged partially underneath and behind the rock, was a cell phone.

"Chief!" she called out. "I think I found something!"

The splash of water grew louder as Kim and the chief jogged the rest of their way to Amber. When they reached her, she pointed to the device. It must have fallen in—or had been *thrown* in—and had bounced its way down the stream, only to get caught by this large rock.

The chief's brows shot toward his hairline when he spotted it. "Good work, Amber."

"We don't know it's hers," Amber said quickly, even though Amber and the chief knew it was. She moved out of the way to stand with Kim, giving the chief room to fish the phone out and place it in a bag he pulled from his pocket.

Kim blew out a breath and rested her hands on her hips, as if she'd just run a great distance. "How did you even *see* that? Actually, how did you know to come up this stream? You seemed to know exactly where you were going."

An unbidden lie sprung up in her mind. "When Chloe was much younger, she and a friend of hers found this stream one day. She said she comes out here to think sometimes.

It totally slipped my mind the night we found her car. I guess I was hoping there would be some clue that she'd been out here."

"Oh wow," Kim said, sounding impressed now instead of suspicious.

"Her dad doesn't know about it," she added softly, as if this were a secret she didn't want the chief to hear either. "If things between Chloe and her dad really *had* gone sour, I didn't want to give away her safe place if she was here."

Kim nodded, then shivered, folding her arms tight across her body.

"*Chloe!*"

"*Chloe!*"

Amber's gaze moved up past the mossy banks of the stream and scanned the foliage-covered ground again, raking the patchy trunks of the red alders that stretched out in all directions like someone had haphazardly dropped fistfuls of gray toothpicks. Her magic had led her to Chloe's phone, not Chloe herself. Which meant either Chloe didn't *want* to be found, she was out of Amber's magical range, or her life's energy was no longer traceable.

"If that's her phone," came Kim's soft, almost-hushed voice, "what does that mean for *her*?"

When Amber spoke now, no lie crossed her lips. "I don't know."

CHAPTER 6

The chief and Amber, alongside Kim, maintained the ruse of searching for Chloe for another couple of hours. Thanks to Amber's magical intel, she knew Chloe wasn't in these woods. Whether she was in Edgehill at all remained to be seen.

Since the rest of the search unveiled nothing else, Kim's suspicions had ebbed about Amber's ability to find Chloe's cell phone with such ease.

At one point during their search, when Kim was distracted, Chief Brown squatted beside Amber as she pretended to find something of interest under a shrub, and whispered, "Depending on how long the phone has been in the water, it very well might be ruined."

Amber had slumped a little.

"There are labs I could potentially send it out to, but ..." he said, poking at the ground a bit absently with a stick, and then his brows rose suggestively at her.

She stared at him a moment. "Another spell?"

"A spell will probably give us better results than contacting Scuttle's headquarters ever could," he said. "Up for it?"

"Sure," she said, "but I can't do anything like that in front of Kim."

"Of course not," he said, sounding offended that she would

102

even say such a thing. "I'll figure something out." Then he stood and wandered off to examine something at the base of a nearby tree.

When Amber had stood as well and turned around, she'd found Kim several feet away, her head cocked as her gaze flitted from Amber to the chief and back again. She'd offered a small, unreadable smile, and then had gotten back to work.

Around half past eleven, the chief led the way back out of the woods for a scheduled lunch break. The staff of the Sippin' Siamese had apparently been working all morning to prepare a feast of their delicious bar fare. Everyone who had participated could eat as much as they wanted for a flat $5. Anyone who stuck around after that had the opportunity to participate in a potential second search in another section of the woods. Amber wondered if there would be any takers.

The group congregated outside the Sippin' Siamese was a bit more disheveled, and decidedly muddier, than the group who had been here early this morning. Amber heard people ask if their group had found anything, and each time, they were met with solemn shakes of the head. The chief had already asked Kim not to tell anyone about the found cell phone, as he didn't want anyone—especially the mayor—to get overly hopeful that this was a clue, in case it ended up being someone else's phone.

When they had all reached the meeting place, Chief Brown had excused himself to chat with his fellow officers. She guessed he would be telling *them* about the discovered cell phone. Amber and Kim had gotten into the long line that snaked out the Siamese's front door and trailed out past the patio and down the sidewalk.

Kim was silent for a full five minutes while they waited. Finally, Amber couldn't take it anymore.

"Hey," she said, nudging Kim with her elbow. "You okay?"

"Um, yeah. Oh sure. Yeah, I'm okay," Kim said quickly, hands stuffed into the pockets of her puffy coat. Then she fell silent again. Amber mentally counted to ten and told herself she would try again if Kim didn't crack first. She only got to eight. Kim abruptly turned, her back to the street lined with cars, and in a hushed rush said, "I know I was joking earlier about you and the chief, Amber, but oh my God. He's married! You have to stop using your feminine wiles on him or he's going to do something you'll both regret! He clearly is totally smitten with you. Men can be such weak creatures. You have to be careful here. Things could go *so* far south if you keep flirting with him like this."

Amber stared at her friend, wide-eyed. There were very few times in her life that she'd honestly been shocked into silence, and this was definitely in her top three. "*What?*" she finally blurted.

The woman in front of them thankfully had earbuds in and was bopping along to something, oblivious to what Kim had just said, but Amber had no idea if the people behind them had heard.

"Amber! Kim!"

Kim turned to her left and Amber looked behind them to see Ann Marie, Nathan, and Jolene approaching. Nathan waved enthusiastically. Kim returned it. A quick glance at the shocked look of the two women behind Amber told her that they had heard every word of Kim's whispered accusation. Amber offered her best tight-lipped smile, but the women scoffed in unison and turned their attention to each other instead.

Fantastic.

She did her best to maintain idle chitchat with the arrived trio, but she was still reeling. Sure, she'd been worried that people would start to think the very things Kim had just said, but she had hoped her friend would have given her a little more credit.

Granted, when she thought about it from Kim's perspective, it wasn't like she blamed her friend for thinking she and the chief were keeping secrets—they were. But she couldn't let Kim in on the true secret.

As if he sensed that now was the perfect time to make a situation even worse, Amber saw Chief Brown walking down the sidewalk, giving the lined-up people a once-over. He was looking for her; she just knew it.

When he reached their little group, Kim squeaked, which drew the attention of everyone assembled, including the chief.

"You all right, Miss Jones?" he asked her.

She tucked her lips under her teeth and nodded vigorously. *Please don't ask me to come with you! Please …*

"Uh … Miss Blackwood?" the chief said. "Would you accompany me to the station? We need to ask you a few more questions for your statement."

"Do you need to ask *me* anything else, chief?" Kim asked in a voice so high-pitched, Amber winced.

Nathan, Jolene, and Ann Marie watched this exchange with confusion, gazes bouncing between the chief, Amber, and Kim as if they were watching a ping-pong match.

"Uh … not at this time, Miss Jones. But we'll be in touch if we do," he said, then stared pointedly at Amber. "Miss Blackwood?"

She swallowed. "Yes, of course."

As she stepped out of line, Kim gently grabbed Amber's elbow, then dramatically brought her mouth to Amber's ear. "Remember what I said. He is *smitten*. Be careful." Then Kim unhanded her and, too loudly, said, "You two crazy kids don't have too much fun, okay?" She pointed at the chief. "Especially you."

"Oh my God," Amber muttered, her face on fire, and looked at the baffled chief. "Your car?"

"Oh, right!" He waved at the group and thanked them for their help. "Right this way," he said to Amber and led her across the street to his cruiser which was parked a few cars down from where the news van had been.

It only occurred to her now that she had no idea where Connor was. She fired off a quick text to tell him she had a way home and thanked him for the ride this morning.

Only once she and the chief were driving down Korat Road did he speak. "What on earth was going on with Kim?"

There really wasn't a gentle way to put this, so she went with the blunt approach. "She seems to think we're having an affair."

"*What?*" he bellowed, the car swerving as he turned to glare daggers at her.

"Watch out!" she said, pointing ahead.

He tugged on the wheel and only narrowly missed sideswiping a parked car. "Explain," he gritted out.

"You hated me three months ago and—"

"I didn't hate you," he said. "I was just highly suspicious of you."

"Whatever. You went from being highly suspicious to confiding in me—especially after I helped solve Melanie's murder—"

"Solve is a stretch."

She rolled her eyes. "And now we're sneaking into alleys and whispering to each other and now you're supposedly taking me to the station to ask me more questions when she was *there* when you got my statement the first time. It just sounds like a terrible cover for us to have an excuse to sneak away and get it on in the back of your cruiser."

Chief Brown almost hit another parked car.

"Kim says you're clearly smitten with me and I need to back off before you do something we'll both regret."

His nostrils flared. After mulling all of this over for a few seconds, he glanced at her again, this time giving her a quick scan from head to foot, then returned his gaze out the windshield. "No offense, Amber, but ew."

Amber cackled. "It's a total ew for me, too!"

"How dare you," he said, deadpan. "I'm very dashing."

She laughed again.

With a sigh, he said, "I guess I can see how our behavior lately could be seen as suspicious. And it's going to have to continue to be that way until you're ready to tell Kim—or anyone else—about your … gifts."

Amber groaned. "I know."

"But we need to nip this affair thing in the bud," he said. "Jessica will have my hide if this rumor gets back to her."

"Want me to say something to her?"

"*No,*" he said. "I'll talk to her tonight. No idea what I'll say, but I'll figure out something."

Amber knew she would have to come up with something to tell Kim, too.

When Chief Brown and Amber walked into the police station, Carl came bounding over with all the enthusiasm of a golden retriever who hadn't seen his human in a week. "Hi, chief. Hi, Amber. What's the good word? Find anything weird or creepy out there? I keep hearing rumors that Chloe was snatched by a cult."

The chief huffed a breath out of his nostrils.

Amber stifled a laugh. "Hey, Carl."

The waiting area of the station was empty. No one sat in the mismatched chairs or on the lumpy sofa. The water cooler in the corner gave a *glug* as it resettled, bubbles rising up in a rush and popping at the top of its gallon container.

"We might have found something on the search, but nothing definitive yet," the chief said. "I'll debrief you in a few minutes, but first I need to discuss something with Miss Blackwood. Thanks for helping man the phones today."

Carl sighed. "Happy to take one for the team." Then he shielded his mouth with one hand and stage whispered to Amber, "Even though I was a boy scout and can track animals like a *boss.*"

Amber gave a snort, then tried to swallow it back when she saw Chief Brown sneer at her.

"We'll be in my office." Then he moved past Carl. "Good afternoon, Dolores," he said as he walked by the open window in the boxy wooden desk the grouchy woman seemed to live in.

Dolores, or Sour Face according to Amber, said, "Afternoon, chief" in a flat tone. Then her eyes cut to Amber, her frizzy blonde hair wild. She didn't say a word to Amber, as usual, just followed her with her eyes as Amber walked by, like one of those paintings in a *Scooby-Doo* cartoon. Once Amber was out of eyesight, the clack of Dolores's keyboard started up.

"I'll just be answering the phone some more," Carl called after them. "Doing paperwork. *Filing.*"

Chief Brown was muttering to himself as he let Amber and himself into the office. He locked the door behind them. Hopefully, Carl wouldn't come check on them, only to find he couldn't get into the room. Amber had a feeling Carl could get gossip going in town just as well as Kim could.

"I swear he's upset that working here isn't like something he saw on TV."

Amber knew better than to come to Carl's defense, so she said nothing as the chief continued to mutter to himself as he cleared off a spot on his cluttered desk. Before she forgot, Amber reached into her pocket and pulled out Chloe's lipstick tube, placing it near the chief's keyboard. As she did so, she caught sight of the photo that sat facing out on the end of his desk—Jessica, the chief, and Sammy all smiling wide at the camera, Jessica's hand on her belly, hinting at the new baby growing within. Amber truly hoped none of the ridiculous rumors about Amber and the chief ever did anything to wipe those smiles off his family's faces.

"All right," he said, pulling the bagged-up phone out of his pocket. He set it down on a cleared section of his desk and then put his hands on his hips.

Feeling a tad nervous all of a sudden, she said, "Seems like you already have experience with Scuttle?"

The chief groaned. "That site is the bane of law enforcement's existence. They keep virtually nothing on their servers so even if we request a log of a user's communications, they often can't provide us with anything. And it takes them a good six months to tell us they have nothing. We don't have Johnny's last name—assuming that really is his name. We don't have his handle. Seems Chloe kept a lot of this a secret even from her closest friends. We have nothing on that front. We're trying but it's pretty much a dead end already." He sighed, staring down at the device on his desk. "Which is where you come in. What do we do now?"

Amber stood beside him, wondering which would be the best spell to use in a situation like this. She had to remind herself once again that memory spells were her forte, even if she was still unskilled. It made sense to her now that she'd had such success with the memory retrieval spell on Melanie's body—it was something her magic understood instinctively.

Objects from sites of high emotion held energies and memories like an insect preserved in amber. Energy became fused with an object; it only needed the right witch to set it free. When she'd touched her father's watch—the one she'd found under her old house's porch at 543 Ocicat Lane—the desire to know what had happened to her parents had been so strong, her magic had taken it as a command. She'd asked what had happened to her parents while holding an object from that very evening, and the simple act of asking her memory magic to show her had been enough … and she'd been hurtled some*when* else.

She needed to do that again with Chloe's cell phone. "Can I take it out of the bag?" she asked the chief, not taking her focus off the dark screen.

"Sure," he said, defeated.

She picked up the bag, the inside damp, and pulled out the water-logged cell phone. The case was simple, dark blue, and thick, and there was a plastic protective sheet laid over the glass. When Amber turned it over, she found the back designed with giant black-and-white lilies.

As she placed the wet bag back on the desk, keeping the cell in her hand, she said, "I'm going to try a memory retrieval spell." She explained how it worked, then added, "It will only show me the last memory. And it will likely only work once, maybe twice. But if the memory was fused into the phone by a moment of high emotion, that same intensity of energy will be thrust back out at me, draining the object just as quickly as it had been infused."

The chief was silent for a moment. "I'm just going to pretend I understood that." He walked to his desk chair and sat, pulling out a pad of paper and a pen. At Amber's cocked brow, he said, "All this magic stuff still gives me the heebie-jeebies, so I need to be doing something other than watching you otherwise I'm going to break out in hives. What if you start speaking in tongues? I'm very good at taking shorthand in tongues. It was my minor in college."

Amber fought an eye roll. She knew he was being overly dramatic just to amuse her, but there was true unease there, too. "All right, here we go."

Holding the phone in both hands, she relaxed her shoulders, and closed her eyes. Her magic leapt to attention, a physical thing that happily awaited instruction. Amber had to keep her intention true. When she asked her memory magic to show her the phone's last memory, it had to be for a pure reason.

More than wanting to know if Chloe had run away or if someone had taken her, more than Amber wanted to know who could have potentially hurt her, more than wanting to know where she was, Amber wanted to know if Chloe was okay—at least for now. If the mayor had hurt Chloe, if the girl truly wasn't safe back home, she knew in her heart of hearts that she wouldn't rat out Chloe's location to her father, not until she knew more. Her well-being was Amber's only concern.

Her magic sang beneath her skin, ready and willing to search out this answer for her.

Is Chloe Deidrick safe? she asked.

Almost instantaneously, white light tore through her vision.

Unlike the clear vision she received from her father's watch, this vision was different. Distorted. Like sinking to the bottom of a swimming pool and looking up through the undulating surface. There were discernible shapes, the muffled sound of voices, but nothing was truly clear. Perhaps even the phone's ability to hang onto the memories had been disrupted by the corrosive power of water.

The sensations she got now were more like the ones she'd

received from Melanie's body. Feelings associated with colors when the images were too corroded.

Amber heard the steady *swipe-swipe* of windshield wipers. Chloe's crisp, sweet voice sang along to a song on the radio. A carefree and happy sound. The rumble of Chloe's car's wheels on the uneven surface of Blue Point Lane was enough to set Amber's teeth on edge even though she knew instinctively that she still stood in Chief Brown's office.

Then came a yelp and the telltale *thwump thwump thwump* of a flat tire. Chloe cursed colorfully, the foul words interrupted occasionally by the swipe of her wipers. The sound soon stopped, and Amber guessed this was when Chloe pulled over.

A ringing in Amber's ear. Chloe *had* called someone that night.

Ring.

Ring.

"Hey! It's me," said Chloe. "I was on my way to Beth's and I got a flat tire. Any chance you could … come get me? I still want to see you." Amber could hear the wince in Chloe's voice, like she was on unsure footing with this person. Whether it was *because* of the person, or because Chloe was asking him or her to brave the storm, Amber couldn't say. "I can come get my car in the morning; you can drop me back at Beth's later. I'm sure her mom won't mind if I crash there tonight. Yeah, we had a *huge* fight. He's the *last* person I want to talk to right now. Really? Oh, you're the best. I'm halfway up Blue Point Lane, which is a little street off Korat Road. Google the Sippin' Siamese—it's not far from there. No one else is out here, but I'll leave my emergency lights on so you can find me."

Swipe. Swipe.

Chloe hummed to herself as tinny beeps, chimes, and happy music echoed around her. Amber guessed she'd been playing a game on her phone while she waited.

Bright light filled Amber's mind and for a moment, she thought she was going to be yanked back out of the memory, but then she realized it was the arrival of a car behind Chloe's, the high beams on.

Rain pattered down on her head, arms, and face.

A tall figure silhouetted against the bright light, followed by the warm burst of orange anticipation.

The figure moving out of the light to reveal a face she didn't know, followed by the red flare of fear.

"Who are you?" came Chloe's voice. "No, you're not. Who … no. I don't know you. Let go. No!"

A surge of adrenaline as she turned for her car, grabbing the still-open door, only to be grabbed from behind. Strong hands gripped her waist and she screamed, throwing back an elbow. The "oof!" of expelled air in her ear, blowing past her damp hair. The heel of a foot slammed against toes. A curse, a loosening of grip. Then Chloe was off like a shot.

Branches clawed at her face and hair. She stumbled, tripped, got back up.

The person thundered behind her, calling her name.

"No, no, no," Chloe muttered as she ran, breath coming in gasps. From exertion, but from fear, too.

The cell phone's screen lit up—a bright burst of blue in pitch black.

"One bar?" she hissed in disbelief. The screen went black

and then Amber and Chloe were careening in the dark once more, not knowing where she was going. Thunder continued to rumble. When the lightning flashed, it lit up everything out here. It kept Chloe from slamming headlong into a tree, but it also gave her pursuer a way to track her. The rain came down harder now, as if the sky wept for her just like she wanted to do for herself.

The person behind her cursed and called her name. "I just want to talk, Chloe!"

She had to get away.

Then her foot slipped and she went tumbling down into what felt like a river. Her hip hit a large rock and she cried out in pain. It momentarily stunned her; the pain was so acute, her vision swam. And then the person was there, yanking her to her feet. An arm went around Chloe's neck. Her pursuer's chest was flush with Chloe's back.

"Hold still," the gruff voice said. "It didn't have to be like this."

Chloe screamed for help.

Something pressed to the side of her neck, like the round, warm pad of a thumb. Then everything went fuzzy, then black, then back to fuzzy. The threat of unconsciousness tugged at her.

Is she still okay? Amber frantically asked her magic, sensing that her hold on this memory was fading, knowing that the girl's cell phone couldn't hold memories from a location that it hadn't been—wherever Chloe went after the cell phone had ended up in the stream would remain a mystery.

Light slipped in and out of Chloe's vision, and she swayed,

as if she were on a boat. Back and forth. A glimpse of water running over rocks. A mossy shore. Gray toothpick trees.

Chloe groaned.

"Just keep still, kid. I'm not going to hurt you," came a disembodied voice.

"I don't believe you," Chloe croaked.

"I guess I wouldn't believe me either."

"Do you have … a thing for … young girls or something?" she managed, but her words were a bit slurred, as if she was trying as hard as possible to hang onto consciousness.

The man scoffed. "*No.* I got a kid bout your age. I'm just in it for the money, okay? I got nothing against you."

Chloe's stomach roiled.

A pair of hands hung limply, one clutching a cell phone with a blue case designed with black-and-white lilies. The hands seemed to be floating. Every few seconds, there was a glimpse of a man's boots, but only the heels.

Her vision swam again and Chloe whimpered.

Body heavy, hands weak. The cell slipped from Chloe's fingers, unable to hold on any longer.

And then everything went black for good.

White light ripped through Amber's vision and she stumbled back, crashing into a bookshelf. The chief was there in an instant, hands on Amber's shoulders to help her back to her feet.

She was crying, a hand to her chest.

"My God, Amber," the chief said, doing his best to angle his head to get her to look at him. "What happened? Are you okay?"

"Someone took her. I think ... I think someone paid a guy to kidnap her," Amber got out, trying to speak while heaving, trying to keep her tears from turning into sobs. "She called someone to come get her, but the person who showed up wasn't who she was expecting and he chased her through the woods." She placed a hand to her neck, to the spot just below her ear. "He used ... I think he used a pressure point to knock her out. Then he just ... carried her away. She dropped her cell phone when she went unconscious. The guy knew her name, called her 'kid,' and said he wouldn't hurt her. But ... who knows if he meant that. I ..." She swallowed, the threat of tears coming back. "I don't know where she is now. It's possible he took her out of Edgehill."

She started to sink to her knees, but the chief hoisted her up again and guided her to the chair behind his desk.

"Sit," he said. "I'll go get you some water."

Then he was dashing to his door, unlocking it, and hurrying down the hallway, his door still open.

Amber blew out slow and steady breaths, staring at the dark-screened cell phone lying on the floor by the bookshelf. "Where are you now, Chloe?"

This time, the phone didn't have an answer.

117

CHAPTER 7

Once Chief Brown had been convinced Amber was okay—though "okay" was a relative term; her mind had new fodder for even worse nightmares now—Carl had driven her home. If people in town were starting to think there was something inappropriate happening between herself and the chief, they had to minimize the number of times they could possibly be seen together.

Though it was only a little after one in the afternoon, she decided to keep the Quirky Whisker closed for the rest of the day. She was exhausted both from a terrible night of sleep, the search through the woods, and from what her spell had revealed.

When she trudged up the steps to her upstairs studio apartment, Tom was there to greet her at the top. He yowled at her.

Right. She was a whopping hour late to feed him.

He yowled again and then bounded toward his bowl. Alley was sprawled out on the bench seat, one paw hanging over the side. It twitched slightly; she was so deeply asleep, she was dreaming. Tom meowed his protest about Amber taking so long. He was, obviously, starving to death. Didn't she care? Didn't she know that if she didn't feed him in the next thirty seconds, he would expire right there on the floor?

"I'm very sorry, Tom," she said, dropping her phone, wallet, and keys on her dining room table and then going about getting the cats' lunch ready. Alley didn't bother to wake up until there was food in her bowl.

Amber took a long, hot shower, got dressed in her pajamas, pulled the curtains shut, and crawled into bed. After the adrenaline of the memory retrieval spell had worn off, and Amber had been sitting in the passenger seat of Carl's car, fatigue had hit her so hard, she had worried she wasn't going to be able to stay awake long enough to even get into her shop.

But now, warm and comfortable, and with two cats curled up beside her, she was suddenly wide awake, even if her limbs still felt as if they weighed a million pounds each. She couldn't stop replaying those images of Chloe. She had been scared, chased, and then carted off by a man apparently paid to do it.

When the mysterious man had first shown up in the memory, Amber had been sure she could definitely tell the chief that their culprit was male. That would narrow the suspects down by gender, at least. But, based on the man's comments, he hadn't snatched Chloe for his own sick purposes; he simply had been following orders. The suspect pool had widened again. The person the chief needed to find was anyone who had both the money to hire the kidnapper, and the desire to either hurt Chloe, or, Amber supposed, who wanted to use Chloe to get to the mayor.

Unless, of course, this had all been staged *by* the mayor.

Amber's gut told her that Chloe wasn't in Edgehill anymore, but she needed proof of that.

Flinging back her comforter, causing Tom to yowl in

disgust as the blanket was tossed over him and Alley, Amber padded to her coffee table and pulled open one of the two small drawers. She riffled around in one, shut it, then opened the second. At the bottom, she found the map of Edgehill she had purchased when she scried Whitney Sadler's where-abouts, searching for Melanie's killer. When Amber's magic had found Whitney, a small dot had appeared on the map at Whitney's house.

When she'd scried for Whitney, Amber had used a picture of her to focus on. She needed to keep the image of the person she wanted to find fresh in her mind in order for her magic to know what to do. Now, with the memories of her spell so clear, all she would need was to remember that scene of her and Chloe talking in the bathroom.

Clearing a spot on her dining room table—which mostly consisted of shoving her collection of half-finished miniature cat toys to the other side—she laid out the map. In a basket tucked under the window bench seat, she found her amethyst crystal and her personal grimoire. The crystal was supposed to strengthen magic; she would need all the help she could get for this.

After working through a few spells, and tweaking the wording, she stood before her map and, with the crystal held firmly in her hand, recited the incantation. The way her magic reacted, as if it had flowed down her arms, into her crystal, and then out of her in a rush, she knew the spell had worked.

Problem was, no dot appeared on the map.

Amber conducted the spell twice more, each one with

more concise, demanding language, but the result was always the same: Chloe was no longer in Edgehill.

Amber placed the crystal on top of the map and slumped into a wooden dining room chair. Her gaze skirted over the familiar streets of her town, wondering which one the man had taken to get Chloe out. Had he gone north into Marbleglen, or south to Belhaven? Had he not stopped in either town and gone on to cross a state line? Was he planning to smuggle her even farther than that?

When the questions began to drive her batty, she got up to grab her cell phone and called her aunt.

She answered on the second ring. "Hi, Amber."

"Hi, Aunt G," she said, trying to force some cheer into her voice, despite feeling bone-weary. "How are you?"

Chuckling, she said, "Come out with it. What's the matter, little mouse?"

With a sigh, Amber flopped onto her bed. Tom crawled out from under the comforter to drape his body across her stomach. Then she told her aunt the whole story. Aunt Gretchen didn't make a peep until Amber had finished speaking.

"Oh my," she said. "That poor, poor girl."

"Yeah," Amber said. "I wish I had—"

"Don't you dare blame yourself for any of this," her aunt said. "You did what you could for her, but she made her own choices that night."

"So you think this is *her* fault?" Amber said, her voice a little sharper than she'd intended. "That if she had done x, y, and z better, she wouldn't have found herself in that position?"

"Absolutely not," Aunt Gretchen said, a bite to her tone,

too. "The only ones at fault are the sleaze who took her and the sleaze who paid him to do it. What I'm saying is, you cannot control what Chloe would do any more than what that horrible man was going to do. Don't beat yourself up."

Amber sighed.

"Now, what is it you need from *me*?"

"I can't just call my favorite aunt because I want to hear her lovely voice?"

"I'm your only *known* aunt, so don't play that *favorite* nonsense with me."

"Can you walk me through that premonition tincture you use at night?" There was a long pause on the other end of the line. "I know tinctures aren't my strong suit, but if you go through it with me—maybe on video chat so you can watch me—I can make sure I get it right? I'm ... I haven't slept well since that night at Edgar's. With all this Chloe stuff, now my worries about *her* are making their way into my dreams, too. Maybe the premonition tincture will help organize my thoughts a little. Give my energy and magic something to focus on."

Gretchen slowly said, "Tinctures for the mind are already risky. Ones used to affect the mind while asleep even more so. If done incorrectly, it can cause madness, can trap a person in a dream state ..."

"I'll be careful," she said. "I'll have you watch everything I'm doing and if you have *any* hesitation—any at all—I won't take it."

Amber held her breath.

"Fine."

She gently pumped a fist in the air as to not disturb the cats. "How soon can we start?"

"Now?"

Amber smiled. "Now is good."

"I don't know how to do this video chat thing, though. I don't have a video camera. Do I need that Skippy program my friend Norma uses to talk to her grandkids?"

It took Amber a moment to realize her aunt meant Skype, then laughed. "We have a lot to teach each other, Aunt G."

The following morning, Amber hopped on her bike at just after seven to meet Edgar in town for breakfast. They had a tentative plan to meet every Sunday—partly to keep in touch, and partly to ensure Edgar got out of the house for at least a couple of hours a week.

She and Aunt Gretchen had worked on the premonition tincture for hours, but when her first attempt turned the color of black sludge—when it was supposed to be clear with "a hint of pink"—and started to bubble, then shattered the glass bowl she had been using, Aunt Gretchen had suggested they take a break. Attempt two, several hours later, had resulted in a small, fireless explosion that filled Amber's kitchen with thick gray smoke. Tom and Alley both had bolted under the bed for safety.

"Amazing!" Aunt Gretchen had said, her wide eyes taking in the scene in Amber's kitchen from the safety of her own back in Portland. "And I don't mean amazing in a good way.

Amazing as in 'I don't understand how you've managed to get two completely different, yet equally horrible results from the same recipe.'"

"I think my magic is glitching," Amber had said, coughing and swatting away the smoke with a dish towel.

"*Something* is glitching," her aunt had muttered. "You need rest, dear child. Drink some of your sleepy tea—that one doesn't cause comas, does it?—and we'll try again once you're rested."

"Ha-ha." Amber was still waving away smoke, her eyes watering. The smoke smelled a bit like burned plastic. "Henrietta buys it every week and has yet to slip into a coma."

"Wonderful. You should use that as your slogan."

Amber had "accidentally" hung up on Aunt Gretchen after that.

Currently, she was pedaling toward the Catty Melt on Calico Way, not far from the Manx Hotel. It had been difficult to get Edgar to agree to many outings, but when he'd come to the Catty Melt last week and had tried their Buttermilk Catty Cakes, he no longer would hear suggestions for anywhere else. He had ordered three six-cake stacks that morning—on her dime—and had been in so much pain afterwards that they'd had to walk it off for half an hour before he could comfortably get back in his *new* truck and drive home.

When she cruised to a stop outside the Catty Melt, she found Edgar already sitting at one of the tables positioned inside the black iron fence. There were a dozen tables outside, but Edgar was the only person in one of the seats. Four currently closed green-and-yellow striped umbrellas wedged into thick black iron stands were dotted around the patio area. They looked like the closed petals of giant flowers.

Edgar had clearly already ordered coffee and was currently reading a copy of the Sunday edition of the *Edgehill Gazette*.

After securing her bike, she strolled up to the fence-lined patio. "Hey, cousin."

His head snapped up, and for a moment his eyes were wild with fear. But then his gaze settled on her and his features relaxed. Folding his newspaper, he dropped it onto a corner of the table. His out-of-control hair had recently been trimmed, his gray T-shirt didn't have a stain on it, and he wore shoes—on both of his feet. Things were looking up.

Edgar Henbane was a handsome guy when he put in the effort to shower. But, she supposed when one has been driven nearly mad by the voice of a cursed Penhallow trapped in his head, things like hygiene weren't high on the priority list. The fact that he was putting in an effort now spoke volumes. He folded his arms on the table. "You're late."

She rolled her eyes and pushed her way through the unlatched gate. "I am not," she said, taking a seat and pulling the strap of her messenger bag over her head. "How have you been? I see you got a haircut."

He self-consciously rubbed his hand up and down the back of his head. "Does it look okay? Just walking into that place was hard. It's so noisy in there. I was holding onto the sides of my chair so hard when the lady started cutting, I thought I would rip the armrests right off." He rubbed the back of his head again. "I thought it turned out not half bad, though."

"You look great," she said. "Honestly."

He nodded to himself a few times, like he was glad to get confirmation of something he'd already suspected.

"I'm proud of you," she said.

He wrinkled his nose. "For getting a haircut?"

"For trying," she said. "Trying is hard. Especially when Neil is still in there."

Edgar absently tapped the side of his head. "He's not as loud. It's kind of like having a roommate now. I know he's there. I can sense him, but he stays out of my way for the most part."

"Glad to hear it." She jutted her chin toward the newspaper on the table. "Anything interesting in that?"

"Nah," he said. "Just that Chloe Deidrick is still missing, the police are following all leads, and there's currently no evidence of foul play."

Amber pursed her lips and glanced away for a moment.

Edgar leaned forward, looked left, then right, and said, "You know something."

A couple, hand in hand, strolled past the patio, and Amber waited until they were hopefully out of earshot before she said, "Locator spell led me to Chloe's cell phone in a stream. And a memory retrieval one showed me Chloe was kidnapped. I don't know who took her."

Edgar's thick black brows arched up. "Dang."

The waitress came out then to take their order. They both ordered orange juice and Catty Cakes—Edgar's with extra powdered sugar. When she'd left again, Edgar said, "How's the chief going to handle this?"

Amber shrugged. "No idea. I scried for her. She's not in Edgehill anymore."

"Scrying isn't exact, though. If she somehow doesn't want to be found, if she was unconscious when you scried for her, if she's more than ten feet underground—your magic wouldn't find her."

Amber wasn't sure if any of that was comforting or not. "Can you think of anything else I can try? Do you think just *looking* at the Henbane book would—"

"No," he said, shaking his head. "Don't touch the cloak on those things. We have to hope that if they stay cloaked, no one will be able to sense your mother's magical signature. I don't know about you, but I'd rather not deal with another Penhallow for a while."

Amber absently rubbed her throat. "Agreed." After a pause, she tentatively changed the subject. "Any word from your dad?"

Edgar's lip curled a fraction. "Won't answer my letters or my calls—assuming I even have the right address and number. I'd thought he'd materialize if it meant learning more about his sister—I know he doesn't care enough about *me*—but not even the truth about what happened to the great Annabelle Henbane was enough to make him crawl out of his hidey hole." He shrugged, but the tightness of his jaw belied the casual gesture. "Maybe he's dead."

"We'll keep trying," Amber said. "Willow and Aunt G are trying to find him, too."

With a finger running idly along the lip of his coffee cup, he shrugged again. He looked like such a little boy then. A boy who missed his father and who couldn't figure out what he'd done to chase the man away.

Amber wanted to find Raphael Henbane if only so she could give him a quick kick in the pants.

"I can search my books for other possibilities to help with Chloe," he said. "I'm guessing you're going to be your relentless Blackwood self and keep searching until you find her, for better or worse?"

Amber shrugged. "Probably."

"I'll do what I can to help."

They talked about normal things, then—like Amber attempting to cart groceries home on her bike. Yesterday, between disastrous premonition tincture lessons, she'd gotten a few essentials at the store. Somehow, on the way home, the bag's bottom gave out and sent her eggs, bread, assorted vegetables, and a bottle of wine crashing to the asphalt. Amber's cursing had been such a shock to a kid and his mother riding their own bikes ahead of her that the kid looked over his shoulder to see what the fuss was about, slammed into a lamppost, was pitched over his handlebars and crashed to the ground, badly scratching up an elbow and knee in the process. Amber had apologized profusely to him and his mother, but she demanded Amber leave them alone. At least the kid had been wearing a helmet. Amber had eaten a mushy apple and two bread butts for dinner.

Edgar had done his best not to laugh, but a loud chuckle escaped anyway. It was a sound she hadn't heard in a long time. "We need to get you a car, cousin. This is getting ridiculous. You're a threat to children now."

They fell into companionable silence as their food arrived and Edgar stared at his Catty Cakes as if they were the most beautiful thing he'd ever seen. He then proceeded to drown them in so much syrup, his pancakes looked like lily pads floating on the surface of a polluted pond.

While they ate, the patio started to fill up with diners. She didn't have long before she'd have to be back at the Quirky Whisker, but Lily and Daisy were scheduled to open for her on the mornings she met her cousin for breakfast.

She gazed out at Calico Way as it slowly came to life around her. More bikes, more foot traffic, and people milling about in the park across the street. Moms with strollers or toddlers, people walking dogs, a pair of guys playing Frisbee. Life continuing on as usual even though Chloe was missing.

Someone walking past her table interrupted her view and she watched a waitress lead a man to a table on the other end of the patio. He had arrived alone and took a seat with his back to the patio's fence, giving him a view of Calico Way stretching to the west behind Amber. She had just taken a sip of orange juice when the man's focus suddenly snapped to her and she sucked in a breath, which caused her drink to go down the wrong way. She coughed and sputtered.

Downing some water, she wiped her eyes and nose on her napkin.

"You all right?" Edgar asked, a thin dribble of syrup hanging from his chin.

As she motioned to the spot on her own face, he wiped at his chin with the back of his hand. In a hushed tone, she said, "There's a guy who just got here who I saw at Chloe's search yesterday. There's something ... off about him. I don't think he's a Penhallow, but ..."

Edgar made to turn around and Amber shook her head discreetly.

Returning her attention to her food, she cut out a very small wedge of pancake while occasionally shooting glances toward the guy. He was scanning the crowd milling about the sidewalk. Then he picked up his menu.

"Look now," she whispered.

Just as Edgar did so, the guy looked up. He offered a wave. Edgar awkwardly returned the gesture, then turned back around. "Oh, that's totally a cop."

"Really? Like a plainclothes detective?" she asked.

"That or a PI," he said, returning to his sugary mess of a breakfast. "Didn't the chief say the mayor was going to start bringing those guys onto the case if he didn't get answers soon? Maybe they're already here."

Amber didn't like the vibe she was getting from the guy, but she couldn't explain why. Wouldn't more people attempting to find Chloe be a good thing? The chief worried less-reputable PIs could hinder his department's efforts, but if his department currently didn't have any leads, and the only vague one they *did* have was one received by a witch, maybe the chief needed all the help he could get.

She hazarded another quick glance his way, only to find him watching her. Studying her. And he wasn't hiding it. It felt neither flirtatious nor predatory. He simply wanted her to know that he was keeping an eye on her.

She didn't like it one bit.

CHAPTER 8

At lunchtime the following day, Amber knew she should ride her bike into town for a reasonable meal. Lily Bowen had even offered to bring back a sandwich for Amber from the Catty Melt, where she and Daisy were headed for lunch. She had declined, and after closing up her shop, dashed across the street to Purrfectly Scrumptious. Ever since she'd tried Betty's Oreo Dream on the evening of the town hall meeting, she'd been craving another.

All she had in her apartment to eat were rice cakes, condiments, and a bruised apple. She needed, at the very least, to invest in a sturdy bicycle basket so her groceries wouldn't end up spilled all over the street again. But, until then, she was going to eat cupcakes for lunch. She was an adult, dang it, and she could do whatever she wanted.

Plus, her sleep had been plagued by nightmares again and she hadn't slept well; the sugar would help get her through the after-lunch hours at the shop. So, really, the cupcakes were necessary—vital, even.

The door to Purrfectly Scrumptious was propped open, several customers still inside. Amber walked in and caught Betty's eye. The woman nodded at her and held up a hand, motioning that she'd be done soon. Resting against the back wall, Amber waited while Betty and Bobby tended to the last of their customers. Betty boxed up three dozen cupcakes for one order, and half a dozen for another. Bobby joked and chatted with customers while he rang them up.

When Amber thought of Ivy and Miles Henbane—her maternal grandparents—she wondered if they were like Betty and Bobby. A couple who genuinely enjoyed each other even after decades of marriage.

Assuming, of course, that her grandparents were still alive.

Needing to think about something else, she gazed around the always-immaculate shop. Every surface gleamed. The white tile floor was shiny, the chrome and glass display cases were fingerprint- and smudge-free, and the whole place smelled of vanilla and sugar. Amber was still amazed that while so much of the decor in the shop was a light pink—the cabinets, light fixtures, trim around the doors and windows, and the pink-and-gray granite counters—the Harrises had managed to make the place feel completely homey rather than gaudy.

Eyeing the large display case nearest her, Amber could see their supply had almost been bought out. They would be working through lunch to restock the shelves and get another batch into the ovens. How these two managed to run the shop everyday by themselves was even more miraculous than the flavor of Betty's Oreo Dreams.

A few minutes later, Betty closed and locked the door behind a woman who was already halfway through her giant Chocolate Chocolate Surprise, humming happily as she went.

Bobby waved to Amber from behind the counter. "How you holding up?"

"Okay," she said. "You two must be exhausted."

He grinned at her. "It's the good kind of tired. Not to be rude, hon, but I gotta get this batch out of the oven." With another wave, he disappeared through the swinging door at the back.

"Phew!" Betty said, resting her back against the door. "Word must have gotten out that we're in the running for Best in Edgehill, because ever since we got officially nominated, we've been run ragged trying to stay on top of all the orders. To be this busy on a Monday? Goodness."

"Have you changed your mind about hiring some help?" Amber asked.

Betty's daughter had been helping out in the shop up until six months ago, before she and her husband had moved out of state for a job opportunity. Betty and Bobby had been running the place solo ever since. Between needing to replace some of their bigger equipment—a new cupcake freezer, and a larger oven—they worried they'd be unable to also afford to hire an employee.

"If you get the Best of Edgehill designation, you might have to," Amber said. "At least for the Here and Meow—you've never run this place without help during the festival, have you?"

Betty shook her head, gaze flitting around her shop. "Bobby says I'm being stubborn, and he thinks I'm scared to hire anyone but family. But ..." She turned to Amber. "Have you ever wanted something *so badly* you start to get superstitious? What if I hire someone to help in preparation for being busy and then demand grinds to a halt? What if hiring someone jinxes my chances?"

Amber cocked a brow.

Betty sighed loudly. "I know. I'm being irrational. Even though this is only the second Best of, Olivia's success after Lollicat won last year set the bar so high. It showed what's possible if you get the label. I never let myself dream this little bakery would be more than what it is right now … and now the possibilities feel tangible, if that makes sense?"

"It totally does," Amber said. "But your hard work and amazing recipes is what got you here. Nothing—not even hiring someone to help out—is going to jeopardize that. You needed help before you got the nomination; hiring someone now isn't you celebrating your win early or anything like that. You have a successful business, woman! Successful businesses hire help. Period."

Betty nodded absently, but it looked like she was considering the possibility, at least. "I'm almost sixty-five. I should be thinking about retirement, not expanding my business."

"Pfft," Amber commented. "If this is what you want, it doesn't matter how old you are."

Betty smiled at that. "Thank you, sugar," she said. "Now, what can I do for *you*?" She pushed away from the door.

"Got any more of those Oreo Dreams?"

With a laugh, she said, "Sure do." As she went behind the counter to grab Amber's cupcake, she said, "How've you been? Any news about Chloe?"

"Nope." No news Amber could share, anyway. "She's been gone for almost four full days now." She walked to the counter. "Have you caught wind of any interesting gossip since yesterday?"

"Not since yesterday," Betty said. "That woman who just left made me remember something though. It happened on Wednesday evening—the day before Chloe went missing."

Interest piqued, Amber asked, "What kind of something?"

After slapping a sticker to the front of the single-cupcake box to keep it closed, Betty pushed it aside, then placed one hand on the counter, and one on her hip. "Well, on Wednesday, Francine Robins came in here and she was, to put it lightly, a mess."

"Frank's assistant?" Amber asked.

Betty nodded. "Yep. Well, *ex*-assistant. He fired her on Wednesday."

"*Really?*" Amber asked. "She'd been working for him for years. Any idea what happened?"

"I can only guess," Betty said. "But that woman chowing down on a Chocolate Chocolate Surprise as she walked out of here made me think of Francine. On Wednesday, she came in here asking for every variation of a chocolate cupcake I had. Her eyes were a bit puffy, and judging by the bag she carried, it looked like she'd already been to Cat's Creamery for ice cream. I asked her if she was okay, and as I was getting her cakes ready, she just started ranting. She called the mayor a monster and said that he'd fired her for 'being too nosy.' She was just carrying on, so I let her talk—seemed like she just needed to vent. Happens in here more often than you'd think. Then Francine said, 'I *have* to see his finances because I'm the one who's booking all his events! How can that be too nosy!' She paid for her cupcakes, downed a Chocolate Chocolate Surprise in two bites right here at the counter, burst into tears, and left."

"Geez," Amber said.

"Yep," said Betty. "I've always liked the mayor, but now I'm starting to wonder who we have running our town. Apparently even the cause of death of Chloe's mother is suspicious."

"I heard the same thing," Amber said slowly.

Francine Robins had knowledge of the mayor's daily habits, and she was skilled at financial matters. A light bulb went off in Amber's head.

"Hey, can I get a dozen Chocolate Chocolate Surprise, too? All this talk of chocolate has gotten to me."

Betty laughed. "Sure thing, sugar."

After Amber left the shop, she called Lily Bowen and asked if she and Daisy could cover the shop for a little longer after lunch. Once she had confirmation, she let herself into the still-closed Quirky Whisker and placed the cupcakes on the counter. For the next twenty minutes, she set about finding a basket big enough to hold a box of a dozen cupcakes, and then looked up Francine Robins online. After dashing upstairs to feed the cats, she did a quick locator spell on Francine. As Amber hoped, she was at home. Amber knew if she was recently unemployed, that was where *she'd* be.

It would take Amber a good twenty-five minutes to make it to Francine's on her bike. A quick consult with her grimoire later, she threw her messenger bag over her shoulder, called a goodbye to Tom and Alley, grabbed her bribery cupcakes and basket, then hurried out to her small outdoor storage closet. Closing herself in the small space, she conducted a spell to fasten the wide mesh basket to the front of her handlebars. She hoped the spell held for the duration of the ride.

There weren't enough words at her disposal to describe how devastating it would be to drop a dozen of Betty's Chocolate Chocolate Surprise cupcakes.

Once the box was snugly inside, and her own smaller cupcake was resting on top, she wheeled herself out of the storage closet. With her bike resting against the wall, she called Kim, hoping her friend was on her lunch break, too.

"Hey, Amber!" Kim answered almost immediately. "Are you okay? What happened?"

"Yes, I'm fine?"

"Oh, phew," she said. "I guess I'm just not used to hearing from you unless we have a Here and Meow meeting coming up, so I assumed it was bad news."

Amber's face flushed. Once they found Chloe, she and Kim would go out to dinner to just talk about … things. Guys? Yes! They could talk about guys. And Amber could ask about Kim's family. Did she have siblings? Ugh.

Then she realized that the reason she was calling her was related to the Here and Meow and her face flushed even further.

"Are we still looking for a finance person for the committee to replace Whitney?"

"Yes! Do you know of someone?"

"I might," Amber said. "I'm going to meet her now. I just wanted to check with you first; I don't want to step on anyone's toes."

"Step all over them! Please!"

Amber laughed.

"Oh! And while I have you on the phone, can I ask you a *huge* favor?" Kim said. "It's totally last minute, so it's okay if you can't, but there's a Job and Career Fair at Edgehill High tomorrow morning from 11 till about 1. Is there any way you can help Ann Marie with our table? We're trying to snag as many student volunteers as we can and the seniors are going to all be there for the fair. Several teachers are offering extra credit to the students who volunteer for the Here and Meow this year. Ann Marie was going to run it with Chloe but, well ..."

Amber blew out a breath that puffed out her cheeks. Lily and Daisy likely could keep the store running while she helped Ann Marie. Luckily Lily had graduated high school last year, so they were now both more readily available. If Amber needed last-minute help, say, on a Monday morning, they usually could. Besides, Kim's earlier comment about Amber only calling her for Here and Meow details had made her feel horribly guilty. "Sure. I can make that work. Just email me details."

Kim cheered. "Oh, you're such a doll, Amber, I swear. I'll be in touch soon!"

After disconnecting the call, Amber scrolled through her contacts again. She jammed earbuds into her ears, then hit dial. When it started ringing, she shoved her phone into the front pocket of her messenger bag. She had already started pedaling down Russian Blue Avenue by the time the chief answered.

"Hey, Amber," the chief said, somewhat cautiously. "What's up?"

"Do you have a revised policy on when I'm allowed to interview potential witnesses?"

His pause was so long, Amber worried she'd managed to hang up on him on accident. "Uhh ... you're not allowed to interview *anyone*, Amber. Why are you breathing so hard?"

"I'm ... biking," she said. "And what if it's more of a ... casual conversation where I ask things that might provide helpful answers?"

"That's an *interview*, Amber. You're not allowed to do those." When Amber didn't reply, he said, "Whatever you're thinking of doing, don't do it."

"I thought you wanted my help! You had me use a locator spell on Chloe's lipstick," she said. "I'm sure that wasn't exactly by the book."

"Yes, but I *asked* you to help. If you do it on your own, it's meddling."

"Is it *really* meddling if I'm just dropping off cupcakes to a very sad woman?"

"What woman?"

"A woman who is currently sad?"

She could feel him glaring at her through the phone. She needed to hang up on him now, but it would be very difficult to do so while she was moving. Releasing the handlebars, she sat straight up, balancing without the use of her hands. All her hours of riding around Edgehill as a bored teenager were paying off. Now, she just hoped she could maintain this without slamming into a parked car while she was distracted. She fished her phone out of the front pocket of her messenger bag.

"Amber ... what are you doing?"

She made a terrible imitation of static. "I ... can't ... reception ... bye." And then she tapped her phone to end the call, wincing. He called back immediately, and she hung up, quickly stuffing her phone back into her bag. He called twice more during her bike ride, but she didn't pick up. She imagined him stomping around his office in a huff. Oh, he was going to be so angry with her.

She'd deal with that later.

Francine lived about a mile from the Deidricks, in a modest one-story house on a quiet street. The house was painted white and had soft blue accents, and there was a small front lawn bisected by a cement walkway that led to a small patio. A large oak tree rose up from the right side of the lawn, its wide branches stretching over most of the house. A Siamese cat sat in a windowsill, eyeing Amber with mild interest as she wheeled up the sidewalk. Amber left her bike on the pathway, and carefully plucked the wide pink box out of the basket, leaving her Oreo Dream inside. Her lower back felt damp from the trek over here and she hoped she wasn't a sweaty mess, or that her hair had turned into a windblown disaster.

As she approached the navy blue front door, the Siamese in the windowsill fled. Amber knocked.

On the way over, she'd worked through any number of things she thought she could ask Francine, but now that she was standing here, holding a very large box of cupcakes, she started to deeply regret her impulsive decision.

The door opened and an extremely disheveled black-haired woman stared out at her. One hand clutched the handle of a wide-rimmed red coffee mug, and the other held fast to the doorknob. The vixen from happy hour night was nowhere to be found. Her hair was piled on top of her head in a messy bun, there was a ring of day-old mascara around her eyes, and she had a ratty red-plaid robe cinched tightly around her waist. Her feet were shoved into black fur-lined slippers.

When Amber just stood there standing at her, Francine finally said, "Sorry, I don't want to buy any cookies," and moved to close the door.

"Oh, no, I'm not selling anything," Amber said quickly. "I'm Amber Blackwood and I'm on the Here and Meow Committee. I wanted to ask if you'd be interested in joining us. These," she said, holding the box out like the offering they were, "are a dozen Chocolate Chocolate Surprise cupcakes from Purrfectly Scrumptious."

Francine blinked at her rapidly. "Are you an angel in disguise?"

"Ha! Hardly."

Stepping back and opening the door further, Francine ushered Amber inside.

The small front entryway had a faux-stone tile flooring, and Amber's boots were directly in the middle of a round forest green mat. A hallway stretched forward from the front door, and on either side of the entryway, arched doorways led both left and right. A bench seat with a plush dark green cushion was pressed against the left wall. It had three cubbyholes below the bench; cream-colored fabric boxes were slotted into spaces on either end. On the opposite wall was a freestanding coat rack, a mirror making up its back. Between a hanging black trench on one side of the mirror and a navy blue peacoat on the other, Amber got confirmation from her reflection that she was, in fact, a windblown mess. How unfortunate.

"Would you like coffee or anything?" Francine asked, redirecting Amber's attention, and hoisting her mug into the air a fraction. Amber wondered if it was *just* coffee in that mug. Given Francine's semi-glassy expression, Amber thought not.

"Oh, no, thank you. I just wanted to chat for a moment, if you have the time."

"I've got nothing but time now," she muttered, then walked through the leftmost archway.

Shrugging to herself, Amber followed Francine into her living room.

Amber guessed the space usually was kept tidy, but at the moment, the beige Berber carpet was littered with kicked-off shoes there, a discarded jacket here, and what had once been a mouse-shaped cat toy festooned with feathers lay gutted under the oval glass coffee table. The parts of the glass surface that weren't dotted with water and coffee rings were heaped with stained glasses, mugs, plates covered in crumbs, and a pizza box from Patch's Pizza, the hint of a few shriveled olives still left in the partly open box.

A white leather couch piled high with blankets had a pair of Siamese cats lying side by side on the far end of it, their blue eyes focused on Amber. White leather wingback chairs were positioned across from each other, the oval coffee table between them. The flat-screen TV on the wall opposite the couch had a paused movie or TV show frozen on a man and woman laughing.

"Sorry about the mess," Francine said, then chugged down the rest of whatever was in her mug before adding it to the collection forming on the coffee table. "It's been a rough few days. A rough *week*, really."

Amber watched as Francine shoved blankets aside on the couch so Amber had a place to sit, then stacked cups and plates on the coffee table to make room for the cupcake box. The moment Amber set it down and sat precariously on the edge of the cleared-off couch cushion, Francine had the box open and was wiggling her fingers over the sea of the twelve perfectly sculpted chocolate frosting swirls, trying to pick which one she should start with. Amber left her bag looped over her shoulder and tucked it close to her side.

Once the cupcake was selected, Francine flopped into one of the wingback chairs, freed the cupcake from its wrapping, and devoured it in three bites, groaning. Amber's stomach growled as she thought of her own sugar lunch still in the basket of her bike. The basket that very well could fall off at any moment, since knowing how long a spell might last was not an exact science. Her grand plan to eat an Oreo Dream for lunch had been derailed for this little impromptu meeting.

"So I wanted to find out what interest you might have in the financial director position with the Here and Meow Committee. It's unpaid, of course, and I can't make any decisions on the staff, as Kimberly Jones would have final say, but I would be happy to pass your name along with a personal recommendation if you think it might be something you'd be interested in."

Francine leaned forward to drop the folded-up cupcake wrapper on top of the box. It took her several long seconds to finally say, "Why me? I know *of* you, but I don't think we've ever had a conversation before today."

Amber winced here, overdoing it a bit for Francine's benefit.

"Well, you know how things are here in Edgehill ... I heard you're no longer working with the mayor's office and thought you might like to join the committee to help prevent gaps in your resume until you find a new position. It's not a *job*, per se, but it's a highly respected event—I know you haven't lived here that long, but it's hard not to know how huge the Here and Meow is. And I figure if you were able stay on top of the finances for the mayor and his campaign, running the finances for the festival would be a breeze. We've needed the additional help since Whitney was arrested."

"Oh ... that's right," she said, wrinkling her nose. "I'm sorry about Melanie. I know enough about you to know you two were close."

Amber nodded slightly. "Thanks."

Francine rested her elbows on her knees, gaze focused on her fur-lined house slippers. "Don't get me wrong," she said after a long pause, raising her head to look at Amber, "I'm flattered you've even come here. Lord knows I could use something to help fill my time and get me out of the house, but I mean ..." She sat straighter to motion at herself, and then at her living room. "I'm a disaster. There *have* to be better candidates than me."

Amber shrugged. "We've all been between jobs before. Nothing a shower and a little tidying up can't fix."

"I was *fired*," Francine said. "I was *dumped*. Day drinking and watching romantic comedies are my new hobbies. Because, as if I couldn't be any more of a mess, I'm heartbroken on top of everything else."

Unsure if she should even bring it up, Amber said, "My

friends and I saw you at the Sippin' Siamese on Thursday with a *very* hot cowboy."

Francine snorted and waved her hand dismissively. "Oh, he was just a distraction."

Chewing on her bottom lip, Amber told herself that she was here to talk about the financial position. Nothing else. Nothing else was any of her business. "Were you dumped by Frank?"

Francine let out such a sudden burst of uproarious laughter that her two cats zipped off the couch and darted away. "Oh my God. No, not him. I was seeing this guy for nearly a year and it turns out the little weasel was only dating me because of my connection to the mayor. When Frank fired me, he was no longer interested." Francine stood long enough to fish another cupcake out of the box. After plopping back into her chair, she said, "I feel like I'm drowning. It's like I've lost control of everything in my life."

Amber frowned, struggling for something to say.

"Everything fell apart spectacularly in a matter of forty-eight hours and I don't know how to get back on track." She devoured the second cupcake, then glared at the wrapper she'd meticulously folded into a tiny square. "I don't know how much help I'd be to the committee. Clearly I'm not the best at making decisions. I've made so many terrible ones lately. *Especially* lately. Men, career … eating habits." She tossed the wrapper onto the coffee table. "It's like I don't even recognize myself anymore."

Amber wasn't sure if the woman was seconds from punching something or bursting into tears. "Just *talking* to Kimberly couldn't hurt, right?" she asked.

"I suppose not."

After a stint of awkward silence, Amber said, "If you were to get the position, as it gets closer to the Here and Meow, the mayor has a tendency to pop in on meetings. Our most recent one was at his house. Would things like that be a problem? Seeing him, I mean?"

Francine shrugged. "It would be fine. I'm mostly just … hurt he fired me after all the work I put into that job. During the campaign, we were practically glued at the hip. And then he fires me for snooping in his personal affairs?" She rolled her eyes. "It was my *job* to be in his personal affairs."

"Did you stumble on something really risqué or something?" Amber asked, still unable to keep her curiosity in check.

Francine laughed. "Hardly. He has monthly payments that go out to someone like clockwork. They've been going out for *years*. So I asked him about it, since they were really starting to cut into his bottom line and I needed to know if we needed to cut back in other areas to help accommodate these payments, whatever they were. I made the mistake of asking what they were for and he *flipped* out. He's usually a super relaxed guy, but *geez*, he's got a temper on him. He started saying these really horrible things to me, so I snapped and said horrible things back, and within ten minutes of me asking about the payments, he'd fired me and practically kicked me out of his office."

"Wow," Amber said, reliving her own experience with Frank's temper. "Can I ask you something?"

"You brought me cupcakes in my time of need. You can ask anything you want."

"It's about him and Chloe," Amber said. "Did you ever see anything that would make you think he was, I don't know, abusive to her?"

"*No*," Francine said emphatically, shaking her head. "He's a monster sometimes—a *monster*—but he and Chloe actually get along really well. They have their little arguments, but what parent and teenager don't? He adores her. I know some people think he had something to do with Chloe's disappearance, but there's no way in this world or in the next that he would ever hurt a hair on that girl's head."

But would he pay someone else *to hurt a hair on her head?* Amber wanted to ask.

"Do you think those monthly payments were alimony?" Amber asked instead. If the "Chloe's mother is still alive" theory was true, then maybe the monthly payments were going to her.

"Nope," Francine said. "Shannon died when Chloe was a baby. Car accident. I have no idea who the payments could be to; he has the most boring social life I've ever seen. He doesn't date. Doesn't really have any close friends. I secretly hope I stumbled on payments from a slush fund to someone who he had an illegitimate kid with or something, but he's honestly so boring and straightlaced, I can't imagine it's anything scandalous."

"Then why fire you just for questioning what the payments were for?" Amber asked.

Francine groaned. "True." Then, in a reluctant tone, she asked, "Have you talked to or seen him lately? I mean, since the disappearance? Any idea how he's doing? Does he look like he's been sleeping? He … he won't return my calls. I just want to know if he's okay. Chloe's his whole world; he has to be a wreck."

Something occurred to Amber then.

"What?" Francine asked, when Amber had done nothing but stare at her.

"How long ago did you fall for Frank?"

Squeezing her eyes shut, Francine dropped her face into her hands. Then she whimpered. "My God, am I really that obvious?" When she finally lowered her hands and shrugged helplessly in Amber's direction, her eyes welled with tears. "Nothing *ever* happened between us, let me point that out right now. He never even flirted with me—at least I don't think he ever did. That man isn't the easiest to read.

"This guy I was seeing was … bad news. Manipulative. Good at gaslighting. But he could also be an amazing listener and was there for me whenever I needed it. Definitely a commitment-phobe though. I kept telling myself he was shy and just needed me to be patient until he was comfortable opening up to me, you know? But he just wasn't that into me. I let myself get strung along like a lovesick idiot. I actually talked to Frank about it a couple times.

"A few months ago, we'd both gotten a little tipsy on wine while working at his office and I came onto him *hard*. He shut me down. I don't even know why I've got it so bad for the stupid wet blanket." Her bottom lip shook, and she worried at a cuticle. "We'd gotten so close over the last few years and I'd really gotten to know Chloe. We've had family dinners together and even went on a little weekend vacation once.

I guess I hoped that whatever Frank was upset about would go on the backburner when Chloe vanished. If something like *this* won't make him reach out to me, I don't know what will. But it's been radio silence. It's like he's written me out of his life. Like I don't matter to him anymore. Why do I keep falling for guys who don't want me?"

Amber wished she had an answer for her. All she knew was that she'd grown uncomfortable now that the adrenaline of chasing down a lead had worn off.

"Good gracious," Francine said, rubbing her face with both hands and smearing her old mascara even further. "I'm sorry I just dumped all that on you. I really need to stop day drinking."

Amber managed a faint laugh. It was time to leave this poor woman alone. She stood, and her still-strapped-on messenger bag tapped lightly against her thigh. "It's not a problem. Everyone needs to vent sometimes. Thanks for talking to me. If you're interested in that position …"

Francine stood, too. "Yes, please tell Kimberly I'd love to meet with her to chat. Let me get you my card."

Amber walked with Francine out of the living room. As Amber waited in the small entryway, Francine headed into the rightmost hallway, calling an "I'll be right back!" over her shoulder.

Glancing around the small space, Amber caught sight of her mess of a reflection again and turned her back on it, shuddering slightly. She needed to start carrying a brush in her bag when she rode her bike long distances. She looked like a woman who had come creeping out of the woods where all her friends were squirrels.

Francine was back in less than a minute and handed the card over.

Amber took it and said, "Thanks again for meeting with me. I'm sure Kim will be in touch soon."

When Amber made it outside, she was relieved to find her bike's basket still attached. Once she'd freed her lunch from its pink box and its wrapper, she walked her bike down the sidewalk as she ate her cupcake, thinking about her conversation with Francine.

"I feel like I'm drowning. It's like I've lost control of my life," she'd said. *"I hoped that whatever Frank was upset about would go on the backburner when Chloe vanished. If something like this won't make him reach out to me, I don't know what will."*

It wasn't possible that Francine had something to do with Chloe's disappearance, was it? Would Francine threaten the safety of Chloe in a desperate attempt to get Frank back into her life? He'd turned down her advances, fired her, and shut her out. Heartbreak could make a rational person do wholly irrational things, but would it drive someone to stage the kidnapping of an innocent girl?

Amber desperately hoped Chloe, wherever she was, was okay. That she could hold on a little longer until they found her.

Amber needed to perfect this premonition tincture as soon as possible. Maybe it would provide a clue to where Chloe was being held, or by whom. The longer Chloe was missing, the closer she got to being a statistic.

Amber refused to let that happen.

CHAPTER 9

By 10:45 Tuesday morning, Amber and Ann Marie had set up their table for the Job and Career Fair, which was due to begin at 11. Ann Marie had brought a white tablecloth covered in frolicking kittens, which they'd laid over the table they'd been assigned to. They had the Edgehill Fire Department to their right, and Lil Whiskers Daycare on the other. Businesses from all over Edgehill were represented at the fair—some offering summer job opportunities, while others offered internships. Students looking to enter the medical profession could sign up for volunteer programs.

The Here and Meow table was decorated with a handful of Amber's toys—both the animated ones and a few of the smaller non-charmed ones that would serve as table decorations during the Hair Ball. As Amber and Ann Marie sat in their seats side by side behind the table, Amber took in the scene around her.

The fair was being held in the Edgehill High gym, tables ringing the outside edge of the shiny wooden floor of the basketball court. The place was filled with adults laying down tablecloths, neatly stacking flyers and business cards, and setting up clipboards to sign up for one thing or another. The din was already loud and the kids hadn't even joined them yet. The sound of voices echoed around Amber, bouncing off the walls where the bleachers had been stacked away.

"So we're going to need volunteers both for the 5k—to pass out water and also people to direct runners where to go to make sure no one veers off course—and for the Hair Ball," Ann Marie explained. The clipboard in front of Amber was for the Hair Ball. "For the gala, we basically need as many people as we can get to pass out samples to the guests and to clean up. Glorified waitresses and busboys. The gala is so much bigger this year—I didn't realize how many people we would need to help out."

"Got it," Amber said with a nod. "Have you had luck at the fair before? Seems like a great place to do it."

"First year," she said. "Getting a table here was Melanie's idea. So was convincing the teachers to offer extra credit in exchange for helping out."

With a slight smile, Amber nodded. "Sounds like Melanie."

Ann Marie tapped the screen on her phone, which was lying behind a standing flyer holder, the clear plastic box stuffed with maps of the 5k path, each volunteer location marked with an X. "Ten minutes until show time," she said. "Thanks for doing this, by the way. I know Kim only asked you yesterday. I'm worried about her. Last minute isn't how she does things. She's got three of us to help and yet she keeps taking on more and more herself. I just have a feeling she's going to crack soon."

"We have to keep reminding her we're here if she needs us. Maybe we can wear her down by being overly eager to help."

"Speaking of! I heard we have a new finance chair," said

Ann Marie. "Kim said she got in contact with Francine Robins based on your recommendation and she said Francine is sharp as a tack. I wonder if she's still seeing that hot cowboy ..."

Amber laughed. "She's not. She said he was just a distraction."

"I couldn't even get a guy like that to look at me, let alone allow me to use him as a plaything."

"*Same*," Amber agreed. "I guess Francine needed it; she's been a bit of a wreck since the mayor fired her."

"Yeah, sounds like Kim and Francine bonded over the whole unrequited love thing, too," said Ann Marie. "They really hit it off."

Amber cocked her head. "*Kim* has an unrequited love thing?"

Ann Marie quickly turned in her seat and rested her elbow on the back of it, then leaned toward Amber. "You're *kidding*!"

"What?" Amber asked, leaning back a little.

"I thought she'd told everyone that story," Ann Marie said. "Well, far be it from me to share that one. You'll have to ask her yourself."

Amber really needed to plan a girl's night out with Kim and Ann Marie. She could have a social life here if she just tried a little harder.

Within a few minutes, kids started to pour into the gym. News must have gotten out about the extra credit, because by noon, they had over one hundred names spread across their two sign-up forms. Amber had even gotten an order for a custom animated toy from a young woman who wanted an elephant wearing a graduation cap. Amber was kicking herself for not thinking of a series of graduation-themed toys sooner.

When the flood of teens to their table had thinned out, Amber kept getting lost in the many ways she could animate the elephant. Could she charm it to use its trunk to take the cap off its head and wave it around before putting it back?

"Uh-oh," Ann Marie muttered under her breath. "Incoming."

Amber pulled herself out of her thoughts just as a very pretty young woman approached the table. She had dark brown hair, brown eyes, flawless skin, and a smile that looked completely staged.

"Hi, ladies," she said cheerfully, holding out a hand to Amber.

Amber shot a curious look at Ann Marie as Amber shook the young woman's hand. "Hi."

"I already know Ann Marie, but I don't think we've ever formally met," she said. "I'm Dawn Newland."

"As in Victor Newland's daughter?" Amber asked.

Ann Marie muttered something else under her breath that Amber didn't catch.

"That's me!" she said, grinning that rehearsed smile again. And then Amber understood. It was a politician's smile. A smile you wanted to trust but knew deep down you shouldn't. "And you are?"

"Amber Blackwood."

"Oh, right!" said Dawn. "You sell those little kitschy novelty toys, right?"

Amber decided not to dignify that with a response. Instead,

she said, "Are you looking to volunteer? We're nearly out of positions for the 5k, but we still have a few busser slots open for the gala."

Dawn wrinkled her little button nose. "Actually, I wanted to find out if you're the replacement for Ann Marie's volunteer department assistant."

"I'm just helping out today," Amber said. "Keeping Chloe's seat warm until she comes back."

With a scoff, Dawn said, "Oh, c'mon, Amber. We both know Chloe isn't coming back."

Goose bumps rose on Amber's arms, but she did her best to keep her voice neutral. "We do?"

"Uh … yeah," Dawn said. "She ran off with that trashy older boyfriend of hers she was always talking to. I swear it's a miracle she was passing any of her classes. All she ever did was talk to him on Scuttle. Johnny this and Johnny that. Sounds like her dad found out about it and Chloe decided she'd rather be with Johnny than deal with her psycho father, so she took off. She'll show back up when the creep knocks her up and she needs money."

Amber's mouth dropped open.

Ann Marie gasped.

Dawn rolled her eyes. "Chloe Deidrick has been fooling everyone with her little wholesome act for ages. *Just* like her dad. You saw how he flipped out at the town hall meeting. Who *wouldn't* want to get away from a guy with a temper like that? Even if it meant shacking up with a sleaze like Johnny." She offered a dramatic shudder. "I'm the only one who can see through it. So if you want help, Ann Marie, from someone with actual work ethic who won't be on her phone every ten seconds, know you have the perfect candidate right here. You'll have the most efficiently run volunteer program the Here and Meow has ever had, and I'll have something that looks great on my résumé. Win-win." She reached into the small purse slung over her shoulder and pulled out a baby pink business card, placing it in the middle of one of the clipboards where dozens of her classmates had filled in their names. "Call me," she said, tapping the card twice with a pointer finger, its nail painted a light pink that matched her card. "You won't regret it."

She turned to leave but came up short when she almost careened into a man standing behind her. She groaned. "Ugh, what are *you* doing here, *Alan*?"

It was the same man from the day of Chloe's search, and the one who had been watching Amber from across the patio at the Catty Melt. He hadn't looked at her yet; his semi-disgusted expression was focused on the young woman in front of him. "I'm doing my job, *Dawn*."

"I'd hardly call what you do a job," she said, then walked away in a huff before he could reply.

Amber shot a horrified look at Ann Marie. "Well, *she* was a nightmare."

"You have *no* idea," Ann Marie said. "She and Chloe clearly don't get along. Their dads are rivals, so they are too, I guess. At least the way Dawn sees it. Last I heard, both girls are in the running for Miss Here and Meow. Chloe was front runner, but if she doesn't come back before the gala, it looks like the title will go to Dawn."

"Which I'm sure will also look great on her résumé?" Amber said.

A man cleared his throat, and Amber glanced up to meet the intense gaze of the man Edgar had said was most definitely a cop. She'd hoped that if she ignored him, he'd go away.

"Hello," Ann Marie said, all smiles. "Can we help you with something?"

The intense cop stare he always aimed in Amber's direction suddenly transformed as he turned to address Ann Marie. "Are these sign-ups only for high school seniors, or can an old man like me sign up too?" Like a chameleon, now he was charming, had a goofy self-deprecating air, and a smile that could light up a room.

Ann Marie flushed and tucked her hair behind her ears. "Of course," she said, grinning. "We can use all the help we can get. Were you interested in volunteering for the 5k or the gala?"

His smile was wide as his gaze raked over Ann Marie's upturned face. "What's still open?" he asked. Then, with a sultry air, he said, "You can put me anywhere you want me."

"*All* right," Amber said, abruptly standing up, which seemed to snap Ann Marie out of her pheromone daze. "You," she said, pointing at the chameleon, "come with me."

He didn't resist her command.

She stalked past the Lil Whiskers Daycare table and toward the side door she'd come in earlier. Just beyond the door was a locker-lined hallway that was nearly deserted when Amber slammed her way into it. When Amber turned around, she found the man a few feet away, the door closing behind him.

"Who are you?" she asked, arms crossed.

"Alan Peterson," he said without hesitation.

It was such a plain name; it being real or made up seemed equally likely.

"Are you a private investigator?" she asked.

His mouth quirked up a fraction. "I need to work on my appearance if I'm that easy to spot. But, yeah, I am."

"Hired by whom?"

"Not going to tell you that."

"But it's connected to Chloe's disappearance?"

"Yes," he said. "My client is desperate to find her, as I'm sure *you* are."

"We *all* are," she said.

"That's what I mean," he said. "Edgehill is definitely a town full of well-meaning people. You all hope you have something useful to tell the police ... or a PI. Anything that will assist the professionals in finding her." He paused for a long time, then slowly said, "It *is* strange, though ..."

Amber tried not to take the bait, but she couldn't help it. "What is?"

"You're the one who found her phone," he said. "It was a needle in a haystack and yet you found it as if you'd known exactly where it would be."

Amber swallowed, heart thundering in her chest. How could he possibly know that? Who told him? The chief wouldn't. But would Kim? Had he charmed the information out of her as he'd tried to do with Ann Marie? Had he over-heard something? Had he been watching her in the woods when her magic had pulled her toward Chloe's phone?

"Can I ask you something?" When Amber didn't respond,

he said, "What's the … *nature* of your relationship with Chief Owen Brown?"

Her head reeled back. "Excuse me?"

He shrugged. "I just meant he's relatively new to town, isn't he? Do you think a big city cop has been a good fit for a place like Edgehill?"

That wasn't at all what he'd meant and they both knew it.

When it was clear to him that Amber was done talking to him, he fished around in his back pocket and produced a business card which he held out to her between two fingers.

Normally, Amber would have refused the card and told him where to shove it. But seeing it between his fingers, seeing the contact the paper had with his skin, made her reach out and take it.

"Give me a ring if you hear anything interesting anything about Chloe, okay?" he asked, taking a couple steps back. "I promise we're on the same side here."

Amber stayed rooted to the spot as she watched him walk down the hall, hands shoved into his pockets. He looked like your average dad taking a stroll through the halls. Someone passing him would likely assume he was here to pick up his kid—would assume he belonged here.

She looked down at the card in her hand. *Alan Peterson, huh? Well, Alan, let's see whose side you're really on.*

CHAPTER 10

After Amber's conversation with Ann Marie at the Job and Career Fair about Kim's stress level, Amber had a chat with the Bowen sisters later that evening.

The sisters were tall, blonde, and a year apart, though they looked like they could have been twins. Lily, the younger at eighteen, was the more adventurous and extroverted sister, her hair color changing every couple of weeks. Daisy's mid-back length hair was its usual shade of straw this evening, while Lily's came just below her ears and was a soft baby pink.

"For the rest of this week," Amber said, "do you think you two could swing more hours?"

Lily grinned. "Yes! We love it here. We're planning on taking a trip to Europe in six months for my birthday, so we need all the extra cash we can get."

Daisy nodded. "We don't have lives, so we're all yours."

"Speak for yourself!" Lily said, balled fists pressed to her hips. She wore rings on both pinkies today. Then she dropped her hands. "Okay, she's right, we have no lives."

Amber laughed. "Usually I don't either, but I need to be as available as possible to help with the Hair Ball preparations. It's only a week and a half away and we're understaffed."

"Just tell us when you need us and we'll be here," Lily said.

Amber sent them home an hour early—with pay—as a thank you.

After closing, she busied herself with restocking shelves, making a note of which animated toys would need to be replenished soon—the head-tossing horses were especially popular lately—and filled a few of the tea orders that had been called in earlier in the day.

A knock sounded from the front door and Amber nearly dropped her clipboard. Chief Brown stood on the other side of her locked door, hands on his hips.

"Uh-oh," she muttered to herself. It had been nearly a full twenty-four hours since she'd talked to the chief. She wasn't ignoring him so much as she was just not answering his calls. She placed her clipboard and pen on the counter and made her way to the door to unlock it. The chime above the door tinkled as she pulled it open. "Chief ..."

He strode in. "Amber."

When she turned to face him, she found him with his arms crossed, scowl marring his forehead.

"Did you get my voicemail?" he asked.

"Which one? The one where you asked me to call you back? Or the one where you said I was going to give you a coronary?"

He pursed his lips. "Who did you interview yesterday?"

"Francine Robins," she said, then proceeded to tell him about how Francine had been fired, that the mayor could be a "monster," and that there were monthly payments being made to an unknown account.

He sagged a little and then grudgingly said, "That may

actually prove to be useful. But you *have* to stop doing this, Amber. I don't know what … techniques you're using to get information out of people, and I don't want something you do to come back to haunt me."

"I just talked to her. Human to human talking. And there were cupcakes. Without any added magical tinctures. Scout's honor." When he only seemed partly mollified, she changed the subject. "Did you know there's at least one PI in town?"

The chief's brows hiked up. "No. Who is he? Did he talk to you?"

"Yeah, he talked to Ann Marie and me at the job fair. Alan Peterson. He wouldn't say who hired him, only that he's trying to find Chloe, too," she said. "He also seems to think that this—" she motioned between herself and him—"is something worth looking into. *And* he knows I'm the one who found Chloe's phone."

"*What?*" he said. "When were you planning on telling me this?"

"Now?"

"*Amber.*"

"It only happened a few hours ago!" she said. "I didn't know what to do with it."

"Don't do *anything* with it."

"Does 'anything' also include telling you about it? I'm a little fuzzy on the rules right now."

He grunted. "You *are* going to give me a coronary."

They stared at each other.

"Was that it?" she finally asked. "You just came over here to yell at me?"

With a huff, he said, "I was on this side of town to get a cake from Betty. Jessica and I had our daughter last night."

Amber squeaked. "Chief! Congrats!"

Despite how bone-weary he looked, his mouth inched up on one side. "Her name is Isabelle. She's quite possibly the most beautiful thing I've ever seen."

"You're a big softie under that gruff exterior," she said. "I knew it."

He coughed. "Well … uhh … I should go get that cake," he said, moving toward the door again. Just after he opened it, he looked over his shoulder at her and said, "Stop interviewing people."

As she watched the door close after him, something occurred to her and she grabbed the handle before the door could shut. "Chief!"

He turned to her, standing on the curb.

"You didn't come over here to yell at me about Francine, did you? You used that as an excuse to drop by because I wasn't answering your calls. You wanted to tell me about Isabelle."

"No …" he said unconvincingly, dragging the word out. "It was definitely to yell at you."

"Chief Owen Brown, are you and I friends?"

Rolling his eyes, he said, "Don't be ridiculous, Miss Blackwood." But just before he turned away from her to walk across the street to Purrfectly Scrumptious, she caught the hint of a smile.

Once Amber had cleaned up for the night, fed the cats, and taken a shower, she settled onto the couch, the chief's words ringing in her head.

I don't want something you do to come back to haunt me.

Alley was stretched out on her stomach on the back of the couch, purring away behind Amber's head. Tom lay curled up by Amber's side. She stared at Alan Peterson's card lying on her coffee table. One of the problems with conducting spells on a paper object was that spells often only worked once—especially if there wasn't something handwritten on it. Alan's card was made of sturdy white paper, and had his name and phone number clearly printed in a standard, easy-to-read font. No embellishments. Nothing was written or printed on the back. It was wholly impersonal, which was the point, she was sure. But it meant that whatever spell she used on it would have to be stronger than anything she knew how to do on her own. The spell would have to be able to tap into what little of Alan's energy still resided in the card. And the longer Amber debated on what spell to use, the weaker that energy got.

She got up without disturbing the cats, plucked her landline phone off its wall-mounted cradle, and dialed her cousin's number. She'd needed to call him so many times during the last few weeks, now she had it memorized.

He answered quicker than usual. "It's only Tuesday. I don't have to leave the house until Sunday."

"What if it's for a good cause?" she asked. "That cop we saw at the Catty Melt? He's been creeping around town and I want to find out what he's really up to. Want to come over and help me with a memory spell? We can cloak my studio to prevent detection; it'll be easier to keep my little place cloaked during the spell than your whole house."

He didn't respond.

"I'll order a pizza," she offered.

"Two pizzas," he said. "At least one of them needs to have pineapple and green peppers."

"On the *same* pizza?" Amber blurted.

"Do you want my help or not?"

"Pineapple and ... green pepper it is."

"I'll be there in twenty." He hung up.

It took him closer to half an hour to finally arrive, and by the time he did, his abomination of a pizza was already waiting for him, along with a pepperoni for herself. She met him downstairs and let him into her dark shop. He stepped over the threshold with a leather-bound book clutched to his side. As he looked around the Quirky Whisker, the tighter he held to the book, as if it were a life raft.

Edgar had been in Edgehill for years, but this was the first time he'd ever been in her shop.

"My apartment and the pizzas are upstairs," she said, and he flinched slightly, as if her voice had been as loud as a gong.

She led the way up the steps, and when they reached the top landing, Tom and Alley were sitting side by side on the dining room table, watching. Amber had expected Tom to already be under the bed, so she was doubly surprised when Tom offered Edgar a little mew, hopped to the floor, and immediately started to nuzzle against Edgar's pant legs.

"Wow. Tom is usually scared of his own shadow. He's only

really ever been friendly with Willow and Aunt G," she said. "I guess he knows who's family."

Edgar dropped to one knee, placing his grimoire by his feet, and gave Tom a thorough greeting, scratching under his chin and on the sides of his face. Watching Edgar as a bit of the hardened, anxious side of her cousin started to melt away, she saw what he might be like when he was relaxed and not so guarded. The small smile on his face—courtesy of Tom reaching up and gently tapping Edgar's hand every time he had the audacity to stop petting him—shaved off a good five years.

She hoped that over time, Edgar could find peace with himself. That he'd find a way to be happy.

After they'd each had a few slices of pizza—three for Amber and seven for Edgar—they sat side by side on her couch, their grimoires lying on the coffee table, and Alan's business card resting a few inches above them. Edgar flipped through his book until he settled on a page for cloaking spells.

"Okay, so I'm thinking something simple—one with only two levels, as you call them—will be enough for what I have in mind for the card," Edgar said. "We'll both do the incantation. Me first—since mine will likely be stronger—and then yours on top of that. If someone breaks through yours somehow, mine will take more energy to tear down."

Amber swallowed, nodding.

Edgar read the spell and completed both levels in a handful of minutes; it seemed easy enough. He strolled into the kitchen to grab another slice of pizza.

When he was done, she picked up his grimoire and rested it

on her pressed-together knees. She kept her intention clear in her mind—to remain undetected while they pulled a memory from Alan's residual energy—and began to read the words of the spell. Her magic hummed beneath her skin as she read, and then turned to something closer to buzzing when she approached the end of the first "level." Her magic pulsed out of her, and she imagined it as a physical thing again—taking the form of blue snaking smoke that oozed out of her pores like a fine mist. When it happened again at the end of level two, the pulse was a bit stronger and she immediately felt drained. Like a twisted wet rag, squeezed dry.

How had Willow and Aunt Gretchen conducted a spell with *four* levels, and while working under the added pressure that if they failed, Kieran Penhallow would surely kill Amber? She'd always thought of magic like a muscle—one that needed to be trained and strengthened. If that analogy was true, she desperately needed to get her out-of-shape butt into a gym. She grabbed a bottle of water out of the fridge and chugged half of it down while resting against her dining room table, watching Edgar from his place on the couch.

He still didn't look taxed in the slightest. Amber's head felt a little woozy. She polished off the rest of her water.

If Edgar noticed her weakened state, he didn't say anything about it. After he'd finished his eighth slice, he plopped onto the couch again and rested his elbows on his knees. "Now, the spell I think we should try is a memory reveal spell, just like you've done before. But the one you use is very basic. You get your magic to show you the last memory held in an object—and you can only be shown a memory from where the object in question had been. In a way, you saw what happened to Chloe as if you were her phone. We don't want a memory of where this guy's business card has been—we'd likely just see the inside of his wallet.

"What we're doing is tapping into *Alan's* energy stored in the card because he touched it. That's what your magic will be latching onto. But that's why spells like this get tricky. We need specifics. We have to get the date, time, and location of the scene you want to see as exact as we can—if we're off by, say, half an hour, your magic won't know where to go and you'll use up what little energy the card holds and your chance will be gone."

Amber nodded, her palms growing a bit clammy. It felt like she was back in high school in math class before a big test she hadn't studied for. "Okay, let's see ... I've only run into him three times now. He was being a creepshow when we saw him at the Catty Melt, but that doesn't mean he'd been doing anything odd before he went to breakfast. He was at the search for Chloe on Saturday—maybe he talked to his client that morning."

Edgar nodded. "That's good. Saturday the 18th. Now, what time do you want the memory to be from?"

Amber chewed on her bottom lip. "We were told to meet outside the Sippin' Siamese at 8 a.m., and the only thing that was found during the search was Chloe's cell phone—which *I* found—so anything after 8 won't be of any use, probably. If we go too early, though, the memory we get might just be of him sleeping."

"Yep," he said, nodding. "What time did *you* get there?

You saw him across the street before the mayor made his announcement at 8, right?"

"Right. I saw him before the chief and I did the locator spell in the alley—and that was around 7:30. So maybe we should try for 7?"

"That seems reasonable." Edgar grabbed his grimoire, balanced it on his knees, and flipped a few pages. He tapped a page. "All right. This is the one. Basically, slot the details you need into the blank spots. Your intention actually isn't as vital with a spell like this as the details are. Remember: date, time, and location. Sounds like you don't know where he was other than being on the west side of Korat Road, right? We'll just have to hope that's specific enough."

Amber nodded, making her way over to Edgar. She sat beside him and cautiously took his offered grimoire.

"Memory spells are innately easier for Henbanes, so you shouldn't get too wiped out by this one," he said. "But there's a risk you might pass out in the middle of it."

"*What*? Why didn't you mention that sooner?"

"Sorry," he said, wincing. "You already look so freaked out; I didn't want to freak you out more."

She groaned. Well, she couldn't back out now: her curiosity about whether it would work was overpowering her fear. She plucked the business card off the coffee table. While she held it in one hand, she calmly recited the spell, slotting in "Saturday the 18th of March," "seven in the morning," and "the west side of Korat Road" where necessary. As she spoke, she felt her body grow heavier, her thrashing magic rapidly coursing through her limbs like water rushing through a dry riverbed in the middle of a flashflood, and into the card she held.

Edgar's encouraging words of "You got this, Amber" sounded far away and drowned out. Her vision blackened at the edges, but she willed her heavy eyelids to stay open, for her gaze to stay rooted to the words of the spell as she read them as fast as she could.

She was sure she wasn't going to make it—that her magic would be depleted before the spell was complete and the little bit of Alan's energy in the card would evaporate.

But then a brilliant white light tore through her vision and she was hurled some*when* else.

CHAPTER 11

When the light faded, Amber stood on familiar car-lined Korat Road. The sky was a sickly gray, the morning air chilly on her skin even with the hint of sunlight trying to break through the cloud cover.

She lifted her wrist to check her watch. It was a heavy, chunky thing that wasn't really her taste—too flashy—but her brother had been so proud of the purchase, mostly because he'd actually remembered her birthday this year.

Amber froze.

Those memories had come to her so easily, yet they weren't hers. These were *Alan's* memories. Unlike the time she rode along as an unfeeling passenger through her father's memories, Amber felt as if she were truly *here*. She was aware of everything, from the environment around Alan, to what was happening in his mind. It was unnerving. Was this what it was like for Neil's magic, trapped as it was in Edgar's head? It was like being in that in-between place of sleep—almost awake, almost asleep, and fully conscious of the world around her. This was the danger of magic that dealt with the mind—your magic could get trapped. Even though Neil Penhallow was physically in an institution somewhere, at least some of his magic—his essence—was stuck in Edgar's consciousness.

171

What would happen to *her* magic if something went wrong? Could her magic get lost not in a person, but in a certain point in time—looping endlessly through the same small snippet of memory?

Amber could only hope that if her physical body showed some sign of things going sideways, that Edgar could rescue her from being trapped somewhere.

Currently, Alan was standing near the small gaggle of reporters, one of whom was Connor's editor. Alan watched as Amber told Connor to join his fellow reporters, and how Connor quickly hurried away from her. Alan found this dynamic fascinating—were they friends, mere acquaintances, two people trying to remain civil while in the throes of a failing relationship? His gaze lingered on the brunette even though the young man stood only a few feet from Alan now.

When she caught him watching her, a flare of embarrassment bloomed in his chest. He'd gotten so good at blending in, that when someone actually noticed him, it threw him off. His instinct was to turn away and melt back into the crowd, to slip from view and her memory. But something about her intrigued him. He didn't think it was something as simple as attraction. She was beautiful, there was no doubt about that, but it was something else. She'd too quickly homed in on him watching her. She, like him, was overly alert. There was a nervous energy about her—a telltale sign she was hiding something. They were subtle clues, ones others might miss, but he saw them. It could be connected to Chloe, but it just as likely could be something else. Perhaps connected to the young man who'd fled her presence as if he couldn't get away from her fast enough.

When Alan won their staring contest, and she shifted her gaze to her phone instead of him, he deftly stepped behind the large news van and out of her direct line of sight. He waited a minute or two, then peered around the back of the van, expecting her to have met up with the friend she'd so clearly been waiting on, but instead he spotted her being escorted down the sidewalk by the chief of police.

Alan stayed out of sight—despite the pair of them shooting anxious looks over their shoulders periodically—as he watched them duck into an alley. He couldn't see what they were doing, and certainly couldn't hear anything, but at one point, the chief pulled something from his pocket and handed it to her. Within a matter of minutes, the chief was jogging down the alley, leaving her at the end of it. Curious.

Alan's phone rang as he watched the woman walk unsteadily down the length of the alley. She looked a little drunk, honestly, as if she'd forgotten how to walk. Had the chief given her a substance of some kind? It wouldn't be the first time he'd found out a cop was selling drugs he'd been siphoning from an evidence closet.

Alan fished his phone out of his pocket and flipped open the disposable device; he pressed it to his ear without bothering to look at the caller's ID—he rarely programmed numbers into these things anyway. "Peterson."

"Any news?" the female voice asked.

"They're conducting a search of the woods this morning," he said, still watching the woman as she lurched forward a couple steps, then paused, hand to her stomach, before she unsteadily stumbled forward again. "It'll be another half hour at least, I'm guessing. The mayor said eight, but things like this rarely start on time. Even if something like this is highly irregular."

"A search?" the woman asked, her voice a little shrill. Alan didn't even know the woman's name. She'd introduced herself as a concerned citizen who was looking out for Chloe Deidrick's best interest and requested he keep a close eye on the mayor. She'd wired him the agreed-upon fee within an hour. He wasn't necessarily crazy about a client being this anonymous, but it wasn't the first time. And it wasn't as if "Alan Peterson" was his true name anyway. As long as clients paid him, he didn't care what they did—or didn't—call themselves. "Do they expect to find her in the woods? Why didn't you mention this sooner?"

"Because I didn't want you to get worked up over something that might not pan out," he said, watching as the woman in the alley got a hold of her limbs and strode out onto the sidewalk, under control again. "It's very strange that the mayor is pushing for something like this so soon—it's almost as if he expects to find something out there. Like he *knows* something is out there. Guilty people do this all the time—they either get anxious about being caught, or antsy that their crime isn't getting the attention they think it deserves, and then start behaving in a way that points law enforcement in the direction the criminal wants them to go."

"So you *do* think they'll find her?" The woman was in near hysterics now.

"No," he said, sounding more patronizing than he intended. "I'm saying it's very possible that this move on the mayor's part is calculated. Maybe he's staging this elaborate search that pulled in most of the Edgehill police force—and police from nearby towns—as a distraction. Something else could be going on right now and he's making sure most of the town has their backs turned so someone *else* can act with less fear of being caught."

"Caught doing what?"

"I have no idea, lady," he said. "This is all speculation. You're paying me to observe, not to be clairvoyant."

"If you're going to be nasty, I can hire someone else, you know."

Alan rolled his eyes. "No skin off my nose."

While the woman on the other end huffed her indignation, Alan watched a second woman—this one in a ridiculous pink cap—push her way through the crowd to join his mystery woman.

"Keep watching the mayor," the woman on the phone finally said. "I want to know where he goes at night, who comes to his house, who comes to his office. Everything. He covered his tracks when Shannon died and got away with it. Don't let the same thing happen with Chloe."

That was enough to get Alan to tear his gaze away from the pair of brunettes, the mayor's voice amplified now by a megaphone. He jammed a finger into his free ear to hear his client better and rested his back against the side of the van. "You really think he killed Shannon?"

"If he didn't do it himself, he got someone else to do it for him," his client said. "His hands might be clean in the sense that he didn't pull the trigger himself, but his money is dirty."

Alan pursed his lips. "So far the guy has the most boring social life I've ever seen. He doesn't go anywhere after ten at night and is up by six every morning. No one comes to the house. Maybe there's nothing to find."

"Keep watching," she said. "Everyone has secrets."

A white light cut through the memory and Amber gasped, opening her eyes to see her apartment from an unusual angle. Then she realized she was lying on her side on the couch, her feet still on the floor. She slowly pushed herself to sitting, wincing a little as her head started to thrum.

Before her swimming thoughts could solidify into anything coherent, a glass of water and a flattened palm with two small pills were shoved in her face. She followed the arm up to a familiar face whose black brows were pulled together. Edgar.

"You all right, cousin?" he asked.

She swallowed, her mouth parched. She took the pills and water from him. After she'd drained the glass and he'd fetched her a second one, she felt a little better. But she also felt like she'd been hit by a truck.

"You are severely out of shape," he said, staring at her while hinged over with his hands on his knees.

She mustered up enough energy to glare at him.

He grinned. "Ah, there's that Blackwood charm." Standing to full height, he said, "You'll be okay. Just takes practice. And sleep. Sleep will recharge your batteries better than anything else."

Suddenly starving, she carefully got to her feet and shuffled into the kitchen to inhale two slices of cold pizza.

Edgar stood in the doorway of her small kitchen, arms crossed as he leaned a shoulder on the refrigerator. "So, what'd you see?"

She told him that Alan wasn't the PI's real name, and that his client *wasn't* the mayor, but a woman who somehow knew Chloe went missing. "Based on the way she talked—like being clueless about the search that happened on Saturday—she's not local. And whoever she is, she knows about Shannon—the mayor's dead wife—and thinks the mayor had something to do with her death."

"Dang," Edgar said, chewing his bottom lip. "The chief have any idea what happened to Shannon?"

"I don't think so," she said. "Connor doesn't either. He said the *Gazette* is trying to track that down."

"Seems weird that in this day and age, it's so hard to find out what happened to her," Edgar said. "Can't we just Google it?"

Amber laughed. "I'm guessing they already tried that. Plus, with enough money, you can alter whatever narrative you want. Maybe anyone who knew the truth about what happened was paid off to keep it out of the paper."

"Or maybe that creep who stole Chloe out of the woods—and the person who killed Shannon—also gets paid to shut up witnesses for good," Edgar offered.

Crossing her arms tightly across her chest, she fought off a sudden chill. "We have to find out what happened to Shannon."

After Edgar left, Amber was filled with a nervous energy. She knew she should sleep, that her magic—which felt sluggish—needed her to rest. But she couldn't get Alan's client's words out of her head: *His hands might be clean in the sense that he didn't pull the trigger himself, but his money is dirty.*

Had the mayor's dirty money bought the assistance of the man who'd chased Chloe through the woods? But why would the mayor, if he truly adored his daughter as much everyone claimed, kidnap her? It couldn't be simply to keep her away from the mystery boy from Scuttle. It went deeper than that.

She snatched her cell phone off the coffee table and called her aunt using the video function. Her aunt had the ability to figure out technology far faster than Amber had the ability to figure out tinctures.

"Hi, little mouse," Aunt Gretchen said, her face smeared in something mint-green colored.

"Ahh! What on earth is on your face?"

"An exfoliant," she said. "You look like you could use one. Why do you look like death warmed over?"

Amber told her about the memory spell she and Edgar had used.

"Ah, well, that would explain it," she said. "And since you have that wild look in your eye right now, I'm guessing you want to resume work on the premonition tincture? Your mother got that same look. You Henbane women get a bug up your butt about something and you don't give up until you see it through." She sighed. "Go get your supplies, little mouse. Let's see if we can get through the lesson this time without smoke, hmm?"

178

"And you say *I* have the bedside manner of a rotting toadstool," Amber muttered as she propped her phone up on the counter and got to work getting the necessary ingredients together.

Aunt Gretchen merely laughed.

It took two hours, but when Amber added the final pinch of wild asparagus root to the glass bowl, the tincture turned bright red and then, seconds later, the color vanished altogether, leaving behind a bowl of what looked more like water than anything. There was a very faint pink hue.

"Perfect!" Aunt Gretchen said, clapping.

Amber sagged against the counter, staring at the bowl in disbelief. No smoke, no stench of burnt plastic, no black sludge. "It's safe to drink?"

Aunt Gretchen nodded. "For tonight, since you're already so exhausted, I would take a smaller dose. Only a teaspoon in your drink of choice tonight. Tomorrow evening, you can take a full tablespoon. That batch there should last you a couple weeks. Keep it in a sealed container in the fridge and it will hold. If the pink darkens to purple, toss it out and start again."

"Okay," Amber said, rubbing her eyes. "Thanks again, Aunt G. I know I'm not the best student."

"Pah, you're a fine student. Tinctures just aren't your specialty; you're definitely your mother's daughter." Aunt Gretchen smiled warmly at her. "Sleep well, little mouse. I expect a report in the morning."

"Will do," Amber said, yawning so deeply that her eyes watered.

"Remember: read the spell, state the person you wish to

see in your dreams, and then drink the tincture as quickly as you can, keeping your thoughts focused on the person the entire time." Worry lines marred her aunt's forehead.

"I'll be okay, Aunt G," Amber said. "I'll talk to you in the morning. Good night."

Her aunt nodded once, quickly, her expression a little wary. "Good night, my sweet girl."

Amber disconnected the call, got ready for bed, and then stood in the kitchen staring at the innocent-looking liquid in the bowl. It was hard to believe that something that appeared so innocuous had caused her so much trouble—and was something that could potentially let Amber see into the future.

After sealing the tincture away—minus a teaspoon—in an airtight container and storing it in her fridge, Amber poured tonight's portion into a glass of water. Her grimoire, with the new spell she'd gotten from Aunt Gretchen, lay on the counter. Most of the magic was in the tincture itself, but Amber had to fall asleep with her intention true, and Aunt Gretchen had warned her that the tincture would work quickly to knock her out.

She took her glass and her spell book to her bed. Once she was situated, she made sure she had the words memorized, then placed her grimoire on her nightstand. Tom and Alley lay on the foot of the bed, their sides flush, watching her as if they knew something was amiss tonight.

"I'm a little nervous, guys," she told them. "What if I see nothing because her future no longer exists?"

They didn't reply.

She gave the glass a tentative sniff. No scent. After reciting the incantation, she said, "All right, well, here goes nothing. Show me Chloe Deidrick." Then she chugged down the contents of the glass.

Almost immediately, her vision started to blacken at the edges. She had enough time to place her empty glass on her nightstand beside her grimoire, and then she tumbled into sleep.

The windowless room was dark, and the walls were cement and unfinished. A mattress lay in a corner, directly on the floor. The sheets on the bed were clean, the dark blue blanket on top soft and new. There was only one pillow, but it was fluffy. There was no other furniture here. On the wall opposite the bed was the distinct outline of a door, but there was no knob or handle on the inside, just a round, flat metal disc where a knob should have been.

Chloe sat on the mattress with her back to the rough wall and the blanket draped over her knees. She angled her head to the upper right corner of the room, where a black wireless camera was mounted into the ceiling, its all-seeing eye trained on her.

A knock sounded on the door. Four quick raps. Chloe flinched with each one.

Slowly, the door opened, but Chloe made no move toward it.

Blackness lay beyond, but the door didn't open far enough to reveal much.

Chloe reached out and slapped an open palm against the

rough wall. One, two, three, four in quick succession. Then she pulled her hand back to wrap her arm around her knees again.

A square paper plate slid into the room, topped with a piece of buttered toast cut diagonally into two triangles, a scrambled egg, and three pieces of bacon. No silverware. A man's hand reached in to place a plastic cup of water beside the plate. A rolled-up newspaper slid into the room next.

The door quickly closed, and a lock engaged. Four quick knocks followed.

It wasn't until the second set of knocks that Chloe moved. She darted forward on her hands and knees, not for the food, but for the newspaper. She quickly unrolled it, her hands shaking. "Edgehill Gazette" was printed at the top of the paper. The top story was, unsurprisingly, about her. Connor Declan's name was in the byline.

"Mayor Deidrick's Daughter Missing for a Full Week."

The picture featured was of the mayor standing on one of the tables outside the Sippin' Siamese, a megaphone to his lips. Chloe placed a finger on the image of her father, her dark red nail polish chipped. Then she picked up her plate of food and newspaper and went back to her mattress. As she used the toast to scoop up the eggs, she read the article about her. A tear slipped down her nose and landed with a splat on the newspaper below, the ink dissolving.

Amber woke with a start. Sunlight poured in through her bedroom window, spilling over Alley's back as she slept on the window bench seat.

Chloe has been gone for seven days?

Amber checked her cell phone. Today was Wednesday, but

Chloe disappeared on a Thursday. The tincture had worked—it had showed her Chloe's tomorrow. Which meant she was alive and safe now and would be for at least twenty-four hours.

They still had time to find her.

CHAPTER 12

After Amber fed the cats, she called the chief. It wasn't until the phone was ringing that it registered with her that it was just after six in the morning. She had to hope that his job and/ or the new baby in the house would ensure he was awake, and not that he would answer the early morning call in a groggy panic.

"Morning, Amber," the chief said. "Please tell me you're calling at this ungodly hour because you have *good* news."

"Chloe's alive," she said.

She almost heard his posture straighten, fully alert now. "You're sure?"

"Yes. I don't know where she is or who has her, but for at least twenty-four hours, she's okay." She then proceeded to explain how a premonition tincture worked, but he cut her off in the middle of it.

"I think I'm at the point where I don't need the details on how this all works," he said. "The details give me hives."

"Okay, then I won't explain how I found out that the nosy PI in town wasn't hired by the mayor," she said. "Whoever hired Alan Peterson seems to think the mayor can't be trusted. Have you been able to find out anything about Shannon? Is there some way that this client of Alan's is related to Chloe or

Shannon somehow? Who else would be invested enough in Chloe's disappearance other than a family member?"

After a long pause, he said, "There's a news article from a small town in Montana that details Shannon's car accident seventeen years ago. She hit a patch of black ice and her car went into a lake, where she drowned. There were marks on her body that imply she'd suffered physical abuse for a while, but none of her injuries are what killed her—the car pitching into near freezing water is what did that. There's an obituary for her in that paper, too. Nothing else. We have a social security number for her, but when we looked into it, we found it actually belongs to a woman who died twenty years before Shannon was apparently born. It's as if Chloe's mother didn't actually exist."

Amber blinked rapidly. "I don't even know what to say to that."

"Yeah, we're all scratching our heads here, too. Don't know if that means Shannon was in the country illegally so her identity isn't on paper, or if Shannon Pritchard is a fake name," the chief said. "We'll keep looking, but something is definitely fishy here."

"Have you been able to look into those monthly payments Francine mentioned?"

"We're working on that, too. We're also close to getting a search warrant on the Deidrick home; Frank won't let us back in. When Chloe first went missing, Frank consented to have us search the house from top to bottom. With consent, we don't need a warrant. However, when we went back a couple days later, he refused to let us in unless we had one," the chief said.

"But if we're granted one now, it means a judge has reason to believe a second search could prove fruitful."

"That doesn't sound good for Frank."

"Nope," the chief said. "It sure doesn't."

Though the premonition tincture hadn't revealed Chloe's location or the identity of her kidnapper, Amber felt some of the tension leave her shoulders, if only because she knew the girl was safe. Scared and lonely, yes, but she was alive. And, even if her accommodations weren't ideal, they were feeding her and she had a decent place to sleep. And that sense of relief allowed Amber to tend to more of her responsibilities—namely filling all the orders she'd gotten behind on and making a list of all the toys she still needed to make for the Hair Ball.

Sometime while Amber had been getting ready that morning, Kim had texted her with,

> Want to grab lunch with me today? I can pick you up at noon. I'm losing my mind and I'm this close to strangling Ann Marie.

At noon on the dot, Kim pulled up in front of the Quirky Whisker. The Bowen sisters had already left for lunch, so as soon as Amber saw Kim out front, she hurried outside, locked up, and climbed into Kim's car.

"Hi," Kim said. "I've had six cups of coffee."

With that, she pulled out onto Russian Blue Avenue.

"Hi to you, too," Amber said. "Why are you going to strangle Ann Marie?"

"Ugh! Can we not even talk about it? I don't even want to

talk about the Hair Ball. We can talk about literally anything else. I just want this to be a fun lunch outing with someone who I don't want to strangle," Kim said.

Amber winced. "Sure. I—"

"The Hair Ball will go fine, right?" Kim said, punctuating the question with a semi-hysterical laugh. "So many businesses are desperate to be named Best of Edgehill—what if I've planned the whole thing wrong? Everyone is going to hate me!"

"Breathe, Kim," she said. "You'll be fine. Lean on the rest of us, okay? The Bowen girls are ready to take on as many hours as possible to allow *me* the time to help *you*."

Kim nodded vigorously without looking at Amber. "I've missed Melanie so much lately. She was so good under pressure. I'm a mess."

"I miss her, too," Amber said. "But she'd tell us that we're strong women capable of anything we put our minds to."

Kim nodded again.

"So where are we headed?" Amber asked. "Think we have enough time to get Mexican food?"

"Yes! But! Oh, fiddlesticks." She thumped the heel of her palm on the steering wheel. "Can we make a quick stop at Hiss and Hers first? I totally forgot I was supposed to check on their table display. Since we can't have people sample home decor the way we can sample cupcakes, we're having Pawterry House and Hiss and Hers put together table displays using only items from their shops. I need to approve their displays before the Hair Ball. Oh my God, Amber, last night Ann Marie and I went to The Applaws to see the one-man play they'll put on during the gala. It was a *disaster*! They let the owner's son, who is in a creative writing program, write an original play for the gala. It was so bad. I don't know if it was the acting or the writing or both, but it was a total stinker. Half the audience walked out. Now they have to scramble to put something else together in only a week."

Amber winced.

"The table display for Pawterry House is gorgeous, so I have my fingers crossed this will be a good one, too. I don't think I can handle another flop like *Stan Tackles a Unicorn*."

Amber snorted. "I don't even want to know."

"You really don't," Kim said. "I'm scarred for life."

Hiss and Hers was on Himalayan Way, not far from Paws 4 Tea, where Susie Paulson used to work before she was arrested for her role in Melanie's death. Amber wasn't sure she'd ever be able to step inside that shop again.

Kim pulled up outside Hiss and Hers in one of the diagonal parking spots at the curb. When she got out, Amber gave her friend a quick scan. Her long brown hair was pulled back in a French braid; she wore a pair of skinny jeans, a silk floral top, and two *very* mismatched flats. One had blue and white stripes, while the other was leopard print. Amber thought it best not to mention it.

Though Hiss and Hers always gave Amber a sense of claustrophobia because the small space was so jam-packed with items, she loved it because the front of the shop was all windows, letting in a ton of natural light. The shop specialized in unique, repurposed furniture and trinkets. There were dressers that had vintage suitcases as the drawers, couches made out of claw foot bathtubs that had been cut in half lengthwise, and steel drums that had been turned into ottomans. In the middle of the room stood a table draped with a white tablecloth. On top was a rustic springtime display. There were vases made from colorfully painted Mason jars and small tin buckets stuffed with pastel flowers; a wire cupcake tower had been filled with wooden wreaths topped with stuffed birds and eggs to resemble nests; and small repainted birdhouses sat on wide-based wooden candle stands.

"Oh my God, Amber," Kim said softly, grabbing Amber's arm. "It's so cute!"

A voice sounded from ahead of them. "Do you really like it? We're not quite done yet, but it's almost there."

Amber glanced up to see a petite, smiling woman walking their way. Grace Williams, Bethany's mother, had short hair that was so black—given the woman's pale complexion, Amber guessed the color had come from a salon—and a tiny hoop in one nostril. Her eyes were a striking purple thanks to colored contacts.

"It's adorable," Amber said to Grace, shaking her hand.

After releasing Amber's hand, Grace said, "Glad to hear it! We've gone through a dozen displays by now. This last one was mostly Bethany's doing. She painted all the jars, buckets, and stands herself."

Just then, a younger version of Grace emerged from the back of the cluttered shop. Her light brown hair matched her natural complexion, which was a bit paler than what seemed healthy. There were bags under her eyes, and she sniffled periodically as she made her way to her mom's side.

Grace wrapped an arm around her daughter's shoulders.

"Poor thing is still recovering from a nasty bug. She's missed school every day this week."

"I already started getting acceptance letters to college," Bethany said, her voice a little nasal, "so it doesn't feel like I'm missing too much. I think I have senioritis on top of having the flu."

They all laughed.

"Oh, Kim, I wanted to find out if what I'm working on for the centerpieces for the Hair Ball are okay," Grace said. "I know you're in a pinch with those, but I didn't want to start making dozens of them if you don't think they'll work. They're in the back if you want to take a look."

Kim arched her brows at Amber.

"Go ahead," Amber said. "I need to find something for Willow's birthday next month."

With a nod, Kim followed Grace toward the back of the shop. Bethany, eyes closed, was leaning against the small glass cashier counter, which was filled with animals made of smooth river rocks. The poor girl looked like she needed to be in bed, not in the shop.

Amber moved toward the front, where there was a display of brightly painted tin cans that had cooking utensils sprouting from them like flowers.

"Hi ... Amber?"

She glanced over to see Bethany standing a few feet away, pulling her oversize cardigan tighter around her body. "Hey, Bethany."

Bethany's green eyes were red-rimmed; they looked itchy. "You saw Chloe the night she disappeared, right?"

"That's right," Amber said, turning to face her.

190

"She's always really liked you," Bethany said. "Respects you a lot. She was happy she got to be on the Here and Meow Committee partly because she thought it would mean you two could get to be friends now that she was older."

Amber's stomach knotted. "I was happy she joined us, too."

Bethany squeezed herself even tighter. "I heard she was talking to you about Johnny … the guy she'd been talking to on Scuttle?" When Amber nodded, Bethany quickly glanced over her shoulder toward where her mom and Kim were still talking at the back of the store. "I think Johnny did something to her. I can't stop thinking about it."

Amber's brows shot toward her hairline. "Why do you think that?"

"Even if she decided she wanted to, like, elope or something crazy, there's no way she wouldn't tell me or her dad. Even if she and her dad were fighting about her dating Johnny, she'd still eventually call him to tell her where she was. Running off and not saying anything to anyone just isn't how Chloe is," Bethany said. "Something about Johnny always felt really off to me. Did you hear about the hack?"

"Hack?"

"Yeah. I don't know the details 'cause I don't understand how all that stuff works, but some guy hacked into Scuttle and found names and email addresses for all the kids in Edgehill who use it and posted the names online. The list got pulled, I think, but Johnny started talking to Chloe after that list went up. I mean, maybe he's someone from Belhaven who's seen her at a game or something, but maybe it was someone *pretending* to be a kid from Belhaven, you know? Chloe showed me his picture, but it was only that *one* picture. Kinda looks like a stock photo if you ask me. He never sent more than that because he was 'shy.'" Bethany rolled her red-rimmed eyes. "I don't think he's who he said he is."

"Did you tell the police or her dad any of this?"

Bethany vigorously shook her head. "No. If she's really okay, she's going to be *so* mad at me for ratting her out to her dad." She hesitated—opening her mouth and closing it a couple times—before she finally said, "I don't have anything against her dad. He's always been really nice to me and everything. But ... I don't know ... lately things between them have been a little weird? I can't even explain it. Chloe told me she found out something about him, too. She wouldn't tell me what it was; she said she didn't want to get into it until she had all the details, but it's about her mom."

"What about her?"

Bethany glanced over her shoulder again and then took a small step toward Amber and lowered her voice a fraction. "Chloe thinks she was murdered."

Amber's eyes widened. "And she thinks her dad—"

"Chloe didn't act like she thought it was her dad who did it or anything," Bethany said quickly, cutting off Amber's question. "But she would get really anxious when she talked about it—and never talked about it when her dad was home. It's like she didn't want him to know she was looking into it."

"*How* was she looking into it?" Amber asked, wondering what Chloe had been able to find that the police couldn't.

Bethany shrugged, arms still crossed. "I just have a really bad feeling about it all. I think that's why I can't get better. It's like I'm literally worried sick about her. She would never go this long without calling me even if she'd run off with

Johnny—so all I can think is that she *can't* call me. She's my best friend. I don't know what I'll do if—"

Even though the girl had to be contagious, Amber closed the distance and pulled her into a hug. Bethany wrapped her arms tightly around Amber's middle and burst into tears. Amber wished she could tell her that Chloe was alive and safe.

"Shh," Amber said, gently running a hand down Bethany's hair. "Shh. We'll find her, okay? Chloe is a fighter. She'll hang on until we can get her back."

After lunch—during which Kim talked about nothing *but* Hair Ball matters—Amber had nothing on her agenda. She'd expected to get a list of errands from Kim, but when Amber asked for an assignment or seven, Kim had waved her off.

"I've got things covered for today," Kim had said. Amber had been fairly certain Kim's eye had been twitching through most of lunch.

With the Bowen sisters scheduled to run the shop for the rest of the afternoon, Amber called a hello to them just before the shop officially reopened for the afternoon, and then trudged upstairs to get to work on the rest of the cat toys she needed to make. On her way, she called the chief.

"Two phone calls in one day?" he asked, sounding vaguely distracted.

"I just had an interesting conversation with Chloe's best friend." As she fed the cats, she recounted what Bethany had told her. "What could Chloe have found out about her mother? She's got far fewer resources than you do."

"Maybe she was snooping in the house and found something Frank had hidden somewhere," the chief offered.

"Maybe," she said halfheartedly.

The chief was a silent for a long time, though Amber could hear the clack of his fingers on his keyboard, and the occasional sound of drawers rolling open or closed. "I think I have something you can help me with."

She had just sat down at her dining room table to get started on her next batch of cats and froze with a hand reached toward a stack of unpainted plastic pieces. "Is Amber Blackwood a consultant on the case now?"

"A) Don't refer to yourself in the third person: that's weird," he said, "and B) don't get ahead of yourself here. I'll ask for help when we've hit a dead end. Like now. During our preliminary search, Frank was in a heightened emotional state and wouldn't have necessarily thought to dispose of or hide anything incriminating. We found absolutely nothing of note. But we very easily could have missed something that seemed insignificant to us but was very important to him. Maybe whatever we missed, Frank realized his mistake in letting us in and that's why he's demanding a warrant now."

"And you want me to help you find what he might be hiding?" Amber asked.

"Yes," he said. "We spent hours in that house looking in every drawer and cabinet. We searched for secret doors to basements or attics—anywhere someone might be hiding a person—or a body. We were extremely thorough and found nothing, but if a judge is granting us a warrant, I'd like to know I did everything in my power—or yours—to be sure."

He paused, then cautiously asked, "Is there a spell, like the locator one, you could use?"

Swallowing, Amber nodded—then remembered he couldn't see her. "I can come up with something."

"Can you be ready in twenty minutes? I can come pick you up."

He wanted to do this *now*? She kept her voice steady as she said, "See you then."

She kept her cool until the call was disconnected, then she let out a squeak and flailed her arms. What on earth was she thinking? She couldn't use a locator spell on something she didn't even have a name for!

Think, Amber. Think. This is for Chloe.

Based on Amber's conversation with Bethany, it was just as likely that *Chloe* had hidden something in that house. Amber was sure she could tap into Chloe's energy better than she could Frank's. Hopefully the chief wouldn't mind Amber changing the plan on him last minute.

Amber needed a spell like the one she had used on the receptionist at the morgue, where her magic had teased out the young woman's guilty pleasure. Or when her magic had found Susie Paulson's biggest recent regret. Amber needed to locate what Chloe didn't want her father to know she'd found. Assuming, of course, that whatever this thing was—the thing she wouldn't even tell her best friend about—was in the house to find. Assuming it was a thing at all.

Amber consulted her grimoire, finding the spell that most resembled what she needed, and then scribbled down her own variation on a scrap of paper she could take with her.

Stuffing the note into her pocket, she snatched up her purse, phone, keys, and jacket that she'd unceremoniously dumped on a chair not more than ten minutes before and made her way back down the stairs.

Lily and Daisy Bowen were busying themselves with restocking shelves and filling orders.

"Hey, ladies, I'm off again," Amber said. "Thanks again for helping me out this week. I need to give you both a raise."

Daisy grinned. "I wouldn't say no to that."

Just then, Chief Brown's cruiser pulled up out front.

When Amber turned to thank them again, the sisters were sharing a knowing look. *Good grief, not them too!* Amber sighed and then darted out the door.

It wasn't until she was strapped in and she and the chief were headed down Russian Blue Avenue that he spoke. "Jessica got wind of the affair rumor before I could figure out how to bring it up. She heard it in the hospital just hours after Isabelle was born."

"Oh no," Amber said with a groan. "How did she react?"

"She said I have to do chores every night for a week before she'll consider forgiving me. She mentioned something about pulling weeds," he said. "Thing is, I don't think she's actually upset at all—she just wants me to do chores. But in case she is mad, I don't want to risk ticking her off."

"I'm sure you look just as dashing in a pair of gardening gloves," she said.

He cut her an annoyed look out of the corner of his eye, but there was no malice in it. "So, what's your plan for when we get in there?"

"I have a two-part plan. For the first one, can you take a right up here and drive to the end of the street? It's a dead end that's overgrown on three sides."

He stared at her in utter confusion for a split second but did as she asked.

Once he was parked in the secluded location, she said, "Try not to have a coronary, all right?" Then she draped her jacket over her head.

Since she and glamour spells didn't mesh, she decided it best to keep this simple. She would change only her hair color and style—glamoured hair had a tendency to hold longer than facial features—the shape of her nose, and the color of her eyes.

When she removed the jacket from her head, she pulled down the passenger side mirror to examine her handiwork. The chief yelped and smashed himself against the car door as if she now had three heads, rather than just one with blonde hair styled into an A-line bob. Her eyes were green now, instead of brown, and her nose was a bit wider.

When she turned her face to the chief, he flinched again. "You can't tell me not to have a coronary and then do *that*, Amber."

"Sorry!" she said. "But if people are already suspicious of us spending time together, isn't it going to look even weirder to have *me* show up to help the police search the house? I joked about being a consultant on the case, but maybe this—" she said, gesturing to her face, "can be your new consultant. You can call me Cassie."

"My God," he muttered, then gave his head a good shake. Without another word, he pulled out of the secluded area and headed back toward Russian Blue Avenue.

When they were halfway there, she broke the silence. "Instead of looking for something Frank hid, I think we should look for something Chloe might be hiding. Can we be in her room in private? I think even if what we're looking for isn't in Chloe's room, her energy will be strongest there. If I can tap into that, my magic will hopefully be able to lead us in the right direction."

"Got it," he said, though he sounded vaguely queasy. His knuckles were white thanks to his death grip on the steering wheel.

When they pulled up outside the Deidrick home, there was already another squad car there—and the Channel 4 news van. Not to mention a handful of reporters loitering on the sidewalk, one of which was Connor Declan.

"Aw, crap," Amber and the chief said in unison.

"I thought I'd have to deal with the media vultures a little less in a small town ..." he muttered, gaze focused on his rearview mirror. "Well, *Cassie*, I guess this ... alteration was a good plan. Just say you're a consultant on the case if you have to say anything—avoid talking if you can help it. Absolutely don't go into details. If they don't have details, they can't cross-check."

With a nod, she let herself out of the car. A couple of the reporters jogged over when they spotted Chief Brown, holding out recording devices as they asked him what had changed in the case that made a judge agree to issue a warrant.

Is Mayor Deidrick responsible for the disappearance of his daughter?

Is it true that Mayor Deidrick is a suspect in the death of his late wife?

Is there a connection between Chloe's disappearance now and the mysterious death of Shannon Pritchard?

Carl, Garcia, and a handful of other officers joined Amber and the chief as they all moved as a unit toward the house. None of the officers said anything, just marched forward as if the reporters didn't exist. Even goofy Carl was doing a good job of keeping his mouth shut.

When they were a foot from the door, Chief Brown, without breaking stride, said, "We cannot discuss the details of this case at this time," voice loud enough so the gaggle of reporters could hear him.

Amber kept her head down largely because she didn't want to have this fake face of hers recorded and wind up on the news. All she needed was Connor scrutinizing the footage for long enough to realize how similar this face looked to Amber's. Why had she agreed to this so readily?

In a matter of minutes, they were inside the mayor's house. Frank Deidrick was his usual gracious self, but that simmering rage was just below the surface—Amber could see it. She could practically feel it.

"And who is this?" the mayor asked the chief, though Frank's attention was squarely on Amber. "You look very familiar. Have we met before?"

Amber kept her voice high and light. "I don't think so."

"If you would excuse us, mayor," the chief said, a hand on Amber's lower back as he gave her a gentle push toward the hallway that would lead to the staircase. He produced a copy of the warrant and handed it to the mayor as he walked past him. "Please give my officers room to search the premises. Failure to do so will complicate matters for you even further."

The chief barked out orders to his officers. They broke off into pairs as they got their assignments. Amber then followed the chief up the stairs. Chloe's room was to the right of the upstairs bathroom, the door standing open. The chief pulled a pair of white latex gloves out of a pocket and handed them to her, then put on a pair of his own. Once she had them on, he motioned to the bedroom door with his chin. Amber walked in first.

The room had a queen-size bed pushed into a corner on the left side of the room, piled high with fluffy pillows and blankets. Discarded jeans and shirts were strewn on the end of it, as well as on the floor around it, along with jackets, shoes, and socks. A closet with two dark-wood French doors stood open, the rack inside so laden with clothes that the bar the hangers hung from bowed in the middle. The floor of the closet was a jumbled mess of more clothes, shoes, boxes, and bags.

On the right side of the room was a large vanity with a rectangular mirror resting above it. The outside edge of the mirror was hung with fairy lights, a handful of printed-out pictures stuck to the glass. Amber walked to the table, stepping over clothes, books, and shoes.

The pictures featured Chloe and her friends, Chloe laughing more often than not. Amber recognized Bethany Williams in most of the photos, the girls with their arms flung over each other's shoulders or around waists. Almost every picture seemed to be taken at school or in this bedroom—no pictures by lakes or pools on a hot summer day.

The tabletop was littered with what looked like home-work—her laptop, a book with an orange highlighter resting on the open spine, scribbled notes in Chloe's looping scrawl. In a partitioned tray to the right of her schoolwork were makeup pots, eyeshadow pallets, bouquets of brushes, and sticks of lip gloss, lipstick, and mascara. Above the vanity, a giant wooden, painted-black C hung on the wall.

A set of white drawers sat on either side of the vanity, the tops piled with more clothes and framed photos.

"Did the room end up like this after the first search, or …" Amber asked, looking around at the mess.

The chief shut the door, a soft *whoosh* sounding as the door passed over the large navy-blue throw rug that covered most of the floor. He pressed his back against the door. "Nope. I think this is just what it means to be a teenage girl. You were a teenage girl once; your room didn't look like this?"

"Aunt Gretchen was not a fan of clutter," Amber said. "Just think—in seventeen years, Isabelle's room could look like this."

The chief grumbled. "We searched this room thoroughly, even looking for false bottoms in drawers, under her mattress, or things stuffed into the bottom of boxes. Came up empty."

Sticking her gloved hand into her pocket, Amber pulled out her newly crafted spell—one for finding what has been hidden. Namely, finding what Chloe hid from her father specifically. Amber walked back to the vanity and found a picture taped there of Chloe and Frank, the two sitting outside a restaurant, Frank with his arm draped over the back of Chloe's chair, and Chloe with her eyes squeezed shut and her tongue out. *Who had taken the picture?* Amber wondered. *Francine? A friend of Chloe's? A waitress?*

Relaxing her shoulders and doing her best to calm her mind despite the chief's curious gaze boring a hole into the side of her head, Amber uttered the spell. When her magic perked up, waiting eagerly for its assignment, Amber focused her attention on Chloe's face first. *What did you not want*—and then she focused on the easy smile of Frank Deidrick—*him to find?*

Just like with the locator spell, her magic pulled her, as if a rope had been tied tight around her middle and someone on the other end *yanked*. It yanked her backward, away from the vanity and back toward the other side of the room. She almost rolled her ankle as she stepped on a tennis shoe. Her magic was leading her toward the third set of drawers in the room, this one resting against the wall to the left of the closet.

Amber tugged open drawers and riffled through each one, fingers searching for any hidden catches in the tops or bottoms of the drawers, just as the chief and his officers had apparently already done. The chief, thankfully, didn't patronize her for going back over old territory. He kept perfectly quiet as he let her work.

When all the drawers revealed nothing, she took a step back, thinking maybe she'd been wrongly drawn toward the dresser. But her magic gently pulled her forward again.

It was like playing a game of hot/cold with a voiceless disembodied friend. Step back: *Cold!* Step forward: *Warm.*

She peered behind the dresser; the gap between it and the wall was thin. Inching the dresser away from the wall a fraction, she ran her latex-covered fingertips over the dresser's back. *Warm!* her magic urged.

At the base of the dresser, there was a half-oval cut out below the last drawer, leaving an inch space between it and the floor. Amber knew the cutout was for decoration, but she didn't understand what purpose it could serve other than as an entry point for dust bunnies to congregate and be lost forever. Amber lay flat on her stomach and peered into the dark space. *Warmer!* her magic said.

Using the flashlight on her phone, Amber angled the light into the space, revealing a whole herd of dust bunnies, a bottle cap, a lone sock, and a couple of hair ties. With her cheek pressed to the navy blue throw rug, Amber saw a dark yellow something poking out from the top of the small, dark space. She reached her hand in, palm up; the top of the oval cutout was low enough that the wood gently scraped against her forearm. She flicked her wrist up, her fingers searching … searching.

Hot! said her magic, and then her fingertips grasped something smooth. It crinkled like paper.

After a pull here, and a yank there—the unfinished edge of the cutout scraping harder against Amber's skin—something detached from the bottom of the shelf. It sounded like masking tape being ripped off the top of a packing box. A heavy packet of paper hit Amber's gloved hand and she carefully dragged it out, like a waitress carrying a tray on an open palm.

She sat cross-legged on the cluttered floor, her phone lying beside her, and held the half-inch-thick packet with both hands. Nothing was written on the large manila envelope, the small copper prong clasp on the back bent down to keep the flap closed. She had never been more desperate to open anything in her life, but she figured the chief would have to analyze everything first. She glanced up at the chief, who still stood with his back pressed against Chloe's door.

After several moments of him staring at her a little slack-jawed, he said, "Your face is back."

Amber noticed then that her shoulder-length hair was down around her shoulders and back to its usual brown, rather than the blonde A-line bob she'd walked in here with.

The chief walked over with his hand out, the white glove in sharp contrast to his black jacket. A little reluctantly, she handed him the packet. He waded across the sea of clothes to get to Chloe's vanity and placed the envelope on top of Chloe's laptop before picking up both. "Can you change your face back to Cassie's so we don't draw any unnecessary attention to ourselves?"

Shoulders sagging, she got to her feet. All that excitement and work to find the packet and now she would have to go back to the Quirky Whisker. Her curiosity about what Chloe had squirreled away was sure to give Amber an ulcer before the chief ever got around to telling her what was in the envelope.

"We'll need to be here another hour or so before I can feasibly make up an excuse about driving you back to the station," he said. "So stop pouting. In an hour, we'll *both* get to see what's in this thing."

CHAPTER 13

As promised, after an hour of Amber doing her level best to act like she actually belonged on this search-and-seizure job with the chief of police, she and Chief Brown left the Deidrick home. When the chief told Garcia that he needed to take Cassie Westbottom—Amber had almost burst into laughter at the improved last name of her consultant-persona the chief had come up with on the fly—back to her hotel because her flight left in a few hours, Garcia had hardly batted an eye. The officers still had half of the Deidrick house to search, so they would be preoccupied for a while, giving Amber and the chief ample time to find out what was in the manila envelope.

They got into a very involved argument about whether or not it was better for Amber to walk into the police station as Amber, or to keep the Cassie persona going. In the end, they decided that they were thinking about this too hard. While driving along a particularly deserted stretch of road, Amber tossed her jacket over her head and uttered three reversal spells. A shock to the system was a better, quicker way to remove a glamour, but she figured the chief wouldn't readily agree to issue her a quick slap across the face—especially not while he was driving.

"Is it safe?" she asked.

"One second. Car coming in the other direction. Okay … now."

When she emerged, finger-combing her hair as she did, the chief gave her a quick once-over. "Welcome back."

The tension in his shoulders seemed to ease once her face was back to normal. Amber's leg jiggled as she cycled through the possibilities of what Chloe had stuffed away in that envelope. Maybe she too had known about her father's strange monthly payments and had found out who they'd been made to.

The police station was quiet. Dolores was in her wooden box desk, and Amber was sure there was at least one officer holding down the fort while the others were at the Deidrick house.

"Dolores," the chief said in greeting as they walked by.

"Chief," she said, her voice croaky, like a frog who had a bad smoking habit. Then her flat eyes focused on Amber, watching her as she went by.

As usual, once they were out of view, Dolores's keyboard clacking resumed. Amber had decided that she hoped Dolores wasn't actually doing paperwork, but was penning a particularly racy romance novel.

The moment the chief had closed his office door behind them, Amber said, "Hurry and open this thing before I die of anticipation!"

The chief laughed—a sound that surprised him, given the way he froze, his eyes suddenly widening. "You'll have to learn to check your enthusiasm," he said once he sobered, rounding his desk so he could place the laptop and manila envelope on top. He shrugged out of his jacket and draped it over the back of his chair. He unbuttoned the cuffs of his shirt and rolled them up a few inches on either side. "I can't tell you how many times I was sure I'd stumbled on something that would break a case wide open and it ended up being nothing. It's possible that the only thing in here is really angsty lovesick teenage poetry."

Amber winced, not once considering that the contents of the envelope could be anything other than evidence so shocking it would lead to solving Chloe's disappearance. Then her posture deflated. "Enthusiasm has officially been checked."

The chief laughed again, handing her another pair of gloves that he produced from a drawer in his desk. As she pulled them on, the chief donned his own—much faster than she had—and bent up the two metal arms of the clasp on the envelope's back flap.

Check your enthusiasm, she instructed herself when an excited trill flitted in her stomach. *Please don't be angsty poetry.* Please *don't be angsty poetry.*

The chief reached into the envelope and pulled out a stack of papers. Amber walked around to stand next to the chief, up on her tiptoes as she tried to look over his shoulder. "Well, it's not poetry." But he still only stared at the top sheet, not offering her any hint of what they'd found.

"Chief, I swear if you don't tell me what's in there, I really *will* turn you into a hamster!"

He laughed again, and when he looked at her, the corner of his mouth was pulled up.

"Oh my God," she said. "You're dragging this out on purpose."

"Maybe." He cleared a space on his desk and placed the papers on the surface. "You're worse than Sammy when I tell him he has to hold still for a full minute after dinner if he wants a cookie. He's so excited, he practically vibrates."

Amber wanted to call him a creatively offensive name, but her gaze snagged on the top sheet of the pile. "All results for Chloe Deidrick," she read out loud. Then she saw phrases like "census and voter lists," "birth, marriage, and death certificates," and "family trees."

It took a second for it to click.

"She had a DNA test done," Amber said, looking up at the chief then.

"Grab a chair," he said as he sat down, never taking his attention off the stack of paper on his desk.

Amber hurried around his desk to grab one of the chairs, then hustled back over to deposit hers beside his. The chief divided the stack and handed her half, his wide hands looking strained in the latex gloves. When she tugged on the stack he held out to her, he tightened his grip.

"Don't think I'm going to make a habit of this," he said. "Think of this as a thank-you for your help."

"Maybe you're sowing the seed for me to become a witch PI."

"Oh God," he groaned.

"We could have our own buddy cop show! You, the no-nonsense police chief, me, the spunky private investigator who uses her magical talents to get results the police can't find through ordinary means."

He stared at her, expression blank. "You're very weird, Amber Blackwood."

"Thank you," she said, finally able to pull the papers from his grasp.

The printout at the top of Amber's stack was the obituary for Shannon Pritchard. "*Shannon Pritchard, 29, passed away January 19 in Lirkaldy, Montana. She is survived by her daughter Chloe and her husband Frank. She will be missed.*" That was it; nothing about a funeral or a wake. Just an acknowledgement that she'd passed away. The photo of her was small, but even though it was grainy and in black-and-white, the similarity to Chloe was unmistakable.

The next was a form that stated that Chloe's birth certificate wasn't available, as it had been sealed.

What followed was what looked like a screen capture, with a column of names and pictures running down the left side of the page. From what Amber could gather, the site Chloe had submitted her DNA sample to had then sent her a list of people—who were also in the system—who might be a "relationship match" for her. At the top was a box with a star above it that was labeled "Aunt," and said she was a maternal match. The woman's name was Karen Reed.

After that were a couple of pages about Karen, listing her parents, birthday, and her place of birth as Lirkaldy, Montana. Karen had only one sibling: Lilith Reed, who was listed as deceased on January 19th. The date was circled. Amber flipped back to the front of her stack. Shannon Pritchard had also died on January 19th.

"Hey, chief," she said. "You know how you said it was like Shannon Pritchard didn't exist? I think I might have found her real name." She then explained what she'd found.

"Interesting ..." The chief dropped his papers and swiveled toward his computer. After the screen came to life, he clicked through a few programs and keyed "Lilith Reed" and "Lirkaldy" into a search engine that definitely wasn't Google.

As he did that, Amber kept flipping through her own stack, and then landed on a birth certificate of Lilith Reed. A note in Chloe's looping scrawl was written at the bottom of the printout. *Is Lilith my mother? When did she become Shannon Pritchard? Why?*

Amber didn't know much about genealogy sites, but she knew enough to know that one could only get matches if someone else from their family—even if it was a distant cousin—was in the system, too. Lilith/Shannon had died before these sites became popular, but even still, weren't there public records detailing the big events in a person's life? "If Lilith had legally changed her name to Shannon," Amber said, "shouldn't there be a report showing the name change? Why was Chloe's birth certificate sealed?"

The chief was still scrolling through things on his computer and answered her without looking away from his screen. "Birth certificates are often sealed when there's a closed adoption. It's possible that Frank isn't Chloe's biological father, but legally adopted her. If the parents want to keep the biological parent or parents from contacting the child or the child's family post-adoption, they'll request that it's closed. The original birth certificate is altered to list the adoptive parents, and then the original is destroyed."

"Permanently destroyed?" Amber asked.

"Depends on the state," the chief said. "In some cases, yes.

In others, the original exists, but can only be revealed by way of a court order, and not until the child in question is 18."

"Are birth certificates only sealed in closed adoptions?" Amber asked.

"I've seen them sealed when the paternity of the father is wished to be kept a secret," the chief said. "For instance, if the mother and the father have a contentious relationship—especially if they aren't married—and the mother feels threatened by him, the birth certificate can be sealed to prevent the father from knowing about his child. A father can always file for a paternity test if he needs legal proof that a child is his, but once that happens, the location of the mother could potentially be revealed during the process. Keeping the birth certificate sealed could be used as a safety measure to protect mother and child from a dangerous man."

Amber swallowed, an image of the mayor's angry face, standing nose to nose with her, replaying in her head. Francine Robins had called the mayor a "monster." What had he done to earn such a label? What had he said to Chloe the night she disappeared that would have made her feel safer out in a storm than in the house with him?

"I'm not finding much of anything about Lilith Reed," the chief said, breaking through Amber's thoughts. "It's as if she didn't exist either. But it's possible that she paid a lawyer to seal more than Chloe's birth certificate."

"You can do that?" Amber asked.

"Depending on the nature of her situation—maybe," the chief said. "There are also plenty of ways to obtain another identity illegally and then fly under the radar. She could then take jobs that pay under the table, opt not to have a bank account—things like that."

"What would make a person do that?" she asked, though some part of her already knew.

"Given the marks that were found on her body—ones that hadn't killed her but had looked as if they'd been sustained over a long period of time—it's very possible Lilith Reed was in a very bad situation. Perhaps she crafted a new identity out of desperation and self-preservation."

Amber chewed on her bottom lip, staring at the small smile on Shannon's Pritchard's face in the photo beside her very sparse obituary. "*She will be missed*," the obituary said.

Missed by who, Amber wanted to know. By Frank? Had his simmering rage been what caused those marks on Lilith's body? Had she changed her name from Lilith to Shannon to escape him? Had he found her after she'd fled, done something to facilitate her death, and then taken Chloe with him? A man who Lilith, very possibly, had gone through so much trouble to keep Chloe safe from?

Did Frank have Chloe again now?

Amber remembered her vision from the promotion tincture—the scene that would play out tomorrow, on the day that marked seven days since Chloe's disappearance—where Chloe had touched the picture of her father standing on a table outside the Sippin' Siamese, a megaphone to his mouth. A tear had hit the newspaper. Had Chloe been crying because she missed her father and was touched to see that he was doing all he could to find her, or was she crying because the person spearheading her search was the same man who had stolen her—perhaps for the second time?

That evening, Amber paced her studio apartment. The chief told her that she needed to lie low until he had a better idea of what to do with this new information. Amber felt restless. It was hard to know this much and this little at once and be unable to tell anyone about it.

She plopped down on her couch and stared at the sea of miniature cat toys littering her coffee table. She needed at least one hundred and fifty, and had only completed ninety so far. She had a little over a week to get them all done, but she couldn't for the life of her concentrate on anything.

Then she spotted the corner of a small white piece of paper. She unearthed the business card from beneath a small pile of tiny balls of yarn. Alan Peterson's name stared up at her.

All she knew about Alan's client was that it was a woman who knew of Chloe, but wasn't local. Could her aunt, Karen Reed, have found Chloe's whereabouts when they had been matched on the ancestry site? If the mayor had been keeping Chloe on a short leash for most of her life, who else could possibly have any idea how or where to find her?

The chief's voice sounded in Amber's head whenever she thought about trying to contact Karen. Who knew what can of worms *that* could open up?

She slapped the business card against her open palm. The chief didn't want her to harass witnesses, but he couldn't get upset with her over watching someone, could he?

She pulled open the right-hand drawer on her coffee table and fished out her map of Edgehill, spreading it out as best she could on what space was available. Though the spell would work best if she had a picture to work from, she knew there was no point searching for Alan Peterson online. Even if he had a website using his apparently false name, Amber had no idea where the guy had originally come from. Plus, what PI would put his picture online? He needed to be as anonymous as possible.

There wasn't any of Alan's energy left in the business card after Amber had conducted the memory spell, but the mere fact that it had once been his would likely be enough. Amber also, thanks to her handful of interactions with the man, had his face burned into her memory.

With the business card in one hand, and her amethyst crystal in the other, Amber recited the increasingly familiar scrying spell. It took five separate attempts over the course of an hour for the dot representing Alan Peterson to finally pop up on her map. Amber knew this was likely in large part due to Alan not wanting to be found. He was staying not in a hotel, but in a small duplex not far from the Sippin' Siamese. It was an out-of-the-way location, as far as the center of Edgehill went, but she figured Alan wanted it that way. The less he was noticed in town, the less he'd be remembered.

For the rest of the evening, Amber scoured her grimoire for anything that might help her stay out of sight of the crafty PI tomorrow. She was desperate to open her parents' grimoires, but until she and Edgar found a safe place for them, Amber couldn't risk breaking the cloaking spell on either one.

When she could scarcely keep her eyes open any longer, she stuffed her folded sheets of newly crafted spells into her purse, got ready for bed, and prepared her glass of water and premonition tincture. The cats curled up on the bed with her, Tom lying flush with her side, and Alley curled up on a pillow.

Since this was Amber's second dose of the tincture, Aunt Gretchen had said she could take a full tablespoon instead of a teaspoon. Amber almost couldn't guzzle the drink down fast enough, the tincture pulling her into sleep almost immediately.

Her glass hit the floor and the *whomp whomp whomp* of it rolling away across the hardwood floor sounded in her head as loud as a gong as she slipped into a vision of Chloe.

Chloe lay on her mattress, picking at her already badly chipped red nail polish.

Four knocks sounded on the door. Chloe slapped her reply, then flipped the bird to the camera in the corner for good measure, but she didn't bother to get up.

A tray of breakfast and a glass of water were slid into the room, just as before. And, just as before, a paper followed. This time, however, it was an article that looked like it had been scanned and then printed on standard white printer paper. When the door closed, followed by four knocks, Chloe kicked off her blanket and scrambled across the cement floor to snatch up the sheet.

It was a newspaper clipping from almost eighteen years ago. "Local Man Suspected in Death of Woman Found in Lake." It was a short article, but it detailed the mysterious death of a woman who had plunged into Lake Lirkaldy in the dead of winter. At the time of the accident, she didn't have any kind of ID on her, so the article referred to her as Jane Doe. The woman had bruises on her arms, legs, and neck, causing police to speculate that she'd been in an altercation of some kind prior to the accident. She wore only a nightshirt and no shoes. By the time the car had been discovered, it had snowed heavily, covering any sign of what might have happened to cause her to plunge into the freezing-cold lake. It was suspected that she could have been under the influence and hit a patch of black ice. Witnesses were urged to come forward with information.

Chloe flipped the paper over and gasped. Written in thick black letters were the words, "*Who killed your mother? Your father isn't who he says he is.*"

Amber woke with a start, her apartment lit with the first rays of morning.

Whoever took Chloe *wasn't* her father ... but it was someone who wanted to pit Chloe against him.

CHAPTER 14

Thursday marked the one-week anniversary of Chloe's disappearance. Amber and the chief at least had the knowledge that the girl was okay. The mayor and everyone else in Edgehill were on high alert. Thanks to movies and TV, most everyone knew how vital the first 48 hours were in cases like Chloe's. They were well beyond that window now, and Amber wondered how many were fearing the worst—how many were simply waiting for the news confirming that Chloe Deidrick was never coming home.

At 8 a.m. sharp, Amber flipped her shop's sign to open, welcomed her first customer, and then slipped out the door to let the Bowens take over.

A cab pulled up outside the Quirky Whisker a few minutes later. A trip to the car rental place resulted in Amber signing several forms, informing the cashier on three separate occasions that she really didn't want the extra insurance because she was already insured, and finally having a car again. One didn't *need* a car in a town like Edgehill, necessarily, but it helped. And one certainly couldn't conduct covert surveillance while on a bicycle.

After adjusting the seat and mirrors in the rental, she pulled her Edgehill map out of her purse. When she'd checked it before leaving, the Alan Peterson dot was still at his duplex. Now, it appeared to be at Catty Melt. Perhaps Alan was as obsessed with Catty Cakes as Edgar was.

Depositing her purse and map on the passenger seat of the nearly spotless rental car, she made the half hour drive back to Edgehill. By the time she was within the town limits, the Alan dot was on the move again. She checked it at every red light and stop sign, wondering if there was a locator app meant for witches. She was surely going to get in an accident tracking this guy on paper.

The good thing was, she could keep a reasonable distance from him at any given time and still know where he was even if she couldn't actually see him. It would prevent her from being spotted. When the Alan dot stopped in a residential neighborhood not more than two blocks from Balinese Park, she didn't have any guesses as to who Alan might be keeping an eye on.

Turning onto LaPerm Way, Amber also realized she had no idea what Alan's car looked like. The street was deserted— no moms pushing strollers down the sidewalk or people out walking dogs—so she pulled over, noting that Alan was still at least a block away, and cast a quick set of glamour spells, turning herself back into Cassie Westbottom. Then she started her slow creep down the street, hands gripping the steering wheel with her chest pulled toward it. Hopefully Cassie merely looked lost, as opposed to suspicious.

Looking left and right, she finally spotted Alan parked on the right side of the street, baseball cap on and pulled low. He was reading a book, but Amber knew that was likely a ruse. As she went by, she scanned the houses around them, wondering who lived here.

And then, two houses up on the left, she saw a door open, and out walked Chief Brown dressed in plain clothes. Her eyes widened and she quickly averted her gaze, hoping he wouldn't see her. Seconds later, Sammy went bounding out of the house, his wild blond curls bouncing around his head. He went tearing off down the sidewalk, Chief Brown following behind at a leisurely pace, calling out for his son to slow down. Sammy went from full-out run to a light jog, then grabbed a large stick off the ground and started to wave it around like a sword.

Amber watched all this from her rearview mirror as she slowly crept down the street. She pulled over and slunk down in her seat, hand shielding her face. The chief didn't notice her as he walked by on the opposite side of the sidewalk. Amber supposed he was home to help give Jessica a bit of a break while she was home with the newborn. Given how wildly Sammy was flailing his way down the sidewalk, she supposed Jessica could use all the help she could get.

Once the father-and-son pair had rounded the corner—heading, Amber guessed, to Balinese Park—Alan's car, several lengths back from hers, pulled out onto the street and drove past her.

Why was he tailing the chief? But then Amber remembered how he'd questioned what his and Amber's relationship was. Amber shielded her face as he went by, and once he was past her, she pulled out too. Alan parked by the small pond on the south side of the park, where he had a clear view of the chief and Sammy in the play area. Sammy had found a friend and the two were chasing each other around the grass. The chief sat on a bench and watched, looking perfectly content.

Nothing of note happened during the forty-five-minute park trip; the chief had hardly even checked his phone. Then the pair walked back, Sammy still skipping ahead but with at least a little less energy. Instead of following Alan and the chief back to the chief's house, Amber stayed put parked beside the park, casting the glamour spells again—like retouching makeup—to make sure her Cassie face stayed in place a while longer. She supposed she could have glamoured herself to look like someone else entirely, but with her glamour skills being so lacking, she was nervous about pushing it. She watched the map, and only started her car back up when the Alan dot was once again on the move.

This time, she followed Alan to the police station. Amber was glad now that she had Cassie's face on instead of her own. If someone saw her following the chief around, it would only give credence to the affair theory: obsessed Amber Blackwood keeping tabs on her lover. She shuddered.

Two hours into being parked on the side of the road outside a restaurant that didn't open until four P.M., Amber wondered how PIs did this. She had joked with the chief about becoming a witch PI, but how long could someone spend sitting in a parked car before she went loopy? Or overdosed on sugar? She'd already eaten two cupcakes and three granola bars. She'd had two bottles of water and one secret coffee from Coffee Cat, and now very much needed to pee. She would be a terrible PI, she decided.

Remembering then that she had an unfinished candy bar in her purse somewhere, she pulled her purse into her lap and rooted around. She found a small tin of mints—empty. She tossed it over her shoulder in frustration, only realizing a moment later that this wasn't her car. In addition to her wallet and phone, there were wads of small note paper, a few pens, and three tubes of lip gloss. No candy bar. She unzipped an inner pocket, finding both her collection of new spells and her rubber cat. No candy there either.

Then she checked—

She yelped as her passenger side door opened and Alan Peterson plopped down beside her. Clutching her purse to her chest, she resisted the urge to whack him in the head with it.

"Is there a particular reason why you've been following me all morning, Miss Blackwood?"

Crap. Her glamour had worn off. She wasn't sure if it had happened during the two hours of boredom, or suddenly from the shock of the door opening—like being scared out of your hiccups.

"Is your ego really that big that you think I have nothing better to do than follow you around?" she asked, her voice only a *little* shaky.

He cut her a sideways look that very clearly said he didn't believe her for a second. "I would suggest you get some more practice under your belt before you try tailing someone who does this for a living. You're *very* bad at it."

The nerve.

"Why are you following me?" he asked.

"How long has Karen Reed been your client?" she countered.

He cocked a brow at her. "I told you I'm not going to divulge my client's identity."

Amber knew that was because he didn't *know* his client's identity, but she figured he must have done some research; his curiosity about who had hired him had surely piqued his interest, hadn't it? "Who else would have a vested interested in Chloe Deidrick, as isolated as she is here, other than family?"

He stared at her a beat, gaze roaming her face. "How do you know Chloe's aunt?"

So he *did* know. That, or she'd just confirmed his suspicions.

"I don't know her," Amber said. "But she's Chloe's family and Karen's never believed that Frank wasn't involved in her sister's death. She's likely worried Frank has done something to Chloe, too."

"Then why did she contact me days *before* Chloe went missing?" he asked.

Amber's head reared back a fraction. Before Chloe went missing? How would Karen have known then that Chloe was in trouble? Had Chloe contacted her before all this and when communication stopped, Karen got worried?

But unless Chloe had explicitly told her aunt that she felt like she was in danger, hiring a PI seemed like an extreme step.

Amber cycled through the last vision she'd gotten from the premonition tincture. Whoever had taken her wanted Chloe to question her father's character. Someone had it out for Frank. Could this same person have contacted Karen, too? Sowed the seeds of doubt enough that it made her seek Chloe out, and then shortly after finding her, Chloe went missing?

"Karen was tipped off," Amber said. "Someone warned her

something was going to happen to Chloe, so she hired you to figure out what was going on. Was she already missing by the time you got to Edgehill?"

"She had actually called someone else first. When the colleague of mine found out about the nature of this job, he called me and put me in contact with Karen. I mostly work in the Pacific Northwest. I had been working a job in California when Karen called me. I got up here as fast as I could, but, yes, Chloe had already been taken by the time I got here."

Amber nodded to herself.

Alan watched her. "Who are you, Amber? I mean ... what's your vested interest in all this?"

"I've known Chloe for most of her life," Amber said. "Why wouldn't I be worried about her?"

"Most people in these situations don't go through this much trouble," he said.

Amber pursed her lips.

"It all just seems a little fishy," he said, gaze focused out the windshield now, his tone flat and a little disinterested. "The mayor's beloved daughter goes missing, he calls for a public search almost immediately, you and the chief are seen sneaking off together just before that search starts, he gives you something, and then you practically sprint right to the location where the missing girl's phone is." He turned his intense gaze back to her, though his tone remained level and even. "Makes me wonder what you three are up to here ... what Frank Deidrick might have done, and what you and the chief are doing now. Maybe you're not actually worried you said something to Chloe that aided in her decision to run away. Maybe you actually *did* something to her. Or maybe you knew where to find the phone because Frank or Owen did something to her, and you were paid to 'find' it. Does one of them have something on you? A secret they're holding over your head?"

All Amber could do was gape at him.

"What I can't figure out it is why the chief of police would target a seventeen-year-old. He doesn't seem like the type to have a thing for young girls—so I doubt it's that," he said. "My bets are on Frank. Frank gets help from the chief—either directly or bribes him—to get rid of his daughter, and then the chief ropes you in because you owe him something." He tapped a nostril. "I keep thinking your payment might not be in cash."

Did he honestly think she was a drug addict? Goodness.

Given what he'd seen—or thought he'd seen—happen in the alley between her and the chief, she couldn't exactly blame him for coming up with such a wild story, but she was still mildly offended.

"At first glance, I wouldn't have pegged you as a fan of the nose candy, but I've known successful CEOs—millionaires—who hit the white stuff on a regular basis and you'd never know," he said.

"Whoa. Geez," she said, hands up, turning more fully in her seat to look at him. "Look, I'm not on drugs. And even if I was—which I'm *not*—Chief Brown would be the last person I'd get them from. You've been watching him for days, I'm guessing? Has he once given you reason to suspect he's up to anything criminal?"

The hint of a smile tugged at his mouth. "Not once."

Amber pursed her lips. "I'm just confirming all kinds of theories for you, aren't I?"

"One after the other," he said. "So, what, you're just a busy-body citizen going out of your way to help the police on this case, or are you one of these people obsessed with true crime and now you're testing out your so-called knowledge in the real world?"

"You're not very nice."

"It's not my job to be nice." He sized her up again. "You clearly have good instincts, but if you're thinking of changing careers from toy making to crime solving, you really need to consider an internship somewhere. Likely for a long time. I can't stress this enough: you are *terrible* about being incon-spicuous."

"Terrible seems a little harsh," she said.

"Terrible is being generous."

She pursed her lips again. She'd never once considered herself interested in true crime or a job solving it, but she was offended he thought so little of her. Though, at what point had he noticed her? Had he only noticed her once she was Amber, or had he noticed Cassie, too? *Terrible at being inconspicuous.* Had he—or anyone else today—seen her use her glamour spells? She thought she'd been careful, but what if she hadn't been?

Though, she supposed, maybe she'd only been painfully obvious to someone who was trained to notice things out of the ordinary.

"You really think my instincts are good?"

"Yep," he said, focused out the windshield again. "Based on my conversations with my client, I'd deduced she was Chloe's aunt or maybe a distant cousin. I hadn't come anywhere close to a name. What do you know about the Reeds?"

Amber chewed the inside of her cheek. *I promise we're on the same side here*, he'd said to her the morning of the job fair. On a whim, she mentally recited the truth spell she'd used numerous times over the last few weeks. She, Willow, and Aunt Gretchen had needed to be extra cautious with everyone they'd met, not knowing who might have been the Penhallow in disguise. Amber didn't know how effective a spell for truth would be on a man who wasn't even using his real name, but she hoped it would work anyway.

"Alan Peterson," she said, magic humming beneath her skin, "why did you take the job to find Chloe Deidrick?"

"I took this job because my little sister was kidnapped when she was eight," Alan said in a flat, even tone. "I was fourteen and in charge of keeping an eye on her while my parents went out to run errands. Miriam and I had begged my parents to let us stay home; I promised to look after her. After they'd left, a few of my friends came over and we went up to my room to play video games. Miriam asked to play too, but I told her to leave us alone. So she went out front to ride her bike. When my parents came home an hour later, Miriam's bike was lying in the middle of the road and she was gone. They found her body in the woods two weeks later. Missing children cases don't come to me that often, but when they do, I always take them. Every success is my way of apologizing to my sister who I'll never see again."

Amber's mouth had dropped open sometime during the course of his confession—a confession that poured out of the man's mouth so quickly, she wondered if it had been primed and ready, just waiting for someone to ask him the right question.

"Oh my God, Alan," Amber said. "I'm so sorry."

He stared at her as if he'd just found out that *she* was the monster who had kidnapped his sister. "What did you just do?"

Amber cocked her head, doing her best to sound innocent. "What do you mean?"

"I've told that story to almost no one and I just ... blurt that out to you when I've talked to you less than an hour combined?" His eyes were red-rimmed—whether he was going to cry or go into a rage, she couldn't be sure. She was scared of both possibilities.

"I know the Reeds live in Montana," she said, barreling ahead to hopefully distract him from strangling her here in her rental car—she figured the fee for cleaning up blood was exorbitant. "Karen had one sister, Lilith Reed, who died almost eighteen years ago. I believe Lilith changed her name to Shannon Pritchard and lived her life in seclusion after that. Why ... I don't know. For a while, I thought it was because she was scared of Frank. Now I'm not so sure."

He had still been gaping at her, but he sobered up soon enough, snapping his mouth shut. "Why don't you suspect him anymore?"

Amber didn't know how to explain that she'd seen enough through her magic tinctures to know the person who kidnapped Chloe was doing so as a way to punish Frank. "I've talked to several people who know Frank well enough to know he keeps a pretty set schedule. If he had stolen away his own daughter, he wouldn't be able to keep her locked in the house. The police have now done two full searches of the place. If that girl was in the house, they would have found her by now. Which would mean he would have to be keeping her somewhere else. If he was suddenly making routine stops to a second location or a storage facility, someone in town would have noticed. *You* would have noticed."

Lips pressed into a hard line, he nodded.

"In order to find her, we have to figure out who the mayor's enemies are," Amber said. "They know Chloe is his world, so they took that from him. I just can't figure out why."

Though he did so reluctantly, Alan shared his list of suspects with her—people he believed would have it out for Frank Deidrick. Two of her suspects were on that list, too. First was Victor Newland and the second was Johnny, the mystery boyfriend.

"What's your connection to the Newlands?" Amber asked, remembering the disdainful look Victor's daughter had angled at Alan the day of the job fair. "Dawn doesn't seem to be your biggest fan."

Alan sighed. "Remember when Victor abruptly dropped out of the race months before the election?" When Amber nodded, he said, "Frank's team found out Victor had been involved with a young woman close to his own daughter's age. Frank went to Victor privately and told him if he dropped out, he'd keep the affair to himself."

"Oh wow," Amber said.

"The news still made it to Victor's wife though and she agreed to couples counseling and the like, and Victor said he would work on his marriage. So Frank kept the news to himself, Victor dropped out, Frank won virtually unopposed," Alan said. "Victor's wife, months later, hired me and said she thought her husband was up to no good again. Turns out she was right. I presented the evidence and she left him, but she did so in the middle of the night, leaving her daughter behind and not leaving so much as a forwarding address. Dawn, I imagine, is furious with both her parents, but for different reasons, so she projects that anger everywhere else. Like on me."

Amber winced. "Guess that explains why she's such a little monster. I would be too in those circumstances." After a pause, she said, "What do you know about Johnny?"

"Not much," he said. "Of the few kids from Edgehill High I've been able to talk to, they all agree that this Johnny kid wasn't from here."

"Did you hear about the hack?"

Alan cocked his head. "What hack?"

Amber recounted, to the best of her limited ability, what Bethany had told her. "The list got pulled down, but maybe it's still possible to find it."

"I made a dummy Scuttle account," Alan said, wincing slightly. "But no one will talk to me on there. They all said I sounded like a cop."

"Who's terrible at being inconspicuous now?"

"Yeah, yeah," he said, waving away her comment. "Any idea what her handle on there was?"

"No, I didn't think to ask Bethany that," Amber said. "How does that whole anonymous thing work? Don't you have to put in your name and email address when you sign up? That information was what was on the list the hacker compiled."

He stared at her for a beat, as if he thought she was quite simple. "First of all, just because it asks for your name, it doesn't mean you have to give your real one. It's also very easy to create an email address you use solely for sites like this. You don't have to input a phone number when you register. Scuttle is built on a platform of privacy for its users, so not even they keep records of all the interactions. Photos and videos sent through there aren't stored anywhere. It's great for kids, since it's a safe space they can talk to each other where adults aren't going to cramp their style—mostly because the adults don't know it exists, let alone how it works—but it also means child predators have figured out how to pretend to be teenagers and then lure vulnerable teens into very dangerous situations."

Amber's stomach knotted. Is that what happened with Chloe? Even Bethany suspected that "Johnny" was someone posing as a college-aged kid from Belhaven who had lied his way into Chloe's heart. Had the man who had been paid to snatch Chloe also been the one pretending for months to be a boy infatuated with her?

"Second," Alan said, pulling Amber from her thoughts, "if you choose a handle that doesn't have your name anywhere in it, how would anyone know it was you? If I'm on there as ILikeAirplanes, you wouldn't know who I was unless I told you, and even then, you'd just have to believe I was who I said I was."

"Johnny sent her a picture, though," Amber said.

"But only one, and a rather staged one at that," said Alan. "Never one taken in the moment. Why do you suppose that is?"

Amber frowned. "How are you supposed to find out who this Johnny guy really is then?"

Alan shrugged. "It's virtually impossible to track these people down. In emergency cases—like missing kids, sexual assault, and murder—logs of conversations can be obtained with a court order. Sometimes those reveal IP addresses, and those can be traced to physical locations, but it doesn't always lead directly to a suspect. And even that information can take a long time to get."

"What a nightmare," Amber muttered.

"I'll see if I can find the list that hacker posted," Alan said. "Maybe it ended up on the dark web and this Johnny guy bought it."

Amber had liked it better when she'd been blissfully unaware of things like this.

He was quiet for a while after that, tension wrinkling his forehead. She figured he was still a little dismayed that he'd divulged his deep secret about his sister and had done so with an ease that clearly was uncharacteristic for him. "As you now know … cases with kids mean more to me than the paycheck. I try to pretend that a job is a job, but ones like these …"

Amber watched his profile, at the way he clearly was cycling through a wide array of emotions. Did he want to share more with her? Did he not know how? More than likely, he was trying to figure out why he'd been compelled to do so earlier and was completely reluctant again now.

"How do you feel about sharing intel?" he finally asked. "I rarely do this, but clearly something makes me trust you. You're in it for the kid. So am I. I want her found and I'm more than happy to work together to find her. I'll even split the—"

She raised a hand to stop him. "Whatever money Karen pays you, that's all yours. Chloe home safe is all I want."

He nodded once, then placed a hand on the door handle. "You have my number," he said, then climbed out. Before shutting the door, he leaned his head back inside. "And when you're surveilling someone, lock your doors. Any weirdo off the street can slip into your car if you're not paying attention."

Then he shut the door and strode back up the sidewalk, hands in his pockets. Once again, he was reduced to a regular guy out for a casual stroll.

As she pulled away from the curb, she wondered if it would give the chief a coronary to know that she and Alan Peterson the PI were now allies.

I've met some real sleazebags who will do anything they think is necessary to get the information they've been paid to find. Depending on who he gets in here ... well, they could make things even more difficult for us.

She wrinkled her nose.

Maybe it was best to keep this one to herself.

CHAPTER 15

With only a week until the Hair Ball, the Here and Meow meetings were now held weekly instead of every two weeks. With yesterday marking a week since Chloe had disappeared, Kim thought it in bad taste to hold the meeting on Thursday.

So now it was 5:45 on a Friday night and Amber was sitting in her rental car in the parking lot of Purrcolate, wondering if she could claim she'd come down with a horrible case of the flu in order to get out of this. She might have tried had Kim not completely turned into the gala-host equivalent of Bridezilla in the last few days. Between the stress of throwing the town's biggest event next to the Here and Meow, worrying she was going to screw up and disappoint the late Melanie Cole, and dreading the news about Chloe, Kim had become increasingly … difficult. Amber had heard that the unflappable Ann Marie had been reduced to tears yesterday when Kim went on a long rant about why Ann Marie was the largest disappointment in Kim's life. Ann Marie, apparently, had picked up the tablecloths for the gala yesterday, but when she placed the order had accidentally ordered robin's egg *blue* instead of eggshell *white* and Kim had nearly had a heart attack in the middle of the community center when Ann Marie unloaded the first few.

Amber had heard all this from Nathan, who had called Amber last night to warn her that Kim was "on the war path" and to be ready for "possible tears and screaming" at today's meeting. This, plus the very high probability that she'd see Jack Terrence, had made Amber consider packing up and moving to a remote village somewhere.

Instead, she told herself she was strong and fierce and she could get through this. She had a car now, at least, so if this all went really badly, she could drive to Cat's Creamery and buy sixteen gallons of chocolate ice cream to drown her sorrows in.

She climbed out of her car and then marched across the parking lot with confidence. The familiar scent of baking scones washed over her as she pulled open the door.

And all her confidence deflated the moment Jack looked up at her and smiled. No recognition beyond Amber being a customer he liked and wanted to possibly go out with sometime. No memory of the few dates they'd already been on. No memory of the terrifying night on Edgar's property when Amber had almost died.

"Hey, Amber," he said. "Long time, no see."

She wanted to run out of here and never come back. "Hey, Jack," she managed.

Larry stood behind the counter as well, where he'd been restocking the pastry case. He continued to do so, but a slight scowl marred his forehead. Amber could only see half of his face and the way his eyes darted from Amber, to Jack, and back again, his head never moving.

"Can I get you anything besides the usual spread of blueberry scones in there?" Jack asked. "I have a new lemon seed scone I debuted at the junior fashion show. Have you had a chance to try one of those yet?"

She bit her bottom lip. He didn't remember that she'd helped him unload those new scones, because he'd seen the real her and decided he couldn't handle it. "Blueberry is fine," she said, voice cracking. "Thank you."

Then she hurried toward the mottled glass door that led to the conference room reserved for the Here and Meow Committee on evenings like this one. She willed her tears away.

"What'd I say?" she heard Jack ask.

"I don't have the first clue," Larry muttered.

Inside the conference room, the vibe wasn't much better. Amber was right on time, but Ann Marie, Nathan, and Francine were already seated across from Kim, their hands folded in their laps. Francine sat farthest from Amber and craned her neck to look over the heads of both Ann Marie and Nathan so she could offer Amber a small smile. A "thank you for helping me get this position but also why didn't you warn me that Kimberly Jones had gone off the deep end?" kind of smile.

No one spoke. Kim had her elbows on the table, and was massaging her temples in wide, slow circles. From what Amber could see of her friend, she wore a bright orange silk blouse and a black-and-white striped vest over it—like a pirate.

Kim suddenly let an arm fall with a thud and glared at Amber. "I'm so glad you could finally join us. Why don't you take a seat so we can get started, hmm?"

Amber winced and slunk into the chair beside Nathan,

leaving Kim on the opposite side by herself. Nathan whispered "war path" out the side of his mouth.

"Something you want to share with the class, Nathan?" Kim asked.

"Kimberly …" Ann Marie started.

"I need you not to talk right now," Kim said, cutting her off. "I've been on the phone all day trying to sort out the tablecloth debacle."

Ann Marie swallowed whatever she'd been about to say.

Kim huffed out a breath and opened the manila folder she had lying by her arm, pulling out a meeting agenda checklist. "Because we're obviously understaffed at the moment, there is going to be a lot we need to do in the next week. *I've* taken a week off work to make sure we can get it all done."

"Kim, we've all offered to take time off," Amber said. "You know I gave Lily and Daisy more hours this week specifically so I could help you more, but you haven't given me much to do."

"From what *I've* heard," Kim snapped, voice dripping with venom, "the chief has been keeping you *plenty* busy." She punctuated that with a little smile that implied she'd just eaten something exceedingly sour.

So help her, Amber would need to throttle this woman soon.

"Now, if you're all finished interrupting me …"

After half an hour, and Kim's tenth snippy comment, Amber had had enough. She leaned forward, catching the wide-eyed attention of Nathan, Ann Marie, and Francine. "Why don't you three take a little break?"

They shoved away from the table so fast, Nathan's chair hit the wall behind him.

Kim jumped to her feet. "Oh. My. God. Amber, you do *not* have the authority to assign breaks. If we let anarchy rule us, this entire gala will be a disaster and we'll be a laughingstock."

Nathan, Ann Marie, and Francine scurried for the door. Ann Marie had her hands on Nathan's back and was shoving him forward, whisper-hissing, "Go, go, go!" Francine was close behind her.

Kim started for the door as well, her face red and her hands balled into fists at her sides. Amber darted in front of the door just as it closed after Francine. To go with her orange shirt and striped vest, Kim also wore brown pinstripe pants and lime green flats. At least these ones matched each other, Amber supposed.

Kim came up short, chest heaving. Amber was genuinely worried her friend might slap her.

"Kim," Amber said softly, her hands out. "You need to—"

"You don't tell me what I need to do!" Kim snapped. "I'm out there working my butt off to make sure this gala runs smoothly, and when I could really use your help, you're too busy fraternizing with the *chief of police!*"

Amber groaned, tipping her head back. When she looked at Kim again, somehow Kim's face was even redder. "You can't seriously still be hung up on that, Kim! I'm not involved with the chief in any way other than trying to help find Chloe."

"Why? You're not a police officer," Kim said, crossing her arms tight over her chest.

Amber shot a quick look behind her, as if she expected to see Ann Marie, Francine, and Nathan—and maybe even Jack and Larry—with their heads poked into the room, waiting for her answer. Taking Kim by the upper arm, she dragged her to the other side of the conference room.

"Ow, ow, ow," Kim muttered, but she let herself be pulled along.

"Okay, so this is a little embarrassing," Amber said, once she unhanded her, "but I've been snooping around a lot in all the free time I've had—" she shot Kim a pointed look—"and I caught the attention of a PI in town who's investigating Chloe's disappearance."

Kim's eyes doubled in diameter. "Caught his attention how? Who hired him—the mayor?"

"Not the mayor," Amber said. "He won't tell me who his client is. And I was … oh gosh … I was following him around town trying to figure out who his client could be, and while I was on my first stakeout, I was distracted and he just … got into my car and asked why I was following him."

With a dramatic gasp, Kim gently swatted at Amber's arm. "Shut. Up. Was he mad?"

"He was mostly annoyed that I was tailing him when I'm bad at it," she said. "He used the word 'terrible' more than once."

"Rude! It was your first stakeout!"

"That's what I said." Amber lowered her voice. "He says I've got good instincts though, and I figured out a couple of things even before he did, so we're kind of allies now? The chief actually doesn't know that part."

"What kind of things?"

Amber bit her lip, not sure how much to divulge to Kim. "You have to keep this to yourself, okay?" Kim nodded her head so hard, Amber worried it would snap off and roll under the conference room table. "Someone kidnapped Chloe as a way to seek revenge on the mayor."

"*Kidnapped? Revenge?*" Kim loudly blurted, then clapped her hands over her mouth.

Amber shushed her. "We have reason to believe she's okay, but we don't know where she is. So if I've seemed distracted or unavailable this past week, it's because of all this other stuff. I'm trying to help find Chloe."

Kim's bottom lip shook violently and then she launched herself at Amber, throwing her arms around her neck. She dissolved into sobs. "Oh my God, Amber. I'm so sorry I've been such a witch!"

Amber sputtered a laugh, but quickly swallowed it down.

"I've been so, *so* worried about Chloe." She pulled away from Amber, keeping her hands on Amber's elbows. Her face was a splotchy mess, her eyes red. "She's really okay?"

"We're pretty sure, yeah."

Tears streamed down Kim's face. "I'm the reason she snuck out," she blubbered.

"Kim, hon, what are you talking about? She snuck out well after all of us left that night."

It took a few moments for Kim to get herself under control. "A week before, we all met for ice cream after the meeting, remember? Oh, wait, I don't think you could make it that night. Anyway, she was on that stinking phone of hers instead of interacting with the group," she said, sniffling. "So I pulled her aside and asked her if she was okay and who she was so busy texting. She told me she was talking to this guy from

Belhaven she had a huge crush on. She said he wanted to meet her, but she was too scared because she was worried he wouldn't like her in person as much as he did on the app. I told her she was amazing and beautiful and to follow her heart. I told her … I told her when you find someone who you really care about, you had to just go for it no … no matter what." Kim burst into tears again.

Amber let her friend cry on her shoulder for a while. Nathan, Francine, and Ann Marie poked their heads in at one point, heard Kim wail, and then quickly backed out of the room.

When Kim finally pulled herself together, Amber asked, in a very serious and solemn tone, "Did *you* kidnap Chloe?"

Kim was so surprised by the question that it dried up the rest of her tears. "Of course not!"

"Then it's not your fault, okay? It's not your fault that Melanie died, either," Amber said. "You're stressed out and you're taking on too much. You've been so worried about things going sideways that you've shut us all out. You need to *let* us help you. I promise you that we all want this gala to go off without a hitch as much as you do."

"Okay." Kim sniffed. "I think some part of me thought if I did it all myself, I knew it would get done right. I think *I* might have actually told Ann Marie robin's egg blue instead of eggshell white! But I was so mad at myself for possibly getting it wrong that I took it out on her. Oh, I'm the *worst*."

"No, you're not. You're just tired," Amber said. "Now, I need you to come up with a list of things you want us to do. If this tablecloth thing is truly a disaster, send one of us to the nearest town that has what you need."

Kim's chin wobbled a bit. "I'm really sorry."

"I know." Amber grabbed some napkins off the table and handed them to Kim so she could blow her nose. "Also ... what in the *world* are you wearing?"

Glancing down at herself, it was as if Kim suddenly came out of a daze. "Oh my God, Amber! I look like a circus clown!"

"It's ... it's not the best look."

Instead of bursting into tears, Kim erupted in giggles. This sound pulled Ann Marie, Francine, and Nathan back into the room.

"Is it safe?" Nathan asked.

"Oh my God, you guys!" Kim said, running to them with her arms out and enclosing them all in a hug. "I'm sorry I've been such a b-word! Francine, bless your heart for not quitting on me. I'm not normally like this. I promise."

"She's really not," Ann Marie said from somewhere within the group hug.

Kim laughed. "I have so much work for you all to do!"

"It's about dang time," Nathan said.

With the gala being a week away, the businesses selected to compete for the Best of Edgehill competition had to submit what their entries into the contest would be in order for menus and banners to be made on time.

This morning, Amber and Ann Marie had divided the list, getting six each, and had to speak to each business owner to confirm final entry and sample numbers and to take pictures. Amber had been given the first half of the list, largely because Purrfectly Scrumptious was across the street, but also because Ann Marie was so grateful that Amber had snapped Kim out of her Galazilla mode, that she thought it only fair that Amber get all the food-related ones today, plus a pair of clothing shops. The businesses Ann Marie was checking in with were harder to quantify and would rely more on displays, video presentations, photographs, and performances. Ann Marie's would take her most of the day.

Amber would have thought this was a perfect arrangement, had it not been for the fact that Purrcolate was on her list twice. Which meant she'd end up staying there twice as long as she would anywhere else. She wasn't sure which Terrence brother she dreaded seeing more: the rightfully suspicious Larry or the clueless Jack.

She stopped by Purrfectly Scrumptious first. Betty's entry into "Best of" would be three flavors of cupcakes: Chocolate Chocolate Surprise, Raspberry Rhapsody, and, of course, Oreo Dream. For samples, she was making bite-size cupcakes of each flavor. With 100 confirmed attendees, she would make 650 total mini cupcakes, so each person could have a second if they wished, plus a few extra in case any were damaged in transit. Amber was certain there wouldn't be a single one left by the end of the gala, damaged or not.

After Amber had taken her notes and pictures of the three full-size cupcakes Betty had displayed specifically for this meeting, Amber started to pack up her things.

Betty wrung her hands. "I know you can't tell me anything about what the others are presenting, but do you really think I have a shot?"

"Absolutely," Amber said. "And not just because you're my friend."

She exhaled deeply. "Thanks, sugar. Well, I better let you go finish your rounds. I need to figure out the best baking schedule for 650 cupcakes!"

Next, Amber hit the two pizza places. One was best known for its calzone, while the other had a to-die-for deep dish pizza. As Betty had done, there was a full-size available for Amber to sample, take notes about, and photograph. For the gala, there were mini calzones on the menu, as well as a small side salad topped with the restaurant's signature Italian dressing. The other would offer small slices of their pizza and breadsticks. Each restaurant would be serving vegetarian, cheese, pepperoni, and chicken and pesto options. The attendees would vote on which restaurant did each flavor best.

There were salads, quinoa bowls, and plant burgers at the Milk Bowl and Holly's Harvest; elaborate burgers and sweet potato fries from Mews and Brews; and decadent sandwiches from Catty Melt, the bread toasted a golden brown and topped with a thin layer of melted cheese.

For her one nonfood-related business category, Amber swung by Angora Threads to see three upscale dresses made by both Letty Rodriguez and her son, Diego. Their competition, the Shabby Tabby, made more ready-to-wear items—everything from pants to sweaters. Amber left with a vintage-looking dress from Angora that was covered in black smiling cat faces and had a thick band of black that marked off the empire waistline, and from Shabby Tabby, she left with a jumper made of a dark blue material with wide pockets in the shorts. An intricately designed cat adorned one of the pockets, stitched with white and gray thread. The cat was perched above the pocket, its nose focused on what might lay inside, its striped tail arched over its back like a miniature cane. For the gala, models would give the attendees a mini fashion show. The Shabby Tabby owner made sure to let Amber know that they would have an array of models of all body types to help show how widely accessible their clothes were.

Next came the horrible Paulette at Clawsome Coffee, who sneered at Amber the moment she walked in, though she tried to hide it. The last time Amber had seen Paulette, the older woman had disparaged the late Melanie Cole for awarding the Terrence brothers the opportunity to offer after-race treats to the 5k runners the morning of the Here and Meow—and Paulette had done so with so much venom, Amber had stormed out of the coffee shop without her order. She hadn't been back since.

Amber and Paulette kept their exchange icy but professional. Amber felt a sense of smug satisfaction that Paulette clearly wanted to wag her tongue about whatever slight she thought had befallen her now, but had to keep her mouth shut if she didn't want to ruin her chances at winning the "Best of" designation for coffee. Amber knew that if Paulette lost to Purrcolate or Coffee Cat, she was even more likely to suffer a coronary than Chief Brown was over Amber's interview tactics. Paulette almost assuredly would blame Amber for her loss—as if Amber had any say in who won. But if thinking Amber held any kind of authority when it came to assigning a winner made Paulette keep her nasty comments to herself, Amber wouldn't correct her.

Coffee Cat would be offering their toasted marshmallow mocha, white chocolate toffee nut latte, and gingerbread latte as their three samples. Samples for guests would come in small shot glasses adorned with the café's logo, which guests could take home with them.

During her discussion with the café's owner, Amber had tried the gingerbread latte and it had been so good, her knees had nearly buckled.

As she left, she smiled to herself, knowing Paulette had little chance of winning this year.

Which left Purrcolate as her last scheduled visit for the day. Her reasoning had been that if this went horribly awry, she could drive straight home rather than having the bad experience distract her during her other meetings. Armed with her clipboard and the knowledge that she'd faced down Paulette "the She-Demon" Newsom without losing her cool, she marched into Purrcolate for the second time in two days.

When she walked in, Jack was behind the counter as usual, and grinned at her. "Hey."

She approached the counter with all the bravado of a turtle scared into its shell. "Hey," she said, glancing around for Larry. Then she spotted him on the other side of the café, chatting with a couple sitting at one of the tables.

"I'm just about ready," Jack said, redirecting her attention. "I was thinking it might be best to do this in the back room?"

Amber swallowed. "Sure. Whatever's most convenient."

Within a couple minutes, he had ushered her around the counter—in the opposite direction of the conference room—and had lifted the flap in the counter's surface to let her behind it with him. He guided her past a pastry display case on one side, and the coffee and espresso machines on the other, and then toward the swinging black door in the back wall. He pushed it open with his back, smiling at her as he did so, and the ever-present smell of baking scones enveloped her.

She followed him into the kitchen; she'd never been back here before. Against the right wall was a large sink that was flanked on either side by shelving. The rolling cart on the right had large glass containers of what looked like flour and sugar, and clear plastic bins filled with a variety of mixing bowls. Above that were three large mixers lined up in a neat row. Various baking utensils and knives hung on the wall above the mixers. The set of shelves on the other side of the sink was packed tight with colorful rows of plastic bins, bottles, and jars of ingredients.

The wall to the left was taken up by the ovens, currently baking scones and other pastries to golden perfection. Beside the ovens was a tall shelving unit, the racks lined with cooling treats.

All the equipment and furniture were made of stainless steel, except for the massive wooden table in the middle of the room, the underside of which had large tubs of more dry ingredients in them. Two people in white aprons were busy working at the table. A woman was using a giant stainless steel mixer, while a man rolled out dough on the flour-covered surface of the table. Knives, spatulas, mixing bowls, and a dish of chocolate chips littered the work surface. At the end of the table was a plastic cover positioned on top of what Amber assumed was a plate.

"Hey, you two, can you give us a few minutes?" Jack asked.

The pair stopped what they were doing and looked up.

"Oh, for the Best of Edgehill, right?" the woman asked, wiping her hands on a towel hung from her apron's waist. "You got this, J." She smiled warmly at Amber, then made her way out the swinging door.

The guy wiped his hands, too, then walked past Jack, placed both hands on his shoulders and gave them a squeeze and a shake. "Good luck, man."

After the door had swung shut behind him, Jack motioned for her to follow him to the end of the table where the covered plate waited. They stood side by side before it. Amber put down her clipboard and fished a pen and her camera out of her purse.

Placing the camera on the table, she asked, "You're submitting three scone flavors for the competition, right?"

"Yep," Jack said. "I've finally settled on lemon seed, espresso chocolate chunk, and glazed gingerbread."

Amber willed her mouth to stop salivating. After all the food and sugar she'd consumed today, she didn't need any more. But good grief, glazed gingerbread? How was she supposed to *not* eat ten of those? Just as she had with the others, she wrote down the three flavors, the number of each he planned to bring with him, and what his refrigeration and plating requirements were.

When she was done, he said, "Scones, milady" and dramatically removed the cover from the plate. The lemon poppy seed and espresso chocolate chunk scones were both topped with a zigzag of white frosting, while the gingerbread scone was covered in a thin sheet of glaze. He'd garnished each one—thin curls of lemon rind for the first, a small stack of chocolate squares and espresso beans for the second, and a dash of colorful sprinkles over the third.

"This is beautiful," she said, unable to help herself. "Is this the plating you plan to do for each guest?"

"Yep," he said, "though the scones will be half the size."

Amber picked up her camera and snapped as many photos as she could from as many angles as possible, worried she wasn't doing them any justice. When she finished, she found him watching her, that familiar little smile on his face—the one from when he'd still had the "middle-school level crush" on her, when things had been full of hopeful maybes and had been far less complicated. Her bottom lip quivered a fraction, a sure sign that she would cry at any moment, and she took in a deep pull of air. "Okay, I think I have everything I need. Thank you so much for meeting with me," she said quickly, stuffing camera and pen back into her purse.

"Would you like to try one?" Jack asked. "I made the gingerbread one especially for you, actually. I just had a feeling it would be one you'd like."

Goodness, she needed to get out of here. But that scone *did* look amazing.

They reached for it at the same time, their hands colliding over the plate of beautifully plated treats. Their fingers tangled for a moment and they froze, gazes finding each other instantly. Just as quickly, they jumped apart. Not from embarrassment, but because they'd been zapped—like from static electricity.

It sent Amber's magic reeling and she stumbled back a step from the table. Her magic thrashed under her skin, like it always did in highly emotional moments. It instantly pulled up memories from the night at Edgar's. The sleep spell she'd put on Jack, being chased across Edgar's property in the dead of night by Kieran Penhallow, the cursed witch's magic crushing Amber's throat with an unseen hand.

Normally she only had to relive those memories in her nightmares.

"I'm sorry," Amber said. "I have to go."

She'd only made it a few steps when Jack called out to her. "You forgot this."

Turning, she found him holding up her clipboard stuffed with all her notes from the day. She met him halfway and took hold of the board, but Jack didn't immediately let go. It forced her to look into his green eyes, his black brows bunched together over them. The way he looked at her was different than it had been minutes ago—that goofy hopefulness was gone and replaced by something else.

When she gave the board another tug, he relinquished his hold. "Thank you," she muttered before she hurried out of the kitchen, along the length of the counter, ducked underneath the flap, and headed straight for the door, doing her best not to knock anyone off their feet in her haste to get out of the café.

Even after Amber made it back outside, the cool air washing over her blazing hot face, her magic didn't calm. Being outside did, however, remind her that she hadn't sampled any of Purrcolate's coffee. Maybe Ann Marie could come back later in Amber's stead; Amber couldn't go back in there—at least not right now.

She wondered if something Jack wore—a watch or belt or even his shoes—still held onto the energy from that night. By coming in contact with her, it had released the pent-up energy he'd been unknowingly storing, waiting for someone like Amber to unleash it. There had been so much of it. It had likely just felt like a static shock to him—like scooting across a carpet in socked feet and then touching something metal. To her, it had been like a quick, sharp lightning bolt to her system. If that zap had been any more powerful, or had lasted longer than a millisecond, it would have knocked her clear off her feet.

Now her magic was energized and frenzied. Restless. Phantom fingers grazed her neck, circled it, *squeezed*. She anxiously rubbed a hand over the skin, mostly to assure herself that she was in this parking lot alone. Nothing was touching her.

She'd need to perform her color-changing spell on the rubber cat toy a few dozen times to dispel just a fraction of the wild, agitated magic flowing through her, and to quiet the torrent of memories that had been exhumed like a body from a grave.

But, even more than that, she needed to stay the heck away from Jack Terrence.

CHAPTER 16

Saturday evening's premonition tincture showed Chloe in the same windowless room, her back to the wall and her knees pulled to her chest. Four knocks on the door from the outside; four slaps on the wall from Chloe's open palm. A plate of food and a glass of water were pushed into the room, just as usual, but this time, instead of any form of reading material, a single cupcake on a small plate was slid across the floor.

When the door closed and the lock engaged, Chloe didn't scramble off the bed with the same haste as she had in the previous visions. Slowly, she tossed back the comforter, padded across the cement floor on bare feet, and squatted before the offering. The cupcake looked to be plain white cake topped with vanilla frosting. These were no professionally made cupcakes; they were homemade. A small note was tucked under the treat.

"Happy birthday, Chloe!" the note read. "Now we can begin."

As Amber's eyes opened to the bright sunlight of Sunday morning, she knew Chloe Deidrick would turn eighteen tomorrow, and, for some reason, her being of legal age was tied up in why she was kidnapped.

After her weekly early Sunday morning breakfast date with Edgar, Amber put in a half day at the shop alone, allowing the Bowen sisters to have an open morning, before she headed out to her only Here and Meow errand for the day. Though her appointment was at Mews and Brews, she didn't immediately get out of the car when she parked in the lot. Instead, she called the chief's office, rather than his cell phone as usual. She needed him to have access to his files and computer for this call.

He picked up almost immediately. "Chief Brown speaking."

"Blackwood speaking," she replied.

She could hear the hint of a smile in his voice when he asked, "What can I do for you, Amber?"

"I have a weird request."

"Most of your requests are weird."

She decided to ignore that. "When's Chloe's birthday?"

"Why—" Then he stopped himself. "Give me a second …"

Amber did her best not to fidget as she waited.

"April 26th."

"And what's today's date?"

"Amber," he said, "did you hit your head?"

"Humor me."

"March 25th," he said.

"Chloe's *actual* birthday is tomorrow," she said. "And whoever took her knows that. Who would know information like that? Have you found out anything interesting about the Reed family?"

"Not really," he said. "Karen Reed is a schoolteacher in Montana. Her husband is a successful contractor. They live in a modest home. They've got a college-aged kid, but he's there on a sports scholarship. Football, I think."

"And Lilith?" Amber asked.

"Haven't had much luck finding anything about her," he said. "What makes you think Chloe's birthday is tomorrow? Wait … the premonition tincture again?"

"Yep. Why do you suppose the date used as Chloe's birthday is a month off? Same date, just a different month."

"I'm not sure."

"Do you think Frank knows?" She supposed it was possible that the kidnapper was wrong, or messing with Chloe's mind, but given the effort the kidnapper put in so far, Amber was willing to bet this person had done extensive research. "How could Frank be off on his daughter's birthday by a whole month? That's strange, right?"

"Yes," he said slowly, drawing the word out, like he was puzzling something out while he spoke. Then his tone changed, as if he'd been leaning back in his chair and now was sitting up straighter or hunched toward the phone—a conspiratorial tone. "All right. Let's run with this a little bit. I know you have reason to believe Frank isn't guilty of harming Chloe, but the fact that he called for a search—a *public* search—for her so soon after her disappearance still rubs me the wrong way. The best way to destroy evidence is to have a sea of well-meaning civilians go tramping through a place. He either wanted evidence destroyed or he knew there was something out there to find. Whether he wanted more manpower out there to help ensure the thing was found, or something else, I don't know."

"What do you think happened?" she asked. "That someone tipped him off? Called him and told him there was something to find out there?" It was possible that this same person tipped off Karen Reed, too. But why?

"Maybe," he said. "He's just normally such a levelheaded, by-the-book kind of guy. I don't think he's ever gotten so much as a parking ticket. So the rash move to completely bypass my department was not only out of character, it was reckless, especially given the circumstances. Granted, without that reckless move, her cell phone never would have been found … not that we've been able to recover anything from it yet."

"But if it weren't for my locator spell, it's likely no one would have found *anything* that day—especially not her cell phone. Not for a long time, anyway."

"True," he said, punctuated by a weary sigh.

"What if he'd been *forced* to make that rash decision?" When he didn't reply, she assumed he was going to continue to humor her. "Okay, so let's say someone called the mayor and said you have, I don't know, twelve hours to find a present I left for you in the woods. Maybe this person threatens Frank by saying, 'if you don't do x, y, and z as soon as possible, I'll hurt your daughter.' Frank panics, knowing your police force isn't big enough to canvass the entirety of the woods in time, so he mobilizes the town to help him instead."

"But, like you said, the search only turned up a cell phone purely by happenstance," he said.

"What if that was the point? What if whoever the kidnapper

is *wanted* the town and the whole police department looking one way—looking for nothing—so the kidnapper could get Chloe out of Edgehill, or at least to a hideout, without being seen?" It was a theory she'd first heard while in Alan's head, and wondered what the chief thought of it.

"A distraction," the chief said. It was a statement, not a question. "If that's the case, Frank might have facilitated his daughter being smuggled out of town—just a matter of whether he did so knowingly or not."

"This person, whoever it is, knows enough about Edgehill to know that an emergency town hall would mean we'd all show up, and the majority of us would ask 'How high?' when the mayor told us to jump," Amber said. "Does that mean the person who took her is a local? Is there a way to find out who didn't go to the search on Saturday and question them?"

"That's too many people," he said. "We don't have the man-power for that."

Amber sighed.

"As fun as all this speculating is," the chief said after a long pause, "what does any of this have to do with Chloe's birthday? Isn't that where this conversation started?"

"I think in order to figure out who took her, we have to figure out what it means for the kidnapper now that Chloe is eighteen," Amber said.

"Wait a minute," the chief said, and Amber heard papers being flipped. "In that packet of papers from Chloe's room, one of them said her birth certificate was unavailable because it had been sealed, right?"

"Right ..."

Now she heard his fingers flying across his keyboard, and the occasional click of his mouse. "Okay … so assuming Chloe was born in Montana—where both Lilith and Karen were raised, and where Frank supposedly moved here from … in order to get access to a child's original sealed birth certificate, the child has to be eighteen before it can be requested. Only the child or the biological parents can request an original birth certificate."

"What the heck could be on that thing to cause this much trouble?"

"I don't know," he said, "but I'm going to do my best to find out. How does Cassie Westbottom feel about paying Frank Deidrick a visit? Can you be here in an hour?"

Amber grinned. "We totally need a buddy cop show."

He hung up.

The real reason Amber had gone to Mews and Brews at noon hadn't been to chat with the chief of police in their parking lot, but to meet with the owner's son who did all the artwork that hung on the walls. Mews and Brews had a movie theme incorporated into every aspect of the place, but, since this was Edgehill, there was also a feline spin. The owner's son was one of the artists competing for the Best of Edgehill logo design. Whoever won would design the decals that would be displayed in the windows of the winning businesses in each category. They would also be the designer of the commemorative pin that each Here and Meow visitor was eligible to earn if they completed a scavenger hunt over the course of the weekend.

The winner of last year's pin design had ended up getting a gig as an animator on a popular kid's show after one of the show runners happened to be at the Here and Meow with his family, fell in love with the designs the young woman had created, and had tracked her down to get her information. After sending him her portfolio, and he'd extensively pored over her impressive body of work she posted daily on her social media, she'd been hired almost immediately.

Ben Lydon was a twenty-two-year-old with a gangly frame and a mop of wavy red hair. As planned, he was sitting at the first table on the right side of the room. He was bent over his sketchbook, pencil moving quickly across the page.

Amber slid into the booth across from him and he jumped. "Sorry," she said, wincing. It looked like he was working on a portrait of a girl. "What are you working on?"

"Nothing much. It's not done yet," he said, and quickly flipped the book closed. The hint of a beard lined his jaw; he was a very attractive kid, just exceedingly awkward.

They chatted about his design and Amber reminded him what would be expected of him were he to win and gave him a rough outline of what his deadlines would be. It was all things he'd heard before, but Melanie had said she'd worked with enough artists over the years to know that you needed to check in with them often to make sure they stayed on task. She claimed that self-doubt took down more of them than anything else.

While he'd walked her through his plans for the designs, he had opened his sketchbook again. The book faced her right side up, and he flipped the pages occasionally. Amber had only seen the mock-ups from one other artist so far, but she already thought Ben's were far superior. On his application for the competition, he'd said that his dream was to work on graphic novels. She hoped the "Best of" competition helped get him there.

"Oh, and I was thinking for the pin it might be cool …" he said, flipping a few pages, looking for something specific to show her. "It would be cool if instead of—"

He'd flipped a few pages too far and the book fell open to a sketch of Chloe Deidrick's smiling face that was so detailed, for a moment, Amber thought she was looking at a black-and-white photograph. Ben froze.

Slowly, Amber pulled the book a little closer. She flipped the page. And the next. And the next. They were all of Chloe. Page after page. Chloe sitting on a low brick wall eating a sandwich. Chloe laughing with a hand over her mouth and her eyes squeezed shut. Chloe sitting at a bench, reading a book.

When she looked up, Ben was slumped a little against the booth's back, his face almost as red as his hair. "How well do you know Chloe?" she finally asked.

He chewed on is bottom lip, his gaze focused on his hands loosely folded on the tabletop. "Not super well. She was a freshman when I was a senior at Edgehill High. She's friends with my little sister though so she would come by the house a lot. Or I'd pick them up from school or the mall in Belhaven or whatever."

"Admiring her from afar?" Amber asked, trying to keep her voice light and not accusatory. It wasn't a crime to have a crush on someone, after all.

"Yeah, I guess." His gaze flicked up to Amber's and then away just as quickly. "She didn't know I existed though. She was obsessed with that college kid."

"The guy from Scuttle?" Amber asked.

When his gaze met hers this time, it held. "You know about Scuttle?"

Amber shrugged. "Kind of. How does it work? Why would you want to chat anonymously with strangers?"

"Well, everyone has usernames, so some of them are obvious on purpose. Like a buddy of mine is named Oliver Pepper and we all call him Ollie Pepperoni—it's dumb, but we've called him that since we were ten. He's Ollie Pepperoni on Scuttle." When Amber chuckled at that, Ben looked to his right, as if checking to see if anyone was listening in on their conversation, and then leaned forward, the lip of the table pressing against his chest. "And it's *technically* anonymous, but some jerk from Edgehill High hacked the app a few months ago and stole a bunch of info off it—email addresses and stuff. Then he started matching up email addresses with usernames so pretty much everyone knew who was who."

Amber perked up at that. "What was Chloe's name on there?"

"MellowMeowt." Ben flushed a bit deeper, clearly embarrassed that he could recall it so quickly.

"Do you have any idea who this Johnny guy was? What his username was?"

Ben shook his head. "He wasn't from Edgehill, so he wasn't on the list. A couple people on the forum where the list was posted ... we have some guesses on which username was his just based on interactions we've had on there. A few of us are trying to do the armchair detective thing to try to figure out what happened to Chloe, I guess. She was always such a chill girl, you know? Just doesn't seem like her to run off with some guy she'd never met in person before."

Amber agreed. "Any way you could give me some of your guesses on those usernames? I'm actually meeting with the chief later and can pass them on."

"You think it could help find her?" he asked, sitting up a little straighter.

"It might; you never know," Amber said.

Ben tore a sheet out of the back of his sketchbook, then wrote down four usernames. He slid it across the table to her.

Listed were: 005BelHavenGuy, MeowAndLater, Handle-This, and JonathanR055.

Ben said, "I almost asked her out a month or so ago. I signed up to volunteer at the Here and Meow just so I'd have an excuse to talk to her. Then I chickened out. I'm kicking myself now. It's not like I'm such a great catch or anything, but maybe she would have been less into this guy if someone here was trying to sweep her off her feet." His face burned a deep red again. "Sorry. I'm really embarrassed that you saw all my drawings and now I can't shut up. I'm going to go home after this and hide in my room until I'm ninety."

Amber laughed.

He managed a half smile, gathered up his things, and climbed out of the booth. Amber followed suit. "Let me know if anything comes of those usernames, yeah? My armchair detectives and I will keep at it, just in case."

Amber watched him go, hoping one of the names she had stuffed in her pocket would lead them to Chloe.

Amber had a half hour before she had to meet the chief as Cassie Westbottom. She spent ten minutes driving around town, trying to find the best place to hide while she worked through her glamour spells. She had already experienced what happened when she went into a public restroom as one person and left as another—in Mews and Brews, no less. Public places were out. Her own shop was out with the Bowen sisters there.

Finally, she found a lot at the back of a boarded-up Italian restaurant that had actually been excellent, but had shuttered its doors unexpectedly a few months ago when it was discovered that they'd been operating without a license. With the building to her right and an empty lot encircled by a chain-link fence to her left—tall weeds sprouting through cracks in the asphalt—Amber worked through her spells. First was the A-line blonde bob, then the wider nose, then green eyes. She eyed her handiwork in the mirror, gave her new face a nod, and then backed out of the lot again.

She had just pulled up to the stop sign at the mouth of the restaurant's driveway—a force of habit more than a necessity, since the area was deserted—when a car at the stop sign to her right turned into the restaurant's lot. Brow furrowed, she watched as the person behind the wheel eyed her as he inched past her car.

Some part of her expected it to be Alan Peterson. Maybe even the chief somehow.

Who she had not expected to see was Connor Declan. He stopped abruptly, so their driver side windows were lined up—his car facing into the lot and hers out. He rolled down his window. Swallowing, she did the same. This car was a rental. Cassie Westbottom was from out of town, so it both made sense that she might be lost and that she'd be in a rented car.

"Hey," Connor said slowly. "You're Cassie, right?"

Amber nodded. "That's me," she said, hoping this was the same high and light tone she'd given this persona before. She didn't trust her magic with something as complicated as a voice alteration spell. Knowing her luck, she'd sound like a deep-voiced man. Or a goose.

"I thought you caught a flight out of here a few days ago," he said, gaze painstakingly roving over her features.

"I did," Amber said. "But Chief Brown asked me to come back."

"Oh?" he asked. "You're a bit far from the station, aren't you?"

"I got a bit turned around," she said with a laugh.

"I see," he said. "Hey, weird question: did you happen to see Amber Blackwood out here just a few minutes ago? She and I were going to meet up for a late lunch and I thought I saw her turn down here—I figured maybe she forgot the restaurant here was closed."

"I'm not sure I know who that is," Amber said. "I was only in town a day last time, and I only got back last night."

"Right," he said. "Right. Of course. Sorry to bother you.

I hope that you coming back to Edgehill is a *good* sign for this case?"

"Sorry, but I can't discuss details with you," Amber said. "I should be going. Have a good day."

His expression was blank as he said, "You too, *Cassie*."

As Amber drove toward the station, her stomach in knots, only one thought cycled through her head: *He knows, he knows, he knows.*

CHAPTER 17

The chief was standing on the curb outside the station when Amber pulled up. His nose wrinkled a fraction when he spotted her. Not because he was unhappy to see her, she figured, but because the idea of magic still made him twitchy.

"Afternoon, Cassie," he said.

Amber lightened her voice. "Hello, Chief Brown."

He angled his head toward his cruiser and they wordlessly climbed in. After a few blocks, he finally spoke. "What do you think about telling Frank that you're a psychic?"

Amber swiveled toward him. "You're kidding."

"Nope," he said, gaze focused ahead. "I want this to be a casual visit. I don't want Frank to feel like we're ambushing him or make him feel like he needs to lawyer up. I figure I can present you as a psychic consultant, but that we want to keep what you do a secret for now, so as to not make the public think we're resorting to drastic measures. You knowing Chloe's true birthday can be thanks to your abilities. If he *does* know her true birthday, your knowledge of it should be a shock to him. As well as Shannon Pritchard's legal name."

Amber nodded. "Okay, I can do that. If he doesn't react well to any of this, I could always erase his memory of the conversation."

He cut a quick, sharp look at her. "It's a little unnerving how causally you suggested that."

"It's not like I go around erasing people's memories all the time," she said. "I'm just saying it's an option."

He huffed a breath out of his nose like a disgruntled cow but said nothing further.

Once the chief had pulled up to the curb in front of the sunshine yellow mayoral home, Amber flipped down the passenger-side visor to check her reflection. Hints of brown roots were starting to show, and her nose wasn't nearly as wide as it should have been. With two quick spells, Cassie Westbottom was firmly back into place.

"Lord help me," the chief muttered as he climbed out of the car. Just before they reached the door, he whispered, "Try to be ethereal and a little off-putting. You know, like usual." He knocked.

She was ready to offer him a lighthearted insult of her own, but then the front door opened. Frank Deidrick peered out at them. It was a Sunday afternoon, so casual attire wasn't odd, per se, but Amber had never seen the man look anything less than well-groomed. He hadn't shaved, the hems of his sweatpants were dirty, and there was a hole in one of his socks—his big toe nearly poking through. He reminded Amber of Edgar before she'd barged into his life and forced him to leave the house once in a while.

"I'm not in the best state for company," Frank said. "Can we do this tomorrow?" Then his gaze slid to Amber. "Who are you, again?"

Amber thrust out a hand. "Cassandra Westbottom, but

please call me Cassie. I was brought on to be a consultant on the case due to my … unique skill set."

Frank didn't shake Amber's offered hand, but he didn't slam the door in their faces either. His usual charm—the politician X factor—was gone. "What are you? A psychologist? A social worker? Are you here to psychoanalyze me? Get in my head? If you're here to use her to accuse me again, chief, for harming my own daughter, I'll have to ask you to leave. You're no closer now to finding Chloe than you were a week ago. She's not here. I don't know where she is. But wasting your time badgering me won't get you any closer to finding her."

When he moved to close the door, Amber blurted out, "Her mother's name was Lilith, wasn't it?"

Frank gaped at her, then quickly snapped his mouth shut, trying to regain some of his composure. "No. Her mother's name was Shannon."

"I meant her *given* name," Amber said. "She was born Lilith Reed and died in a town in Montana that bore the same name as the lake her car sank in."

All the color drained from Frank's face. "What … how could …" His wide-eyed gaze darted between Amber and the chief.

"Can we come in?" the chief asked.

Without a word, Frank stepped aside. He closed the door behind them, then moved down the short entryway, motioning to the right. "You can have a seat in here. Would you like anything to drink? Ingrid has the day off, but I could probably manage to prepare ice water without screwing it up."

The small sitting room had a dark brown leather loveseat

against the back wall under a pair of windows. The loveseat was flanked by black bookshelves packed with hardback books. A glass coffee table stood on curved black metal legs over a sea-green throw rug; its hue matched the curtains drawn open on the windows. Against the wall nearest them was a dark brown leather recliner that matched the loveseat.

The chief perched on the edge of the recliner's cushion and said, "Nothing for me, thanks," then gestured to the loveseat.

Reluctantly, Frank made his way across the room, side-stepped the coffee table, and sat with his clasped hands pressed between his knees, his head lowered. Amber sat beside him, watching as he absently wiggled his toes, the big one on his right foot poking in and out of the hole in his sock like a rodent's head searching for danger above ground.

Amber started to say something, but she saw the chief from across the room lightly raise his hand to stop her. He wanted Frank to break the silence first.

It took almost a full minute, but he finally did. "How do you know Lilith's name?" His attention was still focused on his hands.

Amber met the chief's gaze across the room and he nodded. She steeled herself, knowing Frank's reaction could go in any number of directions. "I'm a practicing psychic."

Frank's head snapped up. That white-hot rage that was always simmering below his surface caused him to shoot to his feet and whirl to face Chief Brown. "What are you playing at, Owen? This is just insulting. My daughter is missing and you're wasting precious resources and time on … on *this*?" He jabbed a finger in Amber's direction without looking at her.

"She's the real deal, Frank," the chief said calmly. "She wouldn't be here otherwise."

"Lilith Reed was running from something," Amber said. Frank, still standing by the couch, turned to glare down at her. "She changed her name to Shannon Pritchard but found a way to get that change removed from her public record, along with sealing Chloe's birth certificate."

He walked away from her to stand on the other side of the coffee table. He crossed his arms. "You could have found all of that out with enough digging. If you're truly gifted, you'd know what was on that sealed certificate."

"I haven't been shown all of it," Amber said, and Frank scoffed and rolled his eyes, "but I do know her 18th birthday is tomorrow, not a *month* from tomorrow, as her current public paperwork shows."

Frank's arms slipped from their tight grip across his chest and hung limply at his sides. "No one knows that except—" He pressed his hands to the sides of his head. "Have you seen her? Is she okay? Is she alive?"

"Yes," Amber said quickly, cutting off his increasingly panic-sounding questions. "She's alive and being cared for. But she *was* kidnapped; she didn't run away."

Frank gusted out a shaky sigh, then cautiously made his way back to Amber, perching on the end of the cushion. His pressed hands were squeezed between his knees again, but this time his knees were pointing toward her. "Someone … took her?"

"Yes … to get back at you. Someone who knows personal details about you that most others wouldn't," she said.

"Someone who believes they can benefit from her now being legal."

Frank cursed. "Montana's law states that either the birth parents or the child, once he or she turns 18, can request to see the original birth certificate." He shrugged, hands out, as if he was offering this confession on a platter. "Original meaning: I adopted Chloe; I'm not her biological father."

Amber and the chief had already suspected this was a possibility.

"This is the kind of thing Victor Newland threatened me with," Frank said, dropping his hands. "When my own researchers found out scandal-worthy information about his family, he swore he wouldn't stop digging until he found the skeletons in *my* closet."

"What information did you find?" the chief asked. "There's been wide speculation about what made Victor suddenly drop out and Lisa skip town. I didn't realize it was something you found."

Frank lightly shook his head. "I never divulged what I found. It was his choice to drop out, not mine."

Amber scoffed. "Are you really trying to put a politician spin on that? Yes, you kept what you found a secret, but you threatened to sell the information to the *Gazette* if he didn't drop out. That's not you being altruistic. That's blackmail."

Frank worked his jaw. "I didn't want the scandal to ruin his family. I wanted to run a clean campaign."

"If you wanted it to be clean, you wouldn't have gone digging into his life with your 'researchers,'" Amber said. "You wanted to find dirt on him before he could find it on you.

And, lucky for you, I guess, your skeletons are buried a lot deeper than his."

He glared at the chief. "You *did* bring her here to further throw my character into question."

The chief held up his hands in innocence. "Your best bet is that Victor Newland is the person most likely to benefit from Chloe turning eighteen? He gets her to request an original birth certificate and it's revealed that you're not really her father? You think that's Victor's big play?"

Frank started to say something, then hesitated. "Yeah," he said flatly. "That's my best guess."

This reasoning didn't sit well with Amber, and given the pinched expression on the chief's face, he didn't buy it either. What Amber wanted to know was *why* the birth certificate had been sealed. If it was merely a case of Frank adopting Chloe as his own because her biological father was out of the picture, why did that need to be kept a secret? If nothing else, it spoke to the *goodness* of Frank's character that he loved Chloe and Lilith enough that he wasn't hung up on the fact that Chloe wasn't his.

Then she remembered the reasons the chief said a woman might want to have a birth certificate sealed as a matter of safety. Had the potential abuse started before or *after* Frank came into Lilith's life?

"You're lying," Amber said flatly.

Frank glared at her. "Excuse me?"

"It wasn't Victor. Are you protecting someone or are you scared of someone?"

"Neither," Frank ground out. "I gave you my best guess.

You should be harassing Victor Newland, not me. And I don't have to sit in my own house being insulted by a *psychic*."

When he stood up, Amber made a quick decision. Her hand clamped down on his forearm. "Who do you think kidnapped Chloe?" Her magic thrummed beneath her skin, and she uttered the spell she'd used on the chief the morning he told her about Melanie's death. It was a spell to reveal a person's last thought.

Though Frank refused to answer her verbally—he squeezed his lips shut as if the words were a physical thing he could keep trapped in his mouth—his thoughts betrayed him. *Sean Merrill.*

"Who is Sean Merrill?" she asked.

Frank yanked his arm away from her and stumbled off the couch and toward the middle of the room. "How did … how did you do that?"

"She's the real deal," the chief repeated from his spot in the recliner, no hint of alarm or concern in his voice.

Amber watched as Frank paced up and down the length of the small room. His brow would crease and he'd tug at his hair and he'd mutter to himself. Finally, he stopped and faced Amber from his spot on the other side of the coffee table. "I've been doing my best to keep Sean Merrill away from Chloe for seventeen—now eighteen—years."

"Her biological father?" Amber guessed.

"Yes," Frank said, sighing. "The guy has been in and out of jail, though. Last I heard, he was released from prison a couple years ago after completing his sentence for a nonviolent drug offense. A friend back in Montana says she's seen him around.

He works as a gas station attendant … has a girlfriend and a dog. All I know is that the money keeps him away from Chloe."

"So he's dangerous?" the chief asked.

"Yes and no," Frank said. "I'm almost positive he's responsible for the accident that killed Lilith. It's a gut feeling; I have no proof. If he's gone through this much trouble to get Chloe now, he needs her for something. He's not a danger to her only because she's no good to him dead." He pressed a fist to his mouth, as if that last word had made him nauseous.

"Any idea what he needs her *for*?" Amber asked.

"All I have are guesses," Frank said, but he didn't elaborate. Then he began to pace again.

"We're here to help," the chief said. "We can't help you if you don't talk to us."

"But see that's the thing," Frank said, turning to the chief. "A big part of why I'm in this mess is because of cops. I know you're a good guy, Owen. You being a law-abiding family man heading the department here is honestly one of the things that pushed me to run for mayor. But Sean Merrill was a cop too, and he nearly ruined my life."

Amber and the chief shot each other bewildered expressions across the room.

"Can you tell us what happened?" Amber ventured.

It took Frank a while to start talking. "Lilith was twenty-five when she met Sean. They both grew up in Montana, but Sean was from Missoula before moving to Lirkaldy and becoming a cop," said Frank, who had resumed his pacing. The movement seemed to keep his wild emotions in check. "She said life was good for them for the first three years or

272

so. She was going to vet school and he was enjoying his job as an officer. Neither was in any rush to get married or have kids. They had a full social life and lots of friends.

"After three years, they moved into Sean's house, but Lilith said it took a lot of convincing to get Sean to agree to it. She said at first that she thought he was just a commitment-phobe, but then she realized it was because Sean kept really strange hours. She was often up late studying, so when they lived apart, she wouldn't bother him with late-night phone calls, assuming he was asleep. But once they were living together, she would see him leave at two or three in the morning, always claiming it was work-related.

"A year later, Sean was involved in a drug bust gone bad, and he was shot twice in the back and once in the leg. Several bones were shattered; he nearly died. After extensive surgery and physical therapy, he was fully mobile again, though he walked with a limp because of a reconstructed femur. Lilith was by his side for all of it. They ended up drowning in debt.

"Even though he was able to walk, he was deemed unable to work for the police department. He went on disability and developed a terrible drinking habit. Six months after all this, his two a.m. nightly outings started up again."

"An affair?" the chief asked. "Or was he uh … *paying* for companionship?"

Frank shook his head. "Neither. He'd been stockpiling his medications from all his medical procedures and had started selling them to make extra cash. Turns out, when he was out at all hours before, he'd been caught up in drugs then too. He'd developed relationships with local dealers in large part

273

because of the drugs he'd been stealing from the evidence locker at work, and had been in the middle of a deal when a dealer got spooked that Sean was an undercover cop, and that's how he wound up shot."

The chief lightly shook his head, his lip curled as if he smelled something rotten.

"After weeks of this, Lilith finally confronted him about it. Unfortunately, he'd been on a bender before that and went at her with his fists. She went to the police, but her reports fell on deaf ears because Sean had dirt on pretty much every cop in town, plus a gang of loyal thugs who threatened anyone who tried to work against him.

"Lilith was trapped with him, as nearly all their money by then had been eaten up by medical bills. She had to drop out of school. And when she tried to have a say, Sean beat her."

"My God," Amber said, hand to her throat. She'd always felt awful that Chloe didn't know anything about her mother, but now she was glad Chloe had been spared these terrible details.

"She worked several jobs for a long time, one of which paid her under the table. She squirreled away cash; it was easy to keep that from Sean since he was drunk half the time anyway. When she had enough saved up, she left. A few months after that, when she was living in her own apartment in Traver—about a hundred miles or so from Lirkaldy—she and I met at a classic film meetup group."

"What was playing?" Amber asked.

A small, wistful smile graced Frank's mouth. "*Some Like it Hot.*" He was lost in his thoughts for a moment, then continued. "We hit it off almost immediately. She didn't get into details about her past for a while—it was a lot to take in—but we both fell hard. One night, she told me everything and dropped the bomb that she was pregnant. It was Sean's; couldn't have been mine. We kept dating after that, and six months in, I proposed. I didn't care if Chloe wasn't mine. I adored Lilith and wanted to make a go of a family. Lilith was terrified of Sean and what being attached to someone like her could mean for me, so she turned down my proposal."

"But she stayed with you?" Amber asked.

"Yeah," he said. "She tried to leave me. It lasted three days and we were both so miserable, I begged her to come back. I didn't care if we were married. I was too far gone to care about much of anything other than being with her."

The chief spoke up. "Was getting her name legally changed your idea or hers?"

"Mine," he said. "I'd tried law school a while back and even though I'd dropped out, I had a few old classmates I could contact about Lilith's situation. That's where we got the sealed birth certificate idea, too—and to use a false birthdate. Anything we could think of to make it harder for Sean to ever find either one of them. When Chloe was born, I legally adopted her, and we had a new birth certificate written up with Lilith's new name, and mine as the father. Then we sealed it so Sean could never find it and try to claim paternity. We hoped if we made Lilith fall off the map, he'd forget about her and move on."

"But that didn't happen?" Amber asked.

"It worked for a while," he said. "Then one day I get a phone call from a blocked number. I still don't know how he found me, but that guy is incredibly well connected. It was clear he knew I had a tie to Lilith, but he couldn't find her. He said he knew she had a child and assumed it was his but said that he didn't want it. What he *did* want was hush money. If I sent him money monthly, he'd leave us alone. I refused. A day later, when I went out to my car at work to grab lunch, all my tires were slashed. That night, Sean called again and asked if I'd changed my mind. I know you're not supposed to give people like him what they want, but based on what Lilith had told me about him …" Frank shook his head and shrugged. "I just wanted to keep my family safe. So I agreed to pay him."

"*Those* are the payments Francine discovered," Amber said, the words leaving her mouth before she'd realized she was going to say them out loud.

Frank stared at her, bewildered for a moment, then shook this off. Perhaps he'd accepted now that she was "psychic." "Yes, that's what Francine found. I didn't want to get into what they were for or have her start investigating and somehow have something get back to Sean, so I had to let her go. I reacted rashly, but it's hard for me to keep a level head when it affects Chloe. I've been too embarrassed to ask Francine to come back."

"Once the payments were set up," the chief said, getting the conversation back on track, "then he left you alone?"

"For nearly a year," Frank said. "Lilith hated dealing with finances, so she left most of that to me. Which was fine, since I was able to hide the payments from her. The longer it went on, and with all the expenses of a new baby, we started living paycheck to paycheck. She got suspicious one day and checked our account history and figured out pretty quickly what was happening. We got into a huge fight about it and she told me to at least cut the payments in half because we were in danger of going bankrupt. We had moved since then, we'd sealed as many public records as we could, I'd changed my number—we thought we were safe."

Amber's stomach churned.

"He found us within three months," Frank said. "Showed up on our doorstep. He was drunk or high or both … just in a really bad way. I tried to get him to leave. I gave him all the cash I had in my wallet. We were all screaming at each other. Chloe was crying in a back room. God, I was so scared he was there to do something to Chloe. The man is huge. He never got farther than the front entryway; he kept trying to barge his way in and I kept shoving him back. Lilith was yelling that she was going to call the police, that he didn't have his cop friends in this town to save his butt this time. Next thing I know …"

Frank grabbed the hem of his shirt and lifted it, revealing a large, jagged scar on his flat abdomen.

"He *stabbed* you?" Amber asked.

"Yep," Frank said, dropping his shirt. "I went down hard. He stabbed me a second time and I remember lifting my head enough to see this hunting knife's handle sticking out of me and the shock of seeing that was almost worse than the pain. Then I saw the blood soaking into my shirt. I've always been squeamish about blood and even though I tried to get myself to get up and get to Lilith and Chloe, I passed out."

Amber had her hand pressed to her mouth, her eyes wide.

"What happened when you came to?" the chief prodded.

"I was in a pool of blood, Chloe—thank God—was still in the house because I heard her crying in the back, but I couldn't hear Lilith or Sean anymore," Frank said, his chin quivering a fraction. "While I was trying to get up, a neighbor happened to be walking by with her dog—she'd only just gotten home about ten minutes before—and saw me lying in the doorway of the house. She called an ambulance and I was rushed to the hospital for emergency surgery. Gut wounds like mine are often fatal; they said it was a small miracle I survived.

"Lilith was gone. Sean had taken her. I …." Frank blew out a long breath. "I actually never saw her again alive." Tears tracked down his cheeks now. "I tried for months to find her. It was like she disappeared off the face of the earth. We hadn't kept in touch with her family because Lilith was terrified that any contact with them would put them in danger. So when she was gone, I didn't even know how to find them. They didn't know who I was. And then three months after she'd disappeared, her car was found at the bottom of a lake."

Amber and the chief diverted their gaze as Frank broke down. He excused himself for a while. When he came back, his eyes were red and his hairline was damp—she figured he had splashed water on his face. They waited patiently for him to resume his story.

"I was a suspect for a while, since it's usually the partner in cases like this, but my neighbor being a witness to the aftermath of the attack helped me," he said. "I told them about Sean Merrill but there was so little evidence the police could find on him, all they could do was bring him in for questioning. The more I pushed the police to keep looking into him, the more harassment I suffered. Hang-up phone calls at all hours of the day. After days of that, I would file a report. The next day, someone would throw a rock through my window in the middle of the night. I reported that. Police kept surveillance on the house for weeks. The day the surveillance stopped, my tires were slashed again.

"So when I got a phone call from Sean one night and he said he wanted more hush money, I agreed. I picked up another job and got help from neighbors to look after Chloe. After months of payments, the harassing phone calls stopped. No rocks through my windows. The moment it felt like I was safe as long as the payments went out like clockwork, I packed up Chloe in the middle of the night and just … drove. I didn't even know where we were going. After a couple of weeks, we ended up in Edgehill. Payments kept going out, so Sean has left us alone."

"Until now," the chief said. "What's the significance of Chloe turning eighteen?"

"That part I don't know," Frank said. "Lilith told me that she put plans in place to make sure Chloe was taken care of if anything should happen to her—it's something a woman does when she's been involved with scum like Sean Merrill. My guess is, she squirreled away money when she was with me, just as she had with Sean. There could be some hidden account somewhere for Chloe that only becomes available when Chloe turns eighteen. He's never wanted to be her father; all he's ever wanted is money." Frank let out a sound akin to a wounded animal. "I should have told her about him and the adoption. I've spent so long trying to protect her and he found her anyway. I just wish I knew how. I've been racking my brain trying to figure out where I screwed up."

Amber had a feeling she knew how he'd found her. "Do you know anything about the Scuttle app?"

The chief and Frank both looked at her with cocked heads—the chief because he likely didn't know why such a question was relevant at the moment, and Frank because he'd likely never heard of it. Amber relayed what she'd learned of the app, the hack, and the fact that Bethany and Ben Lydon both suspected that "Johnny" wasn't a teenage boy at all.

"You mean it's possible that Sean was talking to her on this app while he pretended to be … interested in her?" Frank asked, his face screwed up in disgust.

"That's one of the theories, yes," the chief said, seamlessly following the flow of the conversation even though she hadn't yet shared with him the list of potential "Johnny" handles she'd gotten from Ben. "It's not as uncommon as you'd hope that men join sites popular with young people with the desire of luring them out into the real world. She was already planning to meet this Johnny person the night she disappeared. It's possible his plan had always been to meet her so he could snatch her for whatever purpose. Maybe her flat tire was planned on his part; maybe it was luck and provided the perfect scenario for him to grab her. If he was aware of any tension between you and Chloe—whether this was Sean or someone else who preys on young girls—he absolutely would have exploited that to get her trust to shift away from you and onto him."

Frank's eyes slipped closed. "I screwed this all up."

"You were trying to do right by your girl," the chief said.

"No one can fault you for that. What we need from you is anything you can tell us about Sean and where he might have taken her. Old addresses, phone numbers, makes and models of cars he might have owned, the names of anyone he may be in contact with."

"We'll also take any prized possession or a photograph of Lilith's," Amber quickly added.

Both men stared at her.

"I believe I might be able to gain some insight into what happened to her the night of the accident, but I need something that may still hold her energy. An object from the site of a traumatic event works best, though those are harder to come by."

"I actually have two of those things," Frank said. "A photograph of her when she was pregnant with Chloe, and a rock I took from the shore of Lake Lirkaldy where her car went into the water. I went to the site a few days after they'd pulled her body out."

Amber tried not to let loose an excited squeak. Inanimate objects from places of highly emotional events were the perfect vessels for stored energy her magic could tap into. "Would you allow me to take both of them with me? I need to be in a location that's been cleansed in a very specific manner for something like this, and I have a location nearby that would suit me well."

He pursed his lips. "Sure. I'll see if I can find anything related to Sean, too. I'll be right back."

When he left the room, the chief angled his head around the open doorway that led into the entryway, presumably watching Frank walk down the hallway, and then the chief was on his feet and hurrying over to her. "Your eyes and the ends of your hair are turning brown," he hissed.

"Oh crap," she muttered, then fished in her bag for her compact. She uttered her glamour spells as quickly as she could, keeping an eye on herself as she worked. The chief stood in front of her with his hands on his hips, shielding her from view.

By the time Frank returned twenty minutes later, Cassie was firmly back in place, and the chief was perusing the spines of the hardback books lining the shelves.

Frank handed the chief a sheet of paper with a few random things scrawled on it, promising to contact him if he thought of anything else. To Amber, he handed a photograph of a beautiful dark-haired woman in a flowy dress and a floppy yellow hat, standing in front of a hedge covered in giant pink flowers. One hand protectively rested on her very pregnant belly, while the other held down her hat. The woman bore such a striking resemblance to Chloe, it made Amber's chest ache. The rock was smooth and heavy in Amber's hand.

They both thanked Frank for talking to them, and Amber followed the chief out the front door and down the pathway to his cruiser waiting at the curb.

As she sat in the passenger seat of the chief's car, she stared down at the rock in her hand, turning it end over end in her palm. She wondered if she'd need to buy Edgar a dozen pizzas to get him to leave his house twice in one day.

CHAPTER 18

Edgar's pizza of choice this time was olive and anchovy. Amber honestly wasn't sure if he was doing this to mess with her, if his tastes were really that terrible, or if this was his really lazy way of getting Tom and Alley a treat. While Amber and Edgar sat on the couch to eat and discuss the Chloe situation, he would sneak little pieces of anchovy to the cats who were sitting under the coffee table. Amber pretended she didn't notice.

"Do you think the same spell I used on Alan's business card will work on these?" Amber asked, pointing to the photograph of Lilith and the rock pinning the picture's corner to the table.

"I don't know," he said. "Just because the rock is from the shore of the lake where her car plunged into the water, it doesn't mean that the energy in it is Lilith's. Any number of traumatic things could have happened there—things even more powerful, energy-wise, than what happened to her. But maybe a memory spell isn't what we need at all."

"What do you mean?" she asked, wiping her greasy fingers on a napkin she then swiped across her mouth.

"Remember: time magic is part of your birthright as a Henbane, too," Edgar said.

"Aren't they kind of the same thing?"

"Memory spells are all about the specifics," Edgar said,

casually dropping a small piece of anchovy on the floor. Tom pounced on it. "Reliving a memory isn't really about time itself, as a memory is something specific to a person. When you're experiencing a memory through a spell, you're tapping into that particular person's energy to see a snapshot of the past from their perspective. If you had relived the night of the fire through Belle's energy, rather than Theo's, the majority of the details would be the same, but they'd feel and look different because you'd be seeing it through a different lens. That's why you need personal objects from a person to experience their memory, because you need *their* energy in order to see through that lens."

Amber nodded. "Okay. So what makes time spells different?"

"You'll still end up seeing a snapshot of the past—or future or present—with time spells, but the lens is a bit of a free-for-all," Edgar said. "With time spells, you're transporting your consciousness to a specific time and then you just … see what you see. I think the energy we need to grab hold of is Lake Lirkaldy's. We need to get your magic to sync with the energy of the place, give it a certain time to take you to, and then cross our fingers that you're shown something helpful."

"And that I don't get stuck there," she joked.

"And that," he said without a hint of humor.

Amber swallowed.

"It's relatively safe," he said. "Whereas you need specifics for memory spells, you need to go a bit broader with time spells. So the fact that we don't know the exact time of the accident is actually a good thing."

Amber's stomach churned.

Apparently sensing that, Edgar awkwardly patted her shoulder. "I won't let anything happen to you, cousin. Who would be there to annoy the crap out of me and buy me pizza?"

"No one," she said, "because you're very grumpy."

He grinned at her. "All right," he said, clapping once and then rubbing his hands together. "We need a picture of the lake for you to focus on in addition to the one of Lilith."

Amber closed the lid of Edgar's horrible pizza, fetched her laptop, and then placed it on top of the box. She did an image search of the lake in January, and pulled up one that featured snow-covered pines, a snowy shore, and a pristine blue-gray lake stretching out beyond the trees, the weak sunlight reflecting off the surface as if it were made of glass. Amber tried not to think about how cold that water must have been when Lilith plunged into it.

While Amber had been searching for a suitable picture of the lake, Edgar had been flipping through a grimoire. Once he found a spell for revealing a truth, Amber set to work crafting something that better suited her needs. Edgar told her to let instinct aid her—that her affinity for time magic would act like a guide. It took nearly two hours, but eventually the words written before her burned a faint orange before returning to black, signifying that the spell was complete.

Amber sat back on the couch with a huff; she was already exhausted and the real work hadn't even begun yet. Without needing to discuss it, they layered her studio apartment in cloaking spells.

"So this one is likely going to knock you on your butt,"

said Edgar once they were done. "I recommend reciting the spell, then lying down. You'll sort of semi-pass out anyway if this works."

"You're supposed to tell me these things sooner!"

"Why? It's not like it would make you change your mind," he said.

She shrugged; he wasn't wrong.

Armed with the spell, her laptop, the photo of Lilith, and the rock, Amber climbed onto her bed, her back against the wall at the head of her bed. With her computer perched on her lap and the screen still open to the icy picture of Lake Lirkaldy, she crossed her feet at the ankles. She laid out the spell on her keyboard and then held the Lilith photograph in one hand and grasped the rock in the other.

Edgar stood beside the bed, arms crossed, as he stared down at her. "Instead of keeping the image of a person in your mind like you're used to, focus on the location and the date. I'm right here if things get iffy."

Blowing out a steadying breath, Amber recited the spell, speaking slowly and enunciating each word with care. Her magic thrummed and she clutched the rock a little tighter, her palm growing clammy against the smooth surface. She tried to imagine the biting, icy air stinging her nose and cheeks; her boots sinking into freezing-cold slush; the creak of branches under the heavy weight of snow. Was the stone in her hand growing warmer, or was her own body heat just seeping into it?

As Amber's eyes slipped closed, she thought of Lilith Reed, of little Chloe in her womb, and of the date January 12th. She could have sworn she heard wind whistling through the trees, the freezing air pulling goose pumps up on her skin. She wanted to rub a warm palm over the pebbled flesh, but her hands were occupied. A drowsiness even more powerful than the one that came after the consumption of a premonition tincture pressed her body into the bed. Her head felt like a bowling ball balanced on a toothpick. She couldn't possibly stay awake.

Her magic, on the other hand, was frenzied. It coursed beneath her skin like a river, a flood, a torrent. Amber felt as if her body was the rock in her hand, and her magic was water rushing around it. It would drown her. It would rush up over her head like a tsunami and she would be swallowed up and carried away.

And then she was there.

She stood on a slight hill, surrounded by snow and the occasional pine tree. Given the waning light, she guessed it to be near dusk. Wind occasionally whispered though the branches, but otherwise it was silent. The lake stretched out before her. On the other side, she could see a road that wove between the trees. Around a bend came a pair of headlights. They were there and not there as the car passed behind the trees, like a staccato flash of a strobe light. It was hard to tell how fast the car was going given the distance from her to the other side of the lake. But then a second car came around the bend, this one moving much faster. The first car accelerated.

Amber watched as the cars drove faster and faster, following the shore of the lake. She lost sight of them for a moment given her vantage point on the hill, but she turned and looked up the short incline behind her. She could just make out the edge of the road a few hundred feet away. The cars were zipping up the road near her now. There was a bang—metal on metal. Engines revved. Another bang. A screech. *Bang.* Amber flinched, then charged up the short incline, her boots slipping and crunching in the snow. She stopped at the edge of the road.

Bang. From her right, she saw a pair of headlights barreling toward her.

The car swerved left, then right.

Bang.

Bang.

The car fishtailed, tires squealing.

It was feet away from Amber now, and she could see the whites of Lilith's eyes as they flicked up to her rearview mirror. The second car slammed into Lilith's car again and she screamed, the sound silent to Amber's ears. Lilith's head jerked forward and smacked into the steering wheel. Her head lolled.

Bang.

The car spun and spun and slipped off the road and down the snowy hill and into the water below with a deafening crash. The driver of the second car slammed on its brakes and threw open the driver's side door.

Amber swallowed hard, her heart racing as the large man stalked down the slight slope. He was bald and barrel-chested. Amber wouldn't have been surprised to learn the man had played football in high school. Even though she knew this giant, burly man couldn't see her, she pulled her head toward her shoulders anyway.

The man stalked past her without so much as a glance. He wore a thick red flannel jacket, heavy pants, and black boots.

He crunched his way to the shore. Amber slowly followed, telling herself that she needed to commit his face to memory. When she was close enough to study his profile, what stood out to her more than anything was the complete lack of emotion on his face. He lit a cigarette and savored it, taking his time, as he watched Lilith's car slowly fill with water, and then sink. When the vehicle made its last gurgle and released an explosion of bubbles, he said, "Good riddance, Lilith. You will *not* be missed." He took a long draw on his cigarette, letting the smoke out slowly. "Thanks in advance for the half-million, though. It'll come in handy. Looks like I'm going to need a new car." He laughed and tossed his unfinished cigarette into the snow, the lit end going out instantly with a little hiss.

Amber darted ahead, her boots slipping on the snow. She committed his license plate to memory just before he drove away. She stood on the side of the road, watching the red of his taillights as they grew smaller and smaller before disappearing and leaving her alone in the quiet once more. She wished she could run to the water's edge, dive in, and swim her way to Lilith's car—to pull her body from the vehicle and wrap her in a blanket and bring her back to Chloe and Frank. But she couldn't do anything other than wait for this vision to end.

When it did, it was so abrupt, she gasped as if waking from a dream. Her apartment and her bed were so warm in contrast to that snowy scene from seventeen years ago, it almost hurt. As if she'd been the one frozen and was now rapidly thawing.

Edgar's face swam into view before her and she stifled a gasp. "Did it work?" he asked. "You were shaking really hard at one point, but I couldn't tell if it was a bad reaction to the spell or if you were cold—I wasn't sure if I should snap you out of it."

"It worked," she breathed. "And I think I know why Sean took Chloe."

It took Amber an hour to recover from the spell. The first twenty minutes had been spent guzzling the glasses of water Edgar brought her. Then he encouraged her to eat two more slices of pizza. After a very long shower and a few more glasses of water, Amber sat down on the bed again and then went into her vision in detail.

"All right," Edgar said, from his seated position on the floor, once she was done. Tom lay before him on his back, his paws flopped onto his chest while Edgar scratched under his chin. "It's been a long time since I've needed to work multiple jobs, but if Lilith really was taking under-the-table gigs as a way to keep a low profile, I'm thinking it's pretty impossible that she'd stashed away half a million dollars in a sock drawer just from scrubbing toilets and washing dishes, right? So where does a small-town girl get that much money?"

"Sean very clearly ran her off the road with the intention of killing her," Amber said, shuddering a little at the memory. "What if her death needed to happen in order for him to get the money?"

"Life insurance?" Edgar asked. "And if he needs Chloe to be eighteen, does that mean money from the policy isn't released until she's legal? Can you even name a minor as a beneficiary? I'm guessing this isn't the first case where something like this has happened: a parent names their kid as the beneficiary, but then the parent dies before the kid can legally claim the money. Are there contingencies in place for stuff like this?"

Amber propped one leg on the bed and pulled her laptop in front of her. The image of Lake Lirkaldy filled the screen. She could still hear the sound of Sean's car slamming into the back of Lilith's. The deafening silence as the car seemed to be suspended in air after it went off the incline before careening into the lake, the splash loud and jarring. She closed the tab.

Several searches about life insurance told her that even if a child was named beneficiary to a life insurance policy, there needed to be an adult custodian and/or guardian named— someone who would be the keeper of the money until the minor was of age, as well as someone who would be the child's caretaker if the parent were to die before the child was legal. Often the custodian and guardian were the same person.

"If Chloe had been named the beneficiary, who was named guardian? Frank seems clueless. Sean wouldn't have been keeping tabs on Chloe all this time, only to snatch her when she was a week from being legal if *he* had been named the guardian," Amber said.

"What about her aunt … Lilith's sister?" Edgar asked.

"Karen Reed," Amber said slowly. "But as far as I've been able to tell, Chloe didn't even know she *had* an aunt—and if she did, she figured that out very recently. Why would Karen stay out of Chloe's life if she'd been named guardian?"

Edgar shrugged helplessly. "Maybe that PI friend of yours would know. If the lady was just a callous jerk like Sean, she wouldn't put in all this money to help find Chloe, right?"

Amber grabbed her cell phone off her bed and dialed Alan. He answered almost immediately. "Peterson."

"Hi. It's Amber Blackwood."

"I know," he said. "What's up?"

She told him her life insurance theory, as well as dropping the name "Sean Merrill" to see if Alan had ever heard of him. He hadn't.

"Has Karen given you any indication that she's been named Chloe's guardian?" Amber asked.

Alan sounded truly perplexed as he said, "No. The impression I got is that someone got in contact with her about three weeks ago—so a little over a week before Chloe went missing—and said, 'You should keep a better eye on your niece. She's not safe in Edgehill.' Karen hadn't ever heard of Edgehill, let alone know anything about her niece. Then a week later, she goes missing. She called me the day of and said something like, 'Someone in Edgehill, Oregon, kidnapped Chloe Deidrick. I need you to find her. I was warned a week ago that something would happen to her and I thought it was a hoax. Now she's missing.' Then she muttered something under her breath to the effect of, 'Dang it, Lilith. This is a lot of responsibility for someone I've never met.'"

"What does Lilith have to do with it?" Amber asked.

"Karen has been very sparse on the details. Without you, I probably still wouldn't know her name," Alan said. "There's more she's not telling me, but I don't know what. Maybe she's as scared of Sean Merrill as Frank is. If Sean was the one who put in the warning phone call to Karen, he did it for a reason. He wanted Chloe on her radar. We have to figure out why."

Amber mulled that over for a moment. "Oh! I have one more thing for you. I know a kid who's active on Scuttle and he thinks he's narrowed down the Sean handle to four. I figured you could do your own research into those to see if there's one that sticks out to you as suspicious?"

"That would be great," he said.

She disconnected the call after she rattled off the four names. When she looked at Edgar, she found him watching her, his head cocked.

"What?" she asked, her cheeks heating for some reason.

"You aren't a relentless pest with just me, huh?" Then his expression softened. "Chloe is lucky to have someone like you looking out for her."

"Thanks," she said. "I just hope we can find her."

Edgar went home half an hour later and suggested that they skip Sunday's breakfast next week since he'd need at least two weeks to recover from today's double venture into town. Amber hadn't told him yet, but she planned to get him out of the house on Saturday for the Hair Ball. She would need to do it soon; she couldn't imagine Edgar Henbane had anything in his closet that remotely resembled "formal wear." Neither of them was skilled enough at glamour spells to create something that could last him all evening, either.

Amber shuddered at the thought of having to escort Edgar on a shopping trip. If he was grumpy now, how awful would he be after trying on his third pair of slacks?

The following day, Amber dropped by the station during her lunch break to give the chief the license plate number she found in her vision, as well as tell him about her life insurance idea. She could have called him last night but hadn't wanted to bug him at such a late hour when there was a new baby in the house—especially when his wife had heard the affair rumors.

Amber waved at Dolores as Amber walked past her desk, but stopped dead in her tracks when she heard, "He's in a meeting." Amber slowly turned toward Sour Face; these were the first words she'd ever said directly *to* Amber. Without looking at her, nor halting her typing, Dolores said, "Wait in the lobby and he'll be with you shortly."

Immediately turning around, Amber plopped down on the saggy couch in the lobby. The water cooler gave a *glug* in greeting. Twenty minutes later, the chief, Carl, and Garcia emerged down the hall from the chief's office. The trio talked for another minute, then the two officers headed for the front door, waving at Amber as they went.

The chief made eye contact with Amber, squinted slightly, and said, "C'mon back, Miss Blackwood."

Once they were in his office and he closed the door behind him, Amber started in right away. "Are you in contact with Karen Reed? Alan thinks she's hiding—"

"Who is Alan?"

Amber winced, forgetting that the chief didn't know about her alliance with the PI. "What?"

"Amber, don't play coy. You know I don't like that."

"Alan Peterson the PI?" she said, one eye squinting slightly. "We're kind of ... sharing intel."

The chief just stared at her.

"I didn't tell you because I knew you'd get mad!"

He released a slow, controlled breath out of his nose. "Coronary."

"Karen Reed is who hired Alan," Amber said, explaining what little Alan knew about his client. "What we can't figure out is why Sean essentially warned Karen about the kidnapping. Why did he want her to start looking into Chloe's disappearance?"

The chief chewed on his bottom lip for a moment, then slid his attention to his computer and keyed in a few things. Then he plucked his phone out of its cradle, dialed a number, and pressed the receiver to his ear. After a minute, he said, "Hello, Karen Reed. This is Owen Brown, chief of police in Edgehill, Oregon. I have a few questions I wanted to ask you. If you could call me back at your earliest convenience, that would be greatly appreciated."

Once he had relayed his number and hung up, Amber told him about her vision and fished a piece of paper out of her purse that had Sean's license plate written on it. "It's from eighteen years ago, so who knows how many other cars he's had since then, but maybe this will help get you DMV records?"

The chief nodded, picking up the paper. "Thanks, this could be really—"

He was interrupted by his phone ringing. He hit a button and said, "Hi, Dolores."

"I have a Karen Reed on the line for you, sir," came the woman's gravelly reply through the phone's speakers.

"Put her through." After hitting another button, he said,

"Hi, Karen, this is Chief Brown. Thank you for calling back so quickly."

"No problem," the woman said, her voice ringing out in the room. "I was glad to hear from you. Is ... is there any news about Chloe?"

"We're chasing down several leads," the chief said. "What I wanted to ask you about is related to your sister Lilith. Would that be okay?"

The pause was long. "Sure," came the soft reply. "I don't know how much help I'll be, though."

"What can you tell me about Sean Merrill?"

Karen let out a sharp, short laugh. "Wow, I haven't heard that name in years. He was someone Lilith dated for a while in her twenties. A cop, if I remember. I think he may have been abusive, but Lilith didn't really talk to me about him. She'd never been very good about keeping up with family. Once she left after high school, it was a miracle if she showed up for holidays. Just a really flighty person. Years went by without me knowing where she'd been—and then I get a call that she was ... that she'd died."

However bitter Karen was, the fact that she still loved her sister was evident in the way her voice broke on that last word.

"When did you find out she'd had Chloe?" he asked.

"Not until after Lilith died," Karen said, bitterness creeping back in. "I got a letter in the mail letting me know I was both the custodian and personal guardian of Chloe Deidrick and her assets, as Chloe was the sole beneficiary of a life insurance policy, but she couldn't make a claim on it until she was eighteen. Lilith left me in charge of Chloe's money, yet I didn't know until that letter that Chloe even existed."

"Why haven't you tried to find her if you're her guardian?" Amber asked before she realized she was going to say the words out loud. Her eyes widened.

The chief shot her a pointed look. "That's my associate, Cassie Westbottom. She's a consultant on the case."

"I don't mean to sound judgmental," Amber said now in Cassie's voice. "We're just trying to figure out who Chloe's inner circle is and who she's been in contact with."

"Lilith had a will in addition to the life insurance policy. In it, she asked that I not contact Chloe until she was eighteen," Karen said. "She said Chloe was safe with her adoptive father, Frank Deidrick, and she didn't want Chloe's childhood to be tainted with the truth of her parentage. That was her phrase, not mine: 'truth of parentage.' She said it was vital that I let Chloe live her life blissfully unaware, and that if I ever cared about her, then I would do this for her. She didn't explain herself beyond that but that was just how Lilith was—very private until she needed something. Even when it was her family."

Amber mulled this over.

"If I can ask …" Karen said, "what does Sean have to do with Chloe and her disappearance?" The slight quaver to her voice made it clear she already had a pretty good guess.

"Sean is Chloe's biological father," the chief said. "And he was, in fact, abusive. So much so that it's what made Lilith change her name and essentially go into hiding. She distanced herself from her family to protect them and Chloe from Sean."

Karen let out a choked sob. Her voice was very soft when she asked, "Did he kill her? Lilith, I mean?"

Amber watched the chief's face as he clearly debated how to answer this.

"We think so, yes," he finally said.

Another sob. "And is he who has Chloe now?"

The chief sighed. "He's on the top of our list of suspects, yes."

"Oh my God," Karen whimpered. "That poor girl." Then she gasped. "Is that who called me to tell me Chloe was in trouble?"

"It's possible," he said. "Do you have any idea why he would have called you to tip you off?"

"I didn't have any clue until just now ..." Karen paused for so long, the chief looked up at Amber and shrugged. "If Sean really *did* kill Lilith, my guess is he thought *he* was on the policy as the beneficiary. You can't name a minor without there being a guardian listed, and by then, Lilith had cut herself off from family, so he probably thought he was a sure bet as to who was listed—maybe she *told* him he was the beneficiary and he was operating under incorrect information. When she died, he wasn't notified about benefits—I was—so he must have realized then that he hadn't been named. When he called me, he asked, 'Are you Chloe Deidrick's guardian?' He'd sounded so formal, I thought maybe it was the police—I mean who else would know I was Chloe's guardian, when Lilith made me promise from the great beyond that I would keep this secret to myself? So I said yes and asked where she was and if she was okay. He said, 'She's in Edgehill' and from my reaction, it was clear I had no idea where that was. Then he told me she was in danger and hung up. Do you suppose he knew I would try to find her once I knew she was in trouble?"

"Maybe," Amber said. "Perhaps he'd been hoping you'd come to Edgehill personally so he could go after you instead. It seems like he'd figured out along the way that you're the one listed as Chloe's guardian. He could have been trying to lure you here—you're unfamiliar with the town; you confirmed that for him. Maybe he assumed you would have been worried enough that you'd drop everything to come find her, possibly leaving your family behind. You'd be in a new place without your support system. Hiring a PI might have been a really good call for your own safety."

"Is it … it *my* fault he took Chloe?" Karen asked, her voice strained. "He called me several days *before* he took Chloe. Did he take her instead of me because she was a closer target?"

"None of this is anyone's fault but Sean's," the chief said. "Do *not* blame yourself for any of this. You abided by your late sister's wishes *and* you made a really smart call in sending in someone experienced to investigate the situation. Sean is *not* the type of man a civilian should interact with."

The chief shot a pointed look at Amber when he said that last part. As if Amber wanted anything to do with the man. The snippet of memory she'd seen of Sean with his flat eyes had been more than enough for her.

Karen cried softly.

Frowning to himself, the chief said, "You've been very helpful, Mrs. Reed. If he contacts you again in any way, please let me know. Or if you think of anything that might help us find Chloe."

"I will," she said, sniffling. "Thank you for calling me."

The chief cradled the phone and leaned back in his chair, arms crossed. He and Amber sat in his quiet office, each staring off in different directions. The reality of the situation sunk in. A father had kidnapped his own daughter because of money. He didn't care about her well-being, nor did he care that the man who had raised her was worried sick about her.

"Even though Isabelle is only days old, I already know I would move heaven and earth for that girl," the chief said softly. "I knew it the moment I saw her. How can Sean do this to Chloe? How could he even *think* it, let alone do it? I've seen horrible things on this job, but the crimes parents inflict on their children are always the hardest to wrap my mind around."

What Amber feared most was what Sean would do once he got the money he wanted. He'd run Lilith off the road when he decided that she would be more beneficial to him dead than alive. A woman who had helped him get back on his feet after he'd been shot, had dropped out of school, and given up on her dreams when his medical bills had overwhelmed them, and who had given him a beautiful little girl.

What would he do to his daughter once she'd served her purpose?

CHAPTER 19

The next two days were filled with so many Hair Ball preparations that Amber only had time to worry about Chloe in the evenings, and even then, she was often hard at work on the remainder of her tiny plastic cats. By the time she flopped into bed, she was asleep almost as soon as her head hit the pillow.

The Here and Meow Committee, even with Francine Robins on board, was made up of five people trying to do the job of ten. They were in charge of everything from making sure they had everything the Best of Edgehill participants needed—while also keeping them on schedule—answering emails from gala attendees, ordering all the decorations, finding enough help to set up the day of, coordinating with all the volunteers—many of whom were high school students—to making sure they knew what to do on the day of the gala, and planning the rehearsal gala for Friday night so they could perfect everything before the actual gala on Saturday.

Amber, Kim, and Francine had to make a road trip into Salem on Wednesday to pick up the new tablecloths—eggshell white this time—which saved them a small fortune in delivery costs. After they stuffed the back of Francine's SUV with the correct cloths, they went out for dinner. Kim and Francine got quite toasted on appletinis and were such a goofy, giggly mess, Amber suggested they walk it off a bit before getting back into the car.

Kim and Francine had an arm linked on either side of Amber now, the two women chatting about their failed love lives.

"I have a confession!" Kim said. "I've been in love with Nathan since high school."

Amber was so shocked by the news that she came up short, causing Kim to whirl around a few inches. Kim laughed.

"Wait. *Our* Nathan?" Amber asked. "Married to Jolene, Nathan?"

Kim tossed her head back, staring at the dark sky. "Yes. Ugh, that Jolene! She's so cool and perfect for Nathan and a total sweetheart. I want to hate her, but I can't." Kim tugged on Amber's arm to get the three of them moving down the sidewalk again. "Did you know that the night they met, Nathan was supposed to go out with *me*?"

"No!" Francine said with a level of indignation only possible after four appletinis.

"Yes!" said Kim, leaning forward a bit so she could look at Francine. "I had the hugest, hugest crush on him in high school. We were also best friends for most of junior and senior year. Like hang-out-most-nights kind of best friends. I was sure we were both just too scared to ruin our friendship with romance, so we were holding back. But, ladies? I pined for him so hard. Wrote poetry and everything. Ugh. So much poetry. Thankfully he's never seen any of it.

"Anyhoo! I finally got up the nerve one day to ask him out. On, you know, a date, date. I couldn't believe it when he said yes. I mean, I could tell he was a little nervous about it, but I figured that was normal since we were so close and we'd be crossing a major line. I had every intention of sticking my tongue *all the way down* that throat of his at the end of the night."

Amber and Francine erupted in laughter.

Kim shot them a goofy smile.

"What *happened*?" Francine asked.

"The night of, I got … uhh … how do you say … I had a very unpleasant stomach situation happen and I had to call him from the bathroom floor and tell him I couldn't make it because I was pretty sure all my organs were trying to leave my body at once."

"Oh no!" Amber said, laughing.

"I *know*. Mortifying," Kim said. "We were supposed to go to this old-school arcade together, and he ended up going by himself because he was bored. And, that night, he met Jolene and basically fell in love with her instantly." Kim fake-wailed as she walked. "I think that's why I told Chloe to just go for it when it came to that guy. You never know what the future holds, you know? If I'd said screw it, I'm going to this stupid arcade even if I'm pale as a ghost and sweating like a pig and need a bathroom every ten seconds, maybe I would be the one married to Nathan right now."

"Maybe," said Amber. "But if he was really the one for you, he'd have come to your house to take care of you while your organs were trying to make their exit. Nathan is totally the kind of a guy to hold your hair while you heave. Jolene told me as much."

Kim sighed. "And I *know* that. If Nathan and I really had a shot, it would have already happened. But even if I know it logically, my heart can't seem to let him go."

"Unrequited love is the literal worst," Francine said. "And I had two cases of it in a matter of a year! But … I don't know … I think you were right to tell Chloe to go for it. If you don't at least *try* at love, you'll never find it."

"True," Kim said.

"Sometimes when you try, you get burned anyway, though," Amber said.

"Also true!" said Kim. "But that's why I have you two. Who needs silly men anyway?"

"Amen!" they chorused in unison.

They had just made it back to the car, Kim and Francine a little more sober now, when Amber's phone rang. The other two women clambered into the car, still laughing and chatting, while Amber stayed outside and answered.

"Hey, Alan."

When Kim and Francine offered wolf whistles in reply to Amber saying a man's name, she rolled her eyes and walked farther away.

"Sorry," she said. "How's it going?"

"Does your cop buddy know Sean Merrill has an alibi for the night Chloe was kidnapped?" he asked.

Amber didn't know if the chief knew that. What she did know was that someone other than Sean had snatched Chloe that night—a man paid to grab the girl. Alan, however, didn't know that though and she couldn't tell him. "I'm not sure. Where was he?"

"Portland," Alan said. "He left Missoula, Montana, a month ago, and has been in Portland ever since. Working at a gas station, just like he did in Montana. He's been coming into work every day since he started three weeks ago. He usually works five to six days a week. It's at least a three-hour drive from Edgehill. The night Chloe was taken, Sean was working from five to midnight, and the next day he was back in by six and worked until noon."

It was a solid alibi, one that very likely could get the guy off the suspect list—or at least shove him further down. The one thing about this hired hand that had never sat well with Amber, though, was that he had to know Edgehill well enough to find Blue Point Lane. That street was notorious for not showing up on GPS.

If it was true that the hastily planned search for Chloe on Saturday morning had been part of Sean's plan to get Chloe out of town undetected, that would also require knowledge of the area. Which Sean didn't have. Was the hired hand a local?

"Is he in a house or an apartment?" Amber asked Alan now.

"Apartment," Alan said. "Tiny place on the second floor. If he's got her there, he'd have to keep her in a closet—assuming a place this small even *has* a closet."

"Wait," she said. "Are you in Portland *now*?"

"Parked across the street from his place," Alan said. "I called in some favors to find as much about Sean Merrill as possible after our last talk. Been watching him since I got here this afternoon. All he does is work. Haven't seen anything strange in his behavior yet."

Amber slumped. Were they wrong about Sean Merrill being the kidnapper? "Thanks for the call," she said. "Let me know if anything changes."

"Same goes for you." He ended the call.

When Amber got back to the car, Kim and Francine immediately stopped talking. The inside of the car smelled like an appletini.

Kim was in the passenger seat and turned toward Amber. "Everything okay? Was it the chief? Was it about Chloe?"

"So you and the chief really *are* buddy-buddy?" Francine asked.

"Oh yes!" said Kim, nodding vigorously. "Amber is basically a consultant on the case now because she's a master detective and she's even friends with a private investigator!"

Amber cut her gaze to Kim in a manner that she hoped conveyed, "*You are* terrible *at keeping secrets, Kimberly Jones.*"

Kim clapped a hand over her mouth. "Oops," she said, her voice muffled.

Francine laughed. "A master detective *and* a fairy godmother. Even though I didn't know her well, Amber somehow found the perfect fit for me with the Here and Meow Committee after I got fired."

"Yeah!" said Kim. "Amber, she's, like, a wizard; thank you so much for finding her for us! Thanks to Miss Robins' fancy math skills, we have a solid financial plan in place to be able to afford John Huntley to perform at the festival this year. We're going to make *bank* if his hot country butt comes to play for us."

Amber snorted, then met Francine's gaze in the rearview mirror. "Frank was a dummy to let you go."

Francine grinned.

Amber was roused from a very deep sleep by the sound of her cell phone ringing. She lurched awake in her dark apartment, then searched for her phone. It wasn't charging on her nightstand. She saw a faint outline of a blue rectangle under her comforter and groped groggily in the sea of twisted sheets and blankets until she found it.

It was 4:15 a.m.

And the chief was calling her.

Amber's stomach dropped into her feet.

"Hello?"

"Hi, Amber," the chief said, with what sounded like wind in the background. "I've been working with some colleagues in Portland and we've got reason to believe Sean is there. They got a call into the station an hour ago from your friend Alan Peterson that Sean left his apartment at three a.m. and went to a house that's currently for sale. Alan looked the house up and realized it's been on the market for three months, but there's no sign out front. Garcia and I are headed there now."

"Oh my God," Amber said, sitting bolt upright.

"Just wanted you to know," he said. "I'll keep you updated."

Amber couldn't sleep for the rest of the night.

CHAPTER 20

It seemed that all of Edgehill was abuzz that Thursday. It marked both two weeks since Chloe had disappeared and the day that Chief Brown had raced off to Portland in the middle of the night to hopefully rescue the girl. Edgehill residents came into the Quirky Whisker with speculation about everything from the involvement of the FBI to the possibility that Johnny from Scuttle was the leader of a group who stole young girls for nefarious purposes.

Amber hadn't heard anything from the chief or Alan Peterson since five that morning and her nerves were shot both from worry and lack of sleep.

Just like every day that week, Amber ran the shop until noon, then passed the torch onto the Bowen sisters so she could help Kim with more Here and Meow duties. With the rehearsal gala happening the next day, there was still a lot of preparation needed at the community center. Amber had only ten plastic cats left to create and had a box of completed ones in her car to drop off at the center later.

Her first task of the day was to pick up the rest of the centerpieces from Grace Williams at Hiss and Hers. Amber was halfway there when Kim called her. She hit a button on her rental car's steering wheel and said, "Hey, Kim. I'm on my way to Hiss and Hers right now. I promise I'll be there soon."

"Oh, forget about that. I have a huge favor!" she said. "I'm stuck at the florist for a bit longer than I planned—the sample arrangement they showed me earlier was nearly all muted blues and purples even though I very specifically said I wanted cheery spring colors. I'm trying not to become Galazilla again. I've got a bunch of deep breathing exercises I'm working on."

Amber laughed. "So what's the favor?"

"Francine has a bunch of glass vases she said we can borrow," Kim said. "We need a couple for displays. Can you grab them from her house? She's got a hair appointment she has to leave for in an hour and I'm not going to make it there in time."

"Yep, no problem," Amber said.

"Ah! You're such a doll," Kim said. "We all need to go out for dinner in the city again when this gala madness is over. I had so much fun the other night. It'll be my treat!"

The call disconnected before Amber could reply.

Amber got across town to Francine's house much faster in her rental car than she had on her bike. When she pulled up out front, one of Francine's Siamese cats was perched in the window again. This time, when Amber walked up the front walk, the cat didn't dart for cover.

Francine pulled the door open before Amber had a chance to knock. "Oh, hey!" she said. "I was expecting Kim a bit later; I don't have the box packed up quite yet."

Amber stepped into the front entryway. "Kim is stuck at the florist for a while so she sent me instead. And no hurry; I can wait."

"Okay, I just need to box them up. They're scattered in the back room and the garage," Francine said. "Feel free to hang out in the living room and watch TV. Help yourself to anything in the fridge." Then she hurried through the rightmost archway.

Amber dropped her purse onto the forest green cushion on the bench seat and wandered through the left archway. The living room, with its elegant white leather couch and two wingback chairs, was tidy now. No clothes were piled on the floor or on the sofa. The coffee table was devoid of everything except for a small stack of coasters, the glass surface gleaming. Amber made her way across the room, passed into the dining room, and then turned right into a spotless modern kitchen.

The kitchen floor was made of grayish brown hardwood, the cabinets were a slate gray with gleaming silver knobs and handles, and a white marble island sat in the middle of the room. A white tile backsplash lined the wall behind the stainless steel sink.

It took Amber a moment to realize that the doors of the refrigerator had been modeled to match the sleek cabinets. She pulled one open and found a bottle of water. As she drank, she noticed that the side of the fridge was covered in pictures and magnets—the only truly personal touch added to the pristine room. There were photograph Christmas cards featuring smiling families with kids and pets, engagement announcements of happy couples on a bench or posed in the middle of a field or on the end of a pier, and wedding invitations. There were school pictures of children that might have been nieces or nephews. And then, wedged underneath several photos, was a tan-colored card with a black ribbon looped through a hole in the top. Something about it was vaguely familiar; a magnet covered the words.

Amber removed the card and as she read the words, her mouth dropped open.

"*To my Kitty Cat, you make every day brighter. Love, Snugglebear.*"

It was the exact same message that Johnny had supposedly written on the card he was going to give Chloe along with half a dozen roses, the night of the storm. *Why the heck did* Francine *have this?*

Amber pulled out her phone and shot a glance through the doorway of the kitchen. Francine was still busy collecting the necessary items, so Amber took a quick picture of the card and sent it to Kim, along with the message, *Kim! Did Chloe ever show you this?*

She tucked her phone into her pocket, affixed the card back onto the fridge, and quickly made her way toward the front entryway. She had to get out of here. She didn't know what Francine had to do with all of this, but Amber didn't want to stick around to find out.

Heart in her throat, she hurried into the front entryway, only to find her purse on the ground, and half of the tan body of a Siamese cat sticking out of it.

"Shoo!" Amber said softly, startling the cat who jumped at the sound. In the cat's haste to escape, her head got caught in one of the purse's straps. Being tangled freaked the poor cat out even further, and it started to thrash around. While Amber did her best to calm the cat so she could free it, she tried to listen for Francine. The cat yowled.

"Minnie?" Francine called from the other room. "Is that you? Did you get stuck in a cabinet again?"

Oh goodness. Should she just she leave her purse here and flee?

The cat yowled again, and during the course of her melt-down, she bucked so violently that the purse collided with the various odds and ends stuffed precariously into the middle cubby of the bench seat Amber's purse had previously been lying on. Everything jammed inside came spilling out. Minnie gave another great yowl, but managed to free herself in the chaos, and darted away, claws scrabbling on the tile entryway.

Amber winced and was about to push the objects back in but stilled when her hand closed around a pointy object wrapped in plastic. The heel of a stiletto shoe. Which wasn't odd in and of itself, but both shoes in the bag were caked in mud. They were made of black and red fabric and were elaborately strappy things. The same shoes Amber had noticed Francine wearing at the Sippin' Siamese the night the Here and Meow Committee had gone to happy hour. The shoes were so caked, Amber doubted they were salvageable. In addition to the flakes of mud at the bottom of the bag were a few dried catkins—like the ones that hung from the trees near the location where Chloe's car had been found.

"Sorry that took so long!" Francine called out. But her good cheer died the moment she saw the bag hanging from one of Amber's fingers. "What are you doing?"

"These are the shoes you were wearing the night Chloe went missing," Amber said, her heart rate ratcheting up even further. "Why are they covered in mud?"

Francine stared at Amber with her lips pressed into a thin line. "The storm was bad that night. Must have stepped in mud on the way to my car."

There were only cement and gravel parking lots near the Sippin' Siamese.

"You left early that night," Amber said. "Did you come back here with the hot cowboy?"

"Yep." She still held the box of vases. Her eyes were flat, her voice even more so.

Amber's phone buzzed in her back pocket. She pulled it out, needing an excuse to look away from Francine's dead-eyed expression.

A text from Kim was on the screen.

What the eff?! Is that on Francine's fridge? Why does SHE have that?

"Everything okay?" Francine asked.

When Amber looked up, Francine was a bit closer than she had been a moment before. "Yep! Is this everything Kim needed?" Amber flung her purse over her shoulder, then grabbed for the box, wrapping her arms around it. Francine relinquished it with little fuss. "Kim says thanks."

Amber had just turned for the door when she felt her phone forcefully pulled from her pocket. The message from Kim was still there; Amber hadn't opened the text thread yet. Before Amber could whirl around, Francine grabbed Amber by the shoulder and spun her around.

"Don't you need this?" she asked, waving the phone in Amber's face. "Without this, you can't tell your cop pal that I knew Johnny."

Amber swallowed. "Did you help him kidnap Chloe?"

Francine's eyes welled with tears. The look told Amber that Francine was working through what to do about this little development, and Amber didn't think whatever Francine was going to decide on would be in Amber's best interest.

Amber thrust the box of vases at Francine, who, startled, instinctively reached out to grab it. While she was distracted, Amber pivoted for the door. A thud and crash and then an arm went around Amber's neck, Francine's bent elbow just below Amber's chin. Francine *squeezed*.

"You can't tell him!" Francine hissed in Amber's ear.

The memory of Kieran's magic closing around Amber's neck was still too fresh. The nightmares were too persistent, never letting her forget how scared she'd been. Francine's arm around Amber's throat pulled all that fear back to the surface.

No.

Amber threw her weight into Francine, who stumbled back, the circular throw rug beneath them slipping as the two women struggled to throw the other off. They hit the ground.

Somehow, Francine still had a tight grip on Amber's neck, one hand used to steady the crook of Francine's elbow against Amber's throat. With Amber's back flush with Francine's chest, Amber felt like she was in a boxing ring, though she didn't think Francine would let go of her if Amber tried to tap out.

Black seeped into Amber's vision. No. No, this couldn't be happening to her again.

Kieran's voice echoed in her head. *Give me the book, Blackwood!*

Amber flung her body to the side in a sudden, violent

jerk and wildly flung her arms out, happy to hit any part of Francine if it meant she'd let her go. Amber bucked and kicked and flailed her arms and *whack*. Pain shot through Amber's elbow, up her forearm, and made her fingers twitch. Francine cursed and suddenly Amber could breathe again. She got to her hands and knees and took in great heaving breaths. Her magic was an out of control storm, a hurricane, a tornado. She flicked her gaze up and found Francine with a palm pressed against an eye. Amber hoped she'd given Francine a black eye. Amber wanted to do a lot worse.

"You'll ruin everything!" Francine growled and lunged.

No.

Amber flung her hands out just as the front door to Francine's house opened. Magic shot out of Amber's hands like a gale-force wind and lifted Francine clear off her feet and sent her sailing several feet off the ground before she hit the ground and slid across the hallway.

"Oh, holy smokes!"

Amber whirled around to find a slack-jawed Kimberly Jones standing in the doorway.

"You … you …" Kim said, gaze darting from Amber to Francine's prone form in the hallway and back to Amber again. "You … you …"

Oh, this couldn't possibly go well. "Kim …"

Kim kicked broken glass out of the way and quickly closed the door, pressing her back against the wood. She visibly swallowed. Amber was almost positive Kim hadn't blinked.

Amber's chest heaved. She was more concerned at this moment that the power behind that blast of magic might have been enough to stop Francine's heart than she was about Kim. But Amber would likely need to deal with Kim's screaming once her adrenaline wore off. "What are you doing here?" was all Amber could think to say.

"Oh my God, Amber," Kim said, coming back to herself. "That picture you sent me! Chloe told me so many times that Johnny calls her Kitty Cat and he calls himself Snugglebear. What are the odds? I was so freaked out about it that I just rushed over here."

There was a groan from behind them and Amber and Kim jumped and whirled toward the hallway. Francine pushed herself to sitting and rested her back against a wall.

Amber was still so angry and her throat hurt and she needed to know what on earth Francine's connection was to all of this. She stalked toward the disoriented woman and squatted in front of her; Francine flinched away. If Francine wasn't clearly in so much pain, Amber was sure she would have run screaming from the house already. Amber lowered her voice so only Francine could hear her. "Tell me everything and I promise I'll consider *not* tossing you across the room again."

Francine swallowed, shying away from Amber a fraction. Mentally, Amber uttered the truth spell she'd been using so much lately, grabbed hold of Francine's forearm—her magic singing from the contact—and then asked, "What role did you play in Chloe Deidrick's kidnapping, Francine Robins?"

"It was all indirect," Francine said, eyes widening as she realized her mouth was working without her permission.

Amber stood, towering over the woman.

Kim gasped, joining them in the hallway, though it looked

as if she was warring between staying or bolting out the front door.

With her head resting against the wall, Francine let out a dejected sigh and said, "I got fooled by 055BelHavenGuy, too—just like Chloe did. At the start of Frank's campaign, he wanted a tutorial on social media. We hit on all the major ones, but he wanted to know how Scuttle worked too. I didn't really know myself, but I knew it was big with the younger crowd, so I created an account. I didn't realize until later that anonymity was what users went for on there, so I posted my actual photo and bio on the site. My Belhaven guy started chatting with me almost right away. He said his name was Johnny and that he thought I was beautiful." She snorted derisively. "After almost a year of talking, we met in person in Portland; he claimed he had a job out there. He gave me flowers; he was really sweet. And we got along great, just as we did in messages, but I didn't have that romantic spark with him, you know?"

Francine raised her brows hopefully in Kim's direction, subtly trying to remind her of the times that they'd bonded over their dating woes. Kim's expression was hard and her arms were folded tight across her chest.

Francine frowned slightly and brought her focus back to Amber. "Johnny said he could tell I was hung up on someone else. We still talked all the time after that; he became one of my closest friends. I told him ... everything. About my job, Frank, Chloe ... and confessed my feelings for Frank.

"After a while, he told me he was an undercover journalist working on an explosive series of stories about corrupt politicians. He said he was drawn to me because of my connection to the mayor. He admitted that at first, he'd just been using me for intel, but once we became such close friends, he confided in me about his research into Frank. He told me Frank wasn't who I thought he was and that he was worried for me because Frank was potentially dangerous. He dropped Shannon Pritchard's name in conversation one day, then mentioned a rumor about hush money payments the next. Johnny's the one who tipped me off to the very thing that ended up getting me fired. But I think he wanted that. He wanted me ticked off and heartbroken so that when he needed me to go through with my part of the plan, I would." She laughed. "I'm so stupid."

"What did you *do*?" Kim asked, more bewildered than anything.

"Johnny—whatever his real name is—convinced me that Frank killed his long-time girlfriend Shannon, but was never caught, and that the hush money payments he was making were to a witness," Francine said.

"You told me you didn't have any idea what the payments were for," Amber said.

"By the time you came to talk to me, that was true again," said Francine. "Chloe was gone. I knew Johnny had lied about nearly everything. I was such a mess that day you came to talk to me. I didn't know what to think. I was in love with Frank, and I knew he adored Chloe, but there was something so fishy about his past, regardless of what Johnny had told me. Johnny had planted a seed of doubt and it was growing like crazy."

Amber still wasn't sure how this all resulted in Francine's

shoes being covered with mud. She knew she had to be patient; Francine was on a roll now, either coerced by the magic still, or by her own guilt, Amber couldn't be sure.

"The night of Chloe's disappearance, Johnny messaged me and thanked me for all my help. He said he had a colleague who was in town and based on everything I'd told him, this so-called colleague had been able to find and interview Chloe for the story, which would make it an even more powerful piece. He said once the explosive exposé hit shelves, he'd give me a finder's fee of sorts since his contact never would have been able to find Chloe without me." Francine wrung her hands. "I'd still been at the bar when I got that message and something in my gut told me something very bad had happened.

"Frank sent me a text that night asking if I'd seen or talked to Chloe—you two were still at the bar. I drove right from the bar down Blue Point Lane since I know her best friend lives down that street. I found her car before you two did."

Amber gaped at her.

"I went walking around that whole area calling for her. Got a few feet into all those trees and bushes. It was dumping buckets by then and I almost rolled my ankle half a dozen times in those dang shoes," Francine said. "I knew it was all my fault. I'd basically given this Johnny guy a blueprint of Edgehill because of how much I talked about it and pictures I'd sent him, thinking I was just sharing my town with a friend. I'd willingly given this guy everything he needed to know about Frank and Chloe. I went home before you two found her car. And then the next day, and the days after that, Chloe was just … gone. I knew I'd irrevocably screwed up then. I helped Chloe get kidnapped even if he had a hired goon do the snatching."

"You didn't turn any of this over to the police?" Amber asked.

Francine shook her head. "I was in so deep. He said he'd been keeping screenshots of our conversations and since I was stupid enough to have a handle that was Francine103R—I mean I used the freaking area code of Edgehill in my name!—I figured it could be pretty easy to prove it's me given how many dang selfies I sent him. He said he could send all the screenshots in anonymously to the police and no one would know where they came from, but I'd be implicated.

"I didn't know how I'd be able to prove any of this from my side. Even though we talked for a year, I don't even know his real name. I don't know what he really wants from Chloe or who he is. There are all these rumors about Johnny being the leader of a sex ring or something! What if I did something to completely ruin Chloe's life? All I know is that he's a con artist and I fell for every one of his lies."

Amber merely stared at her.

"Are you going to press charges?" Francine asked, her chin quivering, as if she was fighting the urge to cry. "I probably should have thought of that before I attacked a friend of the chief of police. I just … I freaked out."

"You *should* be freaked out," Kim said. "The whole town's been losing its mind over this and you never once told anyone you were involved with the guy!"

"Amber showed up here like some kind of angel!" Francine

said, waving a hand in Amber's general direction. "I've felt so isolated here and then I suddenly had friends and a project to lose myself in and I didn't want to ruin that."

Amber couldn't say she didn't know what all of that felt like, but Francine staying quiet could have resulted in things going much worse for Chloe. It still wasn't clear what the girl's fate was, after all.

"Why did you call him Snugglebear?" Amber asked.

Francine turned beet red. "How do you know about that?"

"I saw the card on your fridge."

Sighing, she said, "I made it up. He said he was from Belhaven and he'd been a Belhaven Bear many years ago. Somehow from there, I made up the nickname."

Amber told Francine that Sean had sent a picture of that same card to Chloe, claiming he was going to give her the bouquet the night they met.

Francine winced. "God, that guy is sick. He's sick and I'm an idiot for falling for it."

Amber wanted to say that this kind of thing probably happened to women—and likely quite a few men—all the time. Alan had said that predatory men targeted children through apps like Scuttle; the idea that men like Sean with even worse intentions than acquiring money were out there preying on the young and vulnerable made Amber's stomach twist.

In the brief silence, Francine, who was still sitting with her back pressed against the wall, cocked her head at Amber. "How did you do that earlier? I swear I was on my feet one second, then halfway down the hallway the next. I remember you lifting your hand and—"

Amber locked gazes with her and said, "Sleep."

Francine's eyes rolled back in her head and then her chin dropped to her chest. Her limbs relaxed and breathing deepened.

"Oh, holy smokes!" Kim said beside her.

Amber wasn't sure how to handle Kim. Did she really want to deal with another memory erase spell? Was her skill with memory erase even strong enough?

"Holy smokes, holy smokes!"

Slowly, Amber turned to Kim, trying to figure out the best lie to go with. Would the psychic story still work? Hypnotist?

"Are you a …" Kim swallowed, her balled fists pressed to her cheeks. She looked like a startled goldfish. "Are you a witch? Can you do … magic?"

Amber knew her skills were decent enough that she could erase these last five minutes and make Kim forget this conversation if she started screaming. "Yes."

"Oh. My. God," Kim said. She took one step back, then another, her fists still pressed to her face.

"Listen, Kim," Amber said slowly, priming her magic to dart into Kim's mind and pluck out any memory of this. "It's not—"

Kim squealed and bounced on the balls of het feet. "This is the *coolest* thing that's ever happened!"

"Wait, what?" Amber said, her magic deflating like a soufflé.

"This actually makes so much sense now," Kim said, pacing back and forth across the length of the narrow hallway. "*This* is why you're so secretive! You've been holding onto the most epic secret in the history of the *universe*. Do you have any idea how badly I wish I could do magic? It's like literally my only dream in this life. Holy smokes!" She stopped abruptly to stare at Amber with wide eyes. "Do you have a broom? Can you fly?"

Amber let out a burst of nervous laughter. "No. The chief asked that too."

"Chief *Brown* knows?"

"Yes! That's why we're together so much. Sometimes my … skills can help him out with a case when regular police methods won't work."

"Oh my God, Amber, that's so cool," she said. "And holy smokes I'm sorry I thought you were trying to hook up with him. This is so much better. Also, you two need a TV show."

"Right! I keep trying to suggest that, but he thinks I'm loopy."

Kim stared at Amber now with a giddy sort of delight that was downright unsettling.

"Kimberly, you can't—can *not*—tell anyone about this."

"I won't!" she said, holding up two fingers. "Scouts honor."

"You blurted things to Francine within a couple of days!"

"I was tipsy on appletinis!" Kim said.

Amber pursed her lips.

Kim closed the distance between them and grabbed Amber's hands, giving them a shake. "You can trust me. I promise. I'm feeling a little choked up that you told me at all. I know sharing this with people has to be a big deal and I'm glad I'm one of those people."

"Jack knew," Amber blurted.

Kim's brows shot toward her hairline. "Past tense?"

Amber nodded. "It's a long story, but yes. I can get into all the sordid details of my witch family—"

"Uhh … yes, please, and thank you. Tell me when and where and I'll bring the wine."

Smiling, Amber said, "But Jack learned even more about all this than the chief did and he couldn't handle it and asked to have his memory wiped of all of it. Which meant he couldn't really remember me, either. That's why things have been so weird between him and me lately."

Kim grunted. "Dangit, Jack Terrence. Well, just know *I* can handle it, okay? I promise."

We'll see, she wanted to say. Instead, she smiled and said, "Okay."

"What do we do about her?" Kim asked, letting Amber's hands go and turning to face the now snoring Francine.

"I'll talk to the chief when he's got a free minute. I guess I can just keep her asleep until then?"

"Maybe we should put her on her bed at least?" Kim said. "You grab her feet; I'll grab her shoulders." Then she grinned. "That's how I know we're truly friends now. Only your closest friends will help you move a body."

CHAPTER 21

Amber had just reinforced the sleep spell on Francine, who lay peacefully on her bed, when Amber's cell phone started to ring. It was coming from the front entryway, given how distant it sounded. Francine had been taunting Amber with it before the scuffle. Had it rolled under something?

Muttering a quick locator spell, she was tugged forward. She followed the sensation through Francine's bedroom, past a bathroom, and through a small library-like room before Kim had a chance to catch up with her.

"Oh!" Kim chirped from behind her. "This is like when you found Chloe's phone isn't it?"

"Locator spell," Amber said as she darted into the entryway. The contents of Amber's purse lay strewn on the floor, along with the bag of Francine's mud-caked shoes. Amber's magic helped guide her hand under the bench seat, and she did her best not to slice open her knees on the scattered shards of broken glass vases; the large box Francine had brought Amber lay on its side in the middle of the entryway.

Amber pulled out her phone just as the screen went black. She immediately called the chief back. "Hi?" she said breathlessly.

"We've got her," he said.

Amber slumped to the floor in relief, forgetting all about the glass. "Is she—"

"She's fine. Shaken up, but just fine," he said. "Sean Merrill was arrested at his job at the gas station roughly twenty minutes ago. It'll still be an hour at least before we can head back, but she's safe and she's coming home."

Amber started to cry.

Kim dropped to her knees in front of Amber. "Oh no. Are these happy tears or sad tears?"

"Happy!" Amber said, laughing and crying at the same time.

"Oh thank God!" Kim said, throwing her arms around Amber.

"Oh, and chief?" Amber said, once Kim had unhanded her. "You're going to want to talk to Francine Robins. She unknowingly is how Sean was able to get his guy into Edgehill and out again without being seen. Sean has been working a long con on Francine—also pretending to be Johnny with her—and slowly pumped her for information. I have no idea if she did anything criminal here, but she did try to choke me half to death."

"*What?*"

"She also saw me use my magic and was starting to freak out so I put her to sleep."

He went silent.

"Chief?"

"Put her to sleep like a dog or put her to sleep or ..." he whispered.

"How dare you even ask me that!"

"Call the station and have someone come out to grab her for questioning," he said. "We'll deal with the rest later."

Nodding, she said, "I'm so happy you found her."

She could hear the smile in his voice when he said, "Me too."

Later that day, when the chief had texted Amber that they would be in Edgehill within twenty minutes, Amber, Kim, Ann Marie, Nathan, Jolene, Bobby, and Betty had piled into Ann Marie's minivan with the signs they'd hastily made, and hauled tail to the mayor's house. Somehow, news of Chloe's impending arrival had spread even further than Amber's group, and people were already swarming the sidewalk and lawn in front of the house, as well as across the street. Ann Marie had to park two blocks away.

As Amber's group of eight made their way up the sidewalk, Amber saw that a parking spot was being held at the curb by Bethany Williams and several of her friends directly in front of the house.

Armed with their "Welcome Home!" signs, Amber's group stood on the only open space on the front lawn they could find and chatted anxiously amongst themselves. Bethany turned to Amber several times, waving at her over her shoulder.

When the chief's cruiser pulled up, Bethany and her friends hurried onto the grass. The group of four girls stood in a chain, their hands clasped.

And then Chloe was out of the car and running toward her friends. She collided with Bethany so hard, she almost knocked her friend off her feet. Chloe was then enveloped by the rest of the girls, all five of them crying. The crowd collected outside the mayoral home cheered and clapped and waved their signs.

The front door opened a few moments later and the pained cry of "Chloe?" hushed the crowd. The crying girls let Chloe go and she turned toward her house. Frank, looking no better now than he did the last time Amber saw him, staggered forward a few steps as if waking from a dream. The crowd amassed on the lawn and front path parted, allowing father and daughter to finally see each other.

"Dad!" Chloe cried.

They ran for each other, slamming into a tight embrace in the middle of the pathway. They were both crying and saying, "I'm sorry. I'm so sorry" over and over. Kim burst into tears. Amber wrapped an arm around her waist from one side, and Ann Marie did so from the other.

When Frank and Chloe pulled apart, he had his hands on either side of her face. "I should have talked to you. I should have told you about your mom and Sean instead of trying to protect you from everything."

"I should have talked to you, too," she said. "I'm sorry I snuck out. I just—"

"It doesn't matter," he said. "You're back now and you're safe. That's all I care about." He pulled her into another tight hug as they both dissolved into tears again.

Onlookers diverted their gaze, sniffled, and leaned on one another.

Chloe was the one who broke the embrace this time and stared up at her father. "I'm really glad to see you and everything, Dad, but oh my God, you stink!"

While the Here and Meow Committee ran through their rehearsal gala dinner on Friday night with the scores of volunteers, clothing models, stand-up acts, and actors, Francine Robins was on house arrest until the chief could figure out what to do with her. Amber decided not to press charges for the attack, but the mayor hadn't decided if he wanted to pursue legal action against her for withholding information from the police. The chief didn't think Frank would have much of a case, as very little—if any—of the conversations Sean had with Francine on Scuttle would have been logged by Scuttle itself. It was the nature of the app to be discreet, and Sean had done a great job of covering his tracks online.

Halfway through the rehearsal gala, Chloe had arrived, sneaking in the back so she could see what progress the committee had made in the two weeks she'd been gone. Someone spotted her and pulled her out into the rehearsal and the event turned into a celebration of Chloe's return. There was music, dancing, and Nathan and Jolene snuck off to order a dozen pizzas.

Amber knew that Kim was truly going to be okay when, instead of flipping out that the rehearsal had been derailed, was out in the middle of the makeshift dance floor with the kids, dancing and singing along to the music as if she didn't have a care in the world.

After so many nights of terrible sleep over the last few weeks, Amber couldn't muster up the energy to join in on the dancing. She supposed, too, that she'd been wound so tight over her worry about Chloe, that now that the girl was safe, exhaustion was truly kicking in. She sat at one of the round tables scattered throughout the room. The tablecloths were piled in a back room.

"Make them leave me alone," someone hissed in her ear then plopped down into the creaky chair beside her.

Amber grinned over at Chloe. "I'm honestly impressed you're out and about at all."

Chloe rested her forearms on the edge of the table and picked at her cuticles. The nail polish had all been scraped off by now. "After being cooped up in a place with no windows for two weeks, it's hard for me to even be in my room right now. Being around people helps. It gets a little scary in my head when I'm alone for too long or it's too quiet."

Amber turned more fully in her chair to examine Chloe's profile. "Oh, Chloe. Maybe you should see someone … a professional, I mean."

"My dad already set up an appointment for me this week," she said. "I know I haven't really processed everything yet. I mean, I've told the police—both here and in Portland—the story a billion times already, but I haven't really just sat with it myself, you know?" She finally looked at Amber then.

Bags lined the girl's eyes, her skin was paler than usual, and she had a haunted energy to her that definitely hadn't been there two weeks ago. Two weeks ago, she had been a normal seventeen-year-old girl who had a crush on a boy. Now she knew things about her parents—all of them—that she'd likely rather not know.

"I'm here, too, you know," Amber said. "Anything you need."

Chloe nodded. "I know. I heard you turned into a detective trying to find me." Her smile was small, but rueful. "Thanks."

"Of course," Amber said. "I was beating myself up over it. If it's not me being too nosy ... what happened that night between you and your dad that made you sneak off?"

Chloe wrinkled her nose. "Dad's got a temper ... I don't know if you've ever seen it. It's kind of scary. I've seen him go from happy and joking to furious in a second—over someone taking a parking spot he'd been waiting for, or someone getting his order wrong at a restaurant ... little stuff. But he's never, ever gotten mad at me like that. Until that night. I told him about Johnny and he just ... lost it. Screamed at me about breaking his one rule and that I didn't know this guy well enough to meet him alone." She said all this to her fingers still picking at the loose bits of skin around her nail beds. "He said some mean stuff, too; he said I was reckless just like my mom. I got mad too and asked why he never talked about her and said I wished I had her around instead of him because all his rules were going to drown me."

"Yikes."

Chloe wrinkled her nose again. "Yeah, it was pretty bad. I eventually just started saying whatever he wanted to hear to get him to calm down. Then I went into my room to 'change,' gave it a few minutes, then went out the window." She angled her tired face toward Amber. "I'd never been scared of my dad until that night. It was a really awful feeling. I left mostly because I didn't know how to deal. Plus, all that stuff I found on the ancestry site ... I don't know. I just had to get out of there. And then Johnny ended up not even being who he said he was. God, Amber, I told him so much personal stuff. I'm more embarrassed than mad. I fell for all his crap so easily."

"You're not the only one," Amber said. "It sounds like Sean does this to everyone. He's a garbage human being. Don't feel bad for trusting someone. It's great that you were able to be that open with 'Johnny' … even if he wasn't truthful with you. Being open is a good thing."

Chloe rose an eyebrow at her. "You know I love you, Amber, but you're like the most secretive person I know."

Amber laughed. "Yeah, well, I'm working on taking my own advice. And I love you too, kid." She reached out and ruffled Chloe's hair, just like Amber used to do when Chloe was younger.

Chloe laughed and playfully swatted away Amber's hand. "Have you been in contact with your aunt at all?"

Chloe smiled wider. "Yeah. It was a really awkward conversation because neither one of us could stop crying for very long. But she and her husband … my uncle—gosh, that's weird to say—are going to come to my graduation. She said she's going to bring some pictures of my mom from when she was my age."

Amber's eyes welled up. "I'm glad you're going to meet more of your family."

Chloe sniffed. "Me too." Then she turned fully in her seat and faced Amber, arms wide. "Thanks for not giving up on trying to find me."

Amber threw her arms around her. "Never."

When the next song came blasting through the speakers, the dwindling crowd in the community center cheered.

"Oh, you gotta dance to this one," Chloe said, pulling Amber to her feet. "Let loose, woman!"

I'm working on taking my own advice echoed in her head as she let herself be dragged out into the group.

And Amber danced.

Epilogue

"Everyone? Can I get your attention for a second, please?" Kim asked from atop a chair in the middle of one of the back rooms of the community center. The gala was a black-tie event, so it was a small miracle that Kim had been able to even get onto said chair, while wearing a skintight baby pink dress that hit her calves. Her strappy heels were discarded for now, so she stood on the chair in her stockinged feet.

The room was filled with the Here and Meow Committee members and their plus-ones—Amber had successfully guilted Edgar into attending, and he was currently both in a suit and sulking in a corner—dozens of volunteers, the Best of Edgehill competitors, and a few staff members who worked events at the community center. Mayor Deidrick and Chloe were here, too. The volunteers wore black slacks and crisp white shirts, while everyone else was in their best suits and gowns.

Amber had been trying very hard for the last hour to not gawk at Jack Terrence in his perfectly tailored black suit and red tie. She tried even harder not to notice how often his gaze raked over her in her pale blue gown. Kim had done Amber's hair, piling it on top of her head in an elegant bun that was dotted with little white flowers, much like her own hair.

"I speak on behalf of the Here and Meow Committee when

I say we're so honored to have you all here," Kim said. "You've worked so hard, and I'm thrilled we get to help celebrate Edgehill's finest together. I know a lot of you are anxious about who is going to win tonight, and I know it's cheesy, but the fact that you're all here tonight says so much about what you've accomplished. Be proud, no matter what happens."

Amber caught Betty Harris's eye from across the room in her sequin-covered navy blue dress and gave her an enthusiastic double thumbs-up. Betty laughed and held up two sets of crossed fingers.

"Now, are you all ready to get this thing started?" Kim called out.

Everyone cheered in response.

"Volunteers, with me!" one of the community center staff members called out, then ushered the black-and-white clad group out of the room.

"Everyone but the 'Best of' contestants, follow us so you can find your seat. We'll be letting in the masses soon," Kim said. "Good luck out there!"

Amber helped Kim down from the chair while Ann Marie found Kim's shoes. The Here and Meow Committee, their guests, and the guests of the "Best of" contestants trickled out of the meeting room and down the deserted hallway that Amber and Jack had walked down weeks ago on their way to set up the pastry spread for Olaf Betzen.

She could only hope the Hair Ball went more smoothly than the junior fashion show had.

The back door to the main part of the community center was closed, and Kim stood before it, one hand on the handle.

She peered around at the group huddled behind her. Amber knew she wanted to see what the group's reaction would be— no one outside of the committee, staff, and volunteers had seen the final transformation of the community center into a springtime wonderland.

"Welcome to the Hair Ball," Kim said, and pushed the doors open.

There was a collective intake of breath; Amber, Kim, Ann Marie, and Nathan all grinned at each other.

Twenty round tables draped with eggshell white tablecloths were positioned around the room—ten on one side of the four-foot-wide, light-colored parquet wood pathway that led from the front doors to the stage, and ten on the other. Six chairs made of light-colored wood ringed each table. Each place setting had a gray linen napkin, a set of silverware, and a water glass. Circular wood slices a foot in diameter marked the center of each table, and were topped with small glass vases of blue, purple, and green, each one filled with an array of white tulips, cherry blossoms, and baby's breath. Inch-tall candles, their small flames dancing, were dotted amongst the vases along with Amber's plastic cats. Tented white name cards marked each place setting, the attendee's name written in looping cursive and accompanied by a hand-drawn black silhouette of a cat—each one different than the next. Ben Lydon had drawn them all.

Above their heads, strings of lit bulbs hung from the ceiling.

Though Amber and the rest of the committee had helped decorate every inch of this place, the rustic springtime theme had been all Kim.

As people found their seats, Amber and Kim walked down the parquet floor to the still-closed front door. They had less than a minute before the gala was officially due to start. The pair stopped by the door and smiled at each other.

"Mel would have loved all this," Amber said.

Kim beamed. "I think so too."

Though Amber spent most of the evening helping make sure everything ran smoothly behind the scenes and hardly had a chance to sit down, let alone eat anything, she could tell how well the gala was going. The volunteer waiters and waitresses were polite and helpful. Those bussing the tables were efficient. All the electronic equipment ran as it should; *Stan Tackles a Unicorn* had, mercifully, been swapped out for a hilarious one-woman play; and the models didn't suffer from a single wardrobe malfunction.

Votes were collected for each category once all competitors had offered or shown their contributions, and were then counted immediately in the back by Nathan and Ann Marie. Amber could only imagine how nervous Betty and Jack were.

At the end of the twelfth category—leisure—Henry and Danielle of 98.9 K-Mew were on the stage, microphones to their mouths.

"How's everyone doing tonight? You having a good time?" Henry asked.

The crowd cheered.

"We just got word that the final tallies have been counted

for the Best Of Edgehill," said Danielle. "You all ready to hear the results?"

Another cheer rose up from the crowd.

Now that their work was temporarily done, the Here and Meow Committee all hurried to their tables so they could experience the end of the gala along with everyone else. Amber slid into a chair in between Edgar and Kim.

"First, we'd like to announce the winner of our artist competition," Danielle said. "The winner will be the designer of this year's logo for the Here and Meow, the designer of the 'Best of' stickers that will go on the winner's websites and will be displayed in their shop windows, as well as designing this year's commemorative pin." She paused for dramatic effect, then glanced down at the clipboard she held in her hands. "Ben Lydon!"

The redheaded boy shot to his feet near the front of the room, his hands pressed to either side of his head. A very loud cheer erupted from the same general area; Mama Lydon was quite excited for her talented son.

"Now, we'll be working in reverse just to further torment the folks who shared their delicious treats with us first," Henry said.

A collective, good-natured grumble went through the room.

"The winner for leisure is ... Feline Fine Day Spa!" Danielle called out, reading from the clipboard in her hand, which she then handed to Henry.

The owners of Feline Fine—a young married couple—stood and waved, while the attendees cheered them on. Since Ben had just been chosen as the festival's head designer, the winners of "Best of" wouldn't receive their promotional materials for another three to four weeks. Tonight was just an acknowledgement and celebration of the winners.

"The winner for the hotel category is … Tropical Purradise!" Henry announced.

Just Kitten Comedy Club, Purrfect Pitch, Hiss and Hers, the Milk Bowl, Shabby Tabby, Mews and Brews, and Patch's Pizza were the winners from the next seven categories.

Which left the treats and coffee categories. Amber had been trying to catch Betty's eye for the past twenty minutes, but she was on the other side of the parquet pathway and had her attention focused solely on the emcees. Jack was seated even farther away.

"For the treats category—and this one was very close, folks—the winner is …" Henry read. "Purrfectly Scrumptious!"

Amber wasn't sure if she or Bobby yelped loudest. Bobby helped a sobbing Betty to her feet, her hands pressed to her face and her shoulders heaving. Purrcolate was a well-loved establishment in Edgehill, but Purrfectly Scrumptious was an institution. The crowd was on its feet, cheering for Betty, who seemed to cry harder the more people cheered for her.

"You did it, baby!" Bobby kept shouting. "You did it!"

On the count of three, Amber and Kim yelled at the top of their lungs, "We love you, Betty!"

Betty turned then and waved both hands in the air once she spotted Amber and Kim bouncing around like goons on the other side of the room.

"While it was close for the treats category, the coffee category was even closer. So close in fact that it was a tie between two of the shops, and the third won by one vote," Danielle said. "You all ready?"

Amber bit her lip.

"Coffee Cat!" Danielle called out.

Given Amber's own reaction to the gingerbread latte she'd had recently, she couldn't say she disagreed with the choice, but she did feel bad that Jack had lost both categories.

Once the excitement of the announcement had faded, the attendees were served a full meal. After that, the party started. A bartender's cart was rolled out, the dance floor opened, and Henry and Danielle took full control of the music. It was a celebration for the winners, it was a celebration for a successful gala run with a limited staff, and it was a celebration of Chloe Deidrick being back home with her family: her father and all of Edgehill.

The only thing that would have made the evening more perfect for Amber would have been if Melanie could have been dancing and laughing with her, Kim, and the rest of the Here and Meow Committee.

Once the meal was out of the way and the formality of the evening loosened a bit, Amber tracked down Betty, the two squealing and jumping up and down.

"I knew you could do it!" Amber said.

"I still can't believe it!" said Betty.

"Oh, I just love you both!" Bobby said, his bottom lip shaking as he pulled them into a group hug. As soon as Bobby started crying, both Betty and Amber completely lost it.

When the drinking started, Betty and Bobby made for

the exit. Amber told them that they would go out for celebratory Catty Cakes in the morning.

While Amber stood at the front doors, watching Betty—with Bobby's arm wrapped tight around her shoulder—walk across the parking lot, she caught sight of Chief Brown chatting with Connor Declan. Curiosity piqued, she walked outside, the click of her kitten heels giving her away as she got closer; the lot was mostly deserted at the moment. Older residents had fled before things got too rowdy, while the younger set were just getting started. Both men looked up at her. Chief Brown smiled; Connor did not.

"Well, thank you for talking to me, Chief Brown." Connor offered Amber a curt nod, said, "You look lovely this evening," then turned on his heel and left before she could even think of how to respond.

Amber was still frowning after him when the chief said, "I came by to talk to you—and see how the Hair Ball turned out—but Declan cornered me before I could get in there. I swear the guy had been hiding between two cars waiting for me and popped out just when I went by. Scared the daylights out of me."

"What did he want?" she asked, finally turning to him.

"Usual reporter stuff … wants to interview me about how the takedown of Sean Merrill went," the chief said. "He was asking a lot of questions about you too, though. I'd keep an eye out for him. He's very … suspicious."

Amber recalled the way he'd followed her and found Cassie Westbottom instead. She'd need to sort out the Connor Declan problem later. "What did you want to talk to *me* about?"

"Once the dust settles, I may still need your help with the Chloe case," he said. "That Sean Merrill is a piece of work. As soon as we got him in the interrogation room, we couldn't shut the guy up. He threw everyone he could think of under the bus when he wasn't too busy lying through his teeth. He had the audacity to blame Karen for all of this. Pretty classic psychopath: no empathy, no remorse, and thinks he's smarter than everyone else in the room. He said if Karen had shown up after he'd originally called her, he wouldn't have *needed* to kidnap Chloe."

Amber pursed her lips. It was strange to so deeply hate someone she'd never met. "When Sean messaged her, he used a single photo—who was that?"

"It was a photo he found on some teenage boy's public modeling portfolio," the chief said.

As much as the idea of a police takedown sounded exciting, she was glad she'd never had to lay eyes on the creep. Besides, she would have been so unbelievably angry, her magic very well might have reacted without her permission and maimed him. Kim knowing Amber's secret was bad enough; a group of law enforcement finding out about her abilities wouldn't be ideal. Was maiming a felony?

"The person who kidnapped Chloe is an old friend of his from Lirkaldy—Shane Miller," the chief continued, pulling Amber out of her thoughts. "Sean promised Shane a cut of the half-a-million life insurance payout—upwards of fifty grand—if he snatched Chloe. He drove Chloe to Portland, then ducked out of town once the deed was done. Shane is still at large; no one in Lirkaldy seems to know where the guy could be. I've got your buddy Alan Peterson on the hunt."

"See," she said, "not all PIs are bad."

The chief offered a noncommittal shrug in response. "If we can't find Shane in the usual ways, I'll give you a call. Once Shane hears that he's not getting his money, he might be ticked off enough to come after Chloe again."

Amber nodded, hoping they caught the guy soon.

The chief's attention shifted toward the community center. "I don't have a ticket, but can I see how the Hair Ball turned out? Jessica wanted me to take pictures."

She laughed. "You're the chief of police—I'm pretty sure you can go anywhere you want."

They walked back to the front of the center and stopped on the threshold.

The chief let out a whistle. "You guys did good."

Smiling she said, "Thanks. You did too."

The chief wandered the building for a few minutes, snapping dozens of pictures. When Kim saw them, she came bounding over from the dance floor, her face flush and her hairline a little damp. "Chief! Come dance!"

He stared at her as if she'd just admitted that Marbleglen was a superior town and that they should burn Edgehill to the ground. "No, thank you," he said. "I should be getting back to Jessica and the kids." His gaze flicked to the dance floor full of twirling, laughing, and arm-waving people, and Amber could swear he paled. "Congratulations on the gala, ladies." Then he hurried away even faster than Connor had earlier.

Kim shrugged and grabbed Amber's hand. "You, however, cannot say no!" she said, tugging Amber after her.

Amber spent hours on the dance floor after that, even though her date refused to join her. Edgar stayed seated for most of the evening, though he watched the dancers with a strange kind of longing. Amber danced with Chloe and her friends—which they loved and were completely horrified by at the same time—and she danced with the committee members. At one point, Jolene and Ann Marie led the group of dancers through a popular line dance. It was easy enough that Amber forced the ever-grumpy Edgar onto the dance floor. He grudgingly cooperated and ended up picking up the dance even quicker than Amber had.

More than once, she caught Kim eyeing Edgar as if he was a sandwich and she was starving. Amber had yet to let her know that Edgar, too, was a witch. She was a little worried that that fact would make Edgar even more attractive to her.

She'd have to ask Edgar later how he wanted her to handle that, if at all.

The last dance of the night—just before midnight—was a slow one. Most of the crowd had cleared out of the community center by then. Cabs had been parked out in the lot in anticipation hours ago and were soon whisking drunk Hair Ball guests safely back home. Amber shoved Kim and Edgar together. She spotted a very red-faced Ben Lydon asking Chloe to dance, who happily said yes.

Amber flopped into a chair and kicked off her shoes, watching the remaining two dozen guests sway around the dance floor. Her feet and lower back ached, but she hadn't been this content in a long time. She was also quite sure she could fall asleep sitting up—with her eyes open.

"I thought you weren't much of a dancer," she heard someone say close to her left ear.

She turned that way, but no one was there.

"You looked great out there," he said to her right now. "Happy."

When she turned her head toward his voice, she found Jack Terrence sitting beside her. Her first instinct had been to tell him how sorry she was that he'd lost in both categories tonight, but that intense look from the last time she'd seen him was back, making her apology dry up in her mouth. The memory of the zap she'd felt when their hands touched replayed in her head. Her magic didn't feel haywire at the moment, though her heart hammered.

Then what he'd said caught up with her. "You ... you remember that night at the Sippin' Siamese?"

"Something happened when your hand touched mine. Maybe it screwed with whatever your aunt did," he said. "Because now I remember everything."

Amber swallowed. "Everything?"

His gaze swept across her face and down to her neck. He swallowed hard, too, then looked back up into her eyes. "Everything."

About the Author

Melissa has had a love of stories for as long as she can remember, but only started penning her own during her freshman year of college. She majored in Wildlife, Fish, and Conservation Biology at UCDavis. Yet, while she was neck-deep in organic chemistry and physics, she kept finding herself writing stories in the back of the classroom about fairies and trolls and magic. She finished her degree, but it never captured her heart the way writing did.

Now she owns her own dog walking business (that's sort of wildlife related, right?) by day ... and afternoon and night ... and writes whenever she gets a spare moment. The Microsoft Word app is a gift from the gods!

She alternates mostly between fantasy and mystery (often with a paranormal twist). All her books have some element of "other" to them ... witches, ghosts, UFOs. There's no better way to escape the real world than getting lost in a fictional one.

She lives in Northern California with her very patient boyfriend and way too many pets.

Her debut novel, *The Forgotten Child*, released in October of 2018. She is currently fast at work writing both the Riley Thomas mystery series, and the Witch of Edgehill series.

You can find out more about her upcoming books at: https://melissajacksonbooks.com

Acknowledgements

Thanks again and again to my beta readers! You guys are lifesavers! Thank you, Mom, Krista Hall, Margarita Martinez, Brittany Gray, Christiane Loeffler, Jennifer Laam, Lauren Sprang, Garrett Lemons, Noel Russell, Lindsey Duga, Tristin Milazzo, Jasmine Warren, Kara Klemcke, Bobby Lewis, Mary Studebaker, Samantha Lierer (SSDGM, new Murderino sister), Kimberly Ann Shepard, Jesika Olson, and Stefan Anders. And to Courtney Hanson just for being you.

Thank you, Maggie Hall, for being a design wizard.

Thanks to Michelle Raymond and Clark Kenyon for all the cat-filled formatting.

Thank you to Justin Cohen for being my go-to proofreader.

Many thanks to the crazy talented Victoria Villarreal for bring Amber and Edgehill to life. Hopefully we can work on many more books together!

Thank you to Sam for setting up a place for me to write in the garage when I was going loopy and needed a change of scenery. Thank you for running to the store for energy drinks and chocolate when I need to hit a new over-the-top word count goal. You're the best and I love you. (I'm still upset you turned Dusty into a dog, though.)

And, as always, thank you to my readers. Thank you for pre-ordering, reading, reviewing, and telling your friends about my books. I'm so glad I get to share my stories with you. Onto the next!

Thank you for reading *Pawsitively Secretive*! If you enjoyed this story, please consider leaving a review. Reviews mean the world to authors. Reviews often mean more sales, and more sales means more freedom to write more books.

Continue the series with:

Pawsitively Swindled – Coming soon!

Pawsitively Betrayed – Coming soon!

Other books by Melissa Erin Jackson:

If you're looking for a slightly darker tale, consider *The Forgotten Child*, a haunting paranormal mystery starring a reluctant medium.

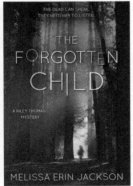

The dead can speak. They need her to listen.

Ever since Riley Thomas, reluctant medium extraordinaire, accidentally released a malevolent spirit from a Ouija board when she was thirteen, she's taken a hard pass on scary movies, haunted houses, and cemeteries. Twelve years later, when her best friend pressures her into spending a paranormal investigation weekend at the infamous Jordanville Ranch—former home of deceased serial killer Orin Jacobs—Riley's still not ready to accept the fact that she can communicate with ghosts.

Shortly after their arrival at the ranch, the spirit of a little boy contacts Riley; a child who went missing—and was never found—in 1973.

In order to put the young boy's spirit to rest, she has to come to grips with her ability. But how can she solve a mystery that happened a decade before she was born? Especially when someone who knows Orin's secrets wants to keep the truth buried—no matter the cost.

Available at Amazon, Kobo, Barnes & Noble, and iBooks. Now available as an audiobook, too!